THE WILD FLOWER

To my husband, who through it all manages to hold the fort down when I'm locked inside these stories. He never fails to accept that there will ALWAYS be another chapter to write. He understands that he has to share me with all the voices in my head and he loves me regardless of the insanity that comes out of me. This is for him.

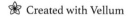

AUTHOR NOTE

Thank you for choosing to read Drew and Maybel's story.
This is part 2 and MUST be read AFTER The Wallflower.
If you're reading this first please grab book 1 and start there
otherwise nothing will make sense. Below are a list of
triggers, that may or may not be spoilers to the book. If you
have any triggers I advise you to read through the list and
make the choice yourself before you continue to read. If
triggers aren't an issue for you then please continue.
Please remember while men like Drew are nice to read in
fictional books, they're not nice to experience in real life. If
you're a victim of domestic violence (physical or mental),
please know there are options available to you and that
you're never alone.
Visit: https://www.thehotline.org/

CONTENT WARNING

Abuse (physical and mental), primal play, blood play, violence, stalking, sexual situations, murder, adoption, mental health issues, conversation surrounding incest, death, grief, dub-con/non-con, domestic violence, child abuse, cancer, bullying, self-harm, cheating, needles, breeding, drug use, suicide, gun violence, kidnapping, poisoning, poverty, blackmail, forced orgasm/pleasure, choking, and marking.

PROLOGUE

Bel

L*ilacs.* The scent tickles my nostrils, wrapping me in comfort. The smell of my mother's perfume surrounded me whenever I curled up on her lap as a kid and snuggled under the blankets while she read a book to me.

I sink deeper into the warmth of my mother's body, promising never to leave her again now that she's here, however fleeting that might be. I grip her tighter, the memory fading like leaves blowing in the wind. I'll hold on to her memory forever. The moment I open my eyes, I know the pain will sweep back in and carry me away, ripping the perfectly constructed figment of solitude right out from under me.

"Maybel?" The deep, dark voice should terrify me but

somehow doesn't. My name echoes around in the concaves of my mind, but I ignore the beacon slipping back into that tranquil space.

"Maybel? Wake up!" the voice calls again, and there's a hard edge this time. Fear strikes me, but I settle quickly because something about that voice is familiar.

The owner is someone my subconscious knows will not hurt me. I cling to the wispy clouds of my dream, slowly evaporating before my eyes. The smell of lilacs, the warmth of my mother's arms around me, the soft thud of her heartbeat beneath my ear... it all slips through my fingers like sand through an hourglass.

Slowly, with the weight of ten cinder blocks on my eyes, I blink them open, then immediately regret it and slam them shut again with a groan. A throbbing sensation slices through my skull as it spears through me like a pencil straight to my pupil.

"Maybel?" A shadow moves above me, blocking out the light. I recognize that voice.

Sebastian. And suddenly, I have a whole other slew of problems I don't know what to do with.

"The light," I croak, my voice raw. "It hurts my head."

The brightness behind my eyelids dims, and it's like someone has pulled a five-pound weight off my face.

"Thank you." I wince while blinking my eyes open once more. It takes a moment to adjust to the room. As soon as they do, I'm struck by his disheveled image, noticing that he's stripped off his tuxedo jacket and his bow tie hangs limply around his neck. He doesn't appear to care.

When our gazes collide, he eases, his shoulders relaxing away from his ears. "Good, you're awake."

I am, but a part of me doesn't want to be, not when the events that transpired earlier come flooding back like a nightmare that refuses to let go.

Sebastian.

Drew.

Mom.

Fuck.

The pressure of it all threatens to suffocate me, and I scramble for the covers, wanting nothing more than to hide beneath them and escape the reality of my life. Sebastian doesn't appear to agree and clamps a hand around my wrist, his hard grip stopping any further advancement. "No fast movements. You have a concussion from the fall, and they had to put in a few stitches to close up the gash on your head."

I attempt to tug my hand from his grasp so I can check for myself, but his unbreakable grip stops me before I can even try. "Let go of me."

His mouth folds down into a straight line, and he slowly relaxes his grip before taking a step back. Just like Drew, he's great at painting an illusion. Though his features may convey a calmness, his body language speaks otherwise. His tense posture is tight, as if he might leap back and grab me the second I twitch the wrong way.

"How's your head feel?"

I nod once, but the action is painful, so I become as still as a statue. "It hurts. In fact, my entire body hurts."

He sighs and smooths his hands down his thighs like he needs something to do, something to focus on. "Yeah, that's probably from when you fainted. I caught you the best I could. It might also be adrenaline. Sometimes after a game, even if I don't take a hit, I'll come home sore, every muscle in my body stiff."

I don't respond and instead look at the other side of the massive hospital room. Everything is beige and white. Sterile and clean. The sheets are soft beneath my fingers, and the beep of the machines next to the bed are muted. It's the complete opposite of all the hospital stays I've had with my mother, where the blankets are scratchy, the walls an off-yellow color, and the machines constantly beep because there aren't enough staff to manage the influx of patients. A place like this will cost more than my entire college degree and then some. I don't know how long I've been here, but I already know I've outstayed my welcome.

"I need to get out of here. I can't afford this." I don't look at him as I speak. The last thing I want to see on his face is disgust or pity. After everything, and even in my current state, I refuse to give up an ounce of dignity.

As if he's finally trusting I won't get up and sprint out of the room, he slumps into the cushy armchair beside my bed. "Don't worry about how much it's going to cost. What you need to worry about is your health."

I shift against the bed and try to hide my wince while I glare at him. "Only someone who *doesn't* have to worry about money says don't worry about money."

A dark spark enters his eyes, reminding me of the first time I saw him at *The Hunt*. Sebastian might appear kind and courteous, but everyone knows his true nature. His beast lingers just below the surface, waiting for the moment he can come out to play. "I said don't fucking worry about it, so don't fucking worry about it. It's all covered. You're not alone anymore, Bel."

My jaw aches as I grit my teeth, and I narrow my eyes at him to make sure he sees the anger, the pain, all of it. I want him to know what it's like to have your still beating heart ripped out of your chest. "I'm not alone. I have my..." A sob rips from my throat, and the pain of the words gouges me, a never-ending wound that refuses to stop bleeding. I clench my jaw tightly and stare up at the ceiling while blinking back tears. "I have my mom. Yeah, I might be poor, but I was never alone. I have the one thing that no amount of money could ever buy—love."

Silence surrounds me, and after a few seconds, I risk glancing at him, even as hot tears slip down my cheeks. There's a crinkle in his brow as he stares at the wall, and it hits me all over again.

My mother is gone.

Gone.

For good.

But I'm not the only one who lost her. *Dammit. Shit.* In a world full of filthy rich assholes, he's the last person I should feel a sliver of sympathy for, but that's not who I am. I might have lost my mother, but so did he. It doesn't matter if he knew less about her than I did. He didn't have to deal with infinite hospital visits and medications. He didn't have bedtimes when she read to him and sang him lullabies.

He didn't have any of those things, but he lost her all the same. At least I had those memories, but he didn't even get that.

I rub my cheeks to wipe at my tears, causing the IV in my hand to pull tight and pinch. The pain helps bring me back to the present.

"If it's okay with you, I'd like to get out of here. I doubt a hospital stay is suitable for the treatment of a concussion."

"It's not, but I wasn't sure what your mental state would be once you were awake, and with the concussion, if you happened to lose it, then medications to sedate you would've been my only other option. The doctor advised me that you should have someone with you for the next couple of days to monitor your condition and make sure you're okay."

Great. Yet another reminder that now, without Mom, I am truly and completely alone. I don't know anything about this man, my so-called brother. Only that he's a dick, and one of Drew's miserable friends, which makes me weary and anxious. I thought I could trust Drew, and look where that fucking got me.

I feel around the sheets for the button to call the nurse and press it hard. The effort makes me pant, and I slump against the soft mattress, my vision going hazy for a moment.

The nurse bustles in, her dark braids coiled on top of her head like a crown. "Oh, you're awake. Let me check your vitals quick, and then I'll get out of your hair."

I roll my head to the side to look at her. Lifting it is just too much effort. "Actually, would it be possible to get the discharge papers going? I'd like to leave."

She gives me a soft smile that doesn't quite reach her eyes. "Sorry, sweetie... but I can't let you leave until the doctor gives me the all clear. Last I checked, he was waiting for your scan results."

I clench my jaw hard enough that it makes the ache in my head worse, then I shift to face Sebastian again. "Okay.

I guess since I'm stuck here, would it be possible to go see my mom?"

His forehead creases, concern etched into his features. *Oh god, what now?* He leans over to brace his elbows on his knees. "Bel, this isn't a conversation that either of us really wants to have right now, but your mental state is very important. I need to make sure that you understand that on our way to the hospital, your mother... *our* mother passed away. Peacefully."

The pain of that statement, the confirmation that this is all real, hits me like a sledgehammer right in the sternum. It's an emotional pain, but I feel it physically along my nerve endings. The air in my lungs stills, and I try to hold the anguish inside. I don't want to keep breaking down, but that's all I can do. The sorrow climbs up my throat, clawing its way out of me. The pain slips past my lips and fills the air with an ear-shattering sob. It's uncontrolled, and agony consumes me, rattling me to the marrow in my bones.

Something cold and wet slips from my eyes and down my cheeks. I can feel the nurse's and Sebastian's eyes on me, and I hate it. The vulnerable state this has left me in makes me feel weak and useless. I'm not used to feeling so helpless.

"Yes," I finally answer, my voice breathy. "I know. I remember everything that happened back at the party." I pin him with a hard expression. "*Everything.*"

He glances across the bed to the nurse. "Can we get a wheelchair, please?"

The woman doesn't ask questions and simply nods once and leaves us alone all over again.

"Wow, so that's what it's like to have money? People just rush off to do your bidding with only a look? No questions or opinions spoken."

The corner of his mouth tips up, and he spears his fingers into his messy curls and shoves them off his forehead. "No, she's a nurse, and to do her job, she would have to have compassion. She knows your mother died, and all she wants to do is help. Can't blame her there. I guess I wonder does being poor mean you have to be an asshole to anyone who does have money? Because if so, I have bad news for you, Bel. You're now one of those people who *has* money."

I lean my head back against the pillow to try to alleviate the throbbing in my head. However, I doubt the throbbing is due to the head injury alone. This entire situation is a migraine in itself. "I don't want your money."

"It's not *my* money. It's yours. Yours, our grandfather's, however you want to word it. He put money in a trust for you and our mother a long time ago. It's just been sitting there for you or her to claim it. Now, it all belongs to you."

Somehow, that hurts worse. I'd rather have my mother here, living and smiling, way more than any amount of money.

"The money doesn't matter. I don't give a shit about any of it. I just want to see her, please." I don't even bother swiping at the tears that cascade down my cheeks. Crying is a permanent feature at this point.

Thankfully, the nurse returns to the room at that moment with the wheelchair. I fight back nausea and dizziness as I push myself up, trying to swing my legs over the edge of the bed. I've barely moved, and Sebastian is already at my side, his gaze hard and unreadable.

"Let me help you," he orders gruffly. I want more than anything to push him away, but I can't bring myself to do it. I need something, someone to hold me together and make sure I don't crack straight down the middle. The nurse grabs a robe and hands it to Sebastian, who helps me put it on. Then he helps untangle the IV tubes and wires to the heart machine before walking me over to the chair.

All the movement makes my head pound more, but I don't care. I need to see her.

Once I'm situated in the wheelchair, Sebastian wheels me out of the room and down the long corridor to the other end. It pays to have money, I see. The rooms are bigger, and the entire place is so quiet. Nothing like the raucous and loud rooms my mom is... *was* usually stuck in.

At the end of the hallway, we turn into another room, and I clamp my hand over my mouth when I spot her lying on the bed with her eyes closed. She looks asleep, and I can almost picture her green eyes opening, joy filling them as she smiles at me. But that will never happen again. I'll never get to experience her smile or the glittering of her eyes. From now on, those things will be just a fragmented memory.

I glance back at Sebastian. "You moved her?"

He nods. "I wanted you to be able to say goodbye. I didn't get to speak with her. The doctors called me, and by the time I made it here, she was already gone. When I realized what was going on, I left to get you. I know how much you love her. Why else would you work your ass off to help pay for her medical bills?"

I swallow around the tennis ball-sized lump in my throat and stare at the dull gray of her skin, the white half-moons of her nails. I'm looking at her body, but I can feel she's not here. No part of her is here in this hospital room any longer. Just the shell of her spirit remains. Time stands still, and it feels like my heart is being ripped out of my chest.

Cold streaks trail down my cheeks faster now, and I cover my face with my hands to try to stop them. *It can't be real. It can't be.* A ragged sob fills the room, the sound both angry and sad. It takes me a moment to realize the noise had come out of me. My lungs deflate, and the throbbing behind my eyes intensifies. I think I'm going to throw up.

"I know it doesn't feel like it right now, but everything will be okay. I promise, and I don't ever break my promises, Bel." Sebastian tries his best to soothe me, but he has no idea what he's saying. How can he think anything will ever be okay? My mother... *our* mother is gone. Dead. Nothing will be okay again. Nothing. Every single breath I inhale and exhale hurts as I try to grapple with the understanding that she's not coming back. That she's not peacefully sleeping in that bed in front of me.

No more cinnamon toast on cold nights. No more drive-throughs where we have to comb the bottoms of our purses for enough change to cover the cost, all while laughing at each new thing we unearth from the depths of our bags. No more watching soap operas in the afternoon while I tease Mom about how cheesy they are. All the memories bottle up, threatening to choke the life out of me. I let out another horrendous sob. I didn't even get to say goodbye. I didn't get to tell her how good of a mom she was. I didn't get to tell her I love her more than anything in this world...

A pair of warm, rough hands grasp me, cradling my cheeks. Sebastian's face swims into view, his image blurry through my tears. "Maybel, breathe. Take a deep breath for me, or we will have to leave the room until you calm down."

I try to do just that, but it's like sucking air through a straw into my lungs. His grip on me tightens, and he squeezes my cheeks tighter, his fingers warm and damp from my tears.

"Come on, Bel. Breathe. You can do it."

I watch as he does it, breathing through his mouth before slowly exhaling out of his nose. I mirror his movements and suck in a ragged breath, then sob it back out. Over and over. I don't know how long I sit there drowning in my grief. Somehow, I make my way to the floor and let the cold seep into my bones. Sebastian's strong arms hold me together, keeping me from shattering. The heavy thud of his heartbeat pulls me back to the present. He eases back, and I notice his cheeks are flushed and a little wet too. "Are you feeling better?"

I don't risk looking at my mother again, not when I can barely breathe as it is. I want to hold her hand and push the hair out of her face, but I can't bring myself to do it. Not when I know she's no longer there.

"Thank you for bringing me to her. I... I just can't do this. I thought I could, but I can't. I can't stand seeing her like this. I want to go home."

He nods once and gently helps me to my feet. Then he glances at someone lingering near the door over my shoulder. "Can you have the doctor get her paperwork ready? I'll have a private doctor visit the house if she needs further care. I think being at home would help her heal better."

"Of course. I'll reach out to the doctor." The voice matches that of the nurse who came to my room earlier. Sebastian gives her a nod, then helps me into the chair. My lip trembles as I bite it, attempting to hold back tears. Losing someone you love, there isn't anything like it. It feels like someone stole a piece of who you are, and there's no way to get it back. Anger and sadness battle it out in my mind as Sebastian wheels me out of the room.

"You can just wear what you have on. I'll order some clothes for you, or we can pick up what you have at the dorms later."

I'm slumped in the chair, barely able to move, let alone think. I don't want to go back to school. I don't want to eat, sleep, or even breathe. I just want my mother back.

He continues talking like I'm actually participating in the conversation. "Don't worry about anything. I'll make the arrangements for her. Right now, I need you to worry about taking care of yourself. If anything happens to you..."

I zone out for a while, stuck in the deep, dark confines of my mind, hiding from the pain, anger, and sadness. I've lost everything. Mom. Drew. Jackie. I have nothing left and no one left to live for. *What's the point anymore?*

A sudden jolt pulls me from my reverie, and I blink and return to the present, realizing that I'm suddenly in a car. *When did he put me in a car?* Disoriented, I shift in the seat and peer out the window. A huge mansion looms outside. This is definitely *not* home.

"This isn't where I live," I whisper.

"It is now. I'm sorry, Bel, I know this is a lot of change all at once," he speaks softly from beside me. "I can't protect you if you are off on your own. You'll have to stay at the family estate from now on so I can keep an eye on you. I don't trust anyone right now."

I wave at the freaking mansion beyond the window. "This doesn't even make sense. You don't even live here. You live at The Mill."

He lets out a slow breath from his nose. "Not anymore. When our grandfather died, I had no option but to step into line as the next heir. My place is here, managing the family affairs. I'll still finish school and do Mill functions, but from now on, I live here. And so do you."

His bossy, domineering tone has returned, but I don't have the strength to fight him. Not today at least.

He exits the car and jogs around to open my door. Gently, as if I'm made of glass, he helps me stand. My legs are jelly, and my knees threaten to buckle beneath my weight. I feel weak, so weak, but I can't be. I can't be weak. The pain in my head has subsided, probably from the pain meds they loaded me with before they removed my IV. If only they had a medication that could ease my heartache...

I hold his forearm but don't lean into him. "Just so you know, I can walk on my own."

"Sure, says the one walking like a newborn fawn." I grimace and glance at his face to find him smiling at me. It's a genuine smile, the kind you give someone you care about.

It's a *lie*. He doesn't care about me. This is all about his image and using me. That's all this is, all it has to be. He helps me up the steps and to the front door. The sprawling mansion is modern, with glass everywhere. Massive black double doors open when Sebastian swipes his hand in front of some sensor near the handle. He leads me into an open foyer with shining marble floors and cathedral ceilings. A chandelier that looks made out of a million diamonds glitters above us. Ahead is a double staircase, and rooms lead off in every direction on the main floor. I can't even be bothered to comment on how over the top and ridiculous this all is. *Who the hell lives like this?*

"I know it's different from what you're used to and that it will take some time to adjust to it, but just know there is *nothing* you cannot have, Bel. I refuse to let you go without."

I don't respond. What is there to say? This is no longer my life. I'm merely a puppet in this play, and someone else is pulling the strings. With more patience than I ever imagined Sebastian having, he guides me up the stairs and down a long hallway. It's decorated in rich florals, expensive fabrics, and precious-looking knickknacks.

The damn hallway alone is bigger than my mom's house.

For one moment, I wonder where everyone is. Does he not have anyone either? In all the time I was messing around with Drew, I never thought to ask questions about his friends. Then again, why would I do that? It's not like we were really ever together.

Sebastian stops at a door near the end of the hall and grabs the silver knob, turning it and pushing it open in one swoop.

Escorting me into the bedroom, he helps me sit on the

edge of the massive king-size bed in the center of the room between two huge windows. I barely give the room a glance, but from what I can see, it's decorated in stately grays and mauves. It's a pretty room, but right now, I don't give a shit about any of that.

It's like I felt too much all at once, and my emotional center has shut down. I've short-circuited my brain, which is a good thing since he turns to me and presses a piece of paper into my hand. I recognize my mom's handwriting scribbled on the front of the white envelope. *What is this?* Sadness suffocates me, and suddenly, I don't want Sebastian to leave.

"I was told to make sure this gets to you. It's from your mother. Feel free to read it when you're ready. Grief takes time to get through, and we all have our own ways of coping. Don't lose your spark, Bel. Don't let this change you. I didn't know our mother at all, but even with that knowledge, I know she wouldn't want you to lose sight of who you are. Use the intercom by the bed if you need anything."

I don't respond. My mouth is dry, my eyes locked on the paper in my hands.

It takes me a long time to gently pry open the back and tug out the thin piece of notebook paper hiding inside. A few pieces of the torn edge from a spiral flutter to the floor. A smile tugs at my lips when my mother's loopy cursive handwriting sprawls across the page.

BABY,

I'm sorry you have to find out this way. I tried to tell you so many times, but you refused to even entertain the idea of me dying. I can't fault you for refusing to accept it. You're as stubborn as your mother sometimes. So this is the backup plan. I hate putting it on you this way, but it's my only option. Sebastian is your brother. I promise everything will make sense soon enough, but all you need to know right now is that I gave him up to keep you safe a long time ago. My only regret is not getting to fall in love with him like I've fallen in love with you. I know this is hard to understand, and you're confused, but hopefully, it will all make sense someday.

Listen to Sebastian. He'll keep you safe, I know it.

Always remember, I love you so much!! You've been the light of my life since the second you opened your eyes. You took care of me when I should have been taking care of you. Well, now Sebastian gets that honor, and the man you decide is yours one day. You will always be so very perfect to me, my little Maybel. Always.

I want you to remember not to let the hard days win. I'm sure there will be plenty of them for you, but always remember I'm there beside you. And I know it's a faraway thought at the moment, but I want you to find love, the kind that awakens the soul and makes you ache for more. I thought I had experienced it once before, but things got cut short. I don't want that for you, sweetie. I want you to experience love for what it is. A valley of highs and lows, and the only person to help guide you is the one standing beside you through it all.

XOXO

Mom

.   .   .

I CLUTCH the letter to my chest and fall back against the mattress. My heart beats, and my lungs inflate, but I feel nothing but pain and loss. There's a hole in my chest that will never be filled, and I don't know how I'll survive with what's left.

1

DREW

I'm a wolf in sheep's clothing. My skin itches, and my stomach tightens like a fist. This is my home, these are my friends, and this is my legacy, yet this blip of a thought tells me I don't belong here. It's not a lie. I could be doing so many other things right now, like begging Bel to speak to me, to forgive me. I've tried sending text messages and showing up at the mansion. I tried breaking in, but Sebastian's stupid security removed me from the premises. Like I haven't been inside that house and a fucking friend of his the majority of my life. Sebastian has practically banned me from seeing her.

Scanning the room, I dart my eyes from person to person. Every single one of the new Mill recruits is pathetic as fuck. A copy-and-paste overlay of every frat boy across this country. I lay across the large wooden throne carved by my great-grandfather, one leg hanging over the arm. Each fucker has five shots in front of them, and they have barely managed to hold them down.

I sweep my leg off the arm of the chair and let my boot hit the ground with a thud. "I'm not even fucking asking you for anything hard. Take five shots and run the five hundred meters across the lawn and back. That's easy compared to what some of the fraternities dish out."

There's a chorus of mutters and moans, and I shove the nearest freshman with my boot against his shoulder. "You, asshole, take your shots and set a good example." I nod toward Sebastian across the room on the oversized velvet armchair looking bored. "Do you want your sponsor to regret bringing you in? Do you want to chase a hare in The Hunt next year? Then get your shit together!" I scream the last bit in his face, and he leans down over his shots, covering his naked skin to protect it like my boot might slip off his shoulder down to his less protected bits.

"Fucking weak," I mutter and stand to go to the bar. I snatch a bottle of bourbon from the top shelf, pop the cork, and take a long drag. The burn of it feels so good while it courses through my cold chest. I keep my gaze on Sebastian as I swallow, thinking about how to approach him without starting another fight.

Lee saunters over, his own bottle of booze in hand. "Is it just me, or are these assholes worse than last year's assholes?"

I snort. "I was just thinking the same thing. Five shots is nothing. That run is nothing."

I raise my voice so the recruits can hear me. "And if these assholes don't get moving soon, I'm going to start adding more shots and wood trails to what needs to get done tonight."

One of the assholes stumbles to his feet, and Lee gives him an appraising look. "You ready, asshole?"

He nods. "Yes, sir."

Lee gives him a saucy wink. "Show me the proof of your daily task, and it better fucking be interesting."

The recruit digs through his clothes on the floor for his phone, opens it, and shoves it at Lee. I lean over his shoulder and look down at the pictures. They each had to fuck five different people today and get proof to be admitted to the initiation.

Lee nods as he scrolls through the photos. "At least you've been thorough, asshole. Your shots are done. Let's go start your run."

Lee signals to Aries, who is monitoring the recruits on the floor still drinking. Seb stands and precedes Lee out the door. The recruit follows them, and I come up behind. A brisk wind howls outside, and the recruit immediately starts shivering as I clutch my fleece tighter around my shoulders and shove my hands into the pockets.

"Get on with it, fuckface. I don't want to get frostbite waiting for you."

Now that football season is over, we start the initiation process for the new recruits. Those who will take over in the coming years as Lee, Seb, and I graduate. It's slim pickings at this point, but someone's bound to have the balls to take over.

I stop next to Sebastian on the starting line, but like I anticipated, he doesn't even spare me a glance. Not until I snatch the bottle of top-shelf vodka from his grasp. Physically, he's here, but mentally, I know he's off in some faraway land, probably plotting my demise.

His eyes shoot to mine and narrow. "Fuck off," he says, low and menacing.

It's not even in the same tone he used to tell me to fuck off in. This tone promises a fight if I push him. And if I'm being honest, I've had just enough alcohol to fucking push him.

In fact, a fight is exactly what I need, because anything would be better than this painful reminder of what I did to Bel, of how I hurt her.

"Where is she?" I question confidently. There's no point in beating around the bush. He knows that I want her, that I'm dying to see even a glimpse of her sunshine blond hair.

He snatches the vodka back, holding it in one hand, his other shoved into his black dress pants. As always, he's dressed like he's about to hit the stock market floor. If I had to guess, I'd say Sebastian really wants to punch me in the face, and maybe that's why he has his hand buried deep in his pocket. To stop himself from giving in to the impulse.

"Perhaps you're deaf. I said fuck. Off."

I step closer, my breath fogging the night air. "Not deaf, buddy, just not listening to your bullshit. She hasn't returned to school for nearly a month. Her academics are important to her. When is she coming back?"

There's a crash as one of the recruits stumbles out of the house naked, racing toward the starting line. He zooms right past us. Finally, someone who is just as ready to get out of here as I am.

I focus my attention back on Seb. "Anyway, as we were discussing, you were just about to tell me when Bel planned to return to school?"

His green eyes narrow to slits. "First, why the fuck

would I ever tell *you*? Second, why do you care so much? If my memory stands correct, you made it painfully clear that she is nothing to you. What, now that she's not trailer trash, you think you can have her back? She's not a fucking toy that you can pass around to your friends."

A hot wash of rage whips through me. "We both know I didn't mean anything I said that day. All I was doing was protecting her from my father. You know how he is, and he's got it in his head to make her pay for sullying our name. I wasn't trying to hurt her. I'm aware that I did, but that wasn't my objective."

I can see the tightening of his jaw, the way the muscle jumps in the dim moonlight. He doesn't respond and instead takes a swig of the liquor.

"Hm...joke's on him. She's fucking higher class than he is now. Karma is a real bitch, isn't she? Was this your daddy's and your plan? He tell you to kiss and make up, so you can marry Bel instead? Everyone knows he lives off your mom's inheritance, and that he had nothing when he started out."

I clench my hands into tight fists. "I'm not talking about him right now. I want to know when Bel will be back at school."

"That's Ms. Arturo to you, dickhead."

I let out a slow breath so I don't punch him in the fucking jaw. He's on my last fucking nerve, and I really don't want to destroy his face. "No, she's my wallflower, and you fucking know it. I'm not going anywhere, and I'm not giving her up."

He smirks. "Hmm...I think you already gave her up. As for when she comes back to school... Let's just say she's waiting for her stitches to heal. The stitches that she had to get after you pushed her and caused her to hit her head. Remember that?"

My stomach cramps. I close my eyes against the image of her falling, of the blood dripping onto the floor. The horror in her eyes, the pain and fear. I did that to her, and I'll never truly forgive myself. I'll spend every day making it up to her if she gives me the chance.

"That was an accident."

"Was calling her white trash an accident too? Because you know what they say about emotional and physical abuse. Physical wounds heal, but it's the emotional wounds that stay with you forever. I wonder how long it'll take for her to heal?"

Another recruit stumbles down the steps of the main house, across the sidewalk, and onto the grass. His glassy eyes barely register us as he races across the line. Being the asshole he is, Sebastian kicks him in his bare flank, sending him stumbling but not fully down. We watch him run until he disappears down the small hill.

Needing a minute to fight back the slowly rising guilt and revulsion of how thoroughly fucked up I am for still wanting her, I turn and walk back into the house.

I snatch one of the recruits who's finishing his last shot. "Let's go, asshole. Time's up."

He struggles and stumbles to his feet, and I drag him out of the house and throw him toward the line. Color me surprised when he doesn't fall and takes off running. Not bad.

I watch him go and then step back inside the house and call out to the remaining stragglers. "You have two minutes to get your asses outside, or you're done. For good."

I turn and watch as Sebastian wanders slowly down the lantern-lined route, and I follow him. He's not getting out of this conversation that easily.

When he pauses, we end up side by side. "Look, everything that happened at that party was fucked up, okay? It didn't go as planned, not at all."

He glances over at me, his features partially hidden in the shadows from the low-lit lanterns. "How is your fiancée, Drew? Have you fucked her yet? Last I saw, she was ready to strip down in the middle of the ballroom in front of everyone. Hell, I bet she'd let me fuck her with you. Two-for-one special."

I clench my teeth and glare off into the dark so I don't take a swing at him. This has been his attitude the few times I've seen him since that night. "That's over with. I made it clear to Spencer and to my father that I won't marry her. He let it drop, for now at least. What are we doing here, man? Is this what years of friendship amounts to?"

Like a bow strung too tightly, he snaps, getting right into my face, his chest bumping against mine. The smell of vodka from his breath burns my eyes. "You fucked her and then threw her away in the most painful way possible. When she needed you most. My fucking *sister*. You expect me to be okay with that? You expect me to choose you over her?"

A snake of danger and pain slithers up my spine. I'm two seconds away from saying *MY* sister, but I don't. I lock the words down because I know that would only start a different kind of fight. "You didn't know she was your sister until a month ago. She's nothing to you. And I'm not asking you to pick me over her or saying that what I did was okay. I'm simply trying to figure out why you're so pissed off at me."

He turns away from me with a shake of his head. "I might not know a lot about her, but she's still my responsibility, my ward. She's my fucking sister, Drew, my sister. I've lost everything, and now I find out I have a sister, a relative that's worthy of giving a fuck about." His voice cracks with raw emotion, and I can understand his desire to protect her. Much like me, he's never had anyone in his life who's worth giving a fuck about. "Anyway, the right thing to do is to protect her, even if that means keeping you away from her. Even if she wanted to see you, which she doesn't."

I sigh, the emotions in my chest all churned up in a gut-wrenching mess. I can't even think about her these days without feeling sick. Not because of her, but because of myself. I've never regretted anything in my life as much as I do the way I treated her that night. I want her back in my life, yes, but not in the same way. I want more, something deeper, something... dare I say like forever. I've already come to terms with the fact that my father needs to be taken care of. I don't know how I'll do that yet, but I'm not giving up Bel for him. He's unpredictable, and proving to him that she was nothing to me put the target back on me and off her.

No matter what, I keep going back to that night—to the betrayal etched into her beautiful features and the pain-stricken look in her eyes. I did that to her, and I hated myself for it. I haven't even been able to look at myself in the mirror since.

The only saving grace is that I haven't had to deal with my father much since then either. I'm worried if I spend longer than five minutes with him, I'll try to kill him, and I'm not quite ready to cross that bridge... *yet.*

"What do you want from me, Seb? I thought I was doing the right thing. I was protecting her," I whisper.

"Nothing. Neither of us wants anything from you. Give it up and leave her alone. That's the only way I'll be able to keep myself from putting a bullet in your head."

The world seems to freeze at his words, but the chill in his eyes tells me he's dead serious. I try not to show him my hurt, but it's almost impossible.

"Are you fucking kidding? Were you not paying attention for the past couple of months? She belongs to me." I lower my voice and step up to him so we are only a few inches apart. "She is *mine.*"

A hand snakes between us and presses me back. Lee inserts himself between us, clearly seeing the war brewing.

"Unless you two are going to make out, back the fuck up. It's obvious neither of you is sharing what happened between the two of you at the party, but I'm done playing referee, trying to keep both of you from killing each other. Now, we have a job to finish here. Let's keep these assholes from dying of alcohol poisoning and frostbite. Otherwise, we'll have a different kind of problem on our hands. Then you two can go back to your respective corners of sulking and brooding."

That was the problem in all this. I have no plans to go anywhere. I let out a long sigh and swipe Lee's bottle of liquor from his hand. Bringing it to my lips, I take a long gulp and barely manage to swallow it.

I lift the bottle, peeking at the label.

"Fucking gin, Lee. Really?"

He eyes me as I wipe my mouth with the back of my hand as if that'll get the terrible taste out of my mouth. "Hey, I don't judge your beverage choices, don't judge mine."

He snatches the bottle back and stands between Seb and I, his body acting as a shield. If Seb and I were really going to fight it out, Lee wouldn't be able to stop us.

Our attention is brought back to the runners as the last of the recruits stagger out of the house, resembling that of drunk toddlers as they race across the lawn. *Fucking finally.* Only a little while longer until I can get out of here. Not that I have anything to look forward to after this. Bel's locked away in an ivory tower, and I have no way of rescuing her.

I'm many things—a heinous villain, devilishly hand-some, an asshole, and prick—

but I'm not dumb. I've been watching Sebastian like a hawk, and I know he's got her stashed away at his house. It's the only viable option. She's not at the dorms or living in her mother's house. I haven't caught even a glimpse of her, and it's that withdrawal, her absence that makes me snappy and irritable. *Fuck me.*

I could always break into the house. I'm not against that... I'd take a charge just to see her beautiful face again. I tried previously and was tossed out on my ass, but that was before. I'm sure they expected it then. As quickly as the thought comes to mind, I shove it away. I'll save that as a last-ditch effort. I'm not quite at the end of my rope yet.

I pull my phone out and peer down at the screen. I've sent her numerous texts, but she only ever tells me to leave her alone or stop messaging her. I've even called. I can't believe she thinks I'd be deterred by her telling me to go away or leave her alone. Maybe if I was a good guy, but I'm not. I'm Drew, the monster she picked to hunt her down in the woods. The man she gave her virginity to and showed all the dark corners of her mind to.

I'm not going anywhere.

Navigating to my messages, I click on her name and then type out another message and hit send. It pings back as undelivered, and I squeeze the phone hard enough to break it while I glare at the ground. I count back from ten...trying to calm myself before I do something stupid like beat the fuck out of my best friend.

Ten. Nine. Eight. Seven. Six. Five. Four. Three. Two. One.

Once I feel a smidge less murderous, I speak.

"Is her cell phone included in her house arrest?"

Seb turns and gives me his typical icy glare that eats through my insides like acid. "She's not under house arrest, fuckwad, and I didn't take shit from her. She threw her phone away because you kept texting her. I was happy to supply her with a brand-new one. One that doesn't have your number in it."

Lee's gaze darts between us, the sides of his mouth turned down into a scowl. "Will you two stop your fucking squabbling and pay attention? I think we just lost one of the fuckers."

One of the recruits lies sprawled out in the grass,

appearing to be passed out only a few feet shy of the finish line. *Not quite, buddy.* I march over and check his pulse, then his fingertips and toes. "He's alive but very drunk."

Not so gently, I haul him to his feet, and a jumble of slurred words slip past his lips while I drag him over to Lee. The guy's knees buckle beneath him as I hand him off, and lucky for him, Lee is quick. Otherwise, he'd be eating dirt again.

I meet Lee's eyes over the kid's shoulder. "Get that number for me, yeah?"

"You missed the finish line by five feet, man," Lee tells him, with a quick nod to me, and then they disappear back toward the house. All over again, it's Seb and me left by ourselves. I turn and find him looking at me. His piercing gaze slices straight through me.

"I UNDERSTAND why you want to protect her, but you can't keep her from me forever. Eventually, she'll have to return to school, and inevitably, I'll see her. I've known you for the majority of my life, and I know you like to think you can control every situation, but you can't. I'm warning you now. I don't give a fuck what you think or how you feel. Bel is *mine*. She was mine before you found out she was your sister, and she'll be mine long after."

He smirks, but it's the serial killer's smirk as he lowers the knife to your throat.

"Sure... but let me share something with you. The Bel who was yours? She's gone. Now that I think about it, what was that nickname you called her? Wallflower?" He taps at his chin like he's lost in thought. "Ahh, yes. I'd say she's more like a wildflower now, and we both know you don't want anything you can't tame. Your best bet is to leave her alone... that is, unless you want our friendship to end and your ass ten feet in the ground."

"Don't make promises you can't keep. You won't kill me. We've been through too much."

He gives me a shove, but I barely feel it.

"Don't tell me what I'll do or not do. If you think I'll stand by and let you treat her like shit, you don't know me at all. When it comes to Bel, I'll do whatever I have to do to protect her. Even kill you, if that's the only way to get rid of you. Family before anything."

I'm not sure how to react, but I continue staring him down, refusing to show an inkling of fear. Sebastian is taking this brother role very seriously, and I don't think he's bluffing. That's the thing, though, neither am I.

Eventually, one of us will have to give...

2

BEL

Time feels different when you're grieving. Like every minute and day that passes is excruciatingly slow. The wound left in my chest from the absence of my mother's presence in my life feels as if it will never heal. Every thought and reminder of her makes my eyes burn, tears forever falling from my eyes. Even when I try to blink them away, my vision is never clear. Every breath I take makes the pain worse and reminds me this isn't a nightmare I can wake up from.

It's been a month since I lost her, but it feels like it's only been seconds. That's how fresh the pain is. I peer around the space that is now called *my* room. Yes, it's my room, but it's not really mine. Nothing about this room says *Bel*. It's perfect, from the painted walls with crown moldings to the silk bedsheets and plush carpeted floor. It's everything I'm not, and it makes me miss my mother and our tiny little house. We didn't have a lot of money, but we had each other. I blink back tears and press my hands into my eye sockets to stop the steady stream of tears from falling.

Think about something else... anything else.

There's a never-ending pile of new clothes, all still with the tags on them, and a stack of paperbacks that sit near the bed on the floor. I look at them with rage. I'm not alone in my grief, but I feel like it. Sebastian thinks he can buy my happiness, and I know this because of his constant need to shower me with gifts—new books, new clothes, new everything.

Those things are nice, but they don't fill the void. Maybe those things work for him, or perhaps that's how he's always coped, but that's not how *I* cope. I can't just buy something new and forget about my problems. *Seb and I are not the same.* Money can solve a lot of issues in a person's life, but it cannot fill the void and loss of someone you love. You can't replace people with objects.

Here and there, I have the desire to leave this room and venture to other parts of the house, but those times are few and far between. I try my best to keep to myself. I don't belong here. I don't need another reminder of exactly how much I don't belong.

Everything in my world is so much darker without her... *without him.*

It's like all the color has been drained from my life. I try not to think about Drew, but if it's not him, then it's my mother, and I'd rather think of the thing that hurts less. I press back against the pillows and stare up at the delicately patterned ceiling, wondering what the hell I'm supposed to do with my life now.

I think back to the conversations with Sebastian in the

past two weeks when he expressed his desire for me to return to class. I wish I could, but I haven't gathered enough courage. Not when there is a risk of seeing Jackie, or Drew, or anyone who knows what happened that night. I don't need their pity.

Like yesterday and the day before that, I roll over on the bed when I get tired of staring at the ceiling and stare at the doorway.

The room is painted a beige color. The bedding, curtains, and trimming—rich people call it trimming, right?—and furniture are all as it was when I moved in: mauves and grays, pretty and understated. I picture it as a hotel room rather than a bedroom.

My bedroom.

My mother would laugh at the frivolity of it all. The ridiculousness of having ten pillows for my bed when I only need a max of two. The insanity that someone comes in to clean my suite almost every day unless I keep them from entering. The preposterousness that someone will deliver food at every meal time without me even having to say a word. For example, someone knocks on the door right now—five o'clock on the dot.

The staff are always on time, and I'm grateful for the food they bring me, but it doesn't change things. The only thing I want off that food tray is the bottle of wine they usually bring with dinner.

I roll off the edge of the bed, my legs protesting after lying in the same position for hours, and open the door. One of the kitchen staff sweeps in. I think it's Heidi, but I'm trying not to get attached to any of them. I'm not staying.

This entire experience has taught me a valuable lesson

—never get comfortable with things because you never know when someone will get tired of playing with you and toss you to the wolves. It's only a matter of time till Sebastian does it. He says he won't, but in this new world, without her, I don't trust anyone or anything.

The woman, who can't be much older than me, wears black slacks and a button-down shirt. I barely blink at her as she leaves the tray on the end of the bed where I prefer it and scampers back out the door without a word.

Something hot scratches inside my chest—guilt maybe for not being nicer, kinder, or not at least saying thank you. My momma raised me better than that, but Drew and the loss of my mother killed off any remaining shred of kindness that I had left. Most days I'm numb to my surroundings, to my thoughts. Sometimes I allow myself to feel things, but it's never good when I do.

"Thank you," I whisper to the empty room.

I swipe the wine bottle off the tray, retreat to my spot nestled in the pillows, and bring the bottle to my lips.

I tip it back and take a long swallow of the bubbly wine.

Sometimes it helps, but most of the time, it doesn't. *But what else can I do?* There's nothing worth holding on to anymore. Reality is far worse than my dreams. My phone pings, and I snatch it off the covers and stare down at the screen with a frown.

It's Drew. *Again.*

I know I should block him. He deserves it. But honestly, I haven't had the heart to do it. I've barely responded to his texts, and the few times I have, it's been with a snarky response that's nothing more than to tell him to fuck off and leave me alone. There was also that time I'd told him I'd send Sebastian after him. He responded almost instantly with an eye roll emoji. I won't lie, that made me smile. It didn't take long for the smile to fade away when I remembered the pain he put me through.

He was very clear he wanted nothing to do with me that night. I reach back and prod at the still sensitive skin on my head. The stitches haven't even come out yet, and he thinks he can text me, and I'll come running to him?

Fuck him. White-hot anger replaces the empty numbness inside me, and I open my phone to reply. To tell him to fuck off in every way that I'm able. My fingers move over the keys as I type out a long response, telling him how I really feel. My heart thunders, beating against my rib cage like it's trying to break free of my body.

I hover over the send button, but then a knock sounds against the door. Before I can open my mouth to respond, Sebastian enters.

Excuse you, sir.

I slap my phone flat on the bed so he won't see the screen and glare at him. "Typically, people wait for permission to enter a room if they knock before entering."

He doesn't respond but sits on the end of the bed near my food, his gaze on the tray. "I'm going to tell the staff to stop sending wine up with your dinner if all you do is drink it and leave the food behind."

I sink back into the pillows and cup the bottle of wine close again. "What do you want from me? I'm not hungry."

He grabs a piece of the chicken on the plate and pops it into his mouth, dragging his attention back to me. "I doubt

I have to tell you this, but you're a fucking mess. You've lost ten pounds this month, ten pounds I don't think you had to lose to begin with. I'm not sure when you last showered, and your hair could use a brushing."

I bring the wine bottle to my lips and tip it back. Taking a long swallow, I keep my gaze on his. I wipe my mouth with the back of my hand. "My weight, or lack thereof, is none of your business. Nor is my personal hygiene, or lack thereof. I think you could use some manners if we're pointing out one another's flaws."

His eyes sweep over me again as he picks at the food on my tray. *Does he not have any food of his own?* It's absurd to be annoyed with him for eating food that I didn't plan to eat anyway, but it's still annoying how he sits here all casually, eating and acting like everything is good. He tilts his head at my phone, his eyes blazing. "Are you talking to him again?"

This entire situation is awkward. His desire to ask questions, to get to know me, to build a relationship. I don't know why he's even trying. We both know he doesn't really give a shit about me. He's not doing this because he cares. Men like him don't do anything for free, and they certainly don't do anything because they care. He can deny it all he wants, but in my eyes, he will always have some hidden agenda.

I wave my phone, the screen thankfully dark. "Also none of your business."

His gaze sharpens, and I resist the urge to flinch. *Show them your fear and they've already won.* "Hate to burst your bubble, sis, but anything concerning you is my business. I'm not about to try to control you or tell you what to do.

Just remember he doesn't give a shit about you. All he cared about was conquering you. Now that you're unattainable, he's angry and throwing a fit like a toddler."

"First of all, don't call me sis ever again. Second of all, I don't want to talk about him. I'm aware that I meant nothing to him. I have a scar that I can see every time I look in the mirror as a damn reminder, so don't lecture me with that bullshit."

He smirks and pops a piece of broccoli into his mouth. "Good. I'm glad you haven't forgotten. But be warned, if he shows up here, I'll kill him. So if you don't want to see his blood on the marble, don't invite him over."

I move to take another swig of the wine, and he swipes the bottle from my hands and brings it to his lips, taking a long chug. My thoughts hover on his warning. Would he really kill his best friend to protect me?

"Hey!" I snap. "That's my dinner, thank you."

He eyes me over the length of the bottle, chugging deeper and deeper. When he finally comes up for air, it's half gone.

"Asshole," I mutter, snatching the bottle back. I know I wouldn't have gotten it back if he didn't want me to have it back. I take a huge gulp of the wine, and as I'm swallowing, some goes down the wrong tube. I start to cough, wine sputtering out of my mouth and down my chin.

"Wow. You're grace personified."

"Fuck off," I mumble while wiping at my mouth, a smile tugging at my lips. His eyes appear to lighten, with a little glimmer of hope.

We've been doing this bickering thing every other day or so since the week after I moved here. I can't pinpoint the exact reason, but it feels...right...normal. Of course it's still awkward as hell while we get to know one another, but a little more of that strange feeling slips away each day. I'm starting to see him, really see him, which terrifies me because that means he's seeing me. I guess this is what siblings are supposed to do? And maybe for a few seconds when he's here giving me shit, I don't feel quite as alone as I have felt since I lost everything.

This thought hardens me again, and I pull my knees to my chest and cradle the wine between my thighs. "Did you need something, or did you just come by to make sure I'm still alive?"

He shrugs and grabs a crescent roll off my tray. Then he stands and throws himself into the armchair across from my bed. "Doing the brotherly thing. You know, making sure you haven't hung yourself from the shower rod, annoying you, the usual brother shit."

I almost smile. "There aren't any shower rods in this house. Everything is stainless steel, ceramic, and marble. There would never be something so basic as a shower curtain in this house."

He snorts. "Fair." He holds his hand out for the bottle, and slowly, begrudgingly, I slip the bottle into his grasp.

"Don't drink it all."

"If I do, I'll have someone bring you another bottle."

We sit in silence that doesn't quite feel as fraught until he stands, crosses the room, and hits a switch to light the fireplace.

It comes to life in a blaze of fire, and then he sits down again. "Don't tell me you don't enjoy this."

I barely withhold an eye roll. "You mean, how can

someone who never had anything not appreciate that they have everything now?"

"That's not what I said."

I make a noise and snag the bottle back to take another drink. "He's been texting me."

The silence in the room suddenly feels heavier, the silence descending for a split second over the backdrop of the crackling fire.

His tone is a little more serious with his next question. "Have you been answering him?"

I stare at my feet and the chipped polish I haven't bothered to refresh in the past month. "No, not really. I haven't been encouraging him if that's what you mean. When I do respond, which is rare, I tell him to leave me alone."

Anger flashes in his eyes. "Why haven't you blocked him?" he mutters. "I should have blocked him myself. In fact, give me your phone. I'll get you a new one with a different number, and I'll personally ensure he doesn't get it."

Panic creeps to the surface, and I snatch my phone off the bed and hug it next to the bottle of wine. "You can't. I don't want a new phone. I want to keep this one."

The thought of losing my pictures and the voicemails from mom guts me. They're all I have left, the only physical memories of her. The thought of losing them makes me feel like I've lost her all over again.

My fear and anxiety must be etched into my features because all he does is nod. "Relax, Bel. I won't take your phone. I was just giving you shit. I want to make sure you're okay."

I sag into the pillows again, relief surging through me. "Right, giving me shit. You've become a pro at that."

He sighs and stares off at the fire. "I know it's going to be hard, but I don't think you should see Drew again. He's not good for you, and take it from someone who has been his friend for years. A leopard doesn't change its spots. If he hurt you once, he'll do it again."

"You think I don't know that already? I'm not nearly as dumb as everyone thinks I am."

"I don't think you're dumb at all. I think you're hungry to be loved and accepted, which can, unfortunately, make you an easy target, especially to the wrong kind of people. Drew is not the type of guy you bring home to Mom and Dad."

Well, funnily enough, I have neither of those... I almost say, but bite my tongue.

Drew isn't perfect, and I wouldn't even say he's good, but Sebastian has no idea what we shared. He has no idea how alive I felt with Drew. I'm not agreeing with anything that happened, nor do I think it's okay, but whatever was developing between us was special, and I can't just switch that off or forget it. At least if you aren't a complete psychopath.

We sit in silence, and for one fleeting moment, I wish I still had Jackie... Scratch that. I wish I had someone to talk to who would understand. My heart aches at the loss of my friendship with her, of the loss of my mother and Drew. The pain rips through me, the wound pulsing with life.

I roll my eyes up toward the ceiling so I don't cry and chug back some more wine.

"What do you want, Bel?"

His adoption of my nickname should grate on every nerve ending in my body, but it feels good to have someone call me that. I swallow hard and then look back at him. His green eyes bore into mine.

"I want the pain to go away, for everything to stop hurting so much. For the constant reminder of all I lost to disappear."

"It won't be this way forever. The pain will fade eventually, and each day will hurt a little less than the day before."

"How do you know?" I snap.

The moment I've spoken the words, I regret them. If anyone doesn't deserve my venom, it's him. Sebastian has been kind, patient, and understanding. He's been far more supportive than I ever expected him to be, and he's lost someone as well. His situation is almost worse than my own. At least I have memories of time spent with our mother. He has nothing.

He stands and slips his hands into his pockets. I swear I see a flicker of disappointment in his eyes. "I'll send up more wine if you eat all your dinner."

My mouth opens, and I want to tell him I'm sorry, that I didn't mean to snap at him, but I'm not sure it would matter. He disappears out the door, closing it softly behind him, leaving me with my thoughts.

I know I'm being a bitch, and that I continue to be one even without thinking about it. Unfortunately, it's a trauma mechanism I've developed to protect myself. It's better if I push him away and keep him at arm's length. At least then, when something happens, when he inevitably leaves, it'll hurt a little less than if I let him in all the way. Because the thought of losing literally the only family I have left hurts, even if I barely know anything about him.

My phone pings again, but I refuse to look at it, so I take a long swig of the wine. "Fuck off, Drew," I whisper.

I let out a shuddering breath and lean back into the pillows. My food is getting cold, and the wine is nearly gone. I should eat something, and sadly not because Sebastian told me to, but because I want more wine.

With a sigh, I lean over and crawl to the end of the bed on my knees to sit and eat. Chicken and vegetables—a full meal of nutrients and vitamins. Nothing like my scamper for nutrients vs. cost when I had to shop for myself. This is a long way away from peanut butter sandwiches. I pop a couple of pieces of food into my mouth. I'm overwhelmed with the robust spice from the chicken and veggies.

It's delicious too, of course. Sebastian, I guess our family, has to have the best.

I take another bite and consider what Sebastian hasn't told me about our family. Like how they made their millions and what this will all mean for me when the time comes. What does my future look like as a member of this family? From what I've seen, Sebastian has taken it all onto his shoulders, even as he seems to stumble under the weight of it. He doesn't complain, doesn't even show a sliver of weakness.

He's far stronger than I am. Maybe that has to do with how he was raised? There are so many things I have yet to learn about him and who our family is. It saddens me to think how much time has passed, how many memories we missed out on making. The pinging of my phone drags me from my thoughts, and I check it before I can think better of it. I see Drew's latest unanswered message.

Psycho: *You have one week, Flower. One week to get back to me, or I'm hunting you down, ready or not.*

I drop the phone down onto the bed and stare straight ahead. Was Sebastian lying when he said he would kill Drew? I'm not sure I want to take that chance. While I'm pissed at Drew and kinda sorta want to stab him, the last thing I want is for him to die. Still, he needs to understand that he's no longer in control. I am, and I'm done answering to him.

3

DREW

I was trying to be a gentleman when I gave her a week, but my ability to hold myself back after two days has frayed. I'm itching to touch her porcelain skin. Hell, at this point, I'd take even a glimpse of her. Call me selfish, I don't give a fuck. All I wanted to do was protect her, and like all the good things in my life, it backfired and exploded in my face. I've done everything I possibly can to try to fix this, but with every day that passes, the space between us grows, and I *need* her. I need her so badly it fucking hurts to breathe. It's wrong, but I'd do anything to touch her, hold her in my arms, even if it would result in her pushing me away. I'm just that fuckin' selfish.

I won't apologize for being me or for trying to do the right thing. Not when she has no idea, not even from their brief encounter, what my father is capable of. I can't lie to myself anymore. My life is in shambles, and like a sinking ship, everyone is jumping overboard. I'm the captain, though. I'm supposed to sink with the fucking ship.

Sebastian isn't speaking to me. Lee is keeping his distance so he doesn't feel like he's taking anyone's side, and I don't even think Aries has a fucking clue what is happening. I will say he definitely feels the tension and notices Seb's absence. Per usual, he likes to act as the fixer and keeps trying to get us into the same room to hash it out, but that's been a complete failure so far.

I scrub my hands over my face, letting out a groan of frustration, then I stand and grab a T-shirt from the dresser. *Today is the day. There won't be any more hiding, Flower. I'm going to find you and pluck all your beautiful petals so you can never escape me...* Whatever patience I had is gone now, and since my father has been out of town for a couple of days, this might be my only opportunity to capture her.

It will be a challenge since she's not back at school yet, but I'm confident I can lure her out of Seb's lockdown at home. *Fuck me.* I just *need* to see her. It's fucked, completely fucked, especially after my father's revelation, but I don't care. I need to see her to ensure she's okay. At least that's what I tell myself. Things haven't changed for me, despite all that has happened. Right now, all that matters to me is seeing her and telling her the truth. I have to make her believe me, to make her understand there was no other choice.

I finish dressing and press down on the edge of the bed, shoving my feet into my black boots. I lace them up tight, then grab my jacket and yank up the hood. I've been doing everything I can to keep a lower profile across campus. If I walk to the other side of campus to catch a ride app, then it's less likely someone will report back to dear ole dad, and after the party, I've learned that I can't trust anyone. So fuck people.

My phone vibrates in my pocket as I jog down the stairs, thankful no one is up yet. Before heading out the door, I grab a granola bar and premade protein shake from the fridge. I walk quickly down the long gravel driveway to the main campus. Halfway through my walk, I open my phone and check the messages, hoping against hope that Bel's finally answered me with something other than "fuck off."

I find no such thing. The campus is still pretty quiet, and as I walk, my gaze snags on the library building, but I quickly look away, the memories bubbling up even though I try to block them out. Those bookshelves, the scent of Bel's fear turning me on...

Fuck. I'm fucked up. I don't think I can fix this, not when my own biology is fighting against me here. It's so messed up but I still want her. I still get unbelievably hard when I think about pressing her into those books. I can still feel her pussy clenching around me, tightening, swallowing every drop of cum, proving how much she needs me.

I can't lie and say I haven't stroked my cock to the image of her. In my eyes, it doesn't matter. It doesn't change a fucking thing. I'm sick, fucked up, demented. All I can ask myself is... is it because of my dad?

Does coveting Bel make me a sick and twisted monster like my father? It should. I'm obsessed, unhinged with the desire to fuck and own a woman who I've fallen for that might now be my goddamn *sister*. My stomach twists painfully, and I want to vomit, but I can't ignore the hardness growing between my legs or the way my heartbeat speeds up.

I'm only a few minutes away from the spot where I'm supposed to meet my ride when my phone vibrates again. I'm two seconds from texting the bitch back to tell her off, but one look at the screen and I discover it's a call from an unknown number.

I swallow hard, my heart in my throat, and hit the answer button, hoping, praying, needing it to be my wallflower.

"Mr. Marshall?"

I don't recognize the voice at all, and my hackles are up. "Yes? Who is this?"

"This is Gerald, a member of the nursing staff for your mother. We are unable to get in touch with your father, and we've had an emergency. Would it be possible for you to come and discuss the next steps with her care team at the estate?"

"Next steps?" *What the fucking hell is going on?*

My ride pulls up. I climb in and navigate from the call to change the address in the app. I usually walk around campus, and if I need to go to the estate, my father will send me a car. But maybe it's time I bring one of the cars here to campus. It just seems stupid when I will rarely ever use it. The ride apps get me where I need easily enough.

We pull away, and I press the phone back to my ear. "I'm on my way there now. Is she okay?"

I hope he can't hear the naked fear in my voice, but I don't have the strength to hide it right now.

"I think it's best if you let the doctors discuss things with you, Mr. Marshall."

Instantly, I know this is bad. I tap the driver on the shoulder. "As fast as you can and I'll give you a bigger tip."

The middle-aged man driving nods and hits the accelerator, causing the car to lurch forward. My back flattens against the seat, and I struggle to catch my breath.

"I'll be there in a few minutes," I tell the guy and hang up.

The entire drive takes ten minutes tops, but it feels like an eternity with something so doomful hanging over my head.

The car hasn't even stopped at the gate. The tires are still rolling, but I couldn't give one shit. I jump from the car and rush through the partially open gate. My boots slap against the concrete, but I don't slow.

I run the entire way up the drive and into the house. The house is nothing like Mill house, sprawling across way too much land for being inside the city limits. I barely see the staff or the rooms as I rush toward my mom's suite. By the time I reach the room, a thin sheen of sweat has formed on my brow, and I'm sucking ragged breaths into my lungs.

I notice a man in a white coat standing in the middle of the room, and I stop short. *What the fuck is going on?*

"Where is her usual doctor?" I bark in the way of greeting.

The youngish white man with dark hair and glasses surveys me. "He was unable to complete his employment. I apologize for any confusion. I was hired in his place until

Mrs. Marshall can get a more permanent in-house physician."

The doctor extends his hand. "Dr. Banks. And you are?"

"Drew. Her *son*."

He nods. "It's nice to meet you although I wish it were under better circumstances."

I shake my head. There's no need for pleasantries right now. I just need to *know*. "What's going on? What's wrong?"

He places his hand on my shoulder, and I scowl but resist shrugging his hold off. "At the moment, your mother is stable, but some decisions will need to be made fairly soon. We are currently unable to get ahold of the elder Mr. Marshall. Your mother has you listed as the next of kin and power of attorney."

That's news to me, but I'm not going to question them. Especially when my father is probably off fucking his new mistress or something equally disturbing.

"What's going on?" All I can think of are the worst possible things. "Please, just tell me. Is she dying?"

His mouth settles into a straight line, and he puts on one of those masks people adopt when they have to impart bad news. "I'll be frank with you, it's not looking good. It seems her organs are beginning to shut down. From the testing we've done, she's going to need at least a kidney transplant, if not more, and fairly soon, too. It's best if a direct family member donates, as the viability of the body taking it without severe complications lessens greatly."

The world spins all around me, and I want to punch my father in the face and rip the room apart. How could he let things get to this point? I eye my mother over his shoulder, staring at her unmoving body. I can't help it. My body moves as if on command, my legs carrying me over to her bedside, forcing the doctor to follow with hurried, worried footsteps.

I don't take my eyes off her. I let the image before me burn into my mind. Her eyes are closed, and she's pale, so pale. Her once dark hair is now streaked with gray, the locks settling around her shoulders.

She looks so sick...

"Mom," I whisper.

The doctor continues speaking like I haven't moved or said a word. "We also need to run some additional tests. I've combed through her medical records myself, and it looks like her previous doctor was a little lax when it came to running regular blood work. I don't mean to make matters worse, but I feel this might have been caught much earlier if routine work was done."

I nod and grip my mother's hand gently. Her hand seems too small in mine, too fragile. The coldness of her skin presses against the warmth of my own, and anger and resentment bloom in my cheeks. How could Dad let her get to this point? I knew he hated me, and I knew he had fallen out of love with my mother, given his desire to sleep around all the time, but I never thought he'd let her fucking die on us.

"Do whatever you need to do, Doctor. Just keep her alive."

He moves beside me, but I don't take my eyes off my mother's face. She's been sick for so long now, I feel like I have more memories of her *with* this illness than I do of her without. Tears burn at the back of my eyes. I won't cry. I can't. I'm stronger than that. Crying doesn't fix shit. It's merely a weakness. I can hear my father's voice in my mind, the words ingrained there. The past month has made me question every single thing I know.

But I don't fucking cry. That much I do remember.

The questions stack up, but there are no answers. Are Bel and I really siblings? According to my father, we are. Then there's the mysterious illness that both Bel's mother and my mother have. *None* of this is a coincidence. There is no way. The problem is I have no idea or way of proving that the two incidents are related. Nothing other than a gut instinct.

I watch the doctor on the other side of the bed warily.

Did my father hire him to keep her sick? What about the previous doctor?

Can I trust this man? He seems to care far more than the previous doctor, who wouldn't even pay attention to me whenever I asked a question. Still, I don't trust any of them.

I need answers, but most importantly, I need to keep her with me so we can find out the truth together. She deserves to survive and see my father pay for what he's done to me, her, and Bel. All of it.

My blood pumps with adrenaline and rage. I tug a chair over so I can be closer to her. "Mom, can you hear me?"

I'm met with silence. I squeeze my eyes closed and try my best not to lose it. I rarely get to see her, and I won't be able to stand it if I don't even get to speak to her ever again.

"Mom?" The word comes out like a prayer.

The doctor clears his throat and fiddles with some tubes.

"I don't mean to interrupt, but I need you to sign some forms for us to approve the tests. She's been given a pretty hefty dose of painkillers and has been in and out of it since this morning. Don't take it personally if she doesn't react. It's best for her to stay sedated so there's less risk of stress to the body."

"This seems pretty serious. Should I have her transferred to the hospital?"

He shakes his head. "No, not yet. I can manage everything that has happened so far here at the house. The problem will be if her organs really start shutting down. At that point, we will rush her to the hospital. On the off chance that does happen, I have a release form that I'll have you sign today, just in case."

"Sure. Whatever you need." I nod, focusing my attention back on my mom. "Nothing matters to me more than her. Do whatever you need to do to keep her alive."

"Money doesn't matter. My job is to save lives. That's what doctors do. I'll do my very best to make sure your mom makes it through this." His response is sincere, but I'm not sure if I can trust him or not. The fear lingers in the pit of my stomach.

He bustles around the bed again, and I focus on her sedate features, giving her hand a little squeeze. "Mom?" All I want is for her to speak. Goddammit. I need *one* good thing to happen right now. Fuck. The floor threatens to give out on me, and I'm barely hanging on.

As if someone up there can hear my unspoken prayer, I watch as Mom's eyes flutter and slowly open. She looks right at me, her blue eyes shining like sapphires. "Drew? Is that you?"

I nod and lean down to kiss her cold, dry knuckles. "Yeah. Hi, Mom."

She tries to smile, but it's more of a wince. "Hi," she breathes.

I swallow a hard lump in my throat. "I have never been happier to see your face. I know things have been hard, and I've been gone a lot, but I want you to know that I'm here now. I'm not going anywhere until we get you feeling better."

She shifts her hand to pat my cheek, which is still near her fingers. "You have school and football. Don't worry about me, sweetie. This is nothing but a hiccup in the road."

I eye the doctor on the other side of the bed. He gives me a little shake of the head almost like he knows what I'm going to ask him. *Why haven't they told her what's going on?* If it were me, I'd want to know what the hell people were doing to me. My guess is the fear and her reaction, and what it might do to her body. Anything not to make it worse, right?

"Football is over Mom, and my classes are pretty flexible. I'm stubborn, you know that. The more you tell me not to worry, the more I'll worry. All I want is for you to know I'm not going anywhere, okay?" I don't add what I want to.

As long as my father isn't here.

She tries to smile again, but her lips slip down as if she can't gather the strength to smile, and then she sucks a shallow breath into her lungs. The doctor steps closer and checks her vitals on the monitor stationed at her bedside.

"Try to relax, Victoria. We don't want your blood pressure to go up again."

I'm so confused right now. Since when are the doctors on a first-name basis with her? I turn my gaze to him and watch him cautiously. Something is wrong here, but I can't pinpoint it.

Her eyes drift shut, and I gently shake her hand. "Mom?"

She doesn't respond, and fear kicks me in the chest like a horse. "Mom?"

My heart rate spikes, and I notice the blips on the monitors blink, and the beeping sound speeds up. The doctor jumps into action, lowering her bed to a flat position.

"Scarlett, come here." Dr. Banks calls for one of the nurses.

I shove out of the chair and move out of their way while they rush around the bed, adjusting her body and grabbing a needle to inject something into her IV. Complete helplessness threatens to suffocate me. I can't stand here and watch her die, but at the same time, I can't do a single fucking thing to help her. I'm not a doctor. This is how Bel felt and probably still does. Like a compass with no sense of direction. Lost without a real meaning. I sink deeper into myself, watching with fear as they move around the room.

There's shouting. "What the fuck are you doing? Call an ambulance for her!" Oh, it takes me a second to realize it's me.

Then the damn doctor is in my face. "We can't do that. Not yet. Please understand things are dire, and she should be in the care of a hospital, but I'm not authorized to approve that." He stares at me meaningfully.

"Then fucking do it. I'm the power of attorney, right? Get her to the hospital!"

After a minute, the screeching of the monitors slows to a more steady beat. The doctor rushes around her bed to check her eyes, pulse, and stats again.

I'm vibrating with tension. Only the steady blip of her heartbeat on the monitor keeps me from splitting down the middle.

"What the hell is going on? What was that?" I pepper him with questions, wondering why this asshole hasn't pulled his phone out to call the ambulance yet.

He skirts the bed to approach, slipping his pen light into his white coat pocket. "I know I told you earlier that she's been in and out of it since early this morning, but I believe something else is going on. I'll need to run some more tests to be sure, but her sleepiness and fatigue are much more than a side effect of the meds."

I wave at the bed. "What does that mean?"

His frown deepens, and I can see the despair in his eyes. "She's fallen into a coma, I believe. We need to get these tests done so we can see about helping her recover." He waves me toward a side table. "Let's start with some blood work and go from there."

I strip my jacket as I cross the room and throw myself down in the chair. "Take whatever you need. As long as you can save her life, I don't give a fuck. I can't lose her, Doctor. I can't."

"Let me draw this lab work, and I promise we'll transport her to the hospital. It's important that I do this first since it will help tailor our position once we get there."

"Whatever, Doc. Just do it.

He hums a noise low in his throat and quickly grabs some supplies from a nearby set of drawers. I'm not sure how my blood can help, but I'd give up anything to ensure I don't lose her.

"You're her best chance for hope. You know that, right?"

I glance up at him. There's something in his tone I can't place through the adrenaline and the fear still coursing through me. All I can think is that I can't lose her.

I can't. If I lose her, there is no saying how far off the rails I'll fall. There might not be anything good left for Bel. There might not be anything left for anyone.

4

BEL

Another glorious day soaking in the despair of my trauma.

Different day, same shit.

I stare at the ceiling, wondering how much longer I can sit here, drowning myself in expensive wine. *This isn't me.* I know that. But I'm lost. I let out an obnoxious sigh. If I spend another day in this bed, the staff will start making the bed around me or over me.

I check the clock on my bedside table. Getting myself out of this rut I'm in will require effort. I'm not ready to let go of her, but allowing myself to be happy and leave this miserable place I've put myself in makes me sick to my stomach. *Your life has to go on, Bel,* my mom's voice reminds me. *Don't let this end you.*

I decide to think about something else, anything else. I guess I can make it down for breakfast with Seb if he didn't stay at The Mill last night. The reminder of The Mill leads my thoughts to another person who I'd do better not to even entertain in my thoughts. I can't think about him, or I'll never drag myself out of this bed.

I throw back the covers and sit up, stretching my arms above my head and groaning as I try to work out the stiffness in my back. *That's what you get for lying in bed for a million days.* I shove off the bed and cross the room, walking into the closet. The lights turn on as soon as I step over the threshold, and I run my fingers over the numerous articles of clothing. Something in here has to cost less than my old car.

Money or not, *I'm not eating breakfast in thousand-dollar sweatpants.*

When I find a pair of joggers and a hoodie that still seems suspiciously expensive, I throw them on. After a quick stop in the bathroom for deodorant, I catch my reflection in the mirror. Dark bags are under my eyes, and my once vibrant green eyes look duller now. I'm still me, but something is missing.

I look away from my reflection and pull my long blond hair up into a messy topknot. My fingers graze the tender flesh at the back of my head, and a memory flashes through my mind.

"It's time for you to leave. You can take the trash out yourself, or I can take you out. You are nothing to me and never were. Nothing more than a warm little hole to sink into every once in a while. Now get up and get the fuck out and let us men do our talking."

The hole in my chest throbs, pulsing, blood pouring from the place where he ripped my heart out. A physical scar will always remind me of what happened that day, but eventually, that will fade. What will *not* fade are the memories that Drew left me with. The rage in his eyes, the venom in his words. The pure, unfiltered hate. True or not, the pain he caused me that night will forever linger. I blink back the tears burning at the back of my eyes.

Do not cry for him. He does not deserve your tears.

I take a couple of calming breaths to compose myself. Then I leave the bathroom and walk through my bedroom, heading downstairs. Perhaps I can convince myself that Drew was never a part of my life. *Ha. I wish.* It would be possible if he would leave me alone, but he's like an infestation of fleas. And there's no damn exterminator that could take out Drew Marshall.

On my way downstairs, I take in the sights and sounds of the mansion. Staff bustle around the place like it's a hotel instead of a home. It's amazing to me that it takes all these people to take care of this place. Then again, I'm not surprised due to the size of it. It's just a gross display of wealth to hide the rotten truth beneath the surface. Or maybe that's the grief talking.

By the time I make it to the dining room, I've already considered going back to my room ten times. This place is too big, too over the top. It's not home even though it's more than my mother and I ever had. It still doesn't compare, though.

Stepping into the formal space I've only seen a couple of times since moving in, I drag my eyes to the long table meant for twenty chairs. The soft rug under my bare feet runs the length of the room, from the door to the far wall, with a floor-to-ceiling window that looks out upon the estate.

Seb sits in the first chair on the right side of the table,

holding a dainty teacup. I want to smile at the ridiculously tiny cup, but I don't have the energy.

After a second, he spots me, stands, and pulls out the chair at the head of the table, with its back to the window. It wouldn't be my first choice for seating, but I don't have the energy to argue, so I mutter a thanks and sit.

My ass has barely hit the seat when one of the staff bustles out of a side door with a tray of food and a carafe of coffee with all the fixings.

The contents are distributed around my place setting, and once the maid leaves, I stare down at the sheer mass of food that is about to go to waste. There's no way in *hell* I'm going to eat all of this. My stomach feels weird just looking at it.

As if Sebastian can read my mind, he speaks, "Just eat what you want and leave the rest." It seems like such a ridiculous waste, but I don't bother arguing with him. I pick up a croissant and nibble on it.

"It's good to see you out of your room," he adds casually as he sips his coffee out of that stupid cup.

His tone is too unconcerned, like if he points out that I've left my room, I might make a mad dash back there.

"I'm sick of wallowing." My voice catches. "Don't get me wrong. I still miss my mother more than anything, but I can't lie in that bed any longer. Lying around and doing nothing makes me sick. I need to find my way back to who I am."

I sigh and grab a fork, spearing a piece of egg. I've lost way too much weight in the past month, weight I couldn't afford to lose in the first place. I eye the runny yolk and force myself to take a bite.

"I agree, and I think you should consider going back to school. You can re-enroll at any time. All I need to do is make a phone call to the administration building. I had them hold your spot, and you won't be penalized either." *Of course I won't be.* I withhold an eye roll. Money can buy you anything. Power. *Corruption.* I never asked for any of this, and maybe that's why my mother hid the truth from me. Why didn't she tell me about my brother or family? Maybe it's because she left them all.

I consider everything while chewing the eggs slowly. They don't taste half bad.

It's still disconcerting to me that Sebastian's being so nice after everything that happened between him and me, between Drew and me. He's Drew's best friend, so he should take his side, but if anything, Sebastian appears to be against him now, and I don't know if I can or should trust that.

He might be my only relation left, but I don't expect him to take care of me like a child. In fact, I'm very against it. I'm not going to be anybody's problem.

"I'll figure it out. I mean..." I let out a long sigh. "I'm undecided. The idea of going back to Oakmount terrifies me. It brings back all kinds of memories that I don't want to relive. Plus, I don't even have my laptop or my books."

Maybe I could enroll in online classes instead? No. As antisocial as I like to tell myself I am, I'd miss the library too much. *Hell, I already miss it.* The smell of the books, the quietness. I haven't been back to campus or my dorm room since my mom died, and the thought of going back makes the eggs in my belly churn roughly.

"None of that is a big deal. We can get you new books,

and you already have a new laptop. Those are easy fixes."
He gives me a boyish smile that might have warmed my
heart previously, but now just annoys me.

I hate myself for hating Sebastian.

He keeps throwing around how easy it is to drop thou-
sands of dollars like it's nothing. I might have money now,
not that I've really spent anything, but that doesn't mean I
can switch my brain to his rich boy way of thinking automatically. I refuse to let the concept of money change my
thinking. I'm still Maybel. The quiet, shy bookworm. I'm
still the girl my mom loved.

I place the fork down on the table and look him right
in the eyes. "Look, I know you're trying to help, and I don't
mean to sound ungrateful because I'm not. But I don't
want new books. I want *my* stuff, the stuff my mother and I
worked hard to buy. I refuse to let those things go to waste
and toss them out because I can buy new ones. Then
there's my notes for classes. Those aren't replaceable and
are in my old laptop, as well as a number of notebooks. I
can't replace that stuff without taking the classes over
again."

There. I even did it without hissing at him.

"It's whatever you want, Bel. Do what you like." He
dismisses me without another glance and goes back to
scrolling on his phone and drinking his coffee.

But is it really? I can't help but wonder if there's a
hidden agenda. I also kind of want to smash his
stupid cup.

I pick my fork back up and continue eating while I
watch him cautiously, both wanting to get to know him
better and not getting too close for fear that he'll disap-

pear. His appearance is well put together. Today, he's added a coat and tie to his usual dress slacks and button-down. "Going somewhere?"

He jerks his gaze to mine, then notices me staring at his clothes. "Not really, why?"

"You usually don't give so much banker chic this early in the morning."

His full lips fold into a straight line while he narrows his eyes at me. "If we are commenting on each other's apparel..." His gaze flicks down to my clothing. "You've got the whole stay-at-home-mom style down pat, minus the spit-up on your sweatshirt."

"Thanks, jerk." I eat some more food, feeling a little lighter for the teasing. "Your cup looks like it came out of a toy set."

It feels right, good. Mom would have loved him. I just know it.

My heart seizes in my chest, and I let the fork clatter to the plate. Every time I remember she's gone, it feels like I'm getting hit by a truck all over again.

"You okay?" Seb's deep voice drags me back to reality, and I notice him crouching beside my chair, his hand resting gently on the armrest.

I swallow thickly. "Yeah, I'm fine. Just the usual reminder of her not being here anymore." Emotion clogs my throat, but I refuse to cry. I can't continue with life if I start crying every time I think of her. "If you're good with it, I'm going to grab my coat and head over to the dorm to get my things."

"You never have to ask my permission to leave, Bel. You're not a prisoner here. This is your home, and I'm your brother. I don't want to control you. I just want to keep you safe. Now, do you really think it's a good idea to go back there?" The concern etched into his handsome features makes me pause, and I know he's not lying.

I shrug and try to curl my mouth into something more than a wince. "I don't know if it's a good idea, but it's the only one I have. I can't keep hiding behind the four walls of that bedroom. I can't keep pretending she's not gone. I have to try... I'll just go in, grab my stuff, and leave as quickly as I came. I doubt Jackie will even be there."

The memory of my friend, or who I thought was my friend, burns like drops of acid on my skin.

"I can send someone with you, or maybe I can come with you if that would make you feel more comfortable?"

I shake my head. "No. I'm not going to hide behind you. You might be my brother, but I'm capable of protecting myself, and I'm not scared of Jackie or Drew. At some point, I will have to face them. It's best to get it over and done with."

He nods and returns to his seat, but I can still feel his eyes on me. He's waiting for me to shatter so he can pick up the pieces again, but I'm tired of breaking. Tired of being seen as fragile. Seconds tick by, and I notice the way his jaw tenses. I can see Seb wants to say something or ask something, but he hasn't spoken yet.

"What's up? If your jaw gets any more tense, you'll have to go to the dentist for your broken teeth."

His lips turn up into a smile. "I'm just thinking... do you think I look like her at all?"

My heart lurches in my chest. He's been so focused on helping me survive and overcome the grief that I'm not sure he's even grieved himself. I tend to forget that he, too, lost a parent. A parent he never got the chance to develop a relationship with.

I smile. "Yeah, I can see it now that I'm looking for it."

His green eyes twinkle just like our mother's did, and it's almost too much for me to endure. "Okay, that's enough brotherly love for the day," I joke and stand to head out of the room, hoping a little distance will dissipate the tightness in my chest.

"I know it's hard and even a little uncomfortable... but I want you to know that I'll always be here for you, Bel. I'm pissed that you were here this entire time, practically right under my nose, and I had no idea. Family is something I never had, and I missed out on getting to meet my real mom. I don't want to miss out on developing a relationship with you, too."

Dammit. The pressure on my chest becomes too much, and all I can do is nod. I scurry out of the room before I start to cry. *Stupid tears.*

Once back in my room, I find the place clean and the bed freshly made. I'm tempted to crawl under the covers and forget my plans for the day, but that wouldn't do me any good. I need to pull myself together, to do something other than lie in bed all day. I need to do this for me, for Mom. She wouldn't want me to lie around in bed all day, crying and dwelling on the things I can't change.

I head for the closet and scour through the shelves, looking for a pair of jeans. I pluck a pair off a stack, and it hits me...

What will I do if I see Jackie? Ugh. What if I run into Drew? That would be my luck. Run into *both* of them.

I sigh, pull on the pair of jeans and my heaviest shit-kicker combat boots, and head down to the foyer.

They stored my car around here somewhere, but I haven't been outside much since I arrived. When one of the staff approaches at my lost look, they call a driver to take me to the campus. I don't have the strength to argue, especially if it's an extra pair of hands to help me carry anything I might need to bring back.

The car is something fancy and shiny and smells like old money. The driver opens the door for me, and as I climb inside, my phone vibrates with a text.

Sebastian. Of freaking course.

SEBASTIAN: *Be careful. Call if you need anything.*

I SHAKE my head as I type back.

ME: *Yes, Dad.*

HIS RESPONSE MAKES ME LAUGH.

SEBASTIAN: *Ew. Don't.*

I tuck my phone into my hoodie pocket along with my keys and stare out the window as we drive toward campus. How long has Sebastian's family lived here? I guess I have to get used to calling them our family now even though it feels all wrong.

Why had Mother kept them a secret? Her letter didn't say much besides to trust Sebastian and that he would take care of me. How can I trust her in this when she doesn't know him any better than I do? Did she?

There are so many secrets that they feel like they are eating me alive and crawling under my skin. So many secrets and too many lies.

I'm thinking so hard as we drive to campus that the driver has to clear his throat when he opens the door to alert me to our arrival.

I climb out and give him a nod. "Thanks. I'll have some stuff to bring back to the house with me in a minute."

"Very good, miss."

I guess money really makes people respect you... or at the very least, afraid of you.

Gotta get used to that too.

I sigh and jog up the steps to the dorm building, then scan my card to enter. My body is tense as I walk. My nerves twinge with adrenaline as I walk down the hall to my room—my old room now, I guess. I unlock the door and stop dead when I spot Jackie sitting at the table in the middle of the main room.

We both freeze—her with a spoon halfway to her mouth and me with my keys dangling from my fingers.

She recovers first, as usual. "What the fuck do *you* want?"

Oh hell no, she doesn't get to speak to me that way after she completely betrayed me. "What's wrong, Jackie?

Your sugar daddy tired of you already, now that you have nothing to offer him?"

Her face twists into an angry scowl, and she plops her spoon into her bowl, splattering milk around in an arc.

I shake my head and turn to my room, thankful I locked the door the last time I was here. Everything inside is just as I left it.

It takes a minute to find some tote bags and load them up with books and a few things I want to take. My laptop is too old to be crushed with the books, so I'll have to carry it.

"What, your sugar daddy can't afford to buy you new stuff?" Jackie sneers from the door.

"Sebastian isn't my sugar daddy. He's my brother," I say absently as I pack, refusing to let my anger ride me.

"What?" She sounds like herself with that, and another pang shoots through my chest. God, I miss her just as much as I miss my mom.

I bow my head and squeeze my eyes shut so I don't start crying. I *can't* let her see me cry.

When I've grabbed everything I want, I turn to face her. "Did you need something, or are you just standing there to watch me pack?"

"I don't need a goddamn thing from you. You ruined everything!"

"Me? How did I do that? I'm not the one selling secrets *and* my pussy for money."

She hisses out a breath and stalks toward me. "Oh, aren't you. Pretty sure that's what you've been doing with Drew for months. Selling your snatch for his A's. What would the school think of that if they found out the truth?"

I'm not playing this game with her. The second she gets

in reach, I throw down the doors of all the anger, the heart-break, the hurt I've been bottling up for weeks and throw it straight at her face in the form of my fist into her nose.

It collides with a satisfying crunch, then a thunderbolt of pain shoots into my knuckles and up my arm. Fucking worth it, though.

She doubles over, blood spraying through her fingers. "What the fuck?" she garbles.

I step around her with my bags and place them on the table. Then I strip my key off my key ring and drop both keys and the key card onto the floor near the table. I won't be back here again, that's for damn sure.

"You can tell the school whatever you like. Let's see who they believe...you...or Sebastian Arturo."

The door slams behind me, and my hand stings while I carry the heavy bags, but I feel twenty pounds lighter after that confrontation. She's out of my life for good, and I don't need to open that door again.

Maybe to finally get closure with Drew, I need a confrontation with him as well? I don't feel strong enough for it, but I didn't feel strong enough to face Jackie either.

But maybe with Drew, only one of us will come out hurt, too. I just have to make sure it's not me.

5

DREW

How did this happen? I thought she was doing better, according to the few nurses I could bribe to tell me what her doctor had put in her files. But shit, I should have considered that information would be tainted from the start since my father dictated it. He's always used her as leverage, and while he has control over her, he has control over me, and I fucking hate it.

I watch her sleeping in the hospital bed. We are in a private room back in a secluded corner, and I flinch every time someone walks past the door. I'm waiting for my father to appear, throw around demands, and try to take her home before she's safe.

The steady beat of her heart on the monitor reassures me, and I can't help but wonder if this is how Bel felt all that time with her mom at the hospital. As always, she's not far from my thoughts, even as my mother is my current priority. I think about her a second, the guilt a storm in my head like it always is when I think about her. Then I shove it all away and lean toward my mom's hospital bed, willing her to wake up.

This is the most time I've spent with her consecutively in years. My father started pushing me out toward the end of high school as my mother grew more ill, and I suddenly grew busier and busier with "obligations."

I don't know how long I sit there and watch her. Long enough that the nurse shift switches and the doctor who brought her to the hospital returns.

"Oh," he starts when he spots me in the chair. Like he's surprised to see me. "I'm glad you're here. Once again, I tried to reach your father and I wasn't able to get ahold of him. We got some of the initial test results back. Do you want me to show you, or would you rather I wait until we can reach your father?"

I shake my head. "No, please, anything you have I want to know about."

He nods and turns to face my mother, grabs her charts, and does a few checks. Once he finishes circling her bed, checking her chest, and marking her chart, he tucks the pen into his breast pocket and faces me again. "Now, the main thing you need to know is she's having trouble. Yes, she's unconscious, but it's not the end yet."

I whoosh out an exhale and stare down at my hands, giving myself a moment before I slip back into my mask and meet his eyes. "So what now? Is there anything we can do to fix this?"

He studies me, and there is something in his eyes I can't read when I usually can see right through people. "How long has your mother been having difficulty?"

I snort. *Difficulty.* "She's been in and out of the hospital since I was ten or eleven. For as long as I can remember, she's been fighting one thing or another. It seems to have gotten worse since I went to college, but I try to be there for her as much as I can."

The doctor grabs the stool on the other side of the room to sit on and slides toward me, stopping a couple of feet away. "Drew, can I ask you something more personal?"

"Like what? It depends on what you want to know." If it's for my mom, though, there isn't much I'd hold back.

He frowns, lines growing bolder around his mouth and on his forehead. Something is wrong, and he's not sure how to tell me. A weight sinks from my chest to my stomach and drifts down, down, down like a rock in a lake. *Shit*. He just said she wasn't dying, so...why the hesitation?

"Doctor, whatever the problem is, just spit it out. This dancing around is making it worse." It's making me want to punch something, namely him, but I keep that little bit to myself.

He sits back and squares his shoulders. "Has either of your parents ever discussed if you're adopted?"

I blink, my mouth popping open.

He rushes on. "It's not something I'd usually be at liberty to discuss, but it was *your* blood work, not your mother's, where we found the discrepancies. So, legally, you have the right to know."

I blink again, wheels grinding in my head like an overworked car. "What?" I sputter.

He swallows loudly enough I can hear it, even with the monitors. "Well, we ran your blood work with your mother's, and your father's even, to look for compatibility. The transplant."

"And?" I say since I've been reduced to one-syllable words.

"You weren't a match to either of them. Neither of them is your biological parent."

The room seems to go silent around me as all the air is sucked out of the room. All the abuse, the verbal jabs, the indifference, all on my so-called father's part, was it because he knew all along?

If they aren't my parents, who the hell is?

I can't wrap my head around what he's told me. Everything seems to tilt sideways. Nothing is lining up. There's no axis on which to orient myself.

I stand, and the doctor stands too, keeping his eyes locked on me. He braces his body like he's ready to rush forward at any moment.

I lay a hand on the back of the chair and turn my back to the man. *Shit. Get ahold of yourself. He doesn't need to see you break down. No one can see that.* I have to keep it together no matter what.

Without turning around, I shuffle toward the doorway, needing distance from him. From the truth, too. "I'll come back, Doctor. I need some time to think about this."

He says something, but I don't catch it as I rush out the door and down the hall, racing to the exit before I say or do something to draw attention to myself.

Don't let them see. It's a lesson my father taught me under the weight of his fist, and I've never in my life been grateful for that particular lesson until this very second.

I step out of the hospital's sliding glass doors and take a deep breath of the cold midday air. Then another, using the chill in my lungs to clear my head. I have so many more questions than answers, but at least I can breathe again.

Until that old familiar feeling rises up to choke me once more. The feeling that I can't quite grasp anything, that nothing, *nothing* is in my control.

I hate this goddamn feeling.

I open my phone and pull up the ride app. Since I'm downtown, it only takes minutes for a car to pull up, and there's only one person I need to see right now. Only one person can make this feeling go away.

Bel. My little wallflower.

It hits me like another punch to the face when I'm already fucking down. We can't be related. If he's her father, but not mine...she's not my sister.

It's not like that knowledge would keep me away from her, but a wave of relief washes through me, and suddenly, the urge to see her is even stronger, a driving force pushing me to get to her.

It takes a little while to get to the Arturo estate, and I rush to the gate, punch the intercom, and wait.

"Can I help you?" a male voice says, but it's not Sebastian.

"I'm here to see Maybel."

There's a pause, then... "Ms. Arturo isn't available, especially to you, ever." It's Seb this time for sure. The venom in his voice reaches me even through the tinny intercom line.

"Fucking let me in, Seb. I just want to talk to her," I grit out, balling my fists to keep from grasping the intercom box and shaking it from its base.

"Go away, Drew. You aren't getting near her. I explained

that before, and I'll keep saying it. Go away before I send security out to make you go away."

Fuck him. He's not going to keep me from my flower. I spin and stare at the fence line as a security guard marches down from the gatehouse on the other side.

He looks pressed and polished in a security uniform, so he doesn't travel with the family. Fucking good.

I paste on my good ole boy smile and wave him over. "Hey, man," I call out.

His shoulders relax, and he steps up to the gate, my disarming smile doing its usual work. "You have to leave, sir."

I smile again and swagger toward the gate until I'm within reaching distance. I shoot my hand through the wrought iron, grab his shirt front, and slam him into the gate hard enough to stun him.

"Look," I snarl with enough menace in my tone to ensure he doesn't mistake a single word I speak. "I want *nothing* to do with you or your boss. I want to know where Bel is, that's all. I'm asking nicely, but here in a few moments, I won't be, and then I can't be held responsible for what happens to you after that. So what's it going to be? Are you going to tell me what I want to know, or are we going to see if I can pull your head through these fucking bars?" My grip is tight as I tug him against the iron, adding just enough pressure to press his cheeks against the bars.

He flails, but he's out of shape and useless with the leverage I have over him.

"It really doesn't have to be this way." I tilt my head and narrow my eyes, considering another option. "Unless she's inside, in which case I'll be entering, and you'll be unconscious."

His radio goes off, and I can hear someone asking for his status. Panic fills his eyes, and he fumbles to grab it, but I catch his hand and twist his wrist back. Not hard enough to break it but hard enough to prove a point.

"The girl..." I prompt.

He hisses out a breath and sags in my hold. *Got him.* I smile like the villain who just got the girl. "She's on campus. She went back to school today."

"See, not as hard as you thought..." I release him with a little shove and take a step back, holding my hands up. Before he can right himself, I swivel and take off running down the street, punching a new address into the rideshare app. They won't catch me before I get to her, that's for sure. I kick myself in the ass for not using my bike. This racing around for rides is bullshit. Thankfully, someone is nearby, and I'm hopping in the back of a Kia Sportage a few minutes later.

The guy behind the driver's seat attempts to make small talk, but I'm not about that shit. I need to get to the library and find Bel. Otherwise, all of this will have been for nothing. It feels like it takes years to get back to campus. By the time we're close enough, I'm hot enough to start a fire with my body heat alone.

"Pull over here," I order the guy as the car reaches the edge of the football field. If I get out here, I'll have a straight shot to the library.

He flounders but slows the car. "This isn't the location you asked me to drop you off at." I exhale and shake my head.

"Fucking stop!" I growl, and the car comes to a halt immediately. I'm aware that I'm a little unhinged, but I crave the pretty little blond bookworm who's been trying to hide from me for the past month. Too bad for her, there will be no more hiding.

My desire for her intensifies, and a coil of need winds tighter and tighter the closer I get to her. I force my legs to move faster and break out into a full run toward the library doors. I shove through the double doors, nearly plowing into a group of girls. I can feel their angry glares on me, but I don't give a fuck. My heart hammers against my rib cage as I scan the expansive space for her familiar messy topknot.

Each second that passes without proof that she's here makes my blood pressure climb. Higher and higher it goes. *What if the guard lied?* I suppose I'll have to pay him another visit. I'm tempted to call out to her, but we haven't spoken in a while, and I don't want to scare her away. I remind myself that when it comes to Bel, I'm back at square one. All the work I put in to earning her trust is nothing but dust in the wind now. If I'm going to get her to listen to me, I'll need to approach this differently.

Impatience blooms in my belly as I stalk toward her favorite set of desks. I notice a bag hanging off the chair and a few romance books stacked on the table, but there's no Bel in sight. *Shit.*

Where is she?

I spin on the balls of my feet and scan the area, raking my gaze over every person in the room, shifting behind the desk toward the stacks to get a better look and make sure she's not hiding somewhere. My heart threatens to catapult out of my chest when I spot her standing next to the window.

The streaks of sunlight make her look like she's wearing a halo. I swear to fucking god, I stop breathing for half a second. Piercing green eyes. Blond strands are held haphazardly on the top of her head in a messy bun, just as expected. My tongue darts out of my mouth, and I lick my lips like the true predator I am.

Relax. Don't scare her.

I watch her curiously, missing this so much there aren't even words to describe it. Sebastian was right. The little wallflower has grown into a wildflower. Gone are the over-sized sweatshirts she adored before. She's wearing designer jeans and a tight white top that makes her tits look great, and my mouth waters at the image before me.

Fucking hell, why didn't I put her in better clothes when I had her?

I suck a ragged breath into my lungs. To be anxious or nervous is unlike me, but Bel is different. Always was. I'm so afraid I'm going to fuck this up again, that I'm going to have to force her to do what I want her to do, and we both know that's not what *I* want. I need her submission, her sweet, fragile trust. I swallow the lump in my throat. Here goes nothing.

"Bel," I whisper her name.

Her eyes shift from the book she's holding right to me like she heard me even though we are several feet apart. She has yet to really see me, and I take a hesitant step forward.

"Bel," I say her name a little louder this time. "It's time we talked about things."

That makes the light bulb go off in her head. I watch as her eyes fill with shock or maybe even fear. I can't really be sure which it is when they mirror one another so closely. I choose to go with the second when her foot slides backward. *Fuck me.* I know what she's about to do, and it's so incredibly stupid.

"Don't do it," I snarl, the animalistic beast barely contained under the cold mask I wear. If she wants to tempt me, nothing will do that quite like the thrill of a chase.

Those pretty emerald eyes of hers flick around the library, looking for an exit, a way to escape me, but what she doesn't understand is that she can *never* escape me.

Bel will never be free of me, no matter how much she cries, begs, or pleads.

I inch closer, and just like the gazelle sensing danger, she notices the movement, her gaze ping-ponging between me and the stacks.

Do it. Run, Flower. Run as fast as you can.

Every drop of blood in my body heads south, pumping furiously into my thickened cock. I'm grappling for control over the primal desire to chase her and fuck her into submission but remind myself that this is so much more than sex. I need to rein in my primal instincts, at least for right now, but seeing her again after all this time is harder than I anticipated.

I fucking crave her submission, the softness of her body as I bend her to my will, forcing her to take whatever it is I want to give her. Yes, I fucked up, and I'm man enough to admit that, but I've given her more than enough time and space. I can't keep myself in check anymore. I can't be without her. She's not getting away from me this time.

Like a spooked animal, she takes off, racing in the direction of the stacks.

Just as I anticipated. I take off after her, slipping through the line of chairs, shelves, and tables, heading right for her. She cuts through some bookshelves to the right, and I follow closely like a bloodhound. She's backing herself into a corner.

"Bel, don't do this. There is nowhere you can go that I won't find you, and the last thing you want to do is provoke me, especially when I've gone so long without you. Don't make me do something I don't want to do."

I'm greeted with silence.

A smile tugs at the corner of my lips. *Fuck.*

Flower wants a chase. She'll get a chase.

No matter what, she's not escaping me. Not this time.

6

BEL

*N*o. No. No, no, no. I can't do this right now. *Shit.*
Panic bubbles up and out of me like a boiling
pan of water. I can't do this right now. First, the
altercation with Jackie, and now, Drew is here.

I'm not sure what I've ever done to piss God off, but the
heaping piles of shit he tosses on me *could* stop at any
point. My adrenaline spikes, the thunderous sound of my
heartbeat fills my ears, and I press a hand to my mouth,
forcing myself to keep quiet as I move through the stacks. I
stick close to the bookshelves, hiding in the shadows, and
there are plenty this far back in the library.

"Bel," Drew calls for me softly.

Thankfully, the sound isn't loud enough to carry into
the main library room. I breathe slowly, reminding myself
that he can't hurt me. Not anymore. Not ever again.

If he can't hurt you, why are you running?

Ignoring the thought, I walk slowly, pushing deeper

into the stacks until I'm surrounded by nothing more than old shelves and years of dust and neglect.

It's sad to watch the demise of books and how little people care for them. With the internet, no one comes back to these older tomes, and the school has let them languish. I do my best to think a step ahead, but there's no real hiding from Drew. He's a predator at his most basic instinct. The only thing I can hope to do is stay hidden as long as possible, until he gets tired of searching for me.

Which will be... never.

Ahead, I notice a corner just small enough for me to hide in. *Bingo.* Quickly, I tuck myself behind it, crouching with my back to the shelf. I feel a little safer here. Once in position, I wrap my arms around my middle to keep myself from crumpling into a million pieces.

Why did he have to come here today? Did someone tell him I'd be here? Did Jackie call him?

I grit my teeth, red-hot fury pulsing through me. If she did, I'll...I'll... I don't know what I'll do, but I certainly won't let it go. I'm past the point of breaking. I'm done being used, toyed with, and then discarded like worthless trash. I won't ever be someone's plaything again and *especially* not his.

Whatever he wants from me, he'll have to take by force, which I know Drew will hate to do. He doesn't get pleasure from taking. He gets pleasure from submission, from me giving up complete control and surrendering to him.

My ears catch the shuffle of a boot on the carpet, and my muscles tense as I wait for him to hopefully pass by without a glance.

"Bel," he calls again, his voice a dark caress. It wraps

around me, tightening its grip on my resolve, making it difficult to remember why I hate him so much. Hard-edged and cutting, or soft and sensual, it doesn't matter... I'm always his willing victim somehow.

His voice ignites the embers of desire deep in my gut.

This run-and-hide game is so familiar it hurts. An ache forms in my chest, the pain spreading outward. It's so suffocating I can barely breathe around it.

God, I've missed him.

I swallow hard, and the memory of all he's said comes barreling into me. *No. I can't miss him.* He's an asshole, even worse than I ever thought he could be. I can't remember how many times he warned me, telling me that he wasn't a good guy. I should've believed him. I should've looked at the red flags and ran the fuck away.

Stupid. So stupid. Instead, I let him use and abuse me. Only to be left discarded when he had his fill. *Fuck him.* He made his choice, and he chose wrong. Now, he'll have to deal with the consequences because I refuse to be second best for anyone, let alone Drew Marshall.

The longer I sit here, the more consumed I become with confronting him. This unbearable desire to hurt him the same way he hurt me, even if I know I can't do so physically, fills me.

I need to end this.

To remind him that I'm not fucking around. Before I can contemplate my next move, a pair of strong arms snakes around my middle. I'm momentarily frozen, with fear or anger I'm not sure, but his firm grip on my biceps as he drags me to my feet slaps me back to reality.

Like a wild animal, I thrash against his hold, refusing

to go down without a fight. I claw at the air, barely missing his skin. *Asshole.* I swipe again but only catch the soft cotton material of his T-shirt. With lightning-fast reflexes, he turns me in his grasp, bringing me face-to-face with a beautiful, wicked monster.

"Hello, Wallflower." His voice wraps around me like smoke, snuffing out any hope of escape. His piercing gaze sends a shudder rippling through me.

His tone says hello but the deep timbre catching in his throat says something else entirely. Something dark, sinister, and molten like red-hot lava.

Remember what he did to you.

A mouse caught in a trap. That's what I am right now, and I can't let him win again.

I can't. I open my mouth to tell him to release me, but nothing more than a whimper escapes. *You're nothing to me, Bel.* The memory splinters through my fragile mind, and I let it guide me. I claw at him, trying to slip out of his iron grip.

"Is that really any way to greet someone?" he taunts.

He is absolutely psycho, but I already know that, don't I?

How dare he assume he can touch, taunt, or talk to me as if he didn't smash my heart with a baseball bat in front of everyone we know?

I snarl my lips and bare my teeth. "Let go of me!" I order, my voice cracking.

Leaning forward, he presses his forehead against mine, and I suck a ragged breath into my lungs as his touch burns across my skin. *I can't breathe.* I can't do anything. Like an eerie mist, Drew's everywhere. His scent surrounds me, drowning me in his darkness.

Peppermint and teakwood.

"Or what? What are you going to do, Flower?" His eyes flash, challenging me.

Fight. I'm going to fight.

I claw at him one last time, putting as much effort into it as possible, and this time, I make contact with his skin. I sink my nails into his flesh, dragging them down the length of his throat. Satisfaction fills all the empty spaces in my heart, but it doesn't last long.

Horror soon takes its place when the skin splits beneath my nails. Blood oozes out of the deep scratches that mark his neck.

I freeze with my heart in my throat.

I shouldn't look at him, but I do.

His features are pinched, and where I expect there to be an expression of anger or pain, I find shock and something like adoration in his green eyes.

Only he would find violence adorable.

I won't lie. I'm a little shocked, but this is another reason he needs to stay away from me. I hate this person I become in his presence. I manage to come back first and take a step back, but I quickly realize I have nowhere to go, not with the huge bookshelf behind me and Drew in front of me.

"Oh... Bel." He shakes his head and presses his fingertips to the side of his throat.

When he pulls his hand back, my eyes catch on the smeared blood and dart up to his. He gives me a devastating smile. If I were not weak in the knees already, I would be now.

"I've missed this, but most of all, I've missed *you*. Has it really been so long that you forgot what your fighting does to me? How hard it makes my cock?" he growls, and the sound vibrates through me like the low buzz of a vibrator. "I'm doing my best to be a gentleman, Bel. I'm trying so hard to give you space and time to heal because I know I fucked up, but my patience can only withstand so much. You belong to me, and no amount of fighting or time will change that."

"That's where you're wrong! Everything has changed," I hiss and raise my hands to his chest, giving him a hard shove.

It does nothing. He doesn't move, not even an inch. It's like he's made of rock.

Knowing this, he smirks, closing the breath's length of distance separating us. The old wood bookshelves dig into my back.

I'm trapped.

I tip my head back to look into his eyes. His gaze burns a path across my skin as he studies each freckle, hair, and mark as if he's seeing it for the first time. That same gaze drags down the length of my neck, burning me from the inside out.

"Fuck, Flower. I can't put into words how good it feels to see you. To feel your fucking skin beneath my hands. This entire month has been a never-ending nightmare."

I grit my teeth, and the familiar pricking of tears in my eyes makes it hard to hold his gaze. "A nightmare...?"

"Yes, a nightmare."

I blink back the tears threatening to slip from my eyes. Of course he would make this about *him*. About how much *he* suffered and how badly I treated *him*. How stupid of me to assume he would actually have an ounce of empathy for the things I've gone through in the past month. He's far too selfish for that. Far too consumed with his own wants and needs.

"I don't know why I'm surprised. I guess I thought maybe you'd think of someone else before yourself for once in your life. I thought maybe you might feel bad about what you did, about how deep your actions and words cut me, but if anything, it made you a bigger victim. It made you think *you're* the one who got hurt."

The reminder of the pain he caused me is bone deep.

It's suffocating and throbbing. My heart is in a vise, the life being squeezed out of it.

"That's okay, though. Lesson learned. I see the real you now. What you were trying to show me all along, and I can't fucking *believe* there was ever a part of me that saw good in you." I desire to rip his heart out the same way he ripped my own out, but that will never happen because I'm not even sure he has a heart to rip out. "I'm glad your month has been a nightmare, and I hope the rest of your fucking life is too because you don't deserve happiness." I stab a finger into his firm chest. "You, Andrew Marshall, mean nothing to me, and I hope that realization eats you up inside. You're a coward. Now let me go, and maybe I *won't* tell Sebastian about this."

His response to my hate is the opposite of what I expect.

He leans down so his face is so close that his lips nearly touch mine. His lower body molds, melting into me and not leaving one single inch to the imagination.

I feel everything.

The hard planes of his muscles and each indentation. *All of it.*

But especially the long, hard length of his cock, which digs into my belly.

Instantly, my traitorous body turns to molten fire.

"Hate me or love me, Bel. It doesn't matter to me. I warned you. When I told you I wasn't a good man, I wasn't lying to you. I'm not lying to you now, either. I said those things and did what I had to do to protect you." There's remorse in his eyes, and I hate it. It looks too much like pity, and the last thing I want is Drew Marshall's fucking pity.

"I don't care why you did it."

"You say that, but you don't mean it. Even as badly as you don't want to admit it, you know as much as I do that I did it to protect you. My father... I didn't want him to hurt you. For him to realize how much you mean to me. You'd become another pawn on his chess board, another avenue to control me, and I couldn't let that happen to you. If I have to be the villain in your story, then I will be, but I'm not letting you go."

"I don't belong to you. I belong to *me*. Now let me go."

"No. I have so much more to say."

"Say it to someone else, like your fiancée," I sneer.

"I know you're upset, but let me help. Let me fix this." I can feel the pain splintering through the slow-healing wound. "I'm sorry about your mom. I'm sorry I wasn't there for you. That I wasn't able to take the pain away. I'm so fucking sorry, Bel."

"Stop!" I whimper. It feels like I'm reliving the memory,

experiencing her loss for the first time all over again. "Just fucking *stop!*"

I hate his words and their meaning, but more than that, I hate that small part of me that wants to believe him. He grinds against me, his hard length stoking the flames of desire that flicker in my pulsing core.

No. We can't.

This is wrong. Both morally and ethically. Even after everything that happened, I could expect him to still want me, but after his father's confession? I've replayed the conversation over in my head a million times.

True or not, *this* cannot happen. *We cannot happen.*

Every cell in my body pulses, urging me to let him in and let him soothe the dreaded ache in my core, but I can't. Not only because I despise him but because I don't, which might be as frightening as the revelation that *he might be my brother*.

"What is it that you want me to stop?" he taunts, acting as if he has no idea what he's doing. He can't really think this is okay, can he?

"This is wrong, Drew. And not just because I hate you... but because..."

Bile climbs up my throat. I've tried not to think about Drew being my brother because the thought is...disgusting.

Leaning forward, he nuzzles against my cheek with the tip of his nose and traces a trail down the side of my face, burying his face into the crook of my neck. There's an audible inhale as he breathes me into his lungs like he's missed my scent. It's such a possessive act, one that he has no right doing.

"Because why? Because I might be your brother?"

"Yes," I hiss, my heart rate picking up.

He lifts his head, his eyes glittering with a desire I know all too well. "It's not any different from before. I've already fucked your cunt and filled you with my cum. The truth can't change what's already happened. Why let it stop us now?" He punctuates his question with a thrust of his hips and a quick jerk and lift of mine.

Knocked off balance, I wrap my arms around his neck and my legs around his waist to steady myself. *Damn him.* Once I realize my position, I wiggle, and that causes friction, allowing him to get closer, his length pressing harder against my core.

He licks his lips as he studies mine and grinds into me. *Goddammit.* The friction is delicious, and pleasure zings up my spine.

"Does it really change anything, Bel? Does that knowledge make you want me any less? Because I'll be honest with you..." He flexes his hips, the tip of his dick pressing against my clit. A whimper escapes my parted lips, and he smirks. "It doesn't change a goddamn thing for me. I still want you. No, I still need you. Nothing has changed for me. How fucked up does that make me? How fucked up does it make me to know you might be my sister, yet I can't stop thinking about pinning you to the wall and fucking you until you beg me to stop? About watching my cum drip out of your tight pussy. Fuck, it's wrong, but I don't want to be right, not if it means I have to give you up, give us up."

I gulp, my hips lifting toward him despite his words. He starts to move, grinding against mine harder and faster like he can't get enough. I clutch onto him, my breaths becoming pants under his brutal touch.

"Drew..." I'm assaulted with so many feelings and thoughts.

Pleasure. Fear. Disgust.

This is wrong, but at the same time, nothing has ever felt more right in my life.

"Tell me to stop, Bel. Tell me you don't feel the same way, the same burning desire in your bones, the same animalistic urge to claim, and I'll walk away. "

There are no words to speak, and I'm embarrassed that I can't even manage to say no. Instead, I moan while clutching him tighter, needing him to hold all the fucked-up pieces of my soul together because I know once he's done with me, I'll be nothing more than a vase shattered against the wall.

The pleasure in my core builds, carrying me higher and higher with every swivel of his hips. I grit my teeth and try to stave off the orgasm threatening to barrel through me with every inch he shifts.

"Drew... we... we have to stop..."

"Shhh," he soothes, his body moving faster. "I know it feels wrong, but it's not. You were made for me, and I know you feel it too. And that's okay, Flower, because I have no problem being the bad man. I have no problem with you blaming me for your moral incompetence. If it makes you feel better, you can tell them I forced myself on you. No one has to know how much you want your potential blood brother's cock."

It's so fucking *wrong*, so terribly bad and fucked up, but I can't stop it, nor would I want to. I shake my head and stifle a moan, my teeth sinking into my bottom lip. The coppery tang of blood fills my mouth.

"Come for me, Bel." He bites out the words, his mouth millimeters from mine. "I'm desperate for you, so fucking desperate. Not even the potential knowledge of you being my sister could stop me from wanting you. I don't care if that makes me the most twisted, fucked-up asshole you know. I need you. I want you."

He shifts his mouth to the side of my neck and nips at my tender flesh. My entire body jolts at the eclectic current that ripples over my skin, and my pussy clenches around nothing, aching to be filled.

Why the hell does he always do this to me? Reduce me to nothing more than my most basic animal instinct?

"Tell me you missed me too," he whispers, nipping my earlobe, then sucking it hard. "Tell me."

I shake my head. Shuddering. Inching closer to the finish line. I'm so close to coming, that's all I can think about.

How can I still feel all this for him, with him, when he broke my heart the way he did? With his father's confession looming over us?

A sob claws its way out of my throat, warring with the pleasure spiraling in my core.

"No," I whisper. "I don't want this."

The words mean nothing, not when I continue grinding against him, chasing the high I've missed, something only he can give me, even if I won't admit it.

"I'd believe you. Maybe I'd even take mercy on you and stop if I actually believed you. But I can't, not when you're clawing at me like a cat in heat, grinding your pussy against my cock, your juices seeping into my jeans. The proof is right there, Flower, right on my fucking jeans."

I gulp and shake my head, gripping his shoulders tight, digging in my nails. Fighting the inevitable. *I hate him.* I hate him so much... but at the same time, I want him. I want him more than I've ever wanted anything.

"I wish I was inside your tight cunt right now. So I could feel you squeeze me, silently begging for me to fill you with my cum. It's all I could think about for days, but I'll take this for now. It's better than not having you at all."

I do my best to fight it. Fight him. But fuck, I can't fight the inevitable. I can't fight the pleasure that carries me higher and higher. I'm a star exploding. I start to shudder, and he holds me tighter, like he's trying to hold all the fragile pieces of my heart inside my chest.

A flash of light appears before my eyes, and I'm swept away, my entire body shattering into a million pieces. All over again, I'm breaking for him.

The glass walls I've built around my body since he knocked me down that night are in shards. All of it is crushed to dust as I stifle my moan against his collarbone, my teeth sinking into his shirt as I ride out the last rippling waves of pleasure.

All I can hear is our mutual panting, then my own heartbeat and his with my ear pressed into his neck. As I float back down to reality, I notice he's still rigid, his cock still hard against my leg. He makes no move to do anything about it and simply holds me.

All the fuzzy feelings leave me, and I snap back to my senses. I shove at his chest, and he pulls back an inch, his steel gaze meeting mine.

What the fuck do I do now?

Saying I don't want him would be an outright lie after what just happened. I can't deny that. His fingers trail down my back in a caress, and slowly, so slowly, as if he's trying to kill me, he releases me, and I slide down every inch of the front of his hard, lean body until my feet hit the floor.

My knees shake beneath my weight, but I manage to stand on my own when Drew takes a small step backward. The world spins around me. I know right from wrong, good from bad, but when it comes to Drew, all those things fly out the window. I don't care if he's the good guy or even if he's the bad guy. In fact, I wished I didn't give a shit about him at all, but I can't help it. Not when he makes me feel like a bird that's finally escaped its cage.

I'm about to tell him that we're done, that this cannot happen again when a rush of cold air swirls around me. One moment, Drew's standing in front of me, and the next, he's gone, his body being yanked a few feet away.

My gaze lands on Sebastian's raging expression. *Shit.*

His hand is tangled in the back of Drew's T-shirt, and Sebastian continues dragging him away, stopping only a few feet from the exit of the stacks.

I chase them because while I fully believe Drew deserves whatever he has coming, I don't want Sebastian to think he needs to swoop in and save me.

I'm not a goddamn damsel in distress, and I can fight my own battles.

"Sebastian," I growl. "Stop."

He doesn't even acknowledge me and rolls his wrist to untangle his hand, then shoves Drew, making him stumble a couple of feet backward. I imagine he wouldn't have moved him as much if Drew actually fought back.

Sebastian glares daggers through Drew, a look of pure disgust on his face. Those same eyes turn to me, narrowing to slits. I don't get the disgusted look but more of a disappointed look. "Didn't I tell you to stay away from him?"

Anger sparks in the flint Drew left smoldering.

"First, I do not need you to come rushing in like a damn knight in shining armor. Second, what do you think happened? Do you think I invited him here? The library is a public place. Anyone registered to attend classes can use the building."

His shoulders slump, and he turns his icy glare back to Drew. I don't know how, but it grows colder. "Didn't I fucking tell you to stay away from her? First, you attack one of my security guards, then you come here and try to fuck my sister in public. *My* sister, by the way. *Mine.*"

Shit. I wrap my arms around my middle, trying to ignore the heat filling my cheeks. There's no point in asking him how much he saw since it's obvious he saw more than I would've liked.

"Don't," Drew growls, taking a step toward me. Sebastian shifts his body between us, blocking any further advancement. "Don't," he speaks again, his eyes on me. "There isn't a damn thing to be ashamed of. Get that fucking look off your face."

I lift my chin and direct my glare at him. "I don't think so. He doesn't get to tell me what to do, and neither do you. I don't answer to either of you."

Sebastian crosses his broad arms over his chest.

"Happy? You got to talk to her. Now go jump off a fucking cliff."

Drew's forest-green eyes darken, his muscles tighten, and his hands clench and unclench into fists. He attempts to take another step toward me, but Sebastian physically shoves him back with his chest.

"One more warning, Marshall. Get near her again, and I'll break every fucking bone in your pretty face. And don't tempt me because if anyone knows what I'm capable of, it's you. So do it. Fuck around and find out. *Please.* I'm itching for you to give me a reason to break your nose."

"I'm not scared of you, Sebastian, and I'm certainly not scared of this big brother image you're portraying. Maybel is and always will be mine. Nothing, and especially not you, is going to change that."

Drew and Sebastian glare at each other for a long moment, and something dark and seething passes between them. I swallow hard and shift on my feet, a nervous energy bubbling to the surface. The last thing I need is more attention put on me.

"Can we please not do this? This is a library, not a boxing ring, and I don't want to get thrown out."

I hold my breath, waiting, hoping that I won't have to step between them. A second passes, and then another, but Sebastian is the first to take a step back, followed by Drew. The movement makes it easier for me to breathe, and I suck a ragged breath into my lungs.

Drew's eyes shift back to me, and I glance at him. As soon as our eyes meet, a bolt of electricity rips through me.

Why, after everything he put me through, does my body still react to him like this?

Like there's this visible string attaching us to one another. It's further confirmation that no matter how hard I try to escape him, I'll always be pulled back into his web.

"I'll see you around, Flower." Drew smirks.

"It's time to go, Bel," Sebastian orders, then grabs me by the wrist and starts tugging me back toward the front of the library. For a moment, I'm frozen, unable to respond, but when my brain catches up with my body, I do. I sink my heels into the carpet, forcing him to slow. Then I wrench my arm free of his grasp and take a wobbly step back.

Who does he think he is?

He turns on me, and his eyes bleed with anger, showing me little pieces of a person I haven't seen in a while.

"Don't treat me like that," I whisper.

"I didn't treat you like anything. I'm *protecting* you, Bel. Drew is bad fucking news, or did you forget all about that because he made you come?"

I don't think. All I do is react.

My hand lands against his cheek before I can even stop myself. A red-hot spark of pain flares through my palm, and Sebastian appears just as shocked as me, his features hard as stone.

Tears burn at the back of my eyes. "I... I shouldn't have done that. I'm sorry, it's just..."

"Stop," Sebastian demands. "Don't apologize. I'm a dickhead for saying that."

"No. It's not okay. I don't like that I hit you. I'm not that person, the one who leans into violence. I'm sorry."

A devilish smile tugs at his lips, but I can't see anything but that red mark on his cheek.

"I don't think you know what you're capable of, Maybel. I don't think you see your real power, nor do I think you've reached your full potential."

"Well, what I do know is that I'm not a violent person. Mom taught me better than that."

"I don't think you are either, but violence is needed sometimes. Sometimes you have to protect yourself. Sometimes the spoken word means nothing. What's that saying, actions speak louder than words? It's no wonder a baseball bat to the knees or fist to the eye leaves a much bigger impact than saying, *don't do that again*."

I shake my head and return his grin, the tension easing between us.

"That escalated quickly."

"Hey, I'm not saying I know from personal experience..."

"Sure you don't." I roll my eyes. "Let me get my books and bag, and then we can leave."

Sebastian gestures for me to lead the way, and I do. He follows me, his presence more like a shadow. We enter the main room, and I find all my belongings in the same spot. I stack them up and shove them into my bag while he stands beside me, his hands in his pockets.

"How did you know he would be here?" I ask quietly.

"The guard called it in. Said he was asking about you. I should've known the first chance he got to see you without me there, he'd take it... but for some reason, I thought he might use the last two remaining brain cells in his head to make a better choice."

All I can do is nod. I should've known too and expected it really. Drew's been trying to see me every day since I came home from the hospital. I suppose I was naive to think he'd give me one day of peace.

Out of the corner of my eye, I see Drew walking toward the front doors. As if someone dipped my skin in gasoline and lit a match, my entire body warms at the reminder of his presence. I'm drawn to him.

I want to drown in his darkness and let him breathe life back into me.

With everything put away, I start toward the door, my arms wrapped around my middle and my coat tucked between them. The cool air makes it easier for me to think, and my clouded thoughts appear in a new light.

I can't believe I let him touch me. Again.

Worse, I melted like butter in his hands. I'm so disappointed and disgusted in myself. *He could be your brother.* We make it to the car, and I climb into the passenger seat. Across the parking lot, I watch Drew amble down the sidewalk, hands in pockets, swaggering like the king of the campus.

I guess he is.

Sebastian rushes around the car and climbs into the driver's side, and as we pull away, Drew holds his hand up and gives me a little wave. I jerk my gaze forward, hoping Sebastian didn't catch that, knowing damn well he did. *He sees everything.*

I sink into the leather seat and let my thoughts run rampant. Trapped between them, how will I survive? And what the hell do I do if what he says was true?

If we're related... What does that even mean?

I've had enough surprises, and part of me thinks it's a game to him. The other part says I can't pretend I didn't hear his father's words.

Deep down, I know I need to discover the truth.

And every fiber of my soul hopes he's wrong because otherwise... I can't fathom what it might mean for me and the person I am.

7

DREW

Sometimes in life, you have to be the bigger person even when you don't want to be. I'm learning that. Learning that sometimes it's not always about what *I* want. It sucks, but when you care about someone else's well-being more than your own, that's the result. Sure, I could've beaten the shit out of Sebastian for taking her away from me, but I didn't.

I've caused her enough pain. Even if fighting with him would've made me feel better, I know it would've only ended up hurting her in some way.

I'm actively trying to avoid doing that, at least on the emotional side.

Since the first moment I laid eyes on Bel, she was meant to be mine. The light to my darkness, the perfect mixture of pain and beauty. She gets off on submitting to me and giving me complete control.

Nothing has changed between us, not in the physical sense. She still reacts to my touch as I suspected she would. A person can't turn off their feelings that easily. Parts of her might hate me, but that sick, twisted piece inside her pretty little head craves me. It craves my darkness, my chaos, and mayhem.

A gust of cold wind blows, and I shiver. I'll have to start wearing my jacket soon and making sure my little wallflower remembers hers when she is lost in her books and notes. I turn toward the other side of campus and jog up the driveway to The Mill house. The cold bites into my fingers enough to spur me up the stairs and through the front door at almost a sprint. Not fast enough to miss the plastic cups and trash littering the yard. All I can do is shake my head.

We need to get the new assholes out here to clean. I can only imagine how terrible the inside looks. New inductee time always means more people in the house, more strangers, trash, and mess.

The old me wouldn't have thought much of it, not when it meant more girls would be around to choke on my cock. Now, I want only one girl on her knees for me. And she won't even have a full conversation with me. I mean, it is what it is, but I won't be able to use my dick to subdue her forever. At some point, we need to be adults and talk about this shit rationally.

Sauntering inside, I let the door slam behind me, rattling the antique picture frames on the wall. The sconces, or whatever the fuck they are, rattle too. Looking ahead, I scan the floor. Bodies litter the main room in various states of undress, and I'm thankful I already gave the housekeeper the week off. Business as usual during our induction week, I guess.

She'd be appalled, not that she hasn't seen all of us who live in the house in some state of undress over the past couple of years. Those moments would pale in comparison to this shit. She's learned to ignore a good amount of stuff, and we've learned to make sure she gets a bonus on her paycheck at least once a quarter.

I contemplate my next move, trying to decide whether to wake these bastards up and throw them out or... A loud crash and glass breaking echo down the stairs and into my ears.

Since Sebastian is with Maybel, it has to be Aries or Lee. My money is on Lee since he's always been the more dramatic of my friends outside of Sebastian. I thought that sounded a lot like a body hitting the floor.

Another crash has me on alert, and I'm jogging up the stairs before I think better of it. I've just reached the top of the stairs, turning to walk into Lee's room, when a crystal glass hurtles into the wall opposite Lee's open door.

What the fuck?

"Hey!" I shout.

There's a pause, and Lee pokes his head out the door with a glare. "I wasn't throwing that at you, just in your direction."

I glare at him now. "Wow, great apology. Perfect cadence."

He ducks back into his room, and I follow. "What the hell? Why are you destroying the antique crystal?"

Not that I give a shit about the antique part. I'm more concerned with the cleaning aspect. Without the house-keeper, one of us is going to have to clean that shit up. And it sure as shit won't be me.

Lee sighs, the sound long and loud as the air escapes his mouth. Patience isn't really my strong suit, but I do my best to give him a moment as he clutches a half-empty bottle of bourbon to his bare chest. One look at him, and you can see he's unhinged. His hair is messy, and there are heavy-looking bags under his eyes. He looks like he's been through the wringer.

His basketball shorts ride low on his hips, and I cringe, noticing his feet are bare. "My family thinks I'm getting married. Actually, not *think*. They've *arranged* my marriage. An arranged marriage? Are you fucking kidding me?!"

I sigh and sink to the edge of his bed to consider what he's confessed. "Why?" It's the only thing I can think to ask. I kinda hate that I'm terrible at conversations and emotions. I could learn a few things from Maybel.

Tightening his grip on the bottle of bourbon, he brings it to his lips and takes a massive gulp before extending the bottle out to me. I should decline since it's not even noon yet, but after the morning I've had, I could use a drink.

With his other hand, he wipes at his mouth. "I don't know. Maybe they think I'm running around, fucking men, destroying the family name. Maybe they want me married off to a meek little girl, someone they can control or use to control me."

I snatch the bottle out of his hands and watch as he takes a spot on the edge of the bed beside me. Then I bring the bottle to my lips and take a long pull from it. The rich brown liquid blazes a path of fire down my throat, coating my insides in warmth. I have to say this is so much better than the gin he had before.

"Shit, man."

He drops his head into his hands. "Why is everything so fucking awful right now? Seb is barely here. You're off doing whatever the fuck you're doing. And Aries is out there fucking his way through the cheerleading team." He lifts his head, piercing me with a knowing look. "Which we need to do something about."

Shit. Yeah, we do. Some of the most off-limit girls at the school are on the cheerleading team. Most of them are daughters or granddaughters of alumni. Too innocent, but I guess not as innocent as they like to portray if Aries has started plowing through them, both literally and figuratively. And if left to his own devices, every one of them will be looking to murder him once he's through with them. *Fuck.*

That's a good enough reason for another drink. Bringing the bottle to my lips, I take another long swig. This time, the bourbon burns a little less. "We'll deal with Aries soon. He's not going to have all of them wanting to murder him in just a few days, right?"

Lee snorts and snatches his bottle back. "I think you've forgotten your friend's sexual appetite. Aries is a playboy, and I mean... does it really matter at this point? You and Seb have barely been here for the new inductee week, and when we manage to get you both in the same room, we have to worry about who is going to murder who first. I've been trying to manage it all on my own, but it's getting to a point where shit is out of control. I need you, all of you, and everyone is going through shit, but we can't fuck this up. We can't make a mockery of ourselves or ruin our own image. Fuck our parents. I only give a shit about *us*."

Fuck, he's right. I'm the president of The Mill. Being

present isn't an option but a requirement. I need to step the fuck up, and I need to do so now. I sigh and give him a nod. That's about as much of an apology as he'll get from me.

Lee relaxes next to me. "Great, one fire out. What about the next one? What are you going to do about Bel?"

His question catches me off guard so much that I flinch.

"Going that well, huh? What even happened?"

I shake my head. "I don't want to drag you into any of it. All you need to know is Seb is trying to keep her away from me, and I'm not giving her up. Not at all."

"Fucking fantastic, the two most hardheaded stubborn fucks fighting against each other. What's the point? Why fight when you could work together?"

I snatch the bottle back from him and take a long drink instead of answering right away. Once I swallow, I pin him with a glare. "Yeah, work together to get his sister out from under his thumb long enough to have a fucking conversation? That will go well. He blames me for everything that happened, and I have no problem saying I fucked up. I know what I did hurt her, but I was trying to protect her. He doesn't see it that way. Not that it matters. I think it has more to do with his pride. The slight to his family name is what he's really pissed about. He doesn't even *know* her."

Lee shrugs and leans over to brace his elbows on his knees. "I don't know, man. He's been living in that giant-ass house with her. I'd assume he's learned something about her by now. Plus, with how he saw you treating her before, his reaction isn't really that shocking. If I had a sister, I'd probably do the same. God knows I wouldn't let any of you fucks touch her."

I let out a small laugh, dislodging a thought from my mind. How would I feel if I had a daughter and she was with a man like me? The thought has the opposite reaction of what I thought it would. Instead of disgust, I feel warmth. The idea of having a child with Bel. *My flower.* Fuck... the image of her pregnant, her swollen belly cradled in my hands is there now. It pops into my head, refusing to leave. It won't be today or even next month, but that will be us years from now. It has to be because there is no point in breathing if she isn't a part of my life.

We sit in silence for a few moments. Lee breaks it after a minute. "You know he's under a lot of pressure. More than he used to be now that he's head of the Arturo family. Something he never even wanted. He's just trying to..."

I wait, not encouraging him since I know where this is going.

"He just wants to secure everything. Make sure the last person related to him by blood is safe and protected."

"Okay, so are you telling me to give up?"

Lee doesn't flinch away from my sharp tone.

"No, dickhead. What I'm saying is try not to kill each other in the process and maybe keep Bel out of it. She doesn't know this world, the ruthlessness of it. She's been through enough shit."

I consider what Bel's been through. She's lost her mom. Me. Her piece-of-shit friend Jackie. All she has is Seb, and through all that, she still remains, standing taller with her chin held high. "She's strong enough to handle it."

He lets out a sigh of defeat. "You're missing my point.

Both you and Seb need to be stronger. That way, she doesn't have to handle it. Get me?"

A light bulb goes off in my head. I'm good at being vindictive, at manipulating and getting what I want, but sometimes you need to think deeper, to dive into the emotions of a person. For the first time, I consider what being part of one of the biggest crime families in the world means for Bel. Does she even know what Seb and his family does? What she has inherited, and what her new last name means?

Lee hands me the bottle again and lies back against the mattress. I swear the man is in perpetual motion, unable to stay still for even a second.

"Okay, Dr. Phil. Your turn. What are you going to do about this whole marriage thing, and if so, can I help at all?"

He snorts. "I doubt even if I brought *you* home and declared that we were getting married, my family would be able to get over my sexuality."

I don't understand that. "What's the big deal? You fuck women too, a lot of women from the couple of years we've lived together. And they only get pissy about the men you sleep with?"

He sighs again and rolls onto his side to stare at the wall. The bottle sits upright against his hip now. "Who I sleep with doesn't really matter. They've made up their mind. I know their end goal now. All they want is to marry me off to a suitable girl with the hope I won't bring any more shame to our family name."

"There's nothing wrong with fucking men or women. Don't let them tell you that you're fucked up or a disgrace because you like both. Do whatever the fuck you want to do. Or better yet, whoever."

I fall back onto the mattress and stare up at the intricate detail on the ceiling.

"Do you think this is how our families got so fucked up in the first place? From all the parental meddling until everything became so fucked up that it couldn't be fixed anymore? Like a permanent fucked-up-ness."

Lee shifts, the covers rustling underneath his legs. "Bleak, man. But hell, probably. Defending the family name is so ingrained in all of our families' heads that it's the only thing they consider. No matter what it does to every individual family member along the way. No matter your feelings, thoughts, or beliefs. As long as the name remains untarnished, everyone in said family could be having a mental breakdown."

I can't help but laugh. "Maybe we should all be like Aries and fuck our way through the cheerleaders."

Lee smiles now. "Who says I haven't already?"

Considering how many of them tried to get an invitation to *The Hunt* this year I wasn't so sure he hadn't.

Just outside the door is a crash followed by a curse. *Aries.* A second later, he appears in the doorway, his big body filling the whole frame. His long curls are wild and combed away from his face, and his blue eyes shine with excitement when they land on us.

"What are you bitches doing? Didn't you see the pile of new inductees downstairs sleeping? Why are we not making their lives miserable right now?"

I laugh and shift to interlace my hands behind my head so I can look up at him from a more comfortable angle. "They'll be there a while. We have time. Where have you been?"

Lee and I exchange a knowing look that Aries doesn't appear to miss.

"Where the fuck you think I've been? I'm sure you both remember the McBeth twins on the cheerleading squad. Did you know they make the same noises? It's like fucking surround sound."

The room fills with laughter, and I roll over, laughing so hard my fucking stomach hurts, and tears leak from the corners of my eyes.

Aries stands at the end of the bed with his hands shoved into his letter jacket pockets. "What the fuck are you assholes laughing about?"

I recover first, and Lee wipes at his face with his forearm. I'm still smiling when I answer him. "Nothing, man. Just keep doing what you're doing while the rest of our worlds burn down."

His brow furrows, and he takes a step toward the bed. "Who do I need to kill?"

With the menacing scowl on his face and his dead-serious tone, I wouldn't put it past him. Maybe I should send him after my asshole father.

I consider it. Nah, Aries is all brute force. If I sicced one of my friends on my father, it would be Seb and only Seb. Not only is he strategic but he's also fucking lethal, going straight for the jugular. And best of all, he has zero regrets afterward.

Aries slumps down on the end of the bed, and I consider my options. *Would Seb help me?*

We all know each other's families. What they do, and

how they operate. The thing is, we've always tried to keep all of that far away from our school life and The Mill. At least, the best we can with my father breathing down my neck. Shit is hard enough without adding in the family inheritances. Maybe I already have the solution to dear ole dad. I just need to nut up and ask a friend for help. I smile to myself, feeling like I might actually have the fix.

Something tells me he's a lot less likely to just do what I ask than he was a month ago.

But if my father became a danger to Bel...that...*that* would make Seb act.

8

BEL

It's been a couple of days, but Drew's words and rough touch have stuck with me. Branding me with their memory. I hate that he knows how to awaken all the dormant places in my body and knows exactly what to do to leave me begging for more.

Why is he doing this to me, sparking my desire for him all over again?

I promised myself he wouldn't pull me back in.

I stop brushing my hair and throw the brush at the bathroom counter, where it clatters and bounces into the sink.

Damn him for doing this to me. If he thinks I'll go back to being the meek little wallflower bending to his every whim, he'll be in for one hell of a surprise. The day I lost my mom... I lost a little piece of myself. I swear it died right along with her, and something else bloomed in that spot. Something different, wild, something that would never be taken advantage of again.

Growing sick of myself, I gather my hair up into a messy knot on top of my head and leave the confines of my bedroom to hunt Sebastian down. He spends the majority of his time in the study that used to be his—*our*—grandfather's. Not that I would know much about him. Seb isn't exactly forthcoming with information. I get the eerie feeling he's trying to protect me from something bigger.

Just as I expect, I find him in the study, a mug of coffee on the leather desk blotter, his feet thrown up on the edge of the massive mahogany desk.

The room looks stately. Shelves line both sides of the room, a massive fireplace near the door, and windows on the opposite wall. The space is too dark and formal for me.

How can someone relax long enough to work in here?

I cringe, realizing at the last moment that I've spoken the words out loud.

Seb glances up and smirks. "No one relaxes here. This room is mostly for show. Hell, some of these books haven't even been cracked open."

I give a little sigh and shuffle to the nearest shelf, the hardwood warm under my sock-covered feet. Classics, lots of classics, with a few law books mixed in. Interesting. I tug on a copy of *Twenty Thousand Leagues* and smell the edge of the case. It reminds me of the school library, and the scent comforts me the same way I feel when I go there.

I gently peel open the cover, and the pages stick straight up, signifying that this one has never been opened. *How sad.*

I look from the book to Seb, who is watching me curiously, his feet now on the floor, his shoulders hunched as he braces his elbows on his knees.

"Did you need something?"

Is it too weird that I just want someone to talk to? Someone to help me figure things out? I tuck the book back in its spot and turn to face the desk.

"I need to know the truth. Am I Drew's sister?"

Seb huffs out a breath and rubs at his eyes.

"Do I personally think he's your brother? No."

I fold myself into the chair in front of the desk and stare at him, afraid that if I look away for even a moment, his response might be missed.

"Do you know more than you've told me? About my father? Or about yours?"

Despite our time together, I still can't really read him. His face is doing that *I'm a grumpy hot boy* thing that it usually does. All I can manage to do is frown. While it's wonderful to have a sibling and someone to talk to, that only works if they respond. He of course says nothing.

"Cool. Glad we are sharing."

He blinks, and his mouth shifts to something that looks a lot like a grin. "I'll share what I can when I can, but I promise, I'm not willfully keeping things from you." There's a pause, and he ducks his chin. "Can you...would you be able to tell me more about what our mom was like?"

I won't lie. My heart swells a little in my chest. Since I miss talking to her so much, Mom's never far from my mind. I think the easiest way to keep someone's memory alive even after they pass is to talk about them.

His green eyes mirror my own, and in some ways, it's like looking at my own reflection. Every twitch reminds me that he's trying to keep his emotions in check, and right now, he's doing a terrible job at it. Not that I'm going to hold it against him. I feel like Sebastian has grown more vulnerable with me in many ways. I see sides of him no one else does, or at least not that I've seen, and that makes me want to get closer. It makes me want to build on our connection.

"She had a way of making everything okay. Not enough butter to make cookies, so use water and create a new recipe for our recipe notebook. Not enough money for new school clothes, so go to Goodwill and get double the haul. It was like no matter what the obstacle or problem was, she found a way to make it better. With nothing more than a smile and a hug, she made life easier. It's funny, no matter how poor we were or how much we struggled, I always knew we'd have each other." My voice cracks, emotion ripping through the words. I blink back tears, reminding myself that I don't need to cry every time I talk about her.

Sebastian's throat bobs as he swallows, and his eyes are trained on his hands. I scan his features, and I can see her there so easily now that I know to look for it. Her nose, and the freckles you can barely see that grace his forehead and the bridge of his nose.

I continue when he doesn't say anything. "I don't mind talking about her. It hurts, of course, but I feel like the day I stop talking about her is the day her memory fades away."

The urge to ask him a question in return about the family he grew up with, about the family who obviously wasn't the same as my mom, even though she might have come from them, sits on the tip of my tongue.

Regardless of my curiosity, I know I'm not ready. A tiny

part of me wants to hold on to the image I have of my mother because I know when he starts to tell me things about our family, my thoughts will change, my feelings will get involved, and I don't ever want to see her in a different way.

And while I don't want to admit it out loud, I'm afraid of our family name and what it means. The respect it demands, the violence and blood it holds. I know very little, but I'm not naive enough to think that our family name was built on wholesome ventures. Sebastian's thrown himself into the family business like he has something to prove, and that terrifies me. With Sebastian keeping company like Drew's family, it's clear whatever we're involved in circles around danger, secrets, and violence.

"I'm sorry. I don't mean to be silent. It's just hard for me to wrap my head around. I'm a logical person, my decisions are fact based, and I'm struggling with my anger and regret. There's nothing I can do to change what happened. I can't bring her back, and it kills me. I wish I had more time. I wish I could ask her all the questions... I wish for so much."

My heart breaks for him because while my life with our mother was nothing short of a struggle, it was overflowing with love and warmth. Two things Sebastian clearly had very little of in his upbringing.

I don't know what makes me do it. Maybe he needs to know I'm here and that he's not alone in his struggle. I don't know, but it doesn't matter. I lean forward and place my hand on his. It's nothing more than a caress, but it's enough of a reminder that I'm here for him and for him to look up at me.

His green eyes are misty, and I look away, acting like I don't see the tears forming there. Something tells me he wouldn't want me to comment on his emotions.

"It's okay to feel the way you do. Everyone grieves in their own way, and I can't even imagine how much her loss hurts you. You'd just found out who your mother was and then..." I can't even finish the sentence, its weight pressing down on my chest and making it difficult to breathe or even speak. I give his hand a tiny squeeze, then release it.

The silence surrounding us becomes deafening, and I shoot a wistful glance over the shelves of books. Anything to distract me from his painful expression. He breaks the silence first with a throat clear.

"Do you really want to see him?"

Him. He doesn't have to say his name. It's engraved in every cell of my body. The spotlight is back on me, and I don't like it. I shift in the chair anxiously. I haven't really wrapped my head around my feelings for Drew. Yes, they're still there, and I'd be a liar if I said they weren't, but they're caked in tears, regret, and anger.

I'm propelled back to the scene he walked in on in the library, and the burn of embarrassment blooms in my cheeks without permission.

"It's complicated. I don't really care to see him..."

He slings his feet back up onto the edge of the desk, the rubber soles leaving scuff marks, which he seems completely unconcerned with. Like it's one last rebellion against his grandfather.

He waits for an explanation with one eyebrow cocked.

The emotional turmoil from minutes ago has disappeared completely. How does he *do* that? Turn off his feelings so easily?

I shrug. "I don't know... What is it you want me to say?" I try not to sound as defensive as I feel, but I can't help it. I know Sebastian is angry with Drew, and rightfully so, as am I... but they're best friends. They grew up together. Part of me wonders how he can so easily jump ship after all they've been through.

"Well, for starters, it would be great if you said, 'Please, brother, go ahead and murder him.'"

I let out a sigh. "Sorry, but I'll never say that. I want to hate him. I really do. And part of me does. The heartache is still so fresh sometimes it's like he's breaking my heart all over again just being in his presence. I just...it's hard to erase all the feelings in a month. Especially when he's so..." I meet his eyes, not willing to finish that sentence.

I don't have to explain. If anyone understands the extreme behaviors and psychopathic tendencies of Drew, it would be Seb. Something tells me he's got his own sick and twisted problems. He just does a better job of concealing them.

"I can't stop thinking about what his dad said that night. I need to know the truth, and that means I can't exile Drew out of my life, not completely."

"The truth?" Seb snaps, but there's no real heat in his eyes, only his tone.

"Yeah, about the sister thing. No offense, but I can only take your word for something so long. I get that you don't think it's anything, but I've learned a couple of things in the past month, and one of those things is that sometimes other people know more than you do. I'd feel better talking to him and finding out for myself. Who knows, maybe he knows something we don't."

Seb drums his fingers on the heavy wood desk. "What he knows is how to manipulate people so that he can get whatever he wants. It's what his father taught him, and he's really fucking good at it. He knew exactly what to say to draw you into his web. Then when he had you right where he wanted you, he pounced, leaving you without a way to escape. I mean, look at you now. Even after everything, you *still* let him touch you."

I already know these things. Drew likes to play games, draw me in and push me away. It's always been a cat-and-mouse game with him. It wouldn't be out of character for him to tell me something and give me just enough information each time to keep me crawling back to him. *But would he really do that? After everything?*

Fuck, am I that predictable?

I know the answer the second Seb sees my realization. "I know it's difficult, and you don't have to admit it out loud, but you know I'm right. He'll tell you anything you want to hear so long as you continue playing his game."

I roll my eyes because while this is my brother, and I feel enough of a connection to trust him, he's no different than Drew. "I might look delicate and naive, but I'm far from it. You're my brother, and you can't make me believe you wouldn't do the same thing. If a person is motivated enough, they'll do *anything* to stay in control. So while you're painting him as the villain in all this, I know it wouldn't take more than a little persuasion for you to do something similar. Don't even try to deny it. You don't want me to see him, even if I want to."

He slaps his hand on the desk this time. A crack resembling thunder resonates through the room, and I jolt forward in my seat. In all the time I've been living here, which isn't long but definitely long enough to see someone's personality, Sebastian hasn't ever reacted in anger, at least not toward me.

This is new and, dare I admit, a little scary.

"There's a fucking difference, Bel. I want to keep you safe, but you're making it so damn *difficult*."

I cross my arms over my chest. "You can't just lock me inside my room and throw away the key. I hate to tell you this, but I didn't come here to exchange one prison for another."

"This isn't a prison. You're free to do whatever you want. All I'm saying is I don't want you to willingly walk into dangerous situations."

I scoff. Does he think I'm stupid? Clearly. "You make it sound like I'm trying to hug a bomb or something."

Seb drops his feet to the floor once again and leans over the desk, leveling me with a fierce look that likely makes most men tremble. God knows it's got a similar effect on me. But my pride and refusal to be pushed around are stronger than my fear, and if I'm not letting Drew push me around, I'm not letting Seb do it either, even if he is my brother.

"How do you not see that's exactly what you're doing? Anyone from a million miles away could see that Drew's life is a fucking mess. Then you come along and put yourself right in the middle of all of it. It's only a matter of time before everything implodes. He's going down hard, and if you aren't careful, he'll take you down with him."

I lean my head back and rest it against the wood.

Even with my indifference toward Drew lingering at the back of my mind, I'm reminded that he's also a victim of his father's wrongdoings. He's been abused both physically and mentally, and if one thing in life is true, it's that hurt people always find a way of hurting those they care about.

Still, that doesn't make what happened okay, and it doesn't mean I should allow him back into my life. The ball is in my court now, and I have to decide whether I'm capable of accepting him for who he is, the good and the bad, and forgiving him. The old me never stood a chance against Drew, but the new me... She's fierce and burning with determination for revenge.

This cruel world ripped my petals off, but I'm resilient, and I'm strong enough to stand up to him now. I'm blooming into something deadly, something beautiful. No matter the obstacles, Drew and I will never be able to move forward together if he wants me to remain below him. Queens stand at their king's side, and I won't be anything less than that.

"I'm sorry, okay? This isn't as easy for me to do. I can't just turn my emotions off. When you fall in l... " I want to punch myself in the face for almost admitting that out loud. *Have I fallen in love with Drew?* Yes, and I didn't find it possible to forget those feelings. They were simply buried beneath everything else, but they were still there.

"Drew is very charismatic when he wants to be. You aren't

the first person to fall for him, and you won't be the last. Things take a dark turn when that charm doesn't work anymore. You're only as useful as your purpose, and you saw what happens when your usefulness runs out. I don't want that to happen to you again. I don't want anyone to think they can fuck with you. I need you to be careful and smart. Oh, and I need you to pick out a dress from the stack I'm having delivered. There's a meeting that we need to attend together soon."

My curiosity has piqued, and I'm thankful for a topic change. Talking about falling in love with someone with your brother isn't exactly high on my bucket list.

"A meeting? What kind of meeting?"

"The business type. You're a member of the Arturo family. I know all of this is new and overwhelming, and while I've done my best to take all the pressure off you and keep you in the shadows, you'll need to know about the family businesses and affairs from time to time. I don't want to keep you completely out of the loop. This name-sake is as much yours as it is mine."

Oh. Oh *shit*. Since I'd moved in, he's been very careful to keep me away from it all. To maintain enough distance from what he's working on and my existence. I'm not surprised to be having this conversation. I knew we would get to this point eventually.

"Okay, so pick a dress out. Is there anything I need to know to prepare for this meeting?" I try not to appear nervous, but inside, my anxiety is already gnawing at me.

A small chuckle escapes his lips, and that seems to ease some of my tension. "Do you have to be such a nerd? There's no homework assignment, Bel. I'll walk you through anything you might need to know. We're in this together."

His phone pings loudly from the other side of the desk, and he snatches it up like it owes him money. I watch as his features pinch together, and his brows turn down as he stares at the screen like he's trying to solve a puzzle.

"Is everything okay?"

"Why wouldn't it be?" he questions without looking up from the screen.

I bite my tongue, wanting to point out how both confused and concerned he appears, but I don't get the chance as his phone rings. He turns away from me, bringing it to his ear and answering it. He speaks in a hushed voice and gives me a small wave before walking through the side door.

Uhhh, okay?

"Perfect," I mutter and stand to go out the opposite door and back to my suite. "It's not like we were having a conversation or anything," I say to myself while walking down the long maze of a hall.

I pause at the entrance of my bedroom. I don't want to keep locking myself in that room. I wasn't lying when I told him I didn't exchange one prison for another. I chew on my bottom lip, considering my options.

Despite Sebastian's opinion and feelings toward Drew, he can't answer my questions. And I hope, by now, I'm capable of seeing through Drew's bullshit games. If anything he's said in those texts and at the library is true, then he won't lead me along with some lie. I'm not dumb enough to think he won't try, though. I know there are no guarantees with him. Up one minute, down the next. There's no way I can predict his next move.

I tug my phone out of my pocket and scroll to my text message thread with him. I deleted our old chain, as too many memories were attached to it. It feels like a complete contradiction for me to push him away but then go out of my way to meet up with him. This isn't for anything but answers.

I'm already regretting every swipe of my fingers as I type out the text. There's a long fall-down-a-hole-drop as I hover my fingers over the send button. I don't know if I can do this. If I can handle seeing him again so soon.

You're stronger than you think.

And before I can chicken out, I hit send and wait.

It only takes a few seconds for the dots to show up on the screen and his response to come through.

Me: Meet me tonight, the cabin on The Mill property. I want you to tell me the truth.

Psycho: What time?

I swallow, my stomach churning with anxiety.

Me: 9 p.m.

I think about it a little longer. Do I really want to do this? Meet Drew in a dark cabin, all by myself? It sounds like a terrible start to a horror film.

The pinging of my phone interrupts my thoughts, and I look down at his response. That stupid, annoying part of me that's suffocated by the anger and pain he caused sparks with life, and that distinct warmth that his presence brought me before trickles in slowly as I read his response back to myself.

Psycho: Unless you plan to walk six miles, grab the four-wheeler at the trailhead. There will be a key in it.

Shit. I forgot how far out it is. My phone chimes again, and the next message almost makes me regret messaging him.

Psycho: I knew I'd be seeing you soon, Flower.

Is it possible he said and did all those horrible things to protect me from his father? Possibly... but how can I ever forgive him? How can I ensure that the next time things get tough, he won't push me away again and hurt me?

I can't, and I need to remind myself of that. I need to remember that no matter what, Drew has always been about making himself happy even at the expense of others, and until he shows me otherwise, I'll play defense, ensuring that I don't become a casualty in the sick and twisted game of chess he plays.

9

DREW

My blood and body hum with a tingling of awareness. My small taste of her did nothing to quench my need or hunger for her. I can already hear her heady breaths in my ear and feel her little nails digging into my skin. To pull me closer or push me away, it doesn't really matter. As I leave the house, I only think about seeing her. I didn't realize how much she meant to me until after everything blew the hell up.

What's that cheesy saying? *You don't know what you have until it's gone?* Isn't that the fucking truth? Along the way to the cabin, I wonder why she chose the cabin in the woods as the location to meet. We could've met anywhere, but she chose the most secluded option...

Is she scared of being seen with me? Or is she hiding from her brother?

Probably a little bit of both.

The quiet claws through me, an unusual and unwelcome sensation.

Rivulets of moonlight cut across the path as I stride through the woods. My phone vibrates in my pocket, and I jerk it out to make sure it's not Bel calling to cancel on me. I can't handle that shit right now. There's no way I won't march right up to the mansion and kidnap her. *Fuck, think rationally.*

All rational thinking goes out the window when I see his name on my phone. *Father.* I should change his name to fuckface since it's far more fitting than father. God knows he's treated me like an inconvenience for as long as I can remember.

Fuck him. He's always got a way of ruining everything. This is the first time he's decided to contact me in days, and the only thing I want to say to him is "go fuck yourself." Well, I'd be more than willing to tell him that, more than willing to stand up to him and put him in the ground. Other things are at stake, other people's well-being hanging in the balance, so my selfish desires will have to wait a little longer. I choose not to let him ruin my evening and instead hit the decline button and shove my phone back into my jean pocket. A minute later, my phone buzzes again, telling me he probably left a caring and delightful voicemail.

I push my father to the back of my mind and pick up my pace toward the cabin, scanning the trees in case she is out here too. It's obvious I'm alone. The quiet of nature greets me, and I love it. I enjoy the sound of the wind, the crunching of leaves beneath my boots.

I walk faster to try to burn some of the edge from seeing her at the library. From holding myself back from pulling her away from Seb and ensuring both of them know whom she belongs to. I told her to take the four-wheeler, but I walked the entire way to help curb some of this need in my blood. As I get close to the cabin, the rough wood structure gives way to a spacious clearing of grass that circles the cabin, butting up to a small river. The moonlight glints off it, but my attention is dragged from the beauty of nature and to someone who is just as beautiful.

On the stairs of the cabin, I finally spot her. My Flower.

She's sitting on the top step, a sweater wrapped tight around her slim frame, her sunshine-blond hair tied up in her usual messy knot. My gaze collides with hers, and I don't even have to be a skilled predator to see how anxious she is. Lucky for her, the only time I want to see tears on her face again is when she's choking on my cock. I hurt her once already. I'm not going to get another chance to fix this if I fuck up again.

"Been waiting long?" I ask as I check my watch. By my time, I'm early, so she got here extra early to beat me. *Smart.*

She shrugs one shoulder and tugs her sleeves over her knuckles, wrapping her arms around her middle as if she's trying to hug herself.

"Hi," I whisper, hoping I put everything I'm feeling into that one tiny word.

"Hi," she responds, her shoulders dropping.

I creep up the last couple of steps and pause on the porch. "It'll be warmer inside once I turn on the heat."

She nods, then pushes up from her spot, tucking her chin into her chest, almost like she's trying to avoid looking at me. *What the fuck is going on?*

Why is she suddenly hiding from me? Not even when I stripped her naked in these woods did she hide from me... My temper rises, and I don't know what to do with it, so I angrily jerk the screen door open and unlock the cabin using a key from my key ring. Then I shove the door open and beckon her inside.

I take a calming breath, breathing through my nose. I need to calm down and figure this out. Her steps are hesitant as she walks over the threshold, and I follow her, flicking on the light switch along the way. Soft illumination cuts through the darkness, and I hit the buttons on the digital thermostat to warm up the place.

I don't know how long we'll be here, but I don't want to risk her getting cold.

The gas fireplace roars to life with another flick of a switch. Bel startles at the soft swish of it igniting.

"Sit," I bite out, waving toward the large, comfortable armchair.

"I'm okay, thank you..."

I stalk around the room, circling her because she's got me on edge, and I don't know what to do. I don't know how to react.

Her emerald eyes track my movements until she has to shift to keep me in her line of sight. "What are you doing?"

I shrug. "Good question. What am I doing, Bel? You're the one who asked me to come here. And now you're acting like a scared rabbit I trapped here. You won't even meet my gaze. So naturally, what am I supposed to think but that you want to be hunted?"

She turns enough to put the chair at her back so she

can face me directly. "If I remember correctly, you're the one who has been begging to see me for weeks."

I let out a sigh of defeat. She takes a step toward me and points at my chest, jabbing me hard with her finger. "If you're going to be a dick to me, then you can turn the hell around and leave."

She shakes her head, disbelief pinching her beautiful features. "I can't believe I thought you would actually be honest with me. That you would talk to me and not make this into some stupid game."

I close my hand around her smaller one, completely engulfing it, barely keeping from sighing at the touch of her smooth skin, and lean in. "Honest? You haven't told me what you want so how can I lie to you when I haven't been asked a question?"

In an instant, the disbelief I saw before turns into panic and dread. She looks up at me through thick lashes, her hands twisting in her sweater sleeves. And that's when it hits me.

"This is about what I said in the library, isn't it?"

When her eyes widen, more horror bleeding into their depths, a small sound slips from her lips. It's all the confirmation I need. I advance, trapping her between my forearms and pressing her into the wall. It's my favorite thing to do. To make her helpless and unable to escape me. "What's the point of asking, Bel? You already know it doesn't matter to me. You already know where I stand. I don't care if you're my sister."

I lean in and run my nose along the line of her neck and shoulder, needing to smell her. God, how does she always smell so good? Like lilacs and baby powder. Who knew baby powder could be so mouth-watering?

"I bet," I whisper against her skin, loving how she trembles against me. "Even with the doubt, and disgust, and dread churning in your gut right now, you'd still open your legs for me. You'd still take my cock into your tight cunt. Even if it's wrong, and it's so fucking wrong to think about your *brother* fucking you, but you would. And like I said, I'd do it. I'd do it because rules, morals, and laws wouldn't stop me from owning you. You're mine forever."

As if on instinct, she squeezes her thighs together, and when she releases them, I shove my thigh roughly between them, hiking her body up high enough that she's basically sitting on my knee.

When I trail my mouth toward hers, teasing her lips with my breath, she flinches, and it's enough to allow me to push back an inch. In her green eyes, I see her fear and how much this is eating away at her.

Guilt blooms in my chest.

Fuck. I meet her gaze. "Luckily for you, we aren't related. So you have nothing to feel bad about. You're still a good little girl, Flower."

She flinches like I slapped her and shoves at my chest hard. Of course, I don't give her even an inch, but it's cute how she tries. "What the hell is wrong with you? You beg to see me for weeks, then you manipulate me into coming to meet you!" she screams, and I'm more surprised than anything else, both at her assumption and her raised voice.

I release my arms but keep my thigh pressed tight against her center. "What are you talking about?"

She growls and attempts to shove at me again, but I

grab onto both of her wrists and hold them tight against my chest in one hand. "Watch it, Wallflower. I'm willing to give you some leeway..." I break off, not ready to go there yet. "But I won't allow you to shove me around and throw tantrums like a child."

"A child?" she screeches and tries to pry herself free from my grasp. "I don't think you're ready to have a conversation about maturity, but since you brought it up and want to act tough, let's do this. Should you even be here right now? Aren't you *engaged to be married*? Shouldn't you be doing husbandly things? Planning a wedding? Picking out names for your 2.5 kids and a Labrador Retriever? Not sneaking around the woods with the 'help'?"

Her words are razor-sharp and sting as they slice through me, leaving behind jagged marks. I release her, adding several feet of space between us. I strip out of my jacket because the room is suddenly hot.

It doesn't bother me that she's brought up Spencer and my father. It bothers me that she talks so negatively about herself. It bothers me to be reminded of how I fed into things, how I just went along with my father's demands. My jaw aches as I clench my teeth. Fists clenched, I feel the urge to punch something. Instead, I spin away from her and pace the room so I don't lash out, unleashing a sudden surge of anger on her.

Goddammit. I know I hurt her.

I know I did, but I'm trying to fix this. I want to fix this. I *need* to fix this.

I stab a hand through my hair, pulling on the long strands, willing an answer to come out of my mouth. I want her so bad it hurts to breathe. The mere thought of never having her in my arms again or having to see her with another man makes me want to commit murder. I'd never allow it. If she doesn't want me, fine, but no other man will ever have her either.

"Yeah," she spits. "That's what I thought."

The venom in her tone intensifies my anger, but more than that, it's the fact that she is wrong, and she doesn't even realize it. Quick like a snake, I reach for her, my fingers pressing into her shoulder blades, forcing her back against the wall. A small gasp leaves her parted lips, and I lean right into her face. The air in my lungs stills, and I'm momentarily frozen in time by her beauty.

My delicate little flower that's so fierce and strong. But so damn weak for me still.

"Fuck, you're so beautiful, Bel. Beautiful, and wrong, so fucking wrong, because I'm not fucking engaged to anyone. It was fake. All of it. My father planned it. I never lied to you, not once. Every word I said that night was to protect you."

Her gaze narrows with suspicion, and I can tell she doesn't believe me. She's so caught up in the pain I caused her, in the hateful words that cut her deeper than a knife that she can't see the truth. "Yeah, well the stitches I had to get because of you aren't *fake*. The heartbreak I have because of you isn't *fake*. Surprise, sometimes other people's emotions and reactions to things are real even if your own aren't."

She could've ripped my fucking heart out, and it would've hurt less.

When I pushed her, I didn't anticipate her hitting her head and I replayed that scene a million times over in my mind. It's the one thing I regret more than anything. Physically hurting her like that. But she's right, and she has a very real reason not to trust me, and to be angry. I can't fault her there, and I know I'll have to earn her trust back if we're to have a future together.

Her green eyes glisten with tears, and when she blinks, one slips free, trailing down the apple of her cheek. I can't help myself. I'm not a good fucking man, after all. I might be sorry, and guilt might riddle my soul, but I can't change the fact that her tears turn me on.

I'll forever be sick and twisted.

Cupping her by the cheeks, I trace that single tear with my thumb. Another falls, and then another, and I lean in and lick them away, relishing the salty taste on my tongue.

"Fuck, how can it be possible that you look even more beautiful with tears in your eyes?"

She jerks her head back and then winces when it hits the wall. "There is something *seriously* wrong with you."

"You already knew that, baby, so don't act surprised."

"Oh, I'm not surprised. I'm just wondering why I had any belief that you'd apologize to me. Even if it wasn't a formal apology, I thought you'd offer me *something*. And that when you did, maybe I'd finally be able to say you gave a fuck about me, but I didn't even get that."

I swallow hard and stare down into her face. "What are you talking about? Everything I've done has been to show you I care about you."

I can visibly see her walls going back up, and I can't let her go back there without me finishing what I have to say. "I care about you, Bel. I care about you more than I've cared about anything or anyone in my life." The other words, the ones I'm not quite ready to say despite all the pressure in my chest urging me to do it, stick tight in my throat. "All I ever do is think about you. This past month has killed me, Bel. I wanted to be there for you when your mom..."

"Do not speak about my mother. Ever!" She grits the words through her teeth.

"It's true. I tried to come to the hospital and Sebastian called the police, but I was there. I didn't abandon you, Bel."

I can see it in her eyes. The confusion, pain, and disbelief. She wants to believe me and accept what I've said, but a wall comes up out of nowhere and shuts down any progress I might have made. I swallow hard and shake my head.

She reaches for me, her tiny hands clutch onto my T-shirt, and for a second, I'm confused about where this is going. The look in her eyes is lethal, and I'm hard just staring into the green depths of her gaze, drowning to be this close to her for longer than a minute.

She clenches her fists tight into a ball, then drags me down so we're face-to-face. Only when bright hot pain shoots through my balls and up into my dick, slithering into my stomach, do I realize what's happened.

Fucking shit.

One. Two. Three. Four.

My entire body becomes one big muscle clenching tightly like the string on a bow before I drop to my knees. The pain makes it hard to breathe, and when I hit the wood floor, I roll to my side. I should've anticipated her making a move like this.

My little flower has always been a bit prone to violence lately.

She leans down, her eyes glittering with anger, and I can still see the lust flickering beneath. She wants me, she *still* fucking wants me. Her eyes rake down over my abs, which are now proudly on display from my tucked up shirt, and my still hard dick that's outlined in my jeans. She'll never admit it, at least not right now, but soon.

So fucking soon.

"Stay away from me, Drew. We're done."

"We will never be done." I speak through my teeth.

"We are, and honestly, I'd stop trying because desperation doesn't look good on you." She steps over me and starts walking toward the door.

"Go to the police, get a restraining order..." I force myself to speak even though my breath is labored. "Tell Sebastian so he can put a bullet in my head because the only way you'll ever be free of me is if I'm dead."

"You're pathetic," she sneers over her shoulder.

She has no fucking clue. No idea the lengths I will go when it comes to her.

I gasp for air and shift on the floor, swallowing down the pain. "You can run, Wallflower, but you can't hide, not from me."

She pauses at the door, her hand gripping the handle. Then she twists around and stares down at me. There I see a fire in her eyes that threatens to burn me to fucking ash.

"I'm not trying to hide, Drew. I'm right fucking here, and when you can be honest with me, then maybe we can have a real conversation. Until then, we're done."

When she walks out, I let out another shuddering

breath. The roar of the four-wheeler engine fills my ears. Lying flat on that floor, I don't think I've ever been more attracted to her than I am right now. Even in her anger, she's beautiful, and when she directs it at me... *Fucking hell, it turns me the fuck on.*

My balls ache, and I adjust my still raging hard-on with a twinge of pain.

After a few minutes, I roll over and sit up so I can get the fuck out of this cabin. Memories of Mom laughing with me on the floor before she started to get really sick assault me. This place used to be a sanctuary, but now it's nothing but a house of horrors.

I stand so fast that I'm hit with a wave of dizziness, but I don't slow. The pressure on my chest is too much. I barely manage to turn off the lights and fireplace before walking out the door, slamming it closed behind me, hoping none of the memories inside come home with me.

Once outside, everything feels lighter, and after I lock the door, I turn to face the river and listen to the sound of the rushing water.

I smile, staring up at the night sky. Bel thinks she's calling the shots, but I know she's simply waiting. Waiting for me to hunt her down and make her mine all over again. I will. I'll claim her, and when I do, I'll make sure she understands that nothing and no one will ever come between us again.

10

BEL

School is still taking some getting used to. Things are different in both good and bad ways. Memories of Drew and Jackie overshadow everything. Thankfully, I haven't seen either of them since I restarted classes.

It's also incredibly lonely. But I guess I'd rather be alone than surrounded by people who don't care about me.

At least today is Friday, so once the day is over, I'll be free and won't have to return for two more days. The tiny hairs on the back of my neck stand on end, and I do my best to ignore the desire to peer over my shoulder. It's been like this for a couple of days now, and the whispers are growing increasingly loud. Then there's the fact that I can feel the other students' eyes on me, tracking my movements.

One table over, a leggy brunette sneers at me and snickers about something to one of her friends while I pack my books in my bag. My hair is up in its usual messy bun, my glasses askew as I bend over to grab another book, but my skirt, opaque tights, and soft cashmere sweater are new and fit me perfectly. As does the wool coat and the designer backpack.

Yet somehow, I'm still not good enough for them.

I shove my shiny new laptop into the laptop bag and zip it closed, then shoot the girls a glare and march up the steps toward the door. In the back of my mind, I hear Drew's voice in my head. *They can go fuck themselves.* At least that's something we agree on.

Once out in the hall, I sigh and let my shoulders slip down from my ears. My body relaxes all on its own, as if it knows danger is no longer present.

On the corkboard ahead, there's a flyer, its black ink printed on neon yellow paper. It reads: PARTY AT THE MILL!!!! That must be what had Sebastian's attention this week since he's been mostly absent. I know he still has duties required of him by The Mill, but that doesn't mean I have to like it.

I pull my phone from my coat pocket and start to text the driver as I walk toward the double doors, but I pause as another thought occurs to me. Do I really want to go back to the house and stay there in the echoing quiet all alone? Without Sebastian there, I might as well get an apartment and live alone...

I doubt he'll be there tonight either, given the party at The Mill.

And if he's at the party, that means Drew may or may not be there, depending on how they are doing at the moment. They've been at each other's throats, but it's been a minute since I've discussed anything with Sebastian regarding Drew.

Ahh, fuck it.

I'm thinking too much about this when I should be cutting loose and enjoying myself. There's a party with free alcohol. *I* should be there. I deserve to let go and enjoy myself a little. Who cares if Drew will be there? Maybe he won't be. That's wishful thinking at best.

The Mill isn't but a couple of blocks from here. There's no need to call a driver when I can walk. I hike my bag up my shoulder and head toward the fraternity house.

The closer I get, the more the memories from *The Hunt* assault me. Of the way the branches scratched at my skin, what my bare feet felt like against the soft earth and fallen leaves. The scent of the forest, the scent of *him*. Manly and spicy.

Lost in thought, I don't even realize I've made it to the mansion until the thundering beat of music shakes the ground beneath my feet. *Holy hell*. I'm almost afraid to go inside. I walk up the steps, stopping at the front door. I'm momentarily paralyzed, a deer caught in the headlights of a car that's about to hit her.

Just do it. Go inside.

Taking hold of the door handle, I shove the huge heavy door open and step inside. An onslaught of sensation greets me. The beat of the music pulses through my body, giving me a second heartbeat—

So.*o. Many.* People.

I don't think there's enough room for one more person on the makeshift dance floor. The farther I shove inside, the more I discover. I pass a couple practically having sex on the couch, three games of beer pong, and small groups of people drinking and milling around. I spot some sports equipment near the door and gently ease my bag to the floor, hoping it'll be safe enough there. It's doubtful anyone will be messing with the guys' stuff. Not if they want to walk out of here in one piece. Unpacked and looking less like a nerd, I squeeze into the crowd and hop up onto the bottom step at the far edge of the room to survey the crowd.

I recognize various members of the football team, basketball team, and soccer team, and just everyone I think I've ever seen on campus. Well, except Drew and Sebastian. At least not that I can see.

I spot Lee in the corner, pressing a blonde against the wall, their lips fused. Aries, the other of their little pack I haven't interacted with much, is in the kitchen, pressed between the thighs of a brunette sitting on the counter.

I could ask one of them where Drew or Sebastian are, but I don't want to face either of them right now. Or better yet, do I want to listen to them lecture me on why I shouldn't be at this party in the first place? Like I'm a child who isn't old enough to drink.

No. Tonight is for me.

I want to drink and dance. I want to have some fucking fun and forget how much of a shit show my life is. I shrug out of my coat and toss it onto a teetering pile of jackets and then stroll into the kitchen. I inspect the different liquor bottles on the counter, choosing vodka over gin.

Clutching the bottle to my chest, I creep deeper into the crowd, trying to blend in on the off chance that Drew or Sebastian do show up. Halfway through my walk, I bring the bottle of clear liquid to my lips and tip it back. The first sip burns across my tongue and down the back of my throat, pooling in my belly.

I don't recall when I ate last, and the responsible thing to do would be to eat something before ingesting this much alcohol, but I didn't see any food in the kitchen, just beverages, so I guess that means no dinner for me.

Some guy cuts me off, muttering an apology, and I turn and smile up at him. He's cute. When the man meets my eyes, he freezes, ducks his chin, and practically runs away from me. *What the fuck?*

I blink a few times and take another swig of the vodka.

Okay. Weird. But not the first time my messy bun or glasses have sent guys running. All I can do is shrug. It's not like I need to add another guy into the mix and complicate things further, but there's no harm in flirting a little, right?

Except there isn't any flirting, not when every single guy I attempt to talk to or even look at looks away and runs to the other side of the room. It's infuriating, and only pisses me off more with every attempt I make.

Whatever. I bet Drew warned all the guys away, telling them that if they even looked at me, he'd rip their eyeballs out of their sockets and feed them to their dog, or something just as psychotic. I bring the bottle to my lips and tip it back, taking a hefty gulp. With every drink the burn lessens.

Wading through the crowd, I people watch while continuing to take small sips of the vodka. I can feel the effects of the alcohol starting to kick in. My cheeks fill with warmth and rational thinking flies out the window. I'm halfway across the door when the tiny hairs on the back of my neck stand on end. Immediately, I'm on alert. The room seems to hush as a blast of cold air cuts through the space, and everyone looks toward the front doors as if they're waiting for their king to arrive.

Of course, Drew stands there, his dark gaze scanning the crowd.

Fucking great. Drew wasn't skipping his own party, he just hadn't arrived yet.

My night is ruined. My feet start moving all on their own as I plan to make a beeline to the kitchen where I thought I saw a back door leading outside. Then I pause. Sober Bel would vote to take her vodka and escape, but escaping doesn't do anything.

I have just as much right to be here as he does. I watch him as he shifts through the crowd of people. They seem to move out of the way for him, parting to let him take up all the space he wants.

A god among mere mortals. That's what he is. Who he thinks he is.

Keeping my eyes trained on him, I wait for him to notice me. It'll happen. Any second now, the connection that tethers us will spark, and he'll realize I'm here. He'll scent me in the crowd like a fucking hunting dog. Slowly, so fucking slowly it's almost painful, his eyes move over the crowd, and then *bam.*

His gaze collides with mine.

An electric jolt passes through my body, rippling under my skin. Just one damn look does that to me. *Damn him.* It's pathetic the power he has over me. I hate myself for wanting more.

I love the way that only he can make me break for him, all before piecing me back together again. What I don't love is having my heart broken. I give him my best glare and take another drink, watching as he cocks his head sideways. He studies me like I'm a rare species or something. I try to drag my gaze from his, but it's impossible. We continue staring at each other, neither of us making a move to get closer to the other.

Something sinful, dark, and filthy coils low in my belly, my core clenching involuntarily as if it's preparing itself for something I know nothing about. *No.* I grit my teeth. He doesn't get to ban everyone from even *looking* at me while he stands there, mocking me. Watching me. Controlling my body with nothing more than a flick of his eyes.

I spin on my feet and scan the people nearest me. There's a guy braced near the counter talking to another guy who's across from him on the other side.

He's tall, with sandy brown hair, but since his back is to me, I have no idea what he looks like. *It doesn't matter.* I walk up to him and tap him on the shoulder. He turns on the balls of his feet, and as soon as he's facing me, I grab him by the lapels of his T-shirt and tug him down to my mouth. There's no opportunity for a greeting or to look at each other.

There's only our lips mashing against one another's. The taste of beer and mint fills my mouth, and it's not a bad combination. I wait for something to happen, for the spark to occur, for the butterflies to take flight in my stomach, for my body to awaken the same way it does when Drew touches or kisses me, but it doesn't happen.

Nothing happens.

Not even when his hands snake around my waist to tuck me against his chest, cradling me closer. *Nothing. No spark.* His tongue dips into my mouth, tangling with mine. Deepening the kiss, I sink my fingers into his hair, and again, I wait for the zing.

The dazzle. Anything.

He's not a bad kisser.

There's just no spark. No rush of pleasure. Nothing makes my heart skip a beat or my stomach twist into a knot. *Ugh. He's not Drew.* My frustration and annoyance mounts, and I spin to press him hard against the opposite side of the L-shaped counter. His hand trails lower and lower until it reaches my ass.

Fine. It's all fine.

Except it's not. All I can see in my mind is Drew.

His dark green eyes, perfectly sculpted abs, and thick muscular thighs.

Goddammit. He's probably on his way over to murder us both right now. *Good.* I hope this hurts his heart as much as seeing him with that other girl hurt mine.

A second passes and then another, and I continue kissing the mystery man. I blink my eyes open and peer over his shoulder. I nearly choke on my tongue when I spot Drew standing there, watching us. His body is as still as a statue, and tendrils of ice seep from his eyes.

And fuck, he's staring right into my soul while I kiss another man.

The eye contact is enough to give me that jolt I was missing, the one I was chasing so badly when I let this man grope me. Suddenly, the kiss feels hotter and deeper, and my body awakens with new life. The man kissing me notices the difference as well since his grip on my ass tightens, his other hand tugging me closer.

Shit. His erection grows hard against my belly, and it's like a bucket of cold water dousing the flames of desire. I watch as Drew crosses his arms over his chest, his eyes narrowed to slits, his jaw tight. Fuck. He's going to explode if I keep this up.

Yet I can't stop it. Not when I feel like it's the first time I've been able to do anything to get back at him, to cause him even an ounce of the pain he's dished out to me.

Fuck it. I'm going to hell anyway, might as well make it worth it. I bite the man's lip and pull away, stretching his skin, all while he releases a loud groan of pleasure.

Who knew victory could taste this good?

11

DREW

Anger isn't a big enough word to describe how I feel watching *my* woman kiss another man. It's more like murderous fucking rage. The kind that makes me want to walk across the room, rip the fucker's organs out of his body, and paint her skin with his blood. She's doing her best to prove a point to me, but she has no fucking clue how close to the edge I am.

Oh, you have no idea what type of game you're playing, Flower.

Even from a distance, I can see the flicker of lust and excitement glittering in her eyes. Bel is smart, and she knows exactly what she's doing, antagonizing a different kind of beast. And watching her now, I can only assume that's what she wants. She wants me to lose control, to feel the same pain she felt watching me with Spencer.

There's only one fatal flaw in her plan. My beautiful, angry Flower doesn't realize that no matter what she does,

I'll never leave her. She could cheat, she could sleep with another man, and while I'd burn down the world and kill the fucker with my bare hands while making her watch me do it as punishment, I wouldn't ever let her go.

While I'm irritated this asshole has his hands on her, jealousy isn't really fitting since she is mine and will *always* be mine. It's obvious she doesn't want him, at least to everyone but him. Hell, she didn't even touch him until she spotted me across the room, which might be the only reason I'm letting this charade continue. I kinda want to see how far she's willing to take it.

Clearly, Bel wants a game, and if anyone is willing to play, it's me. I just don't think she realizes who she's playing against. I don't play fair. I play to win, and I always fucking win.

My fists curl of their own accord as the desire to smash the guy in the face amplifies when he squeezes her ass cheeks in his hands.

She's playing with fire, and it's about to burn her.

"Wallflower," I growl even though she can't hear me.

Her sparkling green eyes remain locked on mine. The fucker fondling her doesn't even realize the danger he's in. That's too bad, really because this charade is about to end. Rolling my shoulders, I stalk across the room, partygoers scurry out of my way, and when I reach the fucker, I grip him by the back of the neck, my fingers digging into his skin.

Pulling him backward, I peer down at him, recognizing him immediately as one of our new inductees. Mmm, this just got a lot more interesting. He flinches and then squeezes his eyes closed like a pussy when I whirl him around to face me.

Bel doesn't move. Instead, she stares at me, her chin held high, a look of defiance plastered on her face. "Drew."

"Maybel," I grit her name out through my teeth and then dismiss her, focusing all my attention back on the guy I'm holding hostage. I lean forward, getting right in his face. His panicked gaze darts between us. Poor guy has no idea the shitstorm he got himself into.

"She... she... she grabbed me before I could see who she was... Drew. I promise. I didn't mean to kiss her. If I knew..."

His excuse is fucking laughable at best. Just like the guys who didn't mean to cheat on their wives. *What, did you slip and fall into her vagina?*

I cock my head to the side. "On the off chance I actually believe you, which I don't... But let's say I did, for shits and giggles. Now, I think I can guess what you're going to tell me next because guys like you always say the same shit..."

"I didn't know, man..."

"You didn't know you were grabbing her ass? Or you didn't know who she was?"

"No," he squeals like a pig. "I mean, yes. I knew I was grabbing her ass, but I didn't know who she was. My eyes were closed the entire time."

"Hmm." I lean, still holding him by the nape. "What's your name?"

He gulps. "Harvey."

I nod conspiratorially. "Harvey. Tell me, did she taste

good to you? Did kissing her get your dick hard, Harvey?" I bite off his name.

"Drew." Bel looms, her voice taking a softer tone now.

I already know what she's up to, and if she thinks she'll be able to stop me from following through on tormenting this fucker for touching her, then she's going to be really fucking disappointed. I glance her way for half a second. "No, don't Drew me. You wanted to play, and now we're playing. See what happens when you push me? See what happens when you taunt the beast?"

Her shoulders slump, and she sighs heavily, then takes a long swig of her vodka. "It wasn't his fault. I just grabbed him and kissed him. It's not like he asked to kiss me."

"Yeah, but he didn't stop either. *No one* puts their lips on you. No one touches you. No one fucking breathes near you, or I will kill them. But before I kill them, I will eviscerate them so they understand how grave of a fucking mistake they've made..."

Harvey's body trembles in my grasp, and he slowly lowers his hands to his sides, his eyes wide and filled with fear. I move closer, invading whatever limited space is left, watching his pupils as they dilate further, his heartbeat picking up another beat.

My gaze is on Bel, though. This is all for her. "Tell me, fuckface, what should your punishment be for touching something that isn't yours?"

I feel his heavy gulp under my grasp, and he shakes his head.

"I'm sorry... I'm so sorry... I swear..."

"Not as sorry as you're going to be soon."

The kitchen has cleared out. Some partygoers stand nearby watching the byplay. Others have just moved on to enjoy the beat elsewhere. Music bumps with a heavy bass through the house almost in time with my steadily increasing heartbeat.

I grasp his left hand in my free one, the other still tight around the back of his neck as I curl my grip around his middle finger and twist. The distinct sound of bone crunching is music to my ears. The little pussy screams and drops to his knees. I let him go and crouch down in front of him. "We aren't done here, Harvey. Give me your hand."

He whimpers, and I glance back at Bel, who is standing near my shoulder. Her hand is plastered over her mouth, and she has fresh tears swimming in her eyes. When she sees me looking, she looks away, her gaze focusing on something else.

I stand and snap, "Consequences. This is what happens, Bel. This is what you make me do when you refuse to listen. Now pay attention because next time you let a man touch you, I won't stop at broken bones, baby."

She jerks her chin back to Harvey and me, and I direct my attention back to the poor fool again. I drop down to my haunches again and extend my hand out to him, waiting to see if I'll have to force him or if he'll be a good boy and listen to me. When he places his trembling hand in mine, I feel the sudden rush of accomplishment. I smirk back at Bel. Tears still coat her eyes but not a single tear has fallen. Her mouth is set into a thin line as if she's riding the edge of anger. Good. *Me fucking too.*

No. That's wrong. I'm free-falling into my anger now, and no one better get in my way.

I pat Harvey on the cheek gently, and he flinches away from me. Smart.

"Since you gave me your hand, I'll go easy on you." I snap another finger, then grab his chin and put my face directly in his. "I won't kill you for touching what's mine. And you know what? I won't kick you out of The Mill either, at least not yet."

I breathe in the sharp scent of his sweat and fear. This is where I thrive, where chaos and my demons can come out to play together. Out of the corner of my eye, I see Bel getting ready to make a run for it. Extending my arm out, I grasp her bicep, halting her midstep. There's no way in hell I'm letting her walk away from this. If she doesn't want to suffer the consequences, then maybe she shouldn't have provoked me.

I grin at her. "No, Flower, you don't get to start something and not finish it. Not when his punishment is all your fault. Your act of defiance will mean a world of hurt for little Harvey here."

The man looks like he's going to vomit, his eyes silently pleading for me to release him as they ping-pong between Bel and myself. I know I have to choose to let go of one of them.

I can't continue to teach this fucker a lesson without releasing Bel, but if I release her, she's going to run. Still, if I let this fucker go, he might tell his friends what happened, and I can't have anyone thinking I'm weak.

"Drew." Bel leans in, clearly understanding the dark direction this is going in. She clutches the bottle of vodka in her other hand. "Leave him be, and come with me. Let's go for a walk."

I snort. "Do you think I'm an idiot? All you want is to get my attention off this fucker. I'm not stupid."

Realizing her words are not enough, her small hand trails up my chest, and it takes everything in me not to lean in, sink into these feelings, and let them be *more*. Not when she's only touching me to protect this asshole.

It makes me more inclined to rip his head off and shit down his throat.

A hard slap lands against my back, the impact vibrating through my muscles, and out of the corner of my eye, I catch a flash of curls and wide-ass shoulders belonging to one of my friends. *Aries*. Always the peace-maker. He leans in, smiling.

"Come on, man. Go talk to your girl. I'll take care of this asshole for you."

It's a ruse. I know it. He knows it. Even Harvey knows it. He'll toss him out on his ass and let him run, but he won't be punished as much as I want. It's a battle of choosing what I want more—to talk with Bel and make her under-stand there is no other option but me or to beat this asshole ten feet into the ground.

I glance down at Bel, and even as her voice has soft-ened and her touch burns across my skin, she's still wearing that defiant-as-fuck look, daring me to walk away and let it go. That's fine, though. Harvey's punishment can be given to her instead. I shift my hand to Harvey's face and give him a shove. Stumbling backward, he nearly trips over his own feet. As soon as he realizes he's free, he scur-ries out of the room without looking back.

Coward. Logically, I know he didn't do anything wrong. It's more about looking weak and teaching Bel a lesson.

Aries gives us his signature grin, all pearly white teeth, then snags a bottle of alcohol off the counter and follows him.

Alone, or as close to alone as we're going to get, I tug Bel closer. "You should be happy. I let him go for you."

Those defiant eyes shine, tipping me over the fucking edge. *I'm done.*

With my patience slipping, I tighten my grip and tug her toward the back door. She barely resists, stumbling over her feet a little too easily along the way.

I'm not sure how much she drank before I arrived, but it's obvious it was enough to make her think she could get away with this ludicrous shit. I push the back door open and pull her outside behind me. The cold night air greets us, and the refreshing feel of it on my skin helps to clear away some of the anger clouding my thoughts.

I only stop once we reach the tree line of the woods, putting us far enough away from the house that I can finally hear myself think. There's no one but us and the quietness now. Turning on her, I take her by both arms and gently press her back against one of the towering oak trees. I force myself to be gentle when what I really want is to take her over my knee and spank her ass until it's cherry red.

The second her back meets the trunk, Maybel charges at me. Only my football training and reflexes, grown at the hands of my father's abuse, allow me to catch her wrists before she makes contact with my neck or face.

"Let go of me," she screeches, and I tighten my grasp.

The hand bared in claws relaxes, but the other, with the bottle clutched tight, still holds on.

All I can think then is... *What happened to my flower?*

My subconscious takes a second to remind me.

You smashed her into a million fucking pieces.

"If you stop trying to attack me, then I can let you go, but if you're going to continue being crazy, I'll have to restrain you for both our safety."

Eyes narrowed to slits, she moves closer, her chest pressing into mine. I think she's relaxing, and my own grip goes lax as I prepare to release her, but it's a mistake on my part because all it does is give her room to pull her hand back, giving her the momentum she needs to slap me. My head swings to the sides from the impact.

I grit my teeth and recover quickly, anger seeping into my veins. With lightning-fast reflexes, I wrap my hand around the column of her throat and give it a little squeeze, becoming mesmerized by the fear that slips into her eyes. I crave her fear, her submission. I get off controlling her every breath, and I know it's fucked up and wrong, but I don't care.

"I know I hurt you. I fucking get it, but don't fucking hit me. That's your warning, Bel. Do it again, and I'll put you on your knees."

I release her before I do something crazy, like strangle her until she passes out. Maybe if I kidnap her and trap her somewhere, I can seduce her with enough orgasms to forgive me?

Or piss Sebastian off enough to kill me.

The fear trickles away from Bel, and she's glaring at me again. I take a step back, hoping some distance might cool her off, but she charges forward again, her hand back ready to land another hit. The thing is, I'm sober, faster, and I've been beat the majority of my life.

She's lost the battle before she's even tried. I sidestep her hit, and she misses me, and her hand flies through the air, making a swishing sound. The sting in my cheek reminds me of the first strike she got on me, and when she tries a third time and misses again, I can't help but wonder how she thinks *this* will fix things.

"What are you doing, Maybel? Is this going to help you? Will hurting me fix us?"

I'm close to making good on my promise of putting her on her knees, but I hesitate, wanting to give her a chance. She huffs and takes a long swig of her vodka, which she has somehow managed to keep in her hands, her body remaining upright. Swallowing it down, she continues to glare, her warm breath billowing out in little clouds of smoke.

"I can't believe you would ask me such a stupid question. One measly slap is not going to make up for all the pain you caused me."

It's my turn to huff out a hot exhale. "Okay, and you think kissing another man will help?"

There's something in her eyes now, something closer to guilt, but not quite.

I shake my head. "This is revenge. You want to hurt me so I'll know exactly what it felt like that night you had to see me with Spencer." I lick my lips and cross the space between us, using my body to crowd her all over again. "Did it make you feel better?"

She squeezes her lips shut and simply glares icy daggers at me.

"Truthfully, you don't have to speak. I can see it in your eyes right now. You want me to hurt. You couldn't give a shit about that guy. No, this was a selfish act. Wasn't it? Am I right? Tell me, Bel. Tell me I'm right. Tell me that you thought if you hurt me the same way I hurt you, your pain would be less. *Tell me.*"

"No," she growls, still gritting her teeth. "I knew it wouldn't be less, but it would make me feel better for a little fucking while. And if anyone deserves to feel better, it's me. Boo-hoo, so what if you had to watch me kiss another guy, and yeah, he groped me a little bit, but nothing you went through tonight will ever amount to what *I* felt and went through. You're not the one who had to have stitches in your scalp, and I don't recall anyone that cared about you calling you a whore and throwing dollar bills at you."

"No amount of apologizing will change what happened. I can't undo the past, Bel. All I can do is try to do better, and you're making it increasingly difficult."

"Good!" she sneers. "I don't want you to do better. I want you to leave me alone and realize you can't win me back no matter how hard you try."

I grab her by the wrist, bringing us closer together. My eyes scan her face, the dilation of her pupils, the way her pulse thrums in the side of her neck, and the sharp intake of breath she takes when I get up close. Leaning in close enough that our lips are almost touching, I speak, "I don't have to win you back, Flower. You've always been mine. I'd just prefer your forgiveness over anger, but in the end, I'll take you however I can get you."

"I hate you!" she seethes, her nostrils flaring.

"You don't, but you wish you did, because if you hated me then all of this would be *so* much easier. If you could blame me, if I was the monster you portray me to be, if you really fucking believed the things you tell yourself about me, then this would be done with." She won't admit it, but she knows I'm right.

"Get away from me!" she hisses, struggling in my grasp.

The more she fights me, the harder my cock gets. If she needs to pretend that she hates me, fine. I'll let her have that. By now, she should've realized that she's mine to hurt, fuck, and completely and utterly destroy.

Doing the opposite of what she wants, I tighten my hold on her and walk her backward, trapping her against the tree once again.

I mold my body against hers, pressing all my hard edges to her soft ones. *Fuck, it feels so good.* The tiniest whimper escapes her lips, and my eyes dart to her pretty mouth. Those full lips of hers, begging to be bit and kissed.

"Let go of me! I don't want you. We're over!" she screams.

Her words say one thing, but her body says something else entirely. I can feel her pressing back against me, silently begging me for more. Her body says what she never will, at least not right now. I drag my eyes away from her lips and press my forehead against hers, breathing her in, letting her breathe me in.

A war wages in her green eyes. She wants to push me away, but she also wants to give in. At some point, I'll make the decision for her, but for a little while longer, I'll play her game.

"We're never done, Bel. We weren't done that night at the banquet, and we aren't done now. I don't give a fuck what it takes to make you see that. I will stop at nothing. I will come to your house every single fucking day. I will crawl across the fucking floor on my hands and knees and beg you. I know you're hurting, and I'm sorry. There won't ever be enough words to explain that to you, and I accept that. I accept that I fucked up, even if I thought what I was doing was the right thing. But I want to move forward. I have to, and there's only one way to do that."

"You're forgetting the most fundamental part of all. The opinion of the person who matters most: me."

"I didn't forget you."

"You *did*. You haven't asked me what I wanted in all of this. You think that an apology automatically fixes things like a magic wand simply because you know how to put on the charm, and abracadabra, everything is fixed."

I snarl and tighten my hold. "I'm not expecting it to be fixed."

Lifting her arm, she cuts off my grip, then gives my chest a hard shove back. I barely move, but I let her think she has control.

"It was clear to me that day in the library when we first met that you weren't used to being told no, but I will say it until you understand. I don't want you, Drew. There is no forgiveness to be given. The sooner you realize that, the sooner all of this can end, and we can move on with our lives."

It hurts to hear her say those words, but they change nothing. *She is still mine.*

"Like it or not, I will never let you go. Like I said before, I'd prefer you be mine willingly, but I will take you however I can get you. Do your worst, Flower. Hit me. Hurt me. Fuck other men. I don't give a shit what you do, but that fact will never change. You are mine, and I don't give up what's mine. Not ever."

12

BEL

I can't breathe through the searing heat of his stare, and the way it holds me in place. My knees barely support me as it is.

You are mine, and I don't give up what's mine. Not ever.

He just said those words, and they're all I can hear in my head. Unbeknownst to him, they're the most believable thing he's ever said to me. I know I'm his. I know this because I wanted him. Hell, dare I say I loved him. I mean, part of me, most of me still does, but I'm not telling him that. He doesn't deserve to have that kind of power in his hands.

"Good for you, but you're wasting your time. I don't want you, so unless you plan to force me into everything for the rest of your life, I'd choose otherwise." The words taste bitter on my tongue as I expel them.

"Whatever you say, Flower." His tone is nearly mocking, and I snarl at him when I see the smile on his lips.

I push away from him and his unforgiving grip and spin into the open air, the bottle of vodka my only remaining lifeline. If I plan to sober up, then I'll need to stop drinking, but that's not going to happen with this asshole in front of me.

I can feel his eyes on me. He's watching me, ensuring I don't get too far away. Forever the gatekeeper. That's all he wants is to keep me so that no one else can have me. He doesn't really want me.

"Stop looking at me like that."

"Like what?"

"You know what."

He shakes his head. "No, I really don't. I'm just watching you. I didn't know it was a crime to look at someone."

"Watching someone is not what you're doing. You're stalking me. I'm not your prey."

He doesn't reply, tucking his hands into his jacket pockets before continuing to survey me. A cold breeze whips through the trees, and I bite my bottom lip to stop my teeth from chattering. "Here, take my jacket." He quickly strips his coat from his shoulders, leaving himself in a long-sleeved black Henley.

He doesn't give me the opportunity to object, and instead gently places it over my shoulders. The smoky scent of him wafts from the warmth of the coat, and I want to hug it tight to my chest and just breathe him in. I should toss it on the ground and stomp it into the dirt, but my heart won't let me.

Drew's eyes track me as I pace around him. The trees

are right here, and memories of the night I spent running through those woods come rushing back to me.

What am I doing here, drowning in Drew?

In our relationship, in our history? Why do I put myself through this?

He's never going to give you up. He's never going to stop wanting you.

I suck a ragged breath into my lungs, the cool air melting away a little bit more of the vodka hazing my mind.

I need to think about something else. Anything but us.

Whirling around, I face him and ask, "How's school?"

His forehead wrinkles with confusion, and he cocks his head to the side like he's waiting for me to tell him a joke. "What?"

"School. I stopped tutoring you. Are you passing your classes? Did you find another tutor?"

"Please tell me you're kidding? Do you really care about that? And are we really going to discuss it here...and of all times, *now*?"

I snort and slip on the wet grass, catching myself on a nearby tree trunk. "If you want the truth, Mr. Marshall, no, I don't really give a shit, but you refuse to let me leave, and I'd rather talk about something else."

This makes him clench his jaw. "We need to talk about *us*."

I shake my head and circle the tree with my bottle of vodka. "We've tried that a couple of times, and it failed. I think that ship has sailed."

He steps toward me, and I keep the tree between us as protection.

"Like I already said, I don't care. I'm not going anywhere."

I turn my back to the tree and bring the bottle of vodka to my lips. I take a long swig, chasing the buzz I had earlier, praying it erases the memory of him. I need something to dull the ache in my chest before it swallows me whole.

Off in the distance, there's shouting. We both glance in the direction, and Drew takes a step toward the noise, his eyes tracking dark shapes that appear on the lawn. My glasses are blurry, so I can't quite make the shapes out completely.

Not that it matters. This is the exact distraction I need to get away. If I stand here another second, he'll convince me to go inside with him, and I don't know if I can survive another loss right now. The shouting continues, and I skirt around the tree, which is between us, and in Drew's direct line of sight.

I count down from three in my head.

Three.

Two.

One.

I tighten my grip on the bottle and dart forward, ripping through the tree line and straight into the woods like a real-life Bambi. It's not the same as that night since I've been through the woods before, but that same adrenaline rush fills my veins.

It can't be but a few seconds later before I hear his heavy footfalls crashing through the forest floor behind me, destroying everything in their path. The tiny hairs on the back of my neck lift in warning, reminding me that

Drew is a true predator and that if I run... he will chase me.

Maybe that's what I want? What I need.

The thrill of being caught makes my blood hum and my core clench tightly. A smart girl would end this right here, right now, but I don't *want* to end this.

My muscles burn and ache in protest as I up my pace.

Ahead, I narrowly miss a downed tree, and I catch myself on the trunk of another tree. I forget that one of my hands is occupied with a bottle of vodka, and only realize it after the glass shatters, the liquor spilling down my arm.

Ugh. I clutch the now broken bottleneck in my freezing hands, my subconscious telling me to keep it with me as I continue. My stomach churns around all that liquor, and I pray I don't have to stop and puke.

Don't find me, Drew.

Speaking of him. It doesn't actually take him long to do. Drew's conditioned for this game. Made to hunt the prey. To catch, skin, and eat. A true huntsman if I ever saw one. He's on me in seconds.

His fingers brush against my hand, and I turn and swipe at him. A sharp hiss fills my ears. The sound reminds me of a soda can when you open it. There's a warm spray of something against my hand, and I pause, confused for a half second.

What the hell? I consider stopping to see what it is that is on my hands, but I can't. The need to keep going consumes me. Instead, I speed up, running faster, pushing my small legs harder, while he slows.

"What the fuck, Bel?" he shouts from somewhere behind me.

I can't tell if he's angry or concerned.

Then again, it doesn't matter if he's angry or concerned, right?

If he catches me, the result will be the same. With each of my senses on high alert, I find myself peering over my shoulder, my ears listening for any noise. The cold air pricks at my skin, and my lungs burn with every breath I take.

The hammering of my heartbeat is the only thing I can hear until Drew's angry, almost bitter laughter rips through the trees. It's venomous, evil sounding, and every cell in my body orders me to run and hide. The old me would've done just that, but I'm not scared of the monster hiding in the dark.

I urge myself forward, my muscles tightening and protesting as I force myself to keep going. Branches slap against my arms and midsection, slowing me down, and my feet slip on the wet ground. I can hear his feet trampling the ground behind me.

He's close.

"If you wanted me to chase you, Flower, all you had to do was say so. I'm always up for hunting you down in the forest and making you beg for me to fuck you. I mean, I'm getting hard just reliving one of the best moments of my life. The day I got to claim you."

Fuck, why doesn't he sound winded?

Meanwhile, I feel like I've been running for hours. I slow so I don't trip, and since he doesn't immediately wrap his arm around me and take me to the ground, I assume he's slowed as well. *Shit.* He's definitely toying with me.

"Just." *Inhale. Exhale.* "Let." *Cough. Gasp. Cough.* "Me go."

There's a chuckle near a tree to my left.

I twist, looking in that direction, but he's not there.

"Not a chance. We've been over this, and I understand more than anyone how stubborn and unruly you can be, so I guess I'll have to do my best to show you. What do you think I should do? Bite you? Leave hickeys all over your neck? Take you in the dirt all over again?"

Damn him.

Even if I don't want to be, I'm turned on.

The forest grows quiet, and I slow further. My gut instinct tells me to stop. I don't trust it. It's too quiet. There's not even a stir of underbrush around me.

I stop running and suck air into my lungs like I'm dying. There's a stitch in my side, and nausea sifts through me like sand in an hourglass. Up feels like down, and down feels like up. I can't comprehend what's going on, not until a pair of strong arms circle my waist and lift me off my feet in one move. I'm suspended in the air for half a second before I'm tossed over his shoulder.

A squeak escapes my lips, and I kick out my legs while clawing at him the best I can, the neck of the glass bottle still in my hand. "Let me go!"

"Why would I do that? You ran, I chased, and caught you. Now I get to do whatever I want to you."

A scream climbs out of my throat and pierces the air.

"Fuck, yes. Scream for me, Bel. You know how much I love it."

Asshole.

"I'm not screaming *for* you, idiot. I'm screaming *at* you. Now, let me go." I kick at him, and I could scream thanks to the lord when my foot connects with his knee. He grunts and tumbles to the ground, bringing me down with him.

We land all as one, and he rolls at the last minute to keep my body on top, caring enough not to crush me with his hulking frame. He's first to recover. His rough hands circle my wrists, trapping me. I struggle against him even while knowing I won't be able to break free.

I hate that my nipples are as hard as diamonds, and that I'm dripping with need, but I still fight against the desire. I can't let him break me. *Not again.*

"I have no problem pinning you to the ground and fucking you senseless right now, so if you want to continue to fight, then that's what's going to happen. I've tried to be patient, but I'm past the point of no return. I don't give a fuck anymore. I'll be the bad guy if you need me to be. You can fight me, beg me to stop, tell me you don't want it, but deep down, I know you do, and I know that while your pussy strangles my cock, begging for me to fill it with my cum, all you're doing is lying to both of us."

"Let me up," I growl.

The pressure on my chest is suffocating. I can feel the bottle top tucked between my thumb and forefinger. The glass is sharp enough to cut my skin, and I tighten my hold on it.

He has to let me go, or I might lose my shit.

The feeling of him...

The taste of his lips...

His scent...

It's all too much.

The hard planes of his body pressing against mine feel so good, too good.

"Please... just let me go," I plead.

The pressure on my chest lifts when he shifts his weight off me. My traitorous body chooses to betray me, and the whisper of a whimper slips past my parted lips when my thighs brush the length of his erection.

He's still holding on to me, though his grasp is lax now. In an instant, I can hear his voice in my head, the sinister words he spoke right before he crushed my heart in his hands.

I'll find another tight cunt to keep my cock warm. That's all you ever were to me anyway, a nice, warm hole to fuck.

"Come on, Bel. Are you going to let me in, or do I have to take it from you?"

There's a coldness in his voice, but that's not the effect it has on me. It warms me up all over, and I know the harder I fight, the harder he'll fuck me.

More memories rip through me.

It's time for you to leave. Now, you can take the trash out yourself, or I can take you out. You are nothing to me and never were. Nothing more than a warm hole to sink into every once in a while.

"I'll fuck you into submission if I have to, so don't tempt me because you know damn well I'll do it."

I stare at his grip, his grasp firm. *Tightening.* I'm burned by his touch.

He leans over me, his face hovering above mine. A shiver ripples through me at the sick, twisted look on his face.

"Please let me go!" I beg.

"No, but I do love it when you beg. I just wish you would save it for when my cock is inside you."

The wires in my brain cross, and something inside me snaps. My vision goes black, and for one second, I'm no longer here, no longer held captive by my love for this toxic man. I break free of his hold and strike at him with the hand holding the broken glass shard. I recognize his pain-filled gasp a moment before I can comprehend what I've done.

Time slows down. There's a break in the foggy rage clouding my judgment, and that gives way to shock. He releases me entirely, pushing up onto his knees.

I look at my trembling hands, seeing the blood on them.

What have I done? I scramble back, like a crab, trying to get away.

I cut him. I cut him.

I've never hurt anyone in my life, and now I've cut him. I've drawn his blood.

Look what he turns you into. An animal. A woman out for revenge.

Bile climbs up my throat. I'm both gripped by fear and guilt. *I can't breathe.* My lungs burn as I try to force air inside them. The glass presses against my palm, the weight of it heavier now.

What have I done?

I scramble to my feet, my legs threatening to give out. He's going to kill me. I need to run. Something dangerous and dark electrifies the air, making it hard for me to breathe.

I watch Drew climb to his feet, his movements slow, and I can't stop looking into his eyes. Like a moth drawn to a flame, even while knowing the power the flame has over me, I continue to stare, mesmerized, frozen with fear.

Those green emeralds shine in the slivers of moonlight that make it through the trees, and what they reflect is something far scarier than anything I could've ever imagined—retribution.

13

DREW

I feel the burn of the cut along my skin, proof that she really did cut me, but somehow, I can't make my brain believe that she actually did. The first cut on my arm was nothing more than a graze, but this one is deep enough that the skin pulls when I shift my arm.

I exhale through my nose. "Flower... that wasn't very nice of you."

She peers up at me, her eyes round and wide, the whites circling her entire iris. I watch her throat as she swallows hard and loud.

"I...I asked you to let me go..." Her voice wavers.

"And I told you no. I had no idea you wanted to play so dirty. If I knew, I would've come better prepared."

She blinks a few times, her eyes tracking down to the wound. The vodka on her breath reaches me as her breathing picks up.

Make her pay. Remind her who you are. Who she belongs to.

The predator lingers right at the surface, demanding retribution, but he doesn't understand that there is no reward in any of this if we lose her.

Still, she made her choice, and every choice has a consequence. I snatch her by the wrist and tug her forward until her small frame runs into my chest. She struggles, but I wrap my other hand around her throat and squeeze, just enough to show her that I'm in control.

The more fear that fills her eyes, the harder my cock becomes.

Is it weird, despite her trying to stab me, that I want her hands on me? That I crave her fucking touch like I crave my next breath because she wants to touch me, even if it's out of violence.

The cut on my pec burns, and I bring her hand back to my chest, pressing the shard of glass against my skin. Then I take a step forward, placing my foot between her legs.

Instantly, she scrambles to shift out of the way. *Nope. You're mine now.*

"Oh no. Don't be afraid, Flower. I haven't made you bleed... *not yet.*"

Panic sets in, and her struggle intensifies. I add pressure to her hand, the one with the glass in it. It has yet to break the skin, but it will soon.

"Wallflower..." I warn, squeezing her throat a little tighter.

She uses her other hand to bat at me, and her nails sink into my skin. The pain only heightens my pleasure. She did this to herself, to us. Her declaration was that she doesn't want me, and that she never has. Well, I'm going to prove her fucking wrong.

I caress her plump bottom lip with my thumb, slowly loosening my grip on her throat. I watch as she sucks a ragged breath into her lungs.

As the panic recedes from her gaze, she still appears afraid, but somehow manages to lift her chin in defiance. "I'm not sorry."

"I didn't expect you to be. If this is the only way to lessen the pain you're feeling, I'll let you plant that glass shard right in my fucking heart."

There's a shift in her gaze, a softening, and she flinches. "I don't..."

"I know you want me to feel the pain you felt, but this isn't you, Wallflower. You don't lash out in violence. You don't make others feel pain because you're hurting. Yes, I fucked up and hurt you in a way that no one else in your life ever has. I hurt you when you needed someone most, and I'm sorry. I can't go back in time and change what happened, and I don't know if I would. I don't regret protecting you from my father." I try to keep my voice low and my tone gentle, but it doesn't help.

There's still this frantic energy about her, this need to run, and she jerks her wrists to escape me again, but I tighten my grasp. It might leave bruises, but she's doing it to herself at this point.

"Maybe you don't know me anymore. Maybe I've changed."

My lips turn up at the sides. She's so fucking cute, trying to be this angry, vicious being when that's not who she is. Bel is grace, kindness, sunshine, and equality. But most of all, she is *mine*.

"Changing those parts of you would be like trying to

change the most influential pieces of who you are. You're not the villain, baby, you aren't a killer, and you aren't a monster. Leave those roles to me."

Her beautiful, full lips twist into a mockery of a smile. "Yeah...well...maybe I want to be those things. Maybe I don't want to be the girl who sticks to the shadows. Maybe I don't want to be the victim anymore. A lot of shit has happened recently. Like losing the only person who ever loved me. Or my entire identity being replaced with another."

I could spend an eternity apologizing to her, but it won't change a damn thing. She's not ready to forgive me, and I have to accept that, just as she has to accept that I'm not going anywhere. I lean in, crowding her, and run my lips over the shell of her ear.

Shivers wrack her body, and I love watching the goose bumps erupt across her creamy flesh. Her lip curls, and she snarls like a feral animal. Using the weight of my body and the hand I have held to my chest with the glass shard in it, she pushes against me.

I tighten my grip on her, and instead of putting distance between us, she merely presses the glass deeper into my flesh. A burning sensation zips across my skin, and I bite back a groan of pain.

Gimme your worst, Flower.

Her pretty emerald eyes catch on my chest, on her hand, on the glass, inching deeper into my skin with each heartbeat. Her frightened gaze widens, but she doesn't make a move to pull away. It's almost like the fear and shock have her frozen in time.

"Is this what you need, Flower? Will this bring you

back to me?" I grunt and shift our combined grip even further forward.

The movement pushes the glass deeper, and while there is pain, this satisfying warmth encompasses me, making the pain nothing more than a dull ache. Blood continues seeping out of the wound, its warmth spreading across my soaked T-shirt.

I don't care what I have to do to get her back. Pain is a momentary thing. If she wants to hurt me, then I'll let her. I'll do any-fucking-thing to get her back. *Anything.*

Full lips trembling, she looks like she might cry. Fuck me, she looks beautiful when she cries.

"No, stop...this isn't what I want." The words are a whisper in the wind, and nearly missed, but just because I hear them doesn't mean I acknowledge them. If she wants to make me believe this isn't what she wants, she'll have to do a better job convincing me.

I squeeze her hand to the point of pain and press harder. The glass slides through more muscle, and I suck a breath in through my teeth. Tears swim in her eyes, and I swear my cock gets harder at the image in front of me.

"Drew, stop! This isn't what I want. Hurting you doesn't fix anything."

"Really? I think it does. You've talked to me more in the past few minutes than you have for the past month. I'll take a thousand cuts to my heart if it means you'll stand here talking to me for five more minutes."

Her teary gaze leaves mine, and I see how close those tears are from cascading down her cheeks. The need to show her mercy overwhelms me, and I release my hold on her hand. Pulling away completely, taking the glass with her, the cut in my chest feels empty without something in it. The spot aches and burns with each labored breath I force into my lungs. Fragments of the old Bel shine in her eyes as she drops the broken glass on the ground.

She shakes her head like this is a nightmare she can wake herself up from. I watch as she unravels, her eyes catching on her hands, which are slick with my blood.

"Why did you do that? What the *fuck* is wrong with you?" she snarls angrily, crossing the few feet separating us on wobbly legs.

When I don't respond, she slams her tiny fists against my muscled chest. The air escapes my lungs in a wheeze from the impact.

All I can do is shrug. I don't really have a reason.

"Why not? I hurt you, and you hurt me. Now we're even. Maybe hurting me is what you needed? I was just doing what I thought was right."

"What you thought was right?" Confusion pinches her delicate features.

I nod. "Yeah. Before I showed up at the party, you had an agenda. It was clear you were going to get drunk and party. No one was going to stop you from doing what you wanted to do, so I simply jumped on the crazy train."

Her eyes go to ice. "Crazy train? I'm not *crazy*, Drew. My mother is dead. The man I thought I lo...the man I cared about betrayed me. Broke my fucking heart, actually..."

Her confession burns more than the cuts on my skin. I'm terrified for one blinding moment that I'll never be able to fix what's broken between us. And that's just a reality I refuse to live in.

"You know what? Fuck you. I'm done." She throws her

hands into the air with a frustrated cry. "We're done. I'm not going to be that stupid girl I was before, waiting for you to break my heart all over again. Praying and hoping I was good enough for you when it was never a question of if I was good enough for you, but if you were good enough for me."

I flinch and hope she doesn't notice in the dark. "Bel—"

"No." She turns to walk away. Fear grips my bones. I'm losing her again. She's slipping through my fingers. I reach for her once more, but it's no good.

"Don't touch me," she growls, batting my hands away, slapping at my skin like I'm an annoying fly that refuses to leave. "Don't fucking touch me." Her eyes narrow in a way that proves my point. "I'm leaving."

"No, you're not because you want me as much as I want you. It's twisted, and sick, and fucked up, but this is us, Flower. This is all we got..."

Her jaw clenches, and determination bleeds into every pore. Then like a kitten, she hisses, "Fuck you. Just watch me."

All over again, similar to that first night when I claimed her virginity, something dark and sinister grips me. It digs its claws into my soul, dragging me deep into its depths. I don't want to hurt Bel. I really don't want to, but I need to. Fuck, I need her pain, her tears, her fucking whimpers. I need to hear her begging me to stop, begging me to keep going. I've had enough of her denial and attitude. She can pretend all she fucking wants that she doesn't want me, but her body and her heart will betray her every time.

She's mine, and I'm hers. No matter what she says.

"Bel, I'm warning you now. Run and I'll catch you.

There won't be a damn thing you can do to stop me from taking you down to the dirt and fucking you *so hard* you won't spend a *second* not feeling me splitting you open. I will be written into your skin. Into your bones. So you can no longer say I'm nothing to you."

"You don't own me, and guess what? I don't want you, Drew. I never did. It was all fake. Every single word, emotion, orgasm. Fake."

It's a lie. Of course it's a lie, there's no way a girl who was a virgin before I took her can fake everything she did with me. But it doesn't matter. Every last bit of control gives way, and while I'm trying to be better for her, she's just unleashed something that won't be stuffed back inside until it's had its fill of her.

14

BEL

Like a puma, he pounces on me before I can even step away from him. I need to get away from him. I'm too close to giving in and letting him have his way with me. He turns me in his arms, and I'm trapped. Both obsession and lust reflect at me in his dazed, manic eyes. He's in full-on hunt mode, and nothing will stop him from taking what he wants, not now. Still, I have to try because my heart is on the line, and if I let him in again, I know it'll end in nothing but heartache.

"Let go of me, you sick bastard. I hate you!" I screech, fighting against him. He licks his lips, a mask slipping over his face.

Tilting my chin up with his finger, he whispers, "It's interesting how much 'I hate you' and 'I don't want you' sound like just the opposite. You might say you hate me, but... " His hand snakes between our bodies, and I find myself reacting without thinking as he cups me between the legs, his fingers on my pussy, right over my tights.

Liquid heat and desire gush to my core from this one simple touch. But I come to my senses quickly and grab his wrist. "I don't want you."

He smirks. "Translation: Fuck me, Drew."

I lick my lips, my breathing growing ragged as I try to come up with an escape plan. "I hate you." It's more of a mumble than an actual statement.

He leans in close, his mouth brushing my earlobe. "Translation: I love you."

"*Love*?" I whisper, all the anger flushed out of me now.

The simmering heat from his touch remains, and I know no matter what he does to me, I'll want it. I need his hand on me in a way I'd only started to understand before he ripped out my heart and stomped all over it. Now, my head is a jumble of confusion, and my body is a raging mess of hormones.

I fucking need him, even if I don't want to need him.

"Why won't you leave me alone?"

"I thought I made it clear you couldn't get away from me."

I let out a sigh of frustration. Now we're back to that. A statement I thought was negated by him calling me a cunt to use back in that kitchen.

Which man do I trust? The one who hurt me a month ago or the one who wants to hurt me now?

When a minute of silence passes between us, he unleashes a long, hissing sigh.

"Bel—" His words are cut off when I slash out to shove his hand away and realize too late that the glass in my hand dug into his arm, right below the other wound I had already inflicted.

I jerk my gaze from the blood.

His jaw is set tight, and he grits his teeth. "Flower..."

Like a cobra striking, he snatches my hand and twists it hard. I gasp, and my fingers spasm, releasing the glass. I watch as it falls to the forest floor. *Shit.* I jerk my hand away and cradle it to my chest, then risk another glance at his face. It's different now. Devoid of emotion, blank, even as I watch the blood drip down his forearm and off his fingertips.

He leans in so his face is even with mine, and he licks my lips in a small swipe. "I think it's time for your punishment, Flower..."

I swallow hard and try to slow my breathing. It's pointless since he no doubt already knows I'm so fucking wet my panties are soaked. "What are you going to do?"

He tilts my chin up toward him and captures my mouth in a searing kiss. It's more than a kiss, it's a claim and control on my soul, a command on my existence. I moan and clench my hand around his forearm, the warmth of his blood slipping along my skin.

His lips force mine open, and his tongue slips inside, tangling with mine. I can't do anything but let him guide me to the ground as I submit to the brutality of that kiss. To the brutality of *him*. Yet in the back of my mind, the events from that day play on repeat.

"We can't do this!" I growl against him.

"We can, and we are," he grunts, easily overpowering me.

"Let go of me!" I hiss, but the idea of him letting go of me leaves me cold and disappointed.

"Never. You're mine. Forever." His tone is granite-hard

and laced with need. A need I feel through my entire body as his hand slips from my waist and under my skirt. "I wanted to fuck you nice and slow and show you how much I crave you, but I realized that's not what you need. What you need is darker than that."

"Stop," I exclaim, even as his hand presses against my pussy.

"You want me to take it from you so you don't have to admit how much you wanted me in the first place, and that's fine. You can hate me for it, hate me as you come all over my cock, because to me, your hate and love taste the same."

I barely blink, and he has me turned so my knees are in the piles of leaves, and my ass is in the air. Another blink and my tights are being ripped, the sound echoing through the empty forest. Cold air flashes across the backs of my thighs and ass, the rest of the material still in place.

Did he really just rip a hole in my tights?

Next come my panties, as a loud rip cuts through the night sounds, and I'm so flabbergasted I don't know what to make of it. He's holding the glass I dropped and hacks away at the material, not even nicking my skin once. He shoves the panties and the glass into the pocket of the jacket I'm still wearing. His fingers smooth over my ass cheeks, and with them comes something warm.

Blood. His blood. I should be repulsed at the thought, but I'm not. It drips down onto my skin, and he smears it across my flesh, painting me with it.

"Fuck, Bel, you look so pretty with my blood staining your silky smooth skin."

I hang my head and just try to be glad he can't see my

face right now. Let him think I can't stand him, that I hate him, that I never want him to touch me again, when it's all the opposite. Those same fingers that we're just smearing blood across my ass trail down and enter me all at once. The harsh intrusion knocks the air out of my lungs, but I'm wet enough for it. I shiver as the sensations of pleasure roll through me.

He fucks me hard and fast with two fingers, my cunt making terrible slurping noises as I bite my lip to stop myself from saying his name. *Fuck*. He doesn't hold back, and the pleasure builds, carrying me higher and higher as he plunges in and out. I'm practically panting, my fingers clinging to the dirt and mud, anything to keep me in place.

"I warned you that I was going to punish you Bel, and I wasn't lying. I won't be gentle with you, not this time. You're going to take my cock in your virgin ass." His words interrupt the haze of pleasure zipping through me, and then he pulls his fingers out of me, leaving me with a cold and dejected feeling.

There's a rustling of clothes, and I realize he's pushing his pants down. Now that some of the pleasure has worn off, I comprehend what he said.

You're going to take my cock in your virgin ass.

"Stay with me, Flower," he growls.

"I'm sorry. I didn't mean it..." I plead and try to inch forward, the reality of my actions finally dawning on me.

"But you did, and that's okay because now I'm going to show you exactly who you belong to, who holds the power of your pleasure, and just who it is that makes you feel this way."

I feel his thick cock head at the entrance of my pussy,

and I shudder, knowing what's coming next. Without warning, he snaps his hips forward, entering me in one solid thrust.

"Fuck, I missed this," he groans into the darkness.

He fucks me at a brutal pace, his balls slapping against my clit at the perfect angle, and all I can do is hold on and let him consume me. My own arousal seeps out around his cock and down my thighs.

"Good girl. Your pussy takes my cock so well. Gripping me nice and tight," Drew praises, and it only encourages my lust. With one hand, he holds me in place at the hip, his fingers biting into my flesh, while the other trails up my back.

I wonder what he'll do with it when his thick fingers sink into my hair. Without care, he tugs my head back, the movement making my scalp burn and my eyes water. The injury, still healing, throbs slightly, and I grit my teeth against the pain.

"Drew, oh God." I start to beg for the impending orgasm that sits on the horizon, close enough for me to taste but still out of reach. My body bows, and I can do nothing but bend at the mercy of his touch.

"Fuck, Bel. Fuck. I wanted to make love to you, but I guess that's not what either of us needed." He slams into me, and I swear I feel him in my stomach. "All I want to do is rut deep inside you, filling you with my cum, fucking you until you can't think of anything but me."

He fucks me savagely, and I sink deeper and deeper into the sensations. I'm terrified of the darkness he's clawing out of me, forcing me to acknowledge.

"Mine. You're mine."

All I can do is moan in pleasure.

"Say it. Say you're mine," Drew demands.

My heart clenches in my chest, and the knot low in my belly unravels.

I'm close, so close.

"If you want to come, then you better tell me who you belong to." The words are feral and animalistic, and I succumb to the need faster than I'm willing to admit.

"You. It's you," I cry.

"Yes, Flower. It's me. You belong to me, and no one is going to change that, not even you." I can see the smile on his lips without even turning around and looking.

The hand at my hip slips between our bodies, and then his fingers are on my clit. It takes less than ten seconds for me to explode. Light flashes before my eyes, and my entire body shudders against the cold ground as a moment of pure blessed silence echoes through me.

The grip on my hair is released, and I sag forward with my head hanging low once again.

I'm slowly floating back down to reality when I feel him... *there.* His thick cock is still inside me, and he's rock hard, signifying he hasn't come yet. I'm still loopy from my climax, but I swear I feel his thumb slipping between my ass cheeks.

Hell no. Out of reflex, I jerk forward.

"Nope, you're not going anywhere, Flower. I told you there would be a punishment. The punishment is this. I'm going to take your ass. I'm going to destroy your last virgin hole, forcing you to acknowledge that every part of you now belongs to me." A desperate darkness in his tone tells me nothing will stop this from happening.

He's not asking me; he's telling me, and I don't know if that's terrifying or the biggest turn-on ever. Moving slowly, he works his thumb into my ass, fucking the hole with care I didn't think was possible. It doesn't take long for me to start mewling like a kitten in heat once he's got his thumb in my ass and his cock in my pussy.

Once acclimated to the pressure, he adds another finger, stretching me. I whimper at the intrusion and the burn of pain that zings through me as he fucks me slowly with the digits while thrusting his hips forward at the same time, fucking me with both his cock and his fingers.

"Fuck, your ass is perfect, Flower. I wish you could see it. See how pretty it is being owned by me."

I grit my teeth and curl my nails into the dirt, needing something to anchor against the pleasure-pain combo threatening to rip me to shreds. Tears sting my eyes as a third finger is added to my ass. The muscles resist, trying to push him out.

The pleasure and pain balance is a razor edge, tipping closer to pain at the moment, but little ripples of pleasure zip through my core every time he bottoms out inside me, and I hold on to those as I let him claim me.

"Drew... It hurts..."

"Shhh, I know. It's going to be okay. Stay with me. Breathe through it. This might be a punishment, but I promise I'll make you feel so good. Don't I always know exactly what you need?"

All I can do is whimper, and I focus on keeping myself on all fours instead of sinking down to the dirt to allow him complete control. I breathe through my nose, the burning in my ass becoming increasingly unbearable. I don't want to tell him to stop—

that's weakness—and I don't know that he even would, but I don't know if I can handle anything else, especially not his cock.

"Drew..." I whine.

His fingers ease out of me, and I relax, sucking a ragged breath into my lungs.

"We aren't done yet," he warns.

Slowly, he pulls his cock out of my pussy, and with it comes an embarrassing amount of liquid. I shudder as the thick head of his dick slides between my ass cheeks while one hand gently strokes my back. I let out a groan when he presses the thick head of his cock against the puckered hole. Something warm and wet lands on my ass, the substance slipping down my crack.

What the hell? I'm confused for half a second, and then I glance at him over my shoulder, my eyes refusing to make sense of what I'm seeing.

I watch curiously as he curls his muscled forearm, making the wound bleed just enough that the drops fall perfectly down my ass crack so that he can use them as lube while he takes my ass. It's so endearing that I almost smile. *Almost.*

The pressure against the hole grows, and no matter how much I tell myself to relax, I can't. I just clench up, tighter and tighter.

"Relax, Flower, and I'll be easier for you to take." His tone is soft, gentle, coaxing.

"It burns..." I hiss through my teeth, feeling the muscles protest and stretch around his thick cock.

"It's going to. You're so tight, and I'm not exactly small." His voice is pinched, his breathing labored.

"Drew..." I whimper.

Fucking hell.

"Shhh, I've got you. I'll always have you." His cock stretches me to the point of pain as he slides in another inch, and my entire body trembles. I bite my lip hard to stop myself from begging him to stop. On the fringes of pain are tiny zings of pleasure, like a silver lining, and I focus my attention there. "I wish you could see how well your ass stretches for me. Opening nice and wide."

"Fuuuuuccckkk," I bite out.

"You take my cock so well, Flower. You're so fucking tight. I think I might love your ass more than your pussy."

It seems like years until I feel the heat of his body resting against mine, letting me know he's all the way in. *Fuck. Fuck. How do I do this?*

Sensations like I've never experienced ricochet through me. Pain and pleasure roll up and pour into me, overflowing the edges until I can't think straight. He consumes me.

I scrabble across the dirt, digging in deeper until my fingertips are buried in the earth.

It's too much.

"Fuck, Flower. *Relax.* Every time you tense up, your muscles strangle my cock to the point I think I'm going to burst. I promise you don't want me to come yet because then we'll have to start the process all over again."

My body trembles, and my knees shake, barely keeping

me upright. All he does is laugh darkly, pulling out of me slowly before sliding back in. Fire. It's all I can feel. Fuck, it burns, and my pussy clenches around nothing.

"Drew, please."

"Ah... I love it when you beg. Tell me what you want. You've been a good girl so far, letting me take your ass without complaint. You deserve a reward." He leans over my body and peppers the side of my neck with kisses. "Come on, Bel. You know how much I love it when you beg."

I whimper and swallow hard so I can speak again. "I don't know what I need..."

He hums against my neck and pulls back. "That's okay. I know what you need. I know how to make it better."

Shifting his grip so one hand holds me up and the other curls down over my thighs, he drags his fingertips over my clit.

Fuck. *Yes.* That's what I need.

I shift to give him better access, and of course he notices. "So greedy for my touch. I know what you need. Remember that." He thrums my clit and surges into me, pressing deep. "You feel so good. Too good," he groans.

The pressure is building, my pussy clenching tight even as my other hole is invaded. We're both panting and writhing against one another. Drew presses harder against me, his chest nearly in line with my back. I feel his hot breath against my ear, and I damn near melt to the ground. Before I can comprehend what is happening, Drew's hand is on the side of my head, his touch searing as he presses my face into the dirt.

"I can't even tell you how beautiful you are stuffed with

my cock inside you," he growls into my ear, and with the way he holds me down, forcing me into submission while fucking my ass, I nearly explode. "I need to feel you come, feel your pussy beg for my cum, all while knowing it's your ass that's going to be rewarded, instead. Can you do that for me? Can you come for me? Do it. Be a good girl and come for me."

Filthy, dirty words. But those words add to the raging storm barreling inside me. I squeeze my eyes closed, focusing solely on the pleasure he gives me, forces on me.

I moan and nod the best I can. "Yes. Yes. Yes."

Pistoning his hips faster and harder, he thrusts deeper, taking another piece of my heart each time he does. A position I thought we'd never be in again.

"So good, so fucking good! I'm going to fill your ass with my cum. Tell me to fill your ass with cum."

He presses me harder into the dirt, holding me in place, using me. Tears leak from my eyes, and I know I'm consumed by this man. Owned by him in every way possible.

"Come in my ass. Fill me with your cum!" I pant.

Then I shatter. For half a second, my vision goes black, and my muscles seize up. I'm momentarily trapped in a vortex of pleasure, and all I can do is let it consume me. I'm vaguely aware of his own groans of pleasure, and then I feel the warm heat of his release filling my ass as he slams into me one final time.

I'm exhausted, spent, and can barely remain on my knees. After having destroyed me both physically and mentally, he pulls out of me with tenderness, his release dripping out of my ass and down my thighs.

Just as my body gives out on me, and I fall flat onto my belly in the dirt, the world spins all around me, and I can't help but wonder what I'm supposed to do now.

How can I give up the man I love?

15

DREW

Isn't it weird how our plans don't always work out? How fate sometimes has something else planned for us. I didn't intend on hunting her in the woods, nor did I plan on fucking her ass, but here we are. The presence of pain flares in the back of my mind as soon as I ease my cock from the tight confines of her ass. I revel in the way my cum leaks from her puckered asshole. Fuck, so tight and perfect. I don't regret a fucking thing.

As gently as possible, I pull the skirt over her bare ass cheeks and lift her, taking her into my arms bridal style. Doing so causes the cuts on my forearm to split and bleed more, but I don't care.

It takes a minute to maneuver her into a comfortable position, and then I stand, surveying the woods. I know every inch of this property. I grew up on it and have walked on it way too many times. There's no such thing as getting lost out here, at least for me.

"I can walk," Bel interjects as I start moving.

I pretend as if I didn't hear her and instead tighten my grip on her body. I'm aware of what she can and can't do, but it's more of what I'm willing to let her do on her own.

As I walk, the weight of my actions presses down on me. I don't necessarily feel bad for taking her as I did. She enjoyed it, and I know she did, but I do feel like an asshole for doing so while trying to get back into her good graces.

I keep my pace slow. After all that running, I don't have it in me to jog the entire way back to the house. Plus, the cold night air feels good against my skin. As we near the house, I peer down at her only to catch her staring up at me. There's this soft look in her eyes, and it reminds me of how she used to look at me before I destroyed everything.

"Are you okay?"

She hums against my shirt, hugging my jacket tight around her. "I'm fine. Why?"

"Don't act like that." I shake my head.

"Act like what?"

"Act like I don't give a shit about you. Like I don't want to make sure you aren't hurt. From the very first time I took you in the woods, I made certain you weren't injured. I'm a monster, but I'm not about to risk losing the one thing I want more than anything else."

"If you must know...I'm fine. A little sore, but that's to be expected when someone takes your ass for the first time, right?" The sarcasm rolls off her tongue easily, and I hide my smile as I turn my head to the side.

The lights from the house cut through the trees ahead, and it doesn't take me long to reach the sloping lawn that leads down to the house. It's still lit up from the party, and the place glows with life.

A whole lot of life that I don't want seeing us, but definitely not Bel. I head to the back of the house and slip inside the back door, then hop up the steps and take the back stairs to the second floor. Thankfully, there aren't any partygoers on the second floor.

When we make it inside the bedroom, I slam the door shut behind us and click the lock into place, then carry Bel over to the bed and set her down on the edge of it.

She sits up, her gaze swinging around the room in marvel. I remember then that she's never seen my bedroom before today.

How many times have I taken her in hers, and she hasn't seen mine?

The longer I stare at her, the more I notice her curious gaze sweeping the room. I smile and cross the room, heading into the bathroom.

In the shower, I turn the handles and let the water run, getting the room all steamed up. I strip out of my shirt and glimpse myself in the mirror.

Fuck, Flower got me good. The cut on my chest is deep, as is the one on my arm. They hurt and bleed like a bitch, but I can't find it in my heart to be mad at her. These wounds are artificial compared to those that I gave her.

I lean against the doorjamb of the bathroom and watch her sneaking a peek at the bookshelves across the room. Her dainty fingers dance against the spine of each title as if she's trying to figure out which one she will select.

Of course my little wallflower would go straight to the books.

I smile like the fucker I am, feeling lucky to have her back in my arms, even if it's temporary. I wish I could hold her at this moment forever, watching her sneak around this room, my room, *our* room.

This is my future, our future.

"Come here, Bel. Let me get you out of those clothes and clean you up."

She startles at my voice and shifts away from the shelf, jerking her hand back as if the books will bite her.

"Don't worry about..." She never finishes what she's saying, and part of me thinks that's because she notices me standing there, every inch of my well-defined eight-pack on display. I mean, I could be wrong, but I don't think so.

Slowly, she blinks back to the present, realizing that she was in fact staring at me. "I don't need you to clean me up."

Fuck. Disappointment punches me in the gut. I don't want to beg her to stay, but I *need* her to stay with me. In my space, her sweet scent surrounds me, her presence warming the icy parts of my heart that have never been touched by the sun.

I know I'm changing, even if it's slowly. I've never shared this place with another woman. Then again, I've never had anyone like Bel in my life.

"Come here, please."

A look of defiance touches her face, and she crosses her arms over her chest. "Or what? You'll make me?"

"Don't act like you wouldn't like that. Now if that's how I have to do it, then I will, but I'd prefer if you came to me on your own."

Standing as still as a statue, she stares at me, probably thinking she's won, but she doesn't know I see right through her. Beneath the defiant image she paints is a wavering desire for my touch. I can see it in the way her body leans toward me, craving my touch and warmth. She wants to give in, even if she doesn't want to admit it to herself or me.

And that's the kicker: sometimes admitting that you want something when you feel like it's bad for you is the hardest thing to do.

"When have you ever given a shit about me?"

"Bel, I know you want to hurt me, but do not hurt yourself in an attempt to hurt me. There is never a time when I have not taken care of you. I always make sure you're satisfied, and I saved you from a rapist. Hell, I paid in flesh and blood to keep you safe from my father."

With a grimace, her gaze moves to the floor, and I wonder if that's a little guilt that I see on her face. "Thanks for the offer, but I should go home."

I gesture to my chest. "Fine, but do you think you could at least give me a hand with these before you go?"

She looks up from her shoes and scans the cuts on my arms and chest. Battling against herself, she takes a step forward but then pauses. Dammit. I can't let her slip through my fingers. *I can't.*

"Please..." I add even though the word is foreign and bitter on my tongue.

"Please? When did you learn that word?"

"Oh, this beautiful, sassy, vengeful girl told me I should use it more often. I'm trying to, but I'll be honest, it tastes a lot like weakness. I prefer to make people do things rather than ask, and especially not nicely. Please doesn't really make my messages come across as threatening."

"I should let you bleed out."

"You should."

Her eyes narrow. "I hate you."

"You say that, but I don't think you really hate me. You hate that I hurt you, but more than that, you hate that even after everything, you still want me, want *us*."

"I'm not talking about us. There is no *us*."

"Sure," I agree, just to move on.

She can think whatever she wants, but that doesn't mean it's true. Sometimes the illusion is all the other person needs. The illusion of freedom, of being in control. Bel will always be free, but never of me.

"So do you still want me to help or what?" she questions, annoyance lacing her tone.

"I thought you were going to let me bleed out?" I cock a brow at her.

She rolls her pretty eyes. "I should, but even Sebastian would be upset about that, I think."

I step out of her way and gesture for her to enter the bathroom. Once in the bathroom, she abandons the coat and walks to the double sink to wash her hands. "I wouldn't have thought this place would be so clean."

Her judgment causes me to chuckle. "Yeah, well, my housekeeper is pretty good at her job. How else would a group of twenty something year old men survive?"

This earns me a smile, and it's like watching the sunrise for the first time. I can't help but smile back. The moment she notices, though, it all crumbles to pieces, and the rays of sunshine disappear, leaving me in complete darkness.

I grab some of the first aid stuff from under the bathroom sink and arrange them on the counter. Alcohol.

Bandages. Medical-grade glue. When you get your ass kicked regularly, some of these things become a part of your daily life.

She eyes them each individually and then drags her gaze back to me."We should probably get you cleaned up first."

Dirt and leaves cling to my jeans, and sticky blood coats my skin. "Good idea."

I pop the button on my jeans and grin as she skitters back, bumping into the counter. *Like I wasn't just in her ass, fucking her until she saw stars.* In seconds, I'm naked, and her eyes are on my blood-coated cock.

"If I'm cleaning up, then you should too. The water is nice and hot, and the shower is big enough for ten people."

I can see her mentally weighing her options, her pearly white teeth sinking into her bottom lip. Maybe realizing how unreasonable she's being to allow me to fuck her but not shower with her, she starts stripping out of her clothing. If she wants to keep distance between us, I'm going to keep knocking down those walls one by one until she can face the truth. That I want her and she will be mine.

I watch as she strips because I'm no gentleman, and I continue watching even when she cocks an eyebrow at me, challenging me.

Once we're both naked, I reach for her and ease the elastic from her hair and fluff out the strands, taking my time to feel the heft of her hair and memorize the scent of shampoo wafting off her mane.

Then I pluck her glasses off her face and set them on the counter.

"This means nothing," she murmurs.

I pick her up and carry her into the shower, stopping right under the hot spray. Her tiny body shudders in my arms as she adjusts to the water, and I slowly lower her to her feet.

"How is that?"

She nods, shoving the water off her face. "It's good. Thank you."

When she reaches for the shampoo, I bat her hand away gently and lather her up myself. She gives me a little smile, and only when she's clean do I let her do the same for me. It's a revelation...caring for someone else. She treats me just as tenderly as I treat her, carefully cleaning around each of my wounds. There's nothing sexual about it, more sensual and emotional, but it's the first time I've experienced it, and I want to do it again and again. Once we're all rinsed and clean, we exit the shower, and I gently dry her skin until she's warm and cozy.

Then comes the part I'm a semi-professional at: gluing and bandaging myself up. Bel helps by handing me each item and helping me clean up and toss all the wrappers out. Then I carry her over to the bed, hit the remote for the lights and fireplace, and climb up onto the mattress. I circle her waist with my arm, tucking her into my chest. Facing me, she stares up at me, a mixture of satisfaction and wariness in her eyes. "I guess I'm an idiot tonight because I'm too tired to hate you right now."

Gently, I stroke her hair, the music from the party downstairs a low hum that becomes background noise. I stare into her sparkling green eyes, my chest tight, and I'm overcome with emotions that I've never felt before. I can't lose Bel. I can't. I won't let my dad take anything else from me. I brush a piece of wet hair off her temple. "You're so beautiful, Maybel."

She gulps and shakes her head. "So are you."

A tear slips from the corner of her eye, and I catch it, flicking it away. "What's wrong?"

She sniffles. "Nothing. I'm fine. Just overwhelmed with everything, I guess."

Another tear falls, and I pull her closer, resting my forehead against hers. "It's okay. I promise I will never hurt you again. If anyone else dares to try, I'll be there to rip their hearts from their bodies. I don't expect you to trust me today, or even tomorrow, but eventually, you'll know that I won't let anyone hurt you ever again."

She releases a heavy sigh. "I'm scared."

I nod and tug her by the waist so her body lines up with mine. It's fucking decadent to feel all her bare skin against mine. I had no idea how much I craved it until this moment. It feels so fucking good. And I realize it's not sexual. It's an intimate connection I've never experienced before.

"Bel," I whisper and kiss her lips tenderly, wanting to tell her all the things.

"I know," she whispers in reply.

I nod and continue staring at her, waiting until her eyelids drift closed before I dare close my own eyes. All the while thinking I have a promise to keep now. And the only way I can keep that promise is to get rid of my father... and soon.

16

BEL

*V*oices. *Yelling.*

The combination is nails on a chalkboard rattling around in my brain. Slowly, so I don't disturb the force field, I crack my eyes open and catch sight of soft light filtering through partially open curtains. It's difficult to make out the color without my glasses on, but I know immediately that those curtains are not mine.

There's a pause, then the voices again, roaring in my ears. Moving my hands, I slide them across the silky sheets and up my bare thigh.

Bare thighs.

Oh shit.

Memories from the night before filter back through my mind. The woods, the shower, Drew chasing me, vodka, and kissing someone else. *Jesus.*

Who let me do all these things? I don't do stuff like this.

Guilt slices through me, followed by a wave of nausea that climbs up my throat. I grab the top sheet and jerk it back to untuck it from the end of the bed. I barely manage to wrap it around myself and rush past Drew and Sebastian and into the bathroom, slapping the door closed behind me. My only focus is not throwing up all over myself right now.

Shit. Shit. Shit.

My already battered knees hate me more as I fall to the tiled floor and secure my death grip on the toilet just in time for the entire contents of my stomach to spew out of my mouth.

The velocity to which the vomit escapes my stomach burns my nose and throat. My vision blurs, tears leak from the corners of my eyes, and once I'm certain I won't leave out anything else, I tug the sheet up around my shoulders and huddle into it.

The cold from the floor seeps into my knees, and it feels nice. *Fuck.* There's an incident throbbing at the back of my head, like an annoying person who won't stop kicking a ball at my brain.

That's it. I'm never drinking again.

With a groan, I stand on unsteady legs and cross the room to the brightly lit sink. It's so fucking bright. Even though I can't see much, I swat around the blurry area until I find the taps and twist them on. A moment later, the rush of water fills my ears.

I rinse my mouth out and take a couple of gulps of water. I can't see my hair all that well, but I run my fingers through it a little bit. I'm feeling better already. Maybe I'm not one of those people who suffers from hangovers? I smile to myself, and then I remember...

The voices. Fighting. Drew. Sebastian.

They were standing inside the bedroom arguing about something when I ran past them to get into the bathroom.

Fuck. Damn. Shit.

Sebastian's judgment stings more than anyone's, and I don't want to look weak to him, but I also know that deep down, this was eventually going to happen. If it wasn't obvious before, it is now. I love Drew.

Not trying to fix things or give him a second chance would be stupid, but I can't act weak either. I can't just act like I did before, rolling over and taking whatever he gives me.

With my head hung low, I walk over to the door, and with a sigh, I tug it open. Their voices get louder as I approach them, but neither seems to pay me an ounce of attention.

Cool, does this mean I can go back to sleep?

I cast a glance at Drew first, who has his fists curled tight and his arms hanging down on either side of him. Thankfully, he's not naked but wearing a pair of navy basketball shorts that hang deliciously low on his hips.

"You have no right to come barging in here and demand a single thing from either of us."

The air becomes electrically charged, and I realize just how serious this is. Sebastian takes a step forward, his presence suffocating. My gaze cuts to him, and I notice then that he's already dressed in his usual slacks and perfectly pressed white button-down. Even his shoes are gleaming.

Releasing a heavy sigh, I make a mental note to tell the guy to relax a little. There's no need for all this at...I glance at the clock on the nightstand...the numbers are hard to read. It looks like seven, eight, or nine. Really, it could be any of those times, but I choose to go with the earliest 'cause it sounds better.

It's seven o'clock, and these assholes are arguing.

Sebastian crowds Drew further, but that doesn't matter as Drew doesn't appear to be bothered by it. In fact, he gives Sebastian a challenging smirk. With that smirk alone, my chances of going back to bed swirl down the drain.

There is way too much testosterone in this room right now. My heart stutters in my chest when Sebastian pulls his fist back like he's going to punch Drew. *Shit.* I do the only thing I can think to do and jump between them, my back pressing firmly against Drew's front, bringing me face-to-face with the meanest guard dog ever.

"Sebastian, back the hell off. All this yelling is hurting my head."

Blurry vision makes it hard to see shit, but I can see him clutching a piece of paper in his other hand. I snatch it and shove it at Sebastian's chest.

He hisses out a breath, and Drew huffs against my ear.

I glance up at him. "You too! Both of you, opposite corners, go." I can't read the paper without my glasses, so I wave it toward Drew. "What is this, and why is it making you two scream at each other before we've had coffee?"

He angrily snatches the thick cardstock back and then tosses it on the bench at the end of his bed. "It's ridiculous bullshit, is what it is."

"Ridiculous bullshit that you're keeping a secret? I thought you were trying to be a better person?" I've had enough of the sarcasm and taunting from Sebastian.

Well, I know he means well and wants to protect me. He has no stake in this fight. This is between Drew and me.

I shift my gaze to Drew, looking for an explanation. "What does he mean?"

Drew cuts in front of me, ignoring my question and moving too fast for my addled brain and body to respond.

"I *am* changing fuckface, but it's difficult when there's someone like you breathing down my neck, pointing out every mistake I make, like it's a goddamn intention. I can't just wave a fucking wand and be a class A gentleman, nor would I ever want to be. That's not the person Bel wants either. Now, get the hell out."

I can feel the icy rage rolling off Sebastian, slamming into anything that's in its wake. "The only way I'm leaving is in a body bag or with my sister in hand. She shouldn't even fucking be here."

Okay, that hurts a little bit. Stings even, but this is my life, and I'm an adult who is very capable of making her own choices. That, and I'm really getting tired of being talked about while being in the room, instead of being included in the conversation.

"Excuse me but did you guys forget I'm standing right here? And that I'm a big girl who was caring for herself long before either of you came along? Neither of you have any say over what I choose to do, who I see, or where I go."

I can feel Seb's intense gaze on me even if I can't make out his features with pinpoint precision. "Don't look at me like that!" I scrape out, then cross the room to the bedside table, where I climb out of the sheets and slap my hands around, feeling for my glasses.

My hand brushes a glass of water and a couple of pills

before landing on my glasses. Once I slip them onto my face, I stare down at the water and pills, my heartbeat quickening. He knew between the way he fucked me and the amount of alcohol I drank last night that painkillers would be a necessity the next day, so before he went to bed, he made sure I had them. I look over at him, but he doesn't look back at me. He's locked in a staring contest with Sebastian with his jaw set tight, hard enough to cut stone.

I wonder what they win by not blinking first?

On the other hand, Sebastian has no issues dishing out his cold, callous anger to everyone. His glare darts between the two of us. Then he locks on Drew with a narrowed gaze. "She's good enough to fuck, but not good enough to know your secrets. Yeah, I feel the respect and the desire for forgiveness. More games, more bullshit. Same Marshall drama."

I try not to flinch at each of his spewed words and even worse at the way Drew's fists tighten more and more at every word he speaks. His veins bulge, like they might explode out of his forearms.

What is this all about? Some stupid piece of paper? I step up to the bench, gather the sheet tight around my chest, and pinch the card between my fingers, inspecting it.

It's an invitation of some sort from Drew's dad. That's all I can make out before the invitation is ripped from my hands rudely and crumpled into a ball. Drew tosses the invitation at Sebastian's feet and smirks.

"What the hell, Drew?" I yell.

"He came here to stir up trouble, Bel. That's all this is."

"You're lucky she gives a fuck about you, or you'd

already be in the ground." Sebastian growls, all teeth, and honestly, this is far too serious of a conversation to have before nine o'clock.

"Okay, pause." I step between them and sigh. "If you two must argue, can it be done without me being rolled up in a sheet?"

Sebastian's fingers slice through his hair, and he curses while Drew gives me a long, sweeping gaze that turns my insides to molten lava, even given the situation.

Damn him.

"Can I put some clothes on so we can talk, or are you two going to kill each other while I brush my teeth?"

No response. Go figure. They continue to glare at each other but remain silent.

Great. I snag my clothes off the floor and stare at the ripped tights and mud-stained skirt. *Shit.* Instead of gathering them up to salvage what I can, I cross the room to the dresser on the other side. However, before I can dig into his drawers, I spot a small stack of clothing on top. An Oakmount T-shirt and a pair of basketball shorts. Shit. No underwear.

While I trek back to the bathroom, I refuse to look at either of them. I will not be shamed by this or any of my choices ever again. Men do whatever they want all the time and are never judged. I refuse to be judged.

Dressing quickly, I do my best to ignore the fact that the clothes I'm wearing are not only Drew's but smell like him and search through the bathroom drawers for another toothbrush. I find a bunch of extras in the third drawer and snag one. I brush my teeth and check my reflection in the mirror. I look like me, but happier and stronger. I can do this. I can handle these idiot cavemen.

When I finish brushing, I leave the bathroom and walk back into the bedroom to find them exactly as I left them, staring at one another like statues. Their jaws tense, and each is a pot of boiling water ready to boil over. I hope I won't have to referee them forever.

That's if Drew and I can get through all this bullshit and find happiness on the other side. I want to find a solution to this...tension between us, but I'm afraid we won't ever be able to overcome our trauma.

Turning my attention to Sebastian, I ask, "Can you please give us a minute to talk?"

Sebastian sighs long and loudly, then glances over my shoulder at Drew, even though his words were for me. "I'll be waiting in the hallway to take you home. Make it quick."

"You aren't my boss or my parent, Sebastian. Stop acting like you are," I say as he leaves the room.

He doesn't respond and slams the door behind him when he walks out. The coiled tension in Drew seems to unfurl as he lets his shoulder relax, his fists finally uncurl. His eyes shine with pure discontent, and those eyes eventually find mine.

I wrap my arms around myself, trying not to fall apart.

"What the hell, Drew?" I feel conflicted. "What is this invitation?"

I want to give in to him, to run into his arms and let him hold me, but at the same time, I need to guard my heart and ensure I protect myself from harm.

"All this shit is a stunt to pull us apart. I mean, would it make a difference if I told you I didn't know anything about the invitation? But it's not the invitation he's pissed about. He knew that was coming. It was my father's demand that Sebastian bring you to the meeting."

I shrug. "I don't know. I find that hard to believe. When it comes to your father, you know everything. You're one of his many forever-moving chess pieces."

Drew grimaces as if I slapped him, and a tiny hint of guilt unfurrows.

It's not a lie.

"I know that I've fucked up and followed along with my father's charades before, but I'm done with that shit, Bel. I'm no longer a pawn or chess piece to him. I'm trying to fix this. To do better. *Fuck me, Bel.* Believe me. Believe me when I tell you I didn't know about the meeting or the stupid invitation. Just because I'm his son doesn't mean he tells me everything."

"I get it, and I want to believe you..."

Shaking his head, he presses his fist against his forehead and turns away from me. The suffocating anguish and anger he's feeling wafts off him in waves. He feels helpless, and I know that feeling all too well. I want to fix this for him, but I can't, and while I'm terrified of losing him, all while keeping him at arm's length, I know that at some point, I'll lose him anyway if I don't let him back in.

My fingers itch to touch him, and I curl my fingers into my hand to stop myself.

Heartbeats pass, the tense muscles in his back shift, and he turns around to face me again. Dark green eyes meet mine, and a battle of emotions clashes in their depths.

"Jesus, fuck, you're acting like we have this wonderful

relationship when you know better. Even when I was following along with his bullshit, I was doing it to protect you. I remember you telling me that I didn't mean the things I was saying. You knew then that I cared and was trying to do the right thing."

Every word he speaks tugs on my heartstrings.

I hate how easily I melt for him.

I hate how he draws me into his web at every turn.

I hate that his darkness reaches for the best still secure parts of me as if it wants to consume me. I don't want to be that girl who gets her heart stomped into the ground again. I can't lower my standards and boundaries to be with him. *I won't.*

Drew steps toward me, and I shake my head, stepping back to keep the distance between us.

"No. We aren't doing that. I'm not too proud to admit that the second you touch me, I seem to fold in on myself. On my values and beliefs. Your touch cuts me wide open, leaving me exposed and vulnerable, and I can't be like that right now."

A wolfish grin touches his lips. "That's so poetic, Bel. My touch cuts you wide open?"

There's a seductive edge to his voice that reaches out and grabs me, sinking its claws deep into my skin.

Frustrated, I snap, "This isn't a joke, Drew."

"I never said it was."

"Then why are you smiling and acting like it is? Sebastian wants to kick your ass, and a part of me wants to let him."

He scoffs. "This isn't the first time we've fought, and it

won't be the last time we fight either. We don't know how to talk. Our words are our fists."

"That's stupid and immature."

He shrugs one shoulder. "That's how we deal with it."

I stare at him for a long moment. My heartbeat thunders in my ears. I want him. I want what we had before everything. The slow, beautiful thing that had started between us. I just don't want to get hurt again, and Drew... he's not the safe bet.

He's not the guy you bring home to Mom and Dad. He's not the gentleman who holds the door open for you or gives you flowers on the first date. He's toxic, messy, a walking red flag, a terrifying nightmare you can never escape, and the villain in every fairy tale. And maybe that's why I'm so attracted to him. Other girls want to marry the prince. They want the Cinderella castle and the horse carriage.

All I want is to be loved, but I don't want just any type of love. I want the kind that awakens the soul, that's obsessive, and scary, and filled with fire that you feel in every cell of your body. I never felt or experienced any of that, not before Drew.

"What's the look for?" Drew asks, interrupting my thoughts.

I tug at the hem of the shirt, *his* shirt. "My heart tells me to give us a second chance, but I'm not ready to forgive you yet. I don't know if I can trust you, and all of this makes it worse. When stuff like this—secrets—pop up, and you act all dismissive, it doesn't build trust between us. It tears it down."

It feels like we're saving each other in so many ways,

but when does it end? *When do we stop having to save each other and start to heal?*

"Does it really matter what I say? Sebastian thinks he has it all figured out. He thinks he knows what's going on between us, who I am. He's judging me without knowing a goddamn thing. He knows what my father is like, more than anyone, yet he's the one who is being the hardest on me of everyone. He acts like I wanted to fucking hurt you. Watching your heart break broke me. It fucking broke me, Bel."

I let my instincts guide me, carrying me to him. Reaching for him, I sink my fingers into his hair, tugging his head down to mine and pressing our foreheads together.

"Sebastian's opinion doesn't matter. He's mad that you hurt me and I can understand his feelings since I'm his sister, but the only person who controls me is me. I make my own decisions, Drew, and if I want to give you a second chance, if I want to give us a second chance, then I will make that decision on my own, and he will not have any say in it."

"Good, because I'm not lying to you, Bel. I didn't know about the fucking meeting. I'm trying to fix things. My father disappeared recently, went on some trip, and my mother, she's sick. My father couldn't be reached, so the doctors called me. He left her there to fucking die. He just left." I can see and feel every emotion he's experiencing as if it's my own. The anger and sadness, combined with guilt. I feel for him, so much because while I know that Drew fucked up and hurt me, he wouldn't be here now if he didn't really care about what happened.

"I'm trying to do better. I want you. I want us more than anything, but I can't flip the switch from who I was to who I want to be, who I need to be for you, overnight. It takes time. It's something I have to work on, and I am. I'm dealing with all this shit at once. But having that person held over my head... It makes it difficult for me to move past. I need your forgiveness, Bel, but I need your acceptance too. I need to know we're going to do this together."

I gulp and know he hears it. Letting the moment stretch while I think.

Is it enough?

He takes that moment and grabs me by the hips and pulls me into him, then wraps his arms around my waist, lifting me tight so we are chest to chest. I can only hold his neck and wait until he releases me again. When he does, a long while later, my knees are wobbly.

"Drew..."

He shakes his head. "I'll try, Bel. I'll keep trying, but you need to know something."

I nod, waiting.

His mouth drops to mine, his lips whispering words on my soul without so much as speaking a word. When the kiss breaks, I'm breathless, and my heart feels like it's going to burst out of my chest.

"You're mine. You will always be mine. There is no walking away, even if you think you hate me. There is only us, and I will go to any lengths to ensure you understand that, Bel. I promise I will never let anyone hurt you again. Not my family, not my enemies, no one."

I gasp at his vehemence. The sheer violence of it. Swallowing hard, I try to keep my face neutral. *Shit.* His claims do things to me I shouldn't be feeling. Not when we are starting things out again. When he seems like he's done with his pronouncement, I shake my head and pull away.

For a moment, I don't think he's going to release me, but then his fingers slide off my skin, and he lets me down to the floor again.

"I have to go before Sebastian bursts through the door again, but... it's all or nothing, Drew. I need all of you. I need you to trust me as I'll try to trust you. Otherwise, we can't do this."

His gaze turns hungry as he stares after me as I grab my phone from the floor and head out the door. Seb waits in the hall and gives me one quick assessing glance before turning to the stairs.

All or nothing.

17

DREW

The nightmare called my life makes it hard to see past the despair to the light at the end of the tunnel. Is there any good in my life? There's Bel, the saving grace in my life. The light. I have to do this for her. For my mother. I have to find something to stand for because if I don't, then I'll never be able to finish this. I'll never be able to defeat my father and the demons haunting me.

The invitation I crumpled up and tossed at Sebastian the other day sits heavy in the pocket of my jeans as I walk up the estate stairs and through the front door. The house bustles with life, further proof of my father's return to the house. Glad he finally decided to grace us with his presence, considering Mom almost fucking died.

I clench my fists in my pockets and march through the foyer and straight to my mother's wing of the house. The medical suite doors that lead into her room are open, and I step inside. It's busier than usual, with nurses rushing all around the room. I survey the small crowd of staff for the doctor I spoke to last time, but he's not there. In fact there's no one I recognize in the room.

Except him.

Nope. I turn and walk right out the door again and out into the hallway. If I don't take a second to get my shit together, I'm going to walk right in there and punch him in his stupid smug-ass face. Hell, maybe I should anyway.

At this point, I'm running out of reasons not to. Mom is dying, and there's only so much pain he can inflict on me before it becomes the same ole, same ole each time. Between his tender care and football, I know how to take a punch and get back up without a flinch.

The only reason he's not dead yet is because I don't want to risk my mother being hurt or her care being removed. But a person can only be threatened for so long before they have to take the risk. There is no risk without reward. This probably isn't going to settle me for talking to him. Regardless, I'm here, and it needs to be done. I don't want Bel at the meeting. Not surrounded by thieves, crooks, and criminals. People like me.

When I feel like I won't gut him over my mother's sickbed, I reenter the room.

This time, I pinpoint him immediately. His forehead is scrunched as he reads over a stack of documents. I tug the invitation from my pocket, smooth it the best I can, and walk over to the bed. One look at my mother's sleeping form, and I'm riddled with guilt. Is she still in a coma? She doesn't stir when I brush my hand against her arm. *Fuck.* I've been so stuck in my own shit I haven't checked on her like I should have.

I step toward the bed, surveying the neatly tucked sheets, the hospital corner edges, if only to give myself a second to breathe and reel back in the anger threatening to pull me under. "Why is she here?"

My father looks up, and while there is still an undercurrent of anger threatening to consume me and pull me into its dark web, there's also this tremendous empty hole of loss.

The real reason I hadn't checked on her or returned to the house has more to do with the information I discovered and less to do with my so-called father. I've been trying to wrap my head around the knowledge that if these two aren't my parents, then who are? And why did they lie to me all this time? I glance down at my mother, and somehow, her betrayal hurts so much more than his. I expect him to lie to me, to hurt me, but not her. *Never her.*

His eyebrow arches, and he smirks. "Finally decide to visit her, I see. She'd be touched by your care." There's so much mockery in his tone I want to punch him.

How dare he, after being gone all this time, doing nothing to help her? I grip the handles of the bed and let my icy glare wash over him.

"Are you kidding me? If it wasn't for me, she would be dead. I was the one who took her to the hospital when her condition worsened and you were off doing god knows what. Why is she back? Her fucking organs were failing."

He stares me in the eyes, his gaze penetrating like he's trying to suck my soul out. Something squeezes tight in my chest. *Is he trying to gauge what I know?* Based on that assumption alone and the instinct in my gut, I keep my face as neutral as I can and give him nothing in return.

"Your mother needs routine and rest. She needs to be home with me."

"With you?" I scoff. "This is a joke, right? You act like you give a fuck about her, but you just disappeared off the face of the earth fucking whatever flavor of the week you were on. Glad you dropped Jackie, by the way. She deserves a shallow grave."

He rolls his eyes. "You're being dramatic, as usual, Son."

I flinch and push off the bed, refusing to let him see my reaction. I can't give him even an inkling that I know more than he thinks. After a moment, I spin back around to face him. "She should be at the hospital. It's dangerous for her to be home. She can't receive the complete care that she needs to get better here."

His eyes drop down to the paper now recrushed in my grip. "Where did you get that?"

I look down and remember the reason that I came here to begin with. I throw it at him and watch it flutter to the bed near Mom's feet.

He doesn't move but levels me with his stare. "Why do you have the Arturo invitation?"

I wave at the paper. "Maybe because Sebastian dragged me out of bed this morning to confront me about it? Three days for the annual meeting is all the notice you're giving this time?"

He narrows his eyes and slips his hands into his suit pockets. "The timeframe is always short on these things. We do this to minimize the chance of an attack."

"And you decide to do this now when tensions are already running high between us and the Arturos?"

He sits up a little straighter, his pensive gaze swinging

around the room. "Can everyone please give us the room? We have a couple of personal things to discuss."

Great. Here comes the beating for so much as expressing my opinion.

His eyes are hard and angry, and I meet them head-on. I'm done fucking cowering in front of this man...this goddamn stranger to me. It makes sense now. I always felt there was no way a man as hateful as him could be my father.

Once the medical staff finishes what they are doing and flee the room, two of my father's goons step inside and close the door, locking us inside.

I don't give the man the satisfaction of backing down this time. "Things are tense because you decided to use and discard the Arturo princess. That's on you."

I clench my jaw and glare at him. *This fucking asshole.* "Pretty sure you helped with that. I could have had her leashed quickly, secured mind and body, if you hadn't decided she wasn't good enough the second you saw her."

He shrugs. "Well, then she was nothing more than a server. Good enough to fuck, sure, but not be included in the family. You'll learn, Son, women are only useful when you need them to be. Otherwise, they are nothing to us."

I shake my head at the hypocrisy. "And now that she's the darling princess heir, she's suddenly good enough to be included in business?"

He snorts. "No, of course not. I'm playing Sebastian. If he thinks I care, if he thinks I'm including her, he'll be content. It's the disrespect he's pissed about. Once I fix that, things will go back to normal."

I scan his face. He's fucking serious. He actually believes himself.

A laugh slips out of me, and I shake my head in disbelief. "If you think that inviting Bel to a fucking party is enough to placate Sebastian, you don't know shit about him. He won't stop until you're eviscerated on his table and he's winding your entrails around his fork. If he accepts the invitation and shows up, it will be only long enough to tell you to go fuck yourself while he secures the rest of your allics at his side. He's ruthless, cunning, and once slighted, he doesn't forgive. *Ever.*"

My father pushes from his seat and skirts the bed casually. I feel his guards closing in on my back. Ah, I must have said something that hit a nerve. Normal if you ask me. Such a fragile ego he has. I can't wait to destroy him.

One of the guards' meaty paws wraps around my upper arm, and I jerk free. "Don't fucking touch me. I'm done being a punching bag for any of you."

The other guard moves to grab me, but I duck out of his hold. And right into my father's fist. It comes at my face, and I barely have time to shift so his knuckles glance off my jaw. Pain zings along my lips and neck, up into my temple. *Fuck this guy.*

I stand up straight and glare right back at him, meeting his eyes. Then I do something I haven't tried since I was a scrawny kid thinking I was a man. I lash out, and my fist hits him right under the chin.

"Hmm," he says and spits blood at my feet. "Did someone grow some balls while I was away?"

I know this game all too well. He's baiting me, trying to draw me out, like he always does. My father waves the guards back and walks toward me, each step bringing him deeper into my space. "You might be the big man on campus, but I rule here, in the real world."

Before he can say anything else, I slug him again, this time right across the cheek. I feel the deep ache in my knuckles, letting me know I've probably fractured something, but I don't even care. It feels good to see that flash of anguish overtake his face, even if it's for a mere second. That anguish morphed into fear that soon becomes anger, that's red hot matching my own.

He strikes back, planting his fist right in my gut, and I double over, trying to hold myself upright. *Damn.* I always forget how fucking fast he is. Just once, I want to be stronger, smarter, better than him.

Once I can draw breath into my lungs again, I stand fully, my fists curled. "What do you want? Or is this just you proving a point, beating on me because you can?"

He grasps the bottom of his jacket and jerks it straight. "Maybe a little of both. Maybe you piss me the fuck off when you open your mouth, Drew. If I want to hear your opinion, it'll be with my gun on your tongue. Are we clear?"

Something in me wants to dare him to do it. End this little back-and-forth between us once and for all. Seb, even if he hates me, would make sure my father sees justice if he kills me. At least, I think he would. Bel certainly would.

I don't answer, and my father steps closer, getting in my face. "Are we clear?"

"If you want me dead, then fucking kill me, but we aren't doing this anymore."

His eyes are slits, and his spittle hits my face as he

whispers low and fierce, "We will do anything I damn well want to do. I'll lay you down right here, shoot you in the head, and put you in a bed just like your mother. Keep you alive with absolutely no control, no care except my mercy. How would you like that?"

I shrug, even as my heart hammers into my ribs. "I'd rather be dead if it's all the same to you."

His arm pulls back, and his fist comes flying through the air. This time, I block it with my palm, catching it midair. Air stirs at my back, the guards rushing forward, but my father waves them away. We stare each other down, and he must see something on my face because for the first time I can remember, he takes a step back from *me.*

There's so much power in that one single move. I can barely keep my breathing in check while I wait to see if he's going to try to fuck with me again.

"Get the fuck off the grounds. You can come back for the meeting, as required, but I don't want to see you again. You're also banned from seeing your mother. If you show up here, security will toss you out. You have no business seeing to her care when I'm here. You want to be the big man and make the choices, you'll do it over my dead body."

I chuckle. "I guess we'll see how long it is until you decide to up and leave again, chasing another little piece of tail."

His eyes are dark and malicious as he waves to the guards. "Get him the fuck out of my house." He pins me with another glare. "Let's see how your mother fares under this new spine of yours, shall we?"

The guards seize me, and I thrash, but there are two,

then four, as they pretty much carry me out of the medical suite and outside to the driveway. The cool air hits my skin, and I fly through the air, landing on my ass on the pavement. I'm back up in seconds, watching as they retreat into the mansion.

I try to make sense of everything that just happened, but I can't wrap my head around it. Did I just make the biggest mistake of my life, leaving my mother's already fragile life in his hands entirely? I have no idea, but I do know that my time to kill him is dwindling. I need a plan, but I have few allies and even fewer people willing to go against my father. All I need is one person, though, and I have an idea of who I should ask. I just hope he says yes.

18

BEL

Since I was little, the library is the one place that had the power to calm me. All my worries and fears vanished when I thought of visiting. We never had a lot of money, but the library didn't cost anything, and there was no price to be put on the distraction and enjoyment I'd get from falling into a new book.

It was the break away from reality I needed, and it always seemed to fix any problems. For the first time in my life, that's no longer the case. It doesn't feel the same anymore. I've become accustomed to Drew's stalking and lingering presence, and without him here, the missing pieces become more noticeable.

There is still plenty of lingering and whispering, though. I didn't expect so much spotlight to be put on me or for everyone to find out about Drew's and my torrid love affair and spin it in a soap opera way. I guess I should've anticipated the worst.

I try my best to focus on the words in the textbook in

front of me, but they might as well be printed in a foreign language with how much sense they make. A groan of frustration bubbles out of me when I think of how much more work I need to do and how much I'm not getting done. The stack of worksheets gets smaller every day, but I'm not used to being behind on my work. Schoolwork is the one thing I excel at, and I'm usually so far ahead on that, I'd be doing extra credit.

I frown at the textbook, wishing I could make my memories of Drew disappear, wishing this damn place didn't hold so much of who he and I were inside its walls.

I haven't heard from Drew since the other night when I brought up us being all or nothing. If we're going to do this, then we need to be a team. We need to trust each other, but that means I need to be willing and capable of trusting him. I need to accept what happened, give him my heart again, and hope he doesn't make the same mistake twice. In many ways, I've already done that, but mentally, I'm afraid to cross that line, to speak the words I love you to him in fear that they'll be twisted and used against me.

The mere thought makes me sick to my stomach. A dark shadow falls over the textbooks in front of me, and my heartbeat kicks into overdrive. *Drew.* I both want it to be him and not be him because craving his attention terrifies me. It leaves me vulnerable and weak.

Looking up from the textbook and seeing Sebastian standing there instead of Drew, I'm filled with disappointment and relief.

Stupid emotions. Stupid heart.

"Figured you could use some company and maybe a meal," he announces, dropping a fast-food bag down on the textbook. *How did he know?* My stomach lets out a loud, angry growl right then, and I snatch it from the spot.

His presence is a well-needed interruption. It's not as if I'm doing anything anyway. I can't study because I can't stop thinking about Drew. And thinking about Drew reminds me of all I lost, and now the one place I used to find solace in is no longer an escape for me.

Jesus, I'm a mess.

I rifle through the bag, and someone has the gall to hush me from the other side of the cubicles. I poke my head up and glare. Probably what I should have done when I arrived. But nothing and no one will come between me and this juicy cheeseburger right now.

"I'm going to assume, since you're ravaging around inside that bag like a small raccoon, that the answer is yes? You could use the company and a meal?"

The grin on his face and the sarcasm in his voice make me ignore his question. I maneuver the burger so the paper cradles it and lick my lips before opening my mouth wide to take a bite. I'm not like most girls, which is painfully obvious to anyone who pays attention to me. I'll choose a greasy burger and fries over chicken and leafy greens any day. Nothing against chicken, or lettuce, or girls who like it, but I'm not afraid of a nice meaty burger.

A moan of pure blissful pleasure escapes my mouth at that first bite, and my eyes catch on Sebastian, who is watching me with a wry twist of his lips. Is it embarrassing to enjoy a burger this much? Maybe, but who cares?

"What?" I mumble, mouth full as I chew.

"What a fucking lady you are."

I nearly choke on the bite as I laugh and give him a

nonchalant shrug. "Good thing I never claimed to be anything of the sort."

I peer back into the bag and spot the fries. Perfectly golden shoestring fries. My mouth waters, and I pull them out next, carefully arranging them on a napkin so I don't get grease on my textbooks.

"So what's the real reason you've graced me with your presence and provided me with lunch? And don't say it's because you thought I looked lonely and hungry over here in the corner all by myself," I ask curiously once I've swallowed the massive bite.

He reaches across the table and snags a fry from my pile. I glare at his hand while he raises it to his lips, shoving it inside, and then smiles.

He notices my glare. "Hey, I paid. Technically, those are my fries."

"Don't they say possession is nine-tenths of the law? These are my fries now, bud."

"Bud?"

I shrug. "I was trying it out. Not really feeling it. What about bro?"

He shakes his head and reaches for another fry. I slap his hand away this time and tug the napkin closer to me. His eyes glitter with amusement, and when he leans forward again, I'm sure it's to grab another one of my fries, so I'm ready and willing to defend the fried slabs of potato, but he doesn't reach for mine. Instead, he slides his hand into the bag and pulls out another box of fries.

"Excuse me. You were taking my fries when you already had your own? Rude!"

A chuckle leaves his lips, and for the first time all day, I let my shoulders relax, and my body slouch into the chair. I share this singular moment with him, brother and sister eating fries and burgers together.

I NOTICE the arches on the bag, and it reminds me that this was one of my mom's favorite fast-food places. I wonder what she would think now if she could see me? See us?

I smile, the story sputtering out of me. "One time, Mom and I went to this place. We went a lot, by the way. It was one of her favorites. Anyway, we went there, and she wanted fresh fries. It turned into this whole ordeal."

"What happened?"

There's something in his tone I can't quite place, like he wants more, needs more, but he can't ask or show how much he wants it.

I smile and swipe away a tear that escapes my eye. "Well, the cashier told her she couldn't have fresh fries until they made the next batch. Mom politely told them she'd wait as long as necessary. She was so polite, always polite, because she had to work in food service when I was young to support us. She knows how much it can suck, ya know?"

He nods but doesn't speak, as if he's urging me to continue.

"Well, anyway, we sat there for an hour. She got her fries, and we ate the whole order together. It's a silly little memory, but I loved when she was like that. Healthy and happy even though we never really had enough. Even though life was hard, she always found joy in it."

He looks wistful. "I envy that you have those memories."

I reach out and pat his hand gently. "I'll share her with you at any opportunity. You'll get all the stories. It's not the same, I know, but she'll be a part of our lives this way."

He nods, and I watch as he sucks a ragged breath into his lungs. He leans away like he's closed the subject and moved on already. "Do you know anything about your father?"

I shake my head. "No. I never met him, and there's no name on my birth certificate. I've even gone through some of the papers she had hidden away, looking for any clue she might have left behind. Haven't found anything, what about yours?"

His jaw is tight, and he shakes his head. "I guess we're in for more surprises. Who knows, maybe we have more siblings out there?"

The thought fills me with dread. Needing to change the subject before I get truly weepy, I take another bite of the burger, studying him. *My brother.* How did I not see it before, the way his eyes sparkle like Mom's used to. He even wrinkles his nose the same way she did.

I see her there in his face in so many ways, and it's like she left a little part of herself with me before she went.

"I wanted to talk to you about something," I mumble around another bite.

This confession makes him sit a little straighter in his seat, and he appears to shrug off the playful brother image, pulling on his war armor.

"Do you have to look like you're going into battle? It's just a conversation, not a debate for class or actual war."

His lips barely lift at the sides. "Everything is war, Bel. There's always someone waiting to steal your piece of the pie. That's why it's important to always be vigilant."

And he's now starting to sound like one of the old men at the nursing home who were adorable but riddled with dementia.

"Honesty. It's important to me. I know you don't like Drew, and you think he's bad for me."

He snorts, interrupting me. "Bad is an understatement, but continue..."

I roll my eyes. "He's your best friend, or at least he was. And I know I'm your sister, and family is important to you, but Drew is family too. After everything you've been through together, you should look at each other like brothers. I'm not saying what he did was okay, nor am I saying that he's forgiven."

Sebastian lifts his brow in questioning. "So what are you saying?"

Yeah, what are you saying, Bel? Part of me is worried to tell him that I'm working on trusting Drew again because I know he doesn't support us being together, but I think that's mainly because he doesn't want me hurt. But getting hurt comes with falling in love. No pain, no gain.

"I'm trying to work things out with Drew. I haven't forgiven him, and we have a long road before we're going to be a couple, but I want you to know and hear it from me that we're working on things. I'm not asking for your approval or even support. I just don't want you standing in the way and causing problems."

His body's tense, but he remains sitting, his face

neutral. He's better at masking his emotions than I'll ever be.

"So you're saying you don't give a fuck if I agree or not because you're working this out with Drew, and that's that?"

Okay, when you put it that way, it sounds kind of rude.

I look down at the food in my hands. The remaining bites of burger stare back at me. "Well, kinda, yes. I'm making my own decisions. I want to be in control of my life and what happens. I know you're trying to protect me, but protecting me and being an overbearing brother are different. Not to say you're being overbearing right now, but I can see it heading down that road, and I want to stop it before it gets to that point."

I'm both shocked and surprised when he smiles, the kind that makes his green eyes light up, showing just a little bit of the human he is underneath the hard exterior.

"You're smiling like you're happy."

"Of course I'm happy."

I smirk back at him. "Okay, well, I didn't expect you to take things so well. I half expected you to scold me."

"Scold you? Maybe a little. But that's only because I'm selfish and don't know how to handle having a sibling. I care about you and want to protect you from anything and anyone that might cause you harm or pain. Drew included. It pisses me off that he hurt you, but I'm coming to terms with it and learning to accept things for what they are. If you can change, then so can he."

"Me change? I haven't changed." I grab a fry from the napkin and shove it into my mouth.

Sebastian brushes the blond curls from his forehead,

and it's then I see more of the young, alluring man he is. If only everyone could see this side of him. The side that's both sweet and fierce. "Bel, you've changed so much in the time since our mother passed, and I'm beyond proud of you for it. Proud of you for sticking up for yourself, and for fighting for what you want. Most would've fallen into depression and never escaped it. Yeah, you were sad and wallowed in your misery for a while, but who wouldn't?"

I guess. He continues. "You might not see it, but I do, and I'm sure Drew does too."

The kindness of his words makes me feel all warm inside. "Whoa, slow it down. Someone might overhear us and think you have a heart in that chest of yours."

Something sinister flicks in his gaze. "Let them. It'll be the last thing they ever hear."

I laugh, thinking it's a joke, but soon discover he's serious when his own expression never changes. *Okay...*

"We never really discussed it, but what was that fight with Drew about? He explained to me that he knew nothing about the invitation. He thinks it's just another way his dad is trying to stir the pot and cause issues."

His body tenses, and he clenches his fingers together on the table. "Do you believe him?" *Do I?* The fear of putting my faith in him and him fooling me again terrifies me, but no bone in my body believes Drew is playing along with his father anymore.

"Yes."

"I find it hard to believe he knew nothing. His father wouldn't blindside him to things."

"I think you're wrong. He explained he knew nothing about it, and I believe him. His father is an asshole, and this seems like something he would do. You, more than anyone, once being his best friend, know how his father is."

He narrows his eyes. "Since when are you the number one chick on the Drew Marshall cheering squad? Did he dickmatize you again?"

I snort and shake my head, but he continues, some of the humor in his tone leaking away. "I can't be one hundred percent certain, but his father needs him. He needs him at his side. Not sharing important information would make him look weak unless his intention is to shake things up, which is definitely the feeling I got when the invitation arrived without warning. But it's not the warning I care about since I know this is the season. It's the damn order to bring you. He has no authority over me." His tone holds a good amount of suspicion, and while Drew deserves some of his anger, the majority should be directed at the real monster in all this: his father.

"You've been best friends for the better part of your lives. I've known his dad all of five minutes, and I get the impression he'll do anything he can to get to the top. He doesn't care who he has to hurt, even if it's his own son." I pause and look away for a moment. This conversation is going deeper than I expected. "All I'm saying is don't end your friendship with him for me. Drew has been through a lot, and that's not an excuse for his behavior. But the last thing he needs is another person against him. Besides, I think...I think he misses you."

Sebastian sighs. "Things with Drew are complicated. He's like a brother to me and always will be, but you're my sister. Family always comes first, and if I have to choose to protect you or him, it will be you."

"Why not choose both of us? Why aren't you putting this anger into Drew's father? Yeah, he deserves to have his balls busted, but his dad, he deserves worse."

A sinister smile twists his lips. "And his time will come sooner than he thinks."

"Not soon enough," I mumble under my breath.

"I agree." He sighs and leans back in his chair. "Now back to the invitation because I was going to tell you about it the next time we both got a moment to sit and eat together, but that didn't happen till now, so..."

I scoff. "Are you insinuating that I have trust issues?"

"Insinuating? You have so many issues a therapist would need another therapist just to dissect them all."

"Wow, rude," I squeak through laughter.

Sebastian beams at me. "The invitation we got was for the annual meeting of the families."

I nod like I know what that is. "The families?"

"Yes. The Mill, their founding members, and other well-connected families in the community come together once a year to negotiate and handle certain business ventures."

"So...when you say *families,* you mean like..." I lean forward and whisper very, very softly, "Criminals."

He snickers and shakes his head. "Some of the families are made up of criminals. However, not all of them do illegal dealings."

His penetrating gaze stares at me. I'm not sure what he's waiting for me to do? Freak out or lose my mind maybe? Joke's on him. I've already surpassed my allotted mental breakdowns for the month.

Instead of reacting or asking him why he's looking at me like I might burst into flames, I ask, "Okay, so why do we have to attend this meeting? And if it happens every year, why are you so mad about it?"

"I'm not mad about the meeting or even that it's taking place. I'm annoyed that it's being held by Drew's father," he grits out. "And yes, we'll both be expected to attend. At least if I want to maintain my protection over you."

"Got it. Attendance required, or else."

He sighs and rakes his hands up his face and into his hair. "I mean yes and no. It's easier to protect you if you're with me. They wouldn't dare try anything in my presence, but leaving you home would be the same as leaving you completely alone. It's not done often, but occasionally, a family will steal a bride or force a marriage contract. It's far more ballsy to perform the ceremony beforehand, but like I always say, expect the worst because once the marriage is done, it's done."

I grimace. "Sounds like a great group of people."

His phone buzzes, and he glances at the screen. His face and body instantly change, freeze up, tense, as if he's afraid to move or be caught. Then he clicks the screen off and sets the phone farther away.

"Should I even ask?"

He shakes his head, swallowing hard. "It's nothing. Just my aunt."

"You have an aunt..." I try to consider how she'd be related to me, but he cuts in.

"My uncle's wife. They raised me mostly because my

grandfather never wanted to get into the nitty-gritty of actual child-rearing. But don't worry about it...where was I?"

I lick my lips, wishing I were brave enough to push on this, but the set in his jaw says I shouldn't. "The people at the party...good...?"

"Far from it. We'll have to be careful at the meeting, both before and after. With my grandfather's death still fresh, I'll have to do whatever I can to cement my place as the heir to the family. It's going to be extremely important that we maintain a strong front and show no weakness whatsoever. I need to ensure that all the families under-stand that I'll be as decisive as my grandfather so no one moves in on the business."

I'm tempted to ask what exactly the *business* is. We've skirted around it for so long, but if I'm going to be an active participant in this, I need to know.

Clearing my throat, I demand, "Tell me."

Giving the surrounding space a cautious glance, he leans forward. Most of the seats near us are empty.

"Wait, it's not..." I pause, not wanting to offend him. "It's not like prostitution, is it?"

He shakes his head. "No, it's not that. Not even close." I watch as he slowly eases his hands apart, holding one up before cocking it back like a gun. There's a crushing reality of what that means. *Guns. Weapons.*

"Oh. Okay." Can I live with that? Do I need to know the particulars or...

Shit. The ethical ramifications swirl through my head. Then I jolt..."Does Drew?"

He grins and shakes his head. "Nope. The Marshalls

are too good to dip their toes into the illegal dealing of weapons. Lyle is in charge of the money. Most of the organization's money. But that will change soon after everything went down."

The memory threatens to surge up, and I push it back. "Yeah, I don't think I'm going to hate it if that guy gets knocked down a peg or twenty."

"You and pretty much everyone else. He's just so damn good with the numbers. Or at least his employees are. He's good with people, cajoling them, threatening them, doing whatever it takes to get their money."

I blink. I know someone else who is good with people too. Not that I'd admit I found any similarities between Drew and his father to his face. He seems to hate the man, as I do. As does Seb apparently.

"So why is he holding the meeting if everyone hates him?"

"Good question. He'll be asking himself that question after the meeting too if things go the way I want."

There's so much threat in his tone I sit back, putting some distance between us. I haven't heard that tone since before we found out the truth of our relationship. Back when he thought I was a pretty amusement for Drew.

"Well, tell me what I need to do," I whisper. "I can handle it."

He nods and smiles, his eyes softening, his shoulders slipping down now. "I know. We've got this. Together."

I nod, feeling not so alone anymore. "Together."

19

DREW

The desire to go to her calls to me. I want to see her, to be around her, to hold her, and be beside her, but I can't. Not when I'm like this. In the past, I didn't give a fuck about taking my anger out on her. I used her body as an outlet, and well, I wouldn't have a problem with that so much if she wasn't already fragile enough. I can't risk doing something stupid and breaking the fragile trust building between us.

I pull out my phone and send her a quick text: *I miss you. I care about you. I can't wait to see you.* I clutch my phone for a second, thinking about deleting it. Maybe it sounds stupid or too sappy. But I shake my head, lock my phone, and take a deep breath.

I can't allow my anger to lead me. I've done that before, and it's only ever left a path of chaos in its wake. I need to do better. *I can do better.*

Why didn't I destroy him? Time and time again, I've had the opportunity, occasionally, to take him out, but I've always hesitated. Pussied out. And why? Because he's my father? Before, I could see that, but now that I have the knowledge that I do, there's no reason.

Yeah, he usually has guards with him. Their standing orders are always to punch first and ask questions later. The thought of my fist marks on his skin is enough to reignite the anger I'd started to feel simmering away. I want to crush his throat, slam his face into a wall, and punch him until he can't see straight. All things he's done to me over the years.

I'd take the pain to my hands, my knuckles split from hitting him, all of it. I'd revel in it, and then I'd show Bel so she'd understand what I'd done, that I had stood up to my father, and that I was done playing his little games.

I clench my fists and jog up the steps to the football team's training gym. The heat and anger blazing through me might keep me away from her for now, but I'll see her soon. I need to see her.

A few guys from the team are lifting weights when I enter. Weights line the mirrored room, leaving the middle of the floor open. The scent of sweat and rubber is overwhelming, but I ignore it. It's certainly better than the overfull gym on campus that the rest of the student body can use.

I drop my bag by an empty bench and turn to eye a heavy bag hanging from the ceiling. This is what I need. I'm a damn good football player because I practice. Now, the next time my father comes at me like that, I'll be ready.

I sit on the bench and carefully wrap my hands. While I don't give a shit if they get bruised, I can't let these guys see me being careless with the quarterback hands.

One of the second-string linemen wanders over as I finish up and strip off my jacket.

"Hey, Drew, what's up, man? We haven't seen you around."

I make a noncommittal hum and study the bag. Most of the campus knows it's rush season, and most of the campus has no idea about The Mill, but the rich ones, the football players, the trust-fund kids usually know because of a family legacy at some point. So when I level the guy with a long stare, he nods once and returns to his workout.

I'm known for being brutal on the field, and I sure as shit don't want to invite open questions about my time or my whereabouts.

As I pound the bag, some of the anger begins to fizzle, channeled through my fists, burning away under the pain in my hands, my arms, my abs, as I move.

As always, my thoughts stray back to her. The way she'd look at me right now. I freeze. Well, shit. The way she used to look at me. Now, I feel like I might not know this new Bel at all. She's different, no less appealing to me, but different.

Regardless of how much I want to destroy him, I need answers first. I need to understand the depths of his evil mind and what he's done so I can make sure he doesn't wheedle out of this like he does everything else. All my life, he's gotten away from deplorable and evil things. Shit, I'm no saint, but what my father has done has always been so much worse. I once witnessed him cave a man's skull in by bashing it on the side of his desk like an egg. He didn't even bat an eye or seem fazed by his actions.

I punch the bag and think.

I punch the bag and plan.

I punch the bag and start planning the topple of my father's empire. That bastard is going down soon, but I need more time and more answers.

I hit the bag again, but now that I'm thinking, I unwrap my hands, pack up my headphones, and grab my jacket. I need to start where things have changed.

The hospital.

Before I leave the gym, I toss my bag into my locker so I don't have to lug it with me. It wasn't a long workout, but I need to change and look more presentable. It sells the good ole boy routine better.

I keep clothes at the training center, and it doesn't take long to change into a well-worn pair of jeans, a long-sleeved gray Henley, and one of my favorite pairs of black combat boots. I put a black zip-up hoodie under my letter jacket and leave the center. My hair is wet, and it makes me colder as I walk, but it doesn't matter.

I call a ride app car when I reach the edge of campus before it unfolds into the small town that basically lives to support the school. The hospital isn't too far away, but it's too chilly to walk all the way there, and I don't want to head back to The Mill for my motorcycle if it means running into Seb or explaining what I'm doing to Lee. I'm not ready for either of their unending questions.

The driver only asks my name and doesn't say a word otherwise. Just the way I like them.

At the hospital, I head inside, hands tucked into my pockets, a slight smile playing on my lips. Unassuming is the goal, even if I rarely succeed. Women, though, usually succumb, and are always more helpful than men when it comes to information.

I cross to the section of the hospital my mother was being treated in. Thankfully, this is an exclusive area that usually requires a fat checkbook to use. The nurses and the doctors there remember me with one look. A nurse comes around the desk the second I cut into her line of sight.

"Mr. Marshall, what brings you back? Your mother was moved back to her home medical suite."

I give her a smile, all white flashing teeth and dimples. She immediately relaxes, leaning close.

"Yes, I know she was moved. I just saw her, but I wanted to speak to her doctor if I'm able."

Her forehead wrinkles slightly, and she looks around carefully. "Her doctor is one of ours. He should be there now. Your father requested someone new when he took her away."

"Oh." I sigh and smile and play the part of the forgetting jock. It seems to sell because once again, she relaxes. "I actually wanted to speak to her old doctor. He said he had some information for me the last time we spoke, and I just wanted to follow up with him. A Dr. Brooks, I believe."

She relaxes further as if she was anticipating having to tell me she couldn't help. Now that she can, her reason to live is restored.

She brushes away some stray hairs at her hairline and refreshes her smile. "Just head down this corridor. His office is on the left. If he's not in there, come back here, and I'll page him."

I nod once and head in the direction she's pointed me.

The office has his name outside on a brass plate. I knock on the door, and when there's a muffled noise on the other side, I take it as a request to enter.

The second I shoulder the door open and the doctor catches sight of me, he jumps out of his chair and puts the length of the small room between us. His voice is all panic. "I told them I wouldn't say anything. I'm working like normal. Nothing has changed." Despite his tone, his back is straight, and he meets my eyes squarely. Scared but not going to run.

"Doctor." I mirror his position, holding my own hands up. "I'm not here to hurt you. I only want to ask you a few questions."

He shakes his head back and forth, trying to squeeze between the cabinet and the couch on the other side. "No, I'm not. I told them I wouldn't talk or they'd come back. I can't."

I enter the room and close the door behind me. This sets him practically shaking, but he still doesn't make a move to hurt me or try to get past me. He's got more balls than he thinks.

"Please, Doctor, it's important. You took an oath, didn't you? All I need is information, and no one will know it came from you. Besides, once it comes out that I even have this information, it won't matter anyway."

He looks like he wants to ask questions, but I shake my head gently, discouraging him as gently as I know how.

He still looks scared and hesitant. "What...what do you want to know?"

That tells me he wants to help. He doesn't like leaving my mom in her situation any more than I do.

I ease down on the end of the couch, putting myself a little lower than him. "I just want to know what you know. What did my father want to keep hidden?"

His eyes turn a little darker, a little calmer now, and he eases away from the wall to lock the door and take his desk chair again. "Your father is a monster." He waves at his face where it's battered and bruised.

I chuckle. "Don't get it twisted, Doctor. I'm a monster too, but I love my mother. But yes, I've been on the receiving end of his handiwork as well."

The words threaten to stick tight in my throat. She's not my real mom, a tiny voice blasts in the back of my mind. But she's the only source of kindness, of love, I've had in my life until Bel, and I won't just walk away from her after that.

He gives me a long look and nods. "I think she's being poisoned. Or has been and is currently. It's a long, slow death he's building for her."

I swallow hard. "Is it too late?"

This makes me think of Bel's mom. Her body had lain right down the hall when Seb had it moved from the emergency room. I hadn't been here, but I'd gotten the information out of the nurses then too as I kept track of Bel.

"I don't believe so. When I was working with her, I started to synthesize an antidote, but I didn't get very far when your father returned and requested I leave your mother's care team." The last is bit out, an edge in his voice now.

Good, this doctor has some fight at least.

"What do you need to finish it?"

"More of your Mother's blood. I have to make sure he

hasn't changed things now that I've interfered. You should probably hurry too. It seems like he might want to end it if he thinks he might get caught."

I snort. "My father has always underestimated me. He thinks I'm stupid, or maybe he just has low expectations. Either way, he won't end things just because of me. Not yet."

Doctor Brooks nods, and I consider Bel's mom again. And what I considered that day in the kitchen that made me think we were related. "Doctor, do you know the name of the doctor who was treating Ms. Jacobs before she passed?"

He eyes me and shakes his head. "I can look it up, though."

Once I have what I need from him, I give him my cell phone number and tell him to get to work. I'll pay whatever he needs.

Then I go find the doctor who helped Bel's mom. She's tall and thin with dark hair and dark eyes. Younger than I thought. "Doctor?"

She spins, a professional smile on her face. "Yes, can I help you?"

"I'm a friend of Maybel Jacobs. I was here trying to get some information and then it occurred to me that you might be able to give me an answer."

"I'd be happy to help."

She actually sounds genuine. Imagine that.

"Is it possible that the illness Ms. Jacob's suffered from could have been caused by long-term poison exposure as a young woman?"

She blinks once, her smile slipping away. "Excuse me?"

"I know it's a strange question. But you guys were treating it like a cancer. Could the cancer, or whatever, be caused by poison over a long period?"

There's a moment when she casts her eyes down, considering. "Let me look at the files, but I'm not sure."

The hesitance in her voice is really all the answer I need. "Thank you, Doctor. I appreciate your time."

I walk away, my world spinning. Now, I need to figure out how to tell Bel my father is the one responsible for everything. And then I need to figure out how to keep Seb on a tight leash until this is all done so he doesn't blow shit up before I can begin.

20

BEL

The library still feels weird, but I'm not giving up. I'm still wearing hundred-dollar jeans, and all my textbooks are brand new, even creaking slightly when I open them, which I will admit to no one is really satisfying. My old ones had been open and closed so many times the spines were loose. Nothing loose about these shiny babies.

I also have to admit it's nice to just come to the library and not have to worry about tutoring, about appointments and money. The thought instantly makes me think of Mom, who was always just doing her best, and guilt swamps me.

Here I am, happy about new textbooks, and she's dead. The joy over the book recedes under the heavy weight of my grief. *Shit.* I hate how this happens. One minute, I'm fine, and the next, it hits me like I've forgotten somehow, as fresh and raw as the day I found out.

I stare at the ceiling to keep the tears from falling, and

once I feel like I'm not going to splatter my shiny new books with tears, I try to go back to studying.

A buzzing sound drags me out of the book, and I check my phone. A text from Seb.

SEBASTIAN: I'll meet you at the library.

I ROLL my eyes and shake my head. Not 'Can I meet you at the library?' Nothing so gracious as a request. It makes me sigh but I shoot him a text back.

MAYBEL: Sure, I'll be here. But what if I'd already gone home?

IT TAKES ONLY a minute for him to respond.

SEBASTIAN: Funny, you never leave the library if you can help it. I'll be there soon.

I RETURN my attention to the book in front of me and only stop when the touch of a soft hand resting on my shoulder pulls me out of my fixation.

Sebastian greets me with a nod, then comes around the other side of the table to take the other chair. "Always studying," he says, his voice low since this is a more quiet area at the moment.

"I'm still not completely caught up on things. All the teachers have been very kind to me and are allowing me as much flexibility as I need, but I feel like I won't get back to normal until I'm caught up, and..." I leave off, thinking.

"And?" There's something in his tone, question, and something softer.

I shake my head. "I just want to get caught up."

He studies me. "You miss your friend."

"My friend?" I scoff. "I hope you aren't talking about Jackie. She deserves the hole she's dug for herself."

"Well, I think you'll be happy to know she won't be making any reappearances in your life. I had a chat with her to make certain of it and discovered that she was only helping Drew's dad because he promised her a place at one of his offices when she graduates."

The air squeezes out of my chest. "That's it? She threw away our whole friendship for an internship, with an asshole to boot?"

He shrugs. "You can never really account for people's ambition. I think you're lonely, though, am I right?"

"How could I be lonely with your company and Drew breathing down my neck every few minutes?"

"There are varying degrees of loneliness, Bel. There's the type when you're in a room with a bunch of people but still feel like you have no one, which I think is the worst kind. Then there's the type when you're simply alone and unwilling to make new friends, so you cause your own loneliness."

"I hope you don't think I'm paying you for this session because I'm not."

He smirks. "I'm not trying to psychoanalyze you. I just don't want your loneliness to eat away at you. No offense but you had limited friends before everything happened. Now there's no one."

I frown. "Thanks for the reminder. Can we not talk about how shitty my social life is, or how the only friend I had was secretly sleeping with this psychopath-obsessed man's dad in an attempt to get information about us?"

"It's not meant to be an insult. I was actually hoping to use it as an opening to invite you to hang out this evening. Lee, Aries, and I are going to have some pizza and beer, then hang out and watch some movies. You're coming."

I shake my head. "You do realize you make decrees a lot, right?"

He shrugs. "It's my job to be decisive. I have no room for questions."

I mock his deep voice. "I have no room for questions. Only commands."

This earns me an eye roll, and he helps me gather my books. "Leave this here. I'll have the driver grab it for you and put it in the car while we walk over to The Mill."

I freeze. "The Mill?"

He tugs me along gently. "Don't worry, Drew isn't there."

"You're sure?" While I mean, it would be fine to see him, I know I don't exactly think clearly when he's around. Nor does Seb at the moment. Not exactly a situation for a relaxing evening.

"Are you going to tell me what's going on with Drew? I thought you were going to stay away from him?"

We walk, and I consider how much I actually want to tell him. "Drew is...hard. I can't just turn off caring for him. He wants to be different. He is different with me. But I also don't want to be an idiot and walk into things blindly."

He nods and tucks his hands into his pockets as the wind cuts through the trees heading up to The Mill house. "While I'd love to just say 'stop seeing him,' something tells me that wouldn't go over well. That you'd probably do the opposite just to piss me off."

"Hmm...seems you are getting to know me."

He chuckles. "Doesn't mean I'm not going to tell him to stay away from you. Not that he's been doing that very well either. Drew does what he wants. Always has."

"Sounds like someone else I know."

We enter the house, and a chill skitters down my spine. What if Seb is wrong, and Drew is here anyway? And I have to sit and endure pizza with him and his friends.

Seb leads me into a clean, modern kitchen I still remember from the party, and I plop at the countertop bar. I duck my chin to hide my blush as I remember that night and what happened after I left the party.

Lee stands on the other side, a pizza box in hand, his light hair mussed, his v-neck T-shirt showing off his golden skin.

Aries stands next to him, almost twice as wide, a big dude, his dark curls tucked back with a black elastic headband. They both eye me like a snake they accidentally walked up on.

"Hi," I say.

Lee recovers first and sets the pizza out on the counter. "Pepperoni? Mushrooms? What's your pleasure?" He slaps Aries on the chest. "Don't be rude. Get the lady a beer."

Aries narrows his eyes in suspicion, but he still turns to grab a beer out of the massive stainless steel fridge. He opens it with one hand and plunks it down in front of me. Some foam escapes the top, and I reach to grab it and lick the edge of the bottle when Lee hands me a plate with a couple of slices of pizza on it.

Pizza is pizza in all its beautiful forms so I don't request anything else and finish cleaning up the beer mess while I nibble on the pepperoni and banana pepper piece I pick up first.

Sebastian sits beside me, tosses his jacket on a nearby empty chair, and greets his friends. "Look at us, doing normal happy family shit."

Lee chuckles, and Aries just stares between us like we might randomly attack him at any moment.

Eventually, Aries settles down and pulls a stool to the other side of the counter to sit on. He cradles a plate stacked high with pieces of mushroom and sausage against his chest.

Seb picks at a piece of pepperoni and cheese. Lee doesn't bother with a plate or chair. Instead, he sits on the counter and folds his slice in half, eating it bite by bite.

Once he chews, he eyes everyone. "Yeah, this is fun. Not awkward as fuck or anything."

We all chuckle and eat. Lee tosses another slice on my plate. "How's school going? Are you getting caught up?"

I groan. "Yes. It's easy to study when I don't have to juggle a job and money."

He nods. "Yeah. I can only imagine. We're all spoiled rich boys who've never had to deal with school tuition." He says it as a joke, but there's something under his tone that's darker and has a jagged edge I'm not getting near.

I glance back at Aries, who is stacking his plate again. *Where the hell did he put all that?* I glance among the men. "Did he even eat, or did he just inhale his food like a vacuum?"

They all laugh, even Aries, who then shrugs.

"Why do you think we get so much pizza?" Lee says, waving to the stacked boxes for the four of us. "Drew can have leftovers."

The mention of Drew's name makes the smile slip off my face, and the tension returns to the room.

"Way to go, asshole," Aries mutters to Lee.

Lee doesn't even flinch. "So what is going on between you two? I saw you kiss one of the new kids at the party? He's still alive, by the way, for now. Not sure how long that will last, though."

Seb grabs another slice of piece, this time a sausage and mushroom, even as Aries growls at him. "Let's not dive into that conversation, Lee. Let's just sit and have a nice relaxing dinner."

Aries snorts. "I hate to break it to you, boss, but nothing about dinner is relaxing."

Seb ignores Aries's pointed comment and stares at Lee. "How's life for you? What about your girl? The one your family is setting you up with?"

Lee grumbles under his breath and shoves half a slice of pizza in his mouth. After he swallows, he licks his fingers. "Apparently, we are getting married. Because that works so well in our world. They're calling it an arranged marriage."

I consider his words. "Is that what was happening with Drew and that girl at the party?"

Sebs sighs like he would love anything better than talking about Drew for five minutes. "Yes. His father forced him to spend time with her for some business thing. And he made it very clear that Drew had to do anything and everything she wanted."

I try to think back to that night, but after the head wound, things became a little blurrier.

Lee carries on. "She was a fucking witch. Her slimy hands were all over him, all over us too when we tried to distract her so he could talk to you."

Thinking about Drew makes me want to see him and talk to him. *Why isn't he here?* I should've asked Seb earlier when he said he wouldn't be here why he wouldn't be here? I drag my cell phone out from under the table and tap out a quick text to him.

ME: *Hey, where are you? At The Mill eating pizza.*

I WAIT FOR A RESPONSE, but all it says is delivered. I try not to let the disappointment take root and put my phone away, focusing my attention back on the conversation.

21

DREW

The anger simmers in my veins. Deeper and heavier than before, like a sticky paste. I have more questions than I have answers, and it's frustrating as hell. Playing detective isn't my thing, and having the patience to wait it out is also not standard for me.

My go-to at this point would be to find someone, start a fight, taunt the fucker, and then lay him out, or fuck the first willing girl I find, but neither of those things will get me Bel back, and I'd rather cut off my cock then put it in someone else at this point. So I take myself back to the gym to pound my rage into the bag some more, since my earlier session ended short.

I want to see her. I want to go home, drag her into my bed, and force her sweet little mouth down on my cock. It feels like it's been too long even though it really hasn't.

My phone beeps signaling an incoming text and I pull it out staring down at the screen.

· · ·

FLOWER: Hey, where are you? At The Mill eating pizza.

I'M TEMPTED to toss my evening plans aside and crash their little shit show, but even I know that would be a terrible idea. With the mood I'm in right now, there would be no stopping me from getting into a fight with Sebastian and or kidnapping Bel. I want to do that on almost any day, and today would be the worst when my temper is flaring, and my tolerance for bullshit is at an all-time low. I tell myself I'll text her back later and close the message before sliding the phone back into my pocket.

I'd be shit for conversation right now, and if I'm going to do better by Bel, that means I'm going to rein my temper in and fix my shit before I talk to her. As I walk into the gym, I find there to be fewer people than usual.

There are a couple of the new mill guys a couple of yards ahead who cast glances every so often but none of them go out of their way to converse with me. It's almost like I'm wearing a blinding neon sign that says: ***Don't Fuck With Me.***

I slip a headphone in my ear, but just one. Two would leave me distracted and potentially jumped by one of these fools. Steadying the heavy punching bag between my hands, I breathe deeply, and then rear my arm back and throw my first punch.

My fist slams into the bag hard, rocking it, and I release a long sigh of contempt.

Yes, I need this.

I punch and punch and punch until I'm panting and have to stop, hugging the bag to catch my breath. It feels good but it's not enough. The steady rock of the bag isn't my father's face splitting open under my fists. It's not his eyes swelling shut, or his lip bleeding.

I need something else, something a little more violent and dark than this to quiet the beast that's clawing under my skin, itching to get out. But I can't get what I need quiet yet. There are still some answers I need and things to put into place. I throw a few more punches at the bag but the initial satisfaction tempers. I breathe and catch the new guys whispering and exchanging cash.

I turn to face them. "What's this? Collecting money for the book club?"

One of the kids, Tyson, or Taylor, I can't fucking remember his name glares at me. "Actually, it's for a bet."

For a second I'm just glad they didn't bring hard drugs into my training center. "Bet for what?"

The other one, I don't even bother trying to recall his name, shakes his head at his friend like he doesn't want to tell me.

I take one step toward them and the dumb one raises his hands, cash still in his fists. "It's for a fight, okay. That's it."

I won't lie, my curiosity is piqued. "What kind of a fight?"

"The underground, illegal kind. Every two weeks they have them at the old Sears center, where the mall used to be in Blackthorn."

Well, shit. Why the fuck am I just now hearing about this? I study them for a minute. "You've got business at

Blackthorn, so much so that you know about secret illegal fights?"

He swallows hard and nods. "Yeah? I used to attend, but got kicked out. My sister still goes there and I have a ton of friends there so I try to make visits back to see them when I can."

I shrug and crack my knuckles. "Funny enough I could use a good fight right now. When do they start, and how do I find more information?"

There's a hard edge to his eyes as he takes in my clenched fists. "There's a bookie who takes all the bets in house when you arrive. If you're wanting to place a bet that is. If you're there to fight, you just show up, tell them you want to be included in the pot."

Easy enough. I just can't risk knowledge of me fighting at Blackthorn getting out and back to my father. It would be another black stain on his so-called perfect image.

I reach for the kid closest to me, and grip onto the lapels of his shirt giving him a little shake. I need to make it very clear what will happen if these two squeak to anyone.

"No one hears about this. Understand? If either of you speak a word about this conversation not only will I make sure the cops know about this event but I'll ruin your fucking lives."

I look between the two of them, and even though I'm not touching the other guy his gaze is filled with fright as well. *Good.* They both nod and I release the kid like he's the plague, giving him a shove before wiping my hand off on the front of my shorts. I head back into the locker room, grab my duffel bag and jacket, then jog out of the gym.

Using my phone, I order one of the ride app cars. It's dark but early so I have no trouble getting a car and heading out to Blackthorn University. It shouldn't take long to find the fights if what the assholes told me is right. Blackthorn and Oakmount have always had a long-standing rivalry of sorts. They're a school for the offspring of the elite, just like Oakmount. Everyone wants to send their kids to these schools but have no clue the dark, fucked up shit that takes place behind the scenes.

The website might show a wholesome, fun, top tier university but once the sun goes down things are far from wholesome. I get another ping on my phone from Bel but again, I ignore it. Not because I don't want to talk to her but because I want to talk to her too much.

All or nothing still rings in my ears and I'm not ready to show her everything yet. Especially with this new information I've learned. How do I tell her my father is the one who killed her mother? Slowly. Painfully. But it's his fault and now he's trying to do it to my mother too. I won't fucking allow it.

All of this bullshit over money. How many people has he killed just to hang on to the numbers in his bank account?

I clench my fists, some of the anger spiraling through me tighter. Yes, I need to break someone's face, that will make me feel better.

When we reached the abandoned Sears center I hop out of the car, tuck my hands into my pockets, and wander in the direction of voices. It doesn't take me long to find it, like the kid said, it's a damn party out here. They aren't even trying to hide it. *Interesting.* I wonder who is running this and how I might get involved if I need this in the future.

I cut through the small crowd outside. There's people smoking, conversing, drinking beer, and even some who are merely standing there surveying the crowd. I spot one guy standing at the edge of the crowd.

He's a big dude but I meet his menacing gaze head-on. "I want to fight."

Carefully, he drops his gaze, sizing me up from boot to brow. "Oakmount's golden boy wants to get his hands dirty with us? Should we be honored?"

I narrow my eyes. "I don't care what the fuck you are, or who the fuck you are. I came here for a fight so if you aren't the person I talk to about one then this conversation is over."

There's a murmuring voice in his earpiece. I barely pick up the buzz but I can't make out the words. "Fine, be in the circle at nine. I'll make sure we put on a good show."

"Rules?"

His eyes narrow this time. "You don't seem like the type that follows rules."

I shrug. "When it benefits me, I do, sure."

"Don't kill each other is about the only rule. Unfortunately death is difficult to cover up and comes with a lot of paperwork. Now fuck off."

I smile, all white teeth, and back away toward the circle and the sound of pounding of flesh on flesh.

The crowd is a mix of upper class in my circles, upper class and legal circles I suppose, and lower class, who are mostly the fighters and what looks like bookies by the way they holler at the crowd and toss cash around.

While waiting I keep my eyes peeled for anyone I might know, or anyone I should know. Thankfully I don't recognize anyone here, but that doesn't mean there isn't someone who won't go running to my father when they discover who I am.

My attention swings back to the ring. It's small, and only delineated by an LED circle on the floor marking the boundary and lighting up the fighters in a red hazy glow.

Blood splatters back on the opponents and I can't help but stare, my adrenaline spiking, anticipation curling deep in my gut.

I spot one of the Blackthorn football players across the circle and shoot him the bird. He took down Lee in one of our games this season and all of us have had our eye on him for payback. I wonder if this will be my lucky opportunity.

His knuckles are wrapped, he's in basketball shorts and a tank top. His features are tight, and serious while I'm still in my Henley, jacket, and jeans. I don't need to change to kick his fucking ass into the hard-packed dirt.

It feels like it takes forever but eventually the guy I spoke to steps into the circle, his eyes search the crowd and when they land on me he nods, his head and waves me in. The second I step over the line the football player I'd been watching wanders into the circle with a smirk.

"What do we have here? A little far from home, aren't you Marshall?"

I shrug and study him, looking for any signs of weakness, anything that might give an edge or advantage.

"What made you decide to come and rub shoulders

with us? Doesn't daddy have more important things for you to be doing?"

I shrug off his words, while on the inside I'm seething with rage. "Daddy doesn't have shit to do, because he doesn't own me," I growl.

His eyes narrow with suspicion like he's expecting me to say more. When I don't give it to him he shifts to face me, his fists curled.

"Are we finally done talking?"

Now the lights shift brighter, and I close the distance between us. "If you want to throw the first punch, you know to make it a little more even. I won't judge you. I know you're used to taking cheap shots."

"You fuckin..." He swings and I lean back to dodge the hard right hook. All I can do is grin, taunting him. We dance around each other for a minute and I take my first shot, my fist connecting hard with his ribs.

Oh fuck the give under my knuckles is fucking satisfying.

Not as good as fucking Bel into submission or hearing her sweet moans of pleasure but pretty good. I swing again but he dances out of the way at the last second, and throws a hit of his own, this time aiming for my face. It's nothing to dodge. I'm lightning on my feet. But as I do, his other hand comes out of nowhere, and his knuckles slam hard into my cheek.

White hot fire splits up my cheekbone, radiating into my eye socket. I grit my teeth and swallow the pain down. Not the first time I've been hit, not even the tenth, and my dad hits harder anyway.

The fucker swings again and I block his hit with my

forearm, I take the opportunity to blast him in the gut and when he doubles over in pain, I pull closer, grab him by the back of the head and slam my knee into his face.

The crowd roars with life, and I release him with a shove, taking a couple of steps back. I bounce on the balls of my feet, watching as blood pours from his nose. I get distracted watching as his blood paints the dirt, and he manages to get another hit on me, this time his knuckles slam into my upper ribs.

Pain snakes up my side, and into my chest, and I do my best to hide any wincing. Can't let this fucker think he's got one up on me. We continue to beat on each other until finally he lets his guard down and I lunge forward, my fist connecting with his temple. The hit is hard enough that one moment he's standing there and the next he's out cold, his body a sack of bricks on the ground.

Well shit. My hands are throbbing, my body aches like it hasn't in a long time, but more than that the pressure on my chest is gone. The desire for blood, for pain, it's merely a distant memory now. Of course the crowd goes wild, people cheering, and rushing toward the circle. The guy who told me when to fight steps back into the circle, grabs my arm and raises it in the air signifying that I've won.

All I can do is grin. The guy releases my arm and I let it fall back down to my side, then he turns away from me, taking a stack of money from one of the bookies.

"Looks like you got what it takes, Marshall. Anytime you're looking for a fight let me know." He passes the stack of cash to me, along with a business card that he's placed on top. "Not that you need it, but here's your winnings."

He's right I don't need the cash, not at all.

Which gives me an idea... I can't change the fact that Maybel lost her mother and I wasn't there to support her but maybe I can offer her an alternative, maybe take the money and create a scholarship of some sort. I'll have plenty of time to think about that later.

"Thanks," I mumble, and take the stack, stuffing it into my pocket.

Now that the desire to destroy and hurt is tamped down I can go home, or not since I remember then that Bel is at The Mill and all it will take is one look for me to have her pinned against the wall, my cock sinking deep inside her.

Fucking hell. I run my hands through my sweaty hair, my muscles ache, and I feel like one giant ass bruise. As I look around the space I notice a makeshift bar in the back and walk over to it. Nothing a little alcohol can't fix. I'll just have one or two drinks, to numb the pain a bit. That should buy me enough time, that is unless the guys decide to take her out somewhere. I shake my head, remembering that Sebastian is there and he would never let anything happen to her. Just as I reach the bar a girl in a mini dress with her tits hanging out the top sashays over to me. I watch out of the corner of my eye as she reaches for me, and I react before I can think better of it, my hand circling her slender wrist.

"I'm not interested." I sneer, and release her wrist.

Refusing to take the hint she smiles like I've just become her favorite challenge. "I'm up for a little pain with my pleasure."

My annoyance grows, and it's a weird feeling to have. Before Bel I would've taken her up on the offer, walked her outside in the alley, fucked her until I came and walked back inside without blinking an eye. Now the thought makes my stomach churn. There's only Bel. She's ruined me for anyone else and I wouldn't have it any other way.

"I already said I'm not interested. Don't make me, *make* you disappear."

"Okay, I get it." She rolls her eyes and tosses her brown curls over her shoulder.

I let out a sigh of relief when she turns and walks away. *Finally.* There's a stack of water bottles in front of me and I snag one pressing the cold plastic to my aching cheek. That's going to fucking hurt tomorrow. A deep satisfied sensation settles in my bones. I don't feel it often, except after a brutal game, or after chasing down my little wallflower to punish her.

"Want anything?" The bartender finally notices me.

"Yeah, I'll take a rum and Coke and a couple of shots of tequila."

"You got it." He smiles, and honestly I feel he's way too happy to be working behind the bar at this place but whatever. Nothing can ruin the high I'm on.

He places the beverages down in front of me and I slam back the tequila shots right away. The burn feels so good, and warms me all over.

"Two more." I gesture to him.

He disappears again and I grab the rum and Coke taking a sip of it. My thoughts inevitably turn back to Bel. I can't fucking escape her. Even when I don't want to be thinking about her I find that's all I can do. She's more than an obsession. She's embedded in my DNA, under my skin, a part of who I am.

Removing her existence from my brain, or forgetting about her would be like forgetting who I myself am. My phone vibrates in my pocket and I tug it out looking down at the text on the screen.

FLOWER: I miss you and I hate myself for it.

THE WEIGHT of her words is almost more than I can bear. She misses me and hates herself for it. I consider firing back a text, but decide otherwise. Bel's always been a hands-on learner, and I think maybe she needs me to remind her how much I care for her.

While I'm doing my best not to fuck this up I can't push her away, or keep her at a distance without causing her harm. There's a fine line with her and I'm going to do my very best to make certain she sees how serious I am.

The bartender places the next two shots down on the bar, and I take them slinging them back like they're water. Then I grab my wallet, and toss a couple of bills down on the bar. I'm not sure if my body is up for another challenge tonight but I'm going to do it anyway.

I guess while find out if I can make it into Sebastian's fucking princess tower without getting my ass kicked or otherwise detected. If I have it my way, Bel will be stuffed full of my cock by the night's end. I need her like I need air, like I need the heart beating in my chest.

22

BEL

The scent of mint, sweat, and liquor tickles my nostrils. It wraps around me in an intoxicating haze that makes me shift backward to get closer to it.

I know who the scent belongs to: *Drew.*

It's always Drew.

The palm of his hand cups my throat gently, and I press into his hold, begging for more. Needing his touch more than I need air.

His lips trace my ear, and I shiver at the intimate caress.

"Wallflower..." he whispers, his voice rough and raw.

All I can do is moan and press my body against any piece of hardness I can find. His body, his hand, anything. I just want to touch him and feel his fingers on my skin. I don't know how to explain with words what I want or need from him.

Not that it matters. This is nothing more than a dream.

I let it pull me deeper into the darkness, where there is

nothing more than his scent and his hands on me. *Yes. It feels so good.* Another moan slips free from my lips, and his hand comes up from my throat to cover my mouth.

"Quiet, Flower."

I grind back, but he's no longer there.

Stupid dream not giving me the hard length of him to grind against.

I'm rewarded with his hand instead, as he grips my pussy through my panties. "Oh, fuck me."

I can feel my arousal swirling deep in my core, wetting my panties. I shouldn't have sent him that text earlier. It's fucking with my head, clearly. Shifting in his grasp so I can get closer, he tightens his hold on my pussy.

The pressure and sensation threaten to consume me, and I blink my eyes open with a gasp. *Oh no.* I crash back down to reality real fast, especially when I look up and see a shadowy figure looming over the bed, leaning near my waist.

Panic and fear zip through me, and all I can think is I need to get away, escape. I immediately lash out, hitting the intruder with my fists, a scream making its way up my throat.

The scream never comes, though, as Drew's blurry face swims into view, or at least what I can make out of it. He clamps a hand tight over my mouth, silencing me. Some of the fear washes away, but there's still lingering anxiety.

How did he get in here? Why does he smell like liquor?

"Shh, it's just me, Flower. I'm not going to hurt you. After your little text message, I knew I needed to come see you. I wanted to be here earlier, but I was trying to do the right thing."

All I can do is stare at him in confusion. He, of course, doesn't add any further context, nor does he lift his hand from my mouth so I can ask him what he's talking about.

"Dammit. I always tell myself I'm doing the right thing by giving you time and space, but then I'm reminded all over again how much I fucking need you the next time I see you, and how I never want to let you go."

"Are you okay?" I mumble against his hand, hoping he can make out some of the words. He gently eases his hand back, but only enough to let the words escape my lips.

"Shh, you have to be quiet. You wouldn't want to wake your brother, would you? I don't think I'll make it through another fight with him, but if you want to see me try, we can. I'd rip out my beating heart and throw it into traffic if you asked me to."

Another fight? He's speaking in riddles and even more than that he's worrying me.

I blink, trying to drag myself out of the foggy haze of sleep so I can look at him. I reach for my glasses which are on the nightstand, and slip them onto my face so I can see him properly and figure out what the hell is happening.

Once the glasses are in place, it takes another minute for my brain to make sense of what I'm seeing. I blink and blink again, but he's still standing here. *It wasn't a dream.* I nearly smile, until I notice that his stunningly handsome face is swollen, his cheek already blooming with an ugly bruise. My gaze drops down to his hands, and I notice the knuckles of both hands are red, cracked, and swollen.

"Drew! What happened?" I gasp. He gently lowers his fingers from my mouth tracing my lips before he lets his hand fall away.

"What's wrong?"

I sit up straighter, and the anxious feeling from just a little bit ago festers in my gut. I need to get him an ice pack and figure out who did this to him. My first thought is his father, but it could be anyone really.

"What happened?" I gesture to his face.

He's bruised and battered, but there's a hazy look in his eyes, reminding me of how he looks when he's relaxed. It's similar to that post-orgasm phase.

A boyish grin appears on his lips, but I don't miss the grimace of pain that pinches his features. "It's nothing. Just a few bruises. I needed to do the right thing. I was so mad, and I wanted to see you. I wanted to come here and fuck you, hurt you, but I knew if I did that I'd only be ruining whatever it is that we have left, so I did something else instead."

I fist the sheets, alarm bells ring in my head. I'm afraid to even ask if it was his father that hurt him or if it was some random person. We haven't really ever discussed his father, or the way he spoke to me. We didn't even really talk about what I witnessed that night, but now he's here, battered and bruised looking every ounce of that scared little boy I picture him to be, and I know I have to ask.

"Who did this to you? Was it your father? Because if it was..."

Drew visibly flinches, and I freeze, waiting for him to lash out, to punish me for asking, but he simply shakes his head softly and gives me one of those all-American smiles.

"What would you do, Flower? How would you protect me against the big bad wolf?"

I shrug my shoulders. "I don't know. I'd find a way to

protect you." I realize I've spoken the words out loud, and now there's no taking them back.

"I love your protectiveness, Bel, and that you'd go to war for me even when knowing it's a losing battle."

"It's only a losing battle if you don't try. If you fight back, there's always the chance of winning."

His green eyes shine with adoration, and my heart clenches inside my chest. Every time we're together, he pulls us closer, stitching up the pieces of my soul that he tore to shreds that night.

"It wasn't my father, so stop your worrying. I did this to myself," he jeers with disgust. "None of it matters. I came here to see you, because I had to see you. Had to prove to you that I still care, that even if I wasn't there at The Mill tonight, it doesn't mean that I didn't want to see you."

I'm grateful for his confession. Sometimes Drew can be difficult to read and understand, but from the sounds of it, he was trying to do the right thing, whatever that was. Leaning over, he forces me to lay flat against his upper body, my own legs resting over the side of the bed.

"I had to see you," he repeats, inching closer to nuzzle against my neck.

I'm tempted to ask him why he would ever do something like that to himself but the thought evaporates when I feel his wet tongue against my skin. He alternates between kissing, sucking, and nipping at the sensitive flesh along my throat and collarbone.

I wiggle to get closer to him, to feel the heat of him against me, but he's still fully dressed and the blanket between us is ruining the mood.

I need more. More of him. All of him.

Frustration wins, and I toss the blanket away, and the cold air of the room raises goose bumps on my bare legs.

"Come here," I whine. "I need you closer."

I can practically feel his lips curving into a smile on my skin. "I've been fighting against myself for days. I've wanted to see you, to touch you, but I was afraid I'd hurt you again. The darkness and anger are too close to the surface right now, and I'm trying to do the right thing with you, Bel. I can't use you as a punching bag if I want to keep you by my side, but it's terrifying because you're also the only thing that has the power to calm me."

He pulls back, his hands trailing up my neck, stopping at my cheeks. He cups them and pulls me closer, so our noses are almost touching. "It's like there's so much noise in my head, the voices scream, telling me to let go, to unleash hell, but then you touch me, and everything goes quiet. It's unexplainable. You quiet the demons. In your presence, there are little fragments of light that slice through the darkness, giving me guidance, and at those moments, I think maybe I can be saved. Maybe I can do this. If I can keep the only person who helps me to think instead of acting out by my side. My only hope is that I can protect you from all the bad in my life, including myself."

I can't blink back the tears fast enough, and a few slip free, cascading down my cheeks. Drew's eyes follow the tears before he swipes them away with his thumbs.

"Shhh, don't cry, Flower. I've made you cry enough. The only time I want to see tears in your eyes is when you're choking on my cock."

A bubble of laughter escapes me. "Only you could say

something so sweet and poetic and ruin it in the next sentence with something sexual and vulgar."

The smile he gives me is breathtaking, and I wish I had a camera so I could take a picture of the handsome but incredibly broken man before me.

"What did you expect? A gentleman? Sorry, baby, but no amount of hits to the head would ever convince me to be that way. Plus, you like me like this. You like me being the villain in the story because no one plays the good girl quite as well as you."

"I'm not always a good girl." I grin, feeling feverish.

"Oh I know. You're bad, really fucking bad. My dirty girl. But only for me. It's only me who gets to see you like this. Only me who gets you so wet and horny you can't think straight."

There's a dark husky whisper to his tone that makes me squeeze my thighs together to try to alleviate my need. "Tell me, are you already wet for me? Is that pretty pussy waiting for me to fill it up?"

I clench my thighs again and gulp. "Yes, I need you."

He leans down and nips my bottom lip with his teeth. "My Bel. My beautiful Bel."

The small pain arouses me further, and I reach for him. I sink my hands into his shirt, fisting it, pulling him closer. I *need him closer. I need him inside me.* His absence this evening when I was with his friends made me feel empty, even if I was nervous about seeing him again. Uncertainty and fear of our fragile connection breaking makes me anxious. I want to be with him, but I'm also afraid of being hurt again.

"The only thing that matters to me is you. Keeping you

safe, and protecting you. That's all that matters, you know that right?"

The urgency and fear in his voice makes me pause and I pull back to look at him. "Are you okay, Drew?"

He gives me a sad smile. "Of course, I'm just terrified of losing you. Terrified that I won't be able to protect you. I can't let anything happen to you again. I don't care about anything else. Not about my father or Sebastian. Fuck them all. It's just me and you, Flower."

I'm left even more confused by his riddles, but he finds a way to pull me back in, dragging me down into the dark waters of lust. He's both the life vest that's trying to save me and the wave that's trying to pull me under. His hand snakes around to the back of my head, and I feel his fingers there, tracking the scar that's now forming.

"I never meant for this to happen. I didn't know you were going to fall, and even though I can't go back in time, I'll spend every day making sure you know how much I care about you."

Slowly things start to make sense to me. Remorse, guilt. He's sorry, and this is his way of saying it. I won't lie, it makes me feel cherished and cared for that he's apologizing and trying to own up to his mistakes.

"Shhh, it's okay. I know you want to keep me safe and that you didn't mean for any of those things to happen. I understand that, but for it to be me and you against the world, you must trust me. You have to let me in. We aren't a team if you're trying to fight everything on your own." Some of the sensual haze recedes, and I can look into his beautiful green eyes. "You get that right? Telling me nothing and that it's for my own good does nothing to help me. Worst of all, it does nothing to prepare me for the real threats."

"It's my job to stand between you and threats. Let me fix things, please." His voice is a whisper now as he searches my eyes for something that I can't quite pinpoint. "Let me show you what you mean to me. I can't lose you, Bel. Not after losing everything else. Not after..." He breaks off, and I wait but he doesn't fill in the blanks. "Let me make it up to you. Let me show you what you mean to me."

Those sinfully rough hands of his roam my body, stopping when they reach my ass, which he grips through my sleep shorts.

"Is that your plan then? Death by orgasm and I will follow you willingly into the dark."

He chuckles. "If that's what it takes then I'll do it. It'll be a hardship but I'll take one for the team."

Sobering, I meet his eyes. "I have to know we are in this together. When you hurt me, I lost my mother, my best friend, everything that means anything to me, and I needed you."

He drops his eyes to my mouth, then lower. "I know. Fuck do I know. I'm sorry, Bel. I never wanted to hurt you. Not ever. It was all to keep you safe. It doesn't make it right, and I hate that I wasn't there for you, but I am now. I'm here now. Forever."

I lean up to press my forehead to his. "I need to know we are in this together. That you aren't going to push me away again for my own good."

He shakes his head, rolling his forehead into mine. "I'm done running. If we can fix this, I'm done running. I can't think of anyone but you, always you."

He nips my lips with his teeth, and my lips part on their own admission. His tongue caresses mine, stroking it, and soon he's owning me, deepening the kiss until I'm dizzy and breathless when he lifts his lips.

I'm damn near panting when he pulls away. *Dammit. I'm so fucked right now.* I can't say no to him especially when he's like this, so sweet and present with me.

"Tell me that you believe me?"

I blink up at him. "Believe you?"

"Yes, do you believe me when I say that I can't lose you. That I'm in this with you till the end."

I nod against the raw need in his tone. If this is what he needs and will help him and bring us closer together, I'll do anything.

"Fuck, Flower, you're so perfect. I don't deserve you. I know that but I'm too selfish of an asshole to give you up. I'll never give you up, never again."

His touch, his words, they cut me open, making me want to give into the temptation and throw caution to the wind, because when it comes to Drew I'm helpless.

"What do you want?" I whisper.

"You," he says against my lips. "Only you."

His lips are on mine again, and I feel his fingers dig into my cheeks, guiding me, bending me to his will. There's an urgency to his touch, a desperation that we both feel. I'm consumed by his kiss, and I let him ravage me, own me.

Home. Drew is my home. My solace, my escape. At least, I think I want him to be. I curl my hands up and thread them through his dark hair. The nape of his neck is damp with sweat but I don't care. I just need him close, as close as possible.

He pulls away, breaking the kiss, and I whine in disapproval but then he nips a line down my jaw and neck. I'm shivering and writhing against his body by the time he reaches my collarbone. With a growl against my skin, his lips move over my collarbone, and when he's reached my T-shirt, he grabs the edge of it and rips it to the side, continuing his assault on me. The sensation tingles down my spine, and I clutch him to my chest.

"Drew, please."

"Tell me what you need."

"You."

"Do you? How badly do you want my cock, baby? Bad enough that you're willing to do anything I tell you to?" He leans back this time and slowly eases me into a sitting position.

I nod because I'll agree to whatever he wants as long as he doesn't stop. With a smile, he lifts me off the bed and places me on the floor. For a moment, all I can do is look up at him in confusion.

The floor beneath my thighs is cold, and I yelp, arranging my legs so I can get used to the chill quicker. Staring up at his knees and further to see the hard length of him outlined in his jeans, I try to ignore the pulsing in my core, along with the way my mouth waters. He wants my lips on his cock. I lean forward, reaching for his fly, but he shakes his head and grabs my hand, stopping me.

"Not yet. You get my cock when I give it to you, and you haven't earned it yet, so if you want it, you'll have to be a good girl and do what you're told. Can you do that?"

His hard gaze penetrates the dark crevices of my mind that only he can reach. The places where I submit to him, give in to his pleasure and pain. His commanding voice reminds me of the Drew that stalked me in the library. The Drew I choose to give control over to.

Gently, he brushes strands of hair away from my face, then without warning, he sinks his fingers into my hair. Shivers wrack my body, and when he tightens his grip, a burn of pain ripples across my scalp, but the kiss of pain leads to a promise of pleasure. He tips my head back, and I let myself go, melting into his touch, into his hold.

"Yes," I hiss out. "Yes."

He smirks. "Good, because you know if you're a good girl I'll reward you, won't I?"

I wiggle, and he jerks his chin up. "Shorts and panties off. Scoot forward, and put that pretty pussy on my boot."

"What?" I squeak, taken aback by his demand.

"You heard me, Flower. I want you to ride my boot, to make yourself come."

I'm tempted to say no, tempted to tell him that's disgusting but also insanely hot. I do neither of those things, because I'm certain my brain would short-circuit right now if I didn't get the opportunity to come. Releasing me, he watches through hooded eyes as I shimmy out of my shorts and panties.

Once I sink back down to the floor, naked from the waist down, he pounces on me, his hand spearing back through the locks again. Shifting forward, I maneuver my knees on either side of his foot. I hesitate for a moment, wondering if I'm really going to do this.

"Mmm...good girl," he praises and guides my head with

his fingers. I let myself go limp in his grasp wanting to give into the pleasure.

"Don't be shy. Use it. Ride it. And once your pussy is ready for me. I'll fuck you until I make you come so hard you see stars."

The hammering of my heartbeat echoes in my ears, while my brain tries to cut into the haze, whispering this might be wrong, but my body is full steam ahead. I'm already moving as my brain tries to shift focus. I lean up to roll my hips over the tip of his boot, and in return, he lifts it gently to provide counterpressure.

"Drew…" I moan, unsure of what I should do.

I know he wants me to ride his boot, but I can't help but feel it's wrong. His grip on my hair becomes painful, and I let out a hiss as he jerks my head back, his dark gaze piercing deep into my soul.

"Be a good girl, Bel. Ride my boot until that pretty pussy is messy with arousal and desperate with need, and I'll reward you with my cock."

All I can do is give in to the pleasure.

23

DREW

I'd never seen anything so beautiful in my life as her riding my boot, wetting me with her pretty little pussy. "Jesus Christ, you look so beautiful like this, at my mercy, desperate for me to fill your pussy with my thick cock."

A whimper escapes her, her white teeth sinking into her bottom lip as I tighten my grip on her golden strands. "A little more, Flower. I want to see your juices drip over the sides of my boot before I take you. Get yourself nice and wet so I can slide into you without effort."

Another cute little whimper greets me and I choose to reward her, angling my foot in a way that puts the laces in direct contact with her swollen clit.

Her pouty lips part, and a gasp escapes them when I make contact. I readjust my cock that's painfully pressing against my fly. In just a minute I'll sink inside her wet heat but not yet. Not until she's begging me for it.

This is for her. All for her.

I know exactly what she needs, and how she needs it.

Hard. Brutal. Punishing. Destroying her inch by inch.

"Ride my fucking boot, Flower. More. Spread your legs, and flatten your pussy against my boot."

My encouraging words make her move a little faster, her center grinding harder against the edge of my boot, sending her knees out wider with each movement, like butterfly wings. Fuck she's stunning like this. Her pupils dilated and rimmed with lust, her lips parted, her cheeks rosy with desire, her chest rising and falling rapidly.

She's chasing a high that only I can give her.

"Oh god..." she pants, and I sink my fingers into her hair, tugging hard as I angle her head back, forcing her to look into my eyes.

"Not God, Flower. Drew. Drew fucking Marshall." I nip at her lips.

"Drew," she purrs, correcting herself.

"Good girl," I praise, and tighten my grip watching as she works herself closer and closer to the edge. "You're doing such a good job, Bel. So wet, so fucking perfect."

Her tiny hands grip onto me like I'm an anchor, the only thing capable of keeping her in place at the moment. I love how vulnerable she becomes when her need for pleasure overrides everything else. When her desperation for me consumes her. She has no idea how much it turns me on to see her like this.

Leaning closer, I trail my nose against her throat. The combination of the scents fills my nostrils and zings straight to my cock.

"Are you ready to be fucked?"

"Mhm. I'm ready." She gasps, as I tug on her hair harder.

"What? I didn't hear you," I growl, my own control on the fringe.

I want to be gentle with her. I want to give her what I never could before, but it's harder than I expected. Both because gentle isn't who I am, and because deep down it's not what Bel really wants.

"Please... please... I want your cock," she begs, her green eyes bright with lust.

I shake my head and bring my lips to hers. So close they're almost touching.

"Not good enough. Say it again. Convince me, prove to me how desperate you are for my cock."

Her eyes flutter closed and then open again. "Please, Drew. I need you inside me, filling me up. Please. I'm so empty."

I nip at her bottom lip gently. "Oh, you beg so prettily. How could I ever deny you what you need when you ask me like that? Sit back. Let me see your work."

I release my hold on her hair and watch as she shifts backward, resting on her calves.

There's a little dark mark on my leather boot top, a tiny line rolling over the side. I lick my lips and smile at her. "Perfect, so good, Bel."

She shifts again, and I grasp her around the waist to lift her onto my lap. Her hands thread around my neck, and I plant her right over my dick, which is still trapped in my pants. Immediately, she grinds against me, and I clamp down hard on her hips.

"Not until I'm ready," I snap.

She freezes her fingers tightening around the back of my neck. When I'm sure she's not going to move, I uncurl her hands and peel her shirt off, tossing it to the floor. I can't make my eyes move fast enough. It's like I'm seeing her for the first time all over again.

Creamy white skin. Dusky pink nipples. Tits that are just the perfect size, and a slim belly that leads down to her bare, clean pussy. *My pussy.* She's baring her sweet little body to me.

Fuck.

I ease my hands down the curve of her waist, then back up to weigh her breasts in my hands, kneading them, my thumbs rolling over the pebbled nipples.

Greedily, she presses into my touch, her shoulders sliding back as if she can't do anything but orbit me. I am her sun and moon, and she is my entire fucking universe.

My mouth waters, my hands shaking, trembling as if it's my first time fucking someone. I'd be embarrassed, but there's no need to be embarrassed, not with Bel in my arms.

I slide my hands down her smooth belly and grasp her hips again. She anchors her hands on my shoulders this time.

"Fuck, Flower. I've missed you."

I gently ease her to her feet and catch her elbows when she wobbles, leaning toward me.

"Shhh...if you want my cock, you have to be real quiet."

She nods her head eagerly as if she understands the repercussions.

I quickly lean down to unlace my boots, then shuck my pants, as well as shirt, and stand before her naked. It occurs to me that this might be the first time we've both been naked together. So many times we've peeled off the necessary clothing, but we haven't done this. And even now we have to be quiet or risk Seb's wrath.

Bel whimpers, her eyes raking me from head to toe. Bruises mar my ribs and my face, but she doesn't seem to care as she stares, her mouth wet from biting her lip.

"Come here." I tug her close and grab her soaked panties off the floor.

She steps into my arms with zero hesitation and something in my chest eases with her trust. And I plan to ensure she gets everything she doesn't even know she needs yet.

I hold out the panties that are curled in my fingers and fist her hips to lead her over to the full-length mirror by her bathroom door.

Her eyes go a little wider, a little clearer. "What..."

I press my fingers to her lips. "Remember we have to be quiet."

She blinks and nods. When she opens her mouth to speak again I raise the balled up panties, and press them into her mouth. Her forehead wrinkles in confusion, but she opens wider as I shove them a bit deeper, muffling the noise she makes.

"It's the only way I don't get murdered by your brother tonight, Flower. I know how vocal you can get and I plan to make up for lost time."

I slip a hand down her belly and cup her pussy, slipping one finger inside. She greets me with a moan. Her pussy is so warm and wet that I swear I feel my cock leaking pre-cum. Pulling my finger out of her I grip her by the waist and turn her to face the mirror then slide my hands up to hers and place them flat on the glass.

Leaning into her ear, I whisper. "Look at how beautiful you are while I fuck you."

I knock my knee between her thighs to spread her open and thank all the gods for the squats I have to do for the team because it gives me the strength I need to get the right angle to slide my hard dick along her seam. So wet.

I grip her right thigh and raise it slightly so I can enter her a little easier. It earns me a muffled whimper and I smirk at her in the mirror.

I grit my teeth. The desire to rut into her is consuming but I slowly breach her center and slide into that hot wet sheath. *Fucking hell.* I press deeper, the heat of her gripping me tighter the deeper I go. Her knees are shaking now and I whisper.

"Fuck, you feel so good. Always so good."

When I'm all the way inside her, my balls tucked against her round little ass, I press on her back, folding her forward enough to give me the angle I want. Her hands slide down the mirror, leaving fingerprints on the glass in a straight line.

I slowly ease out of her, watching my cock glisten in the low light of the room. Then I ease back inside, marveling in the way she clenches around me.

She murmurs something, and I grin, pulling her in tight and shoving her away, picking up a brutal pace. "You like it when it hurts, don't you? You want me to abuse your pussy, use her until there's nothing left, until she's swollen and full of my cum, don't you?"

She mumbles something else, and I lose myself to the

feel of her soft skin, the scent of her body, and the way she fucks back against me, slamming her body into mine.

"Nuh-uh, my pace," I growl low.

She stills, and I reward her with a little strum on her clit that makes her knees knock together.

"You'll come first. Then you'll come again, and again until I'm satisfied," I whisper then I pull her forward, and press her face against the glass, my cock slamming deep inside her touching her G-spot. She lets out a muffled scream which I'm unsure if it's from pleasure or pain with how deep I am inside her.

I decide to see how far she lets me take it, knowing that if I'm really hurting her she'll tell me to stop. I press my chest against her, and thrust up, watching as her eyes roll to the back of her head, her tiny toes curling into the carpet.

"Look at what you do to me, to us. Look at how perfectly imperfect we are, baby. How well you take my cock inside your pussy? My dirty girl. Fuck I'm going to fill all your holes with my come just so I can watch it drip out of you."

She whimpers, clutching onto me with one hand while she presses her other hand to the mirror. Reaching around, I thumb her clit again, and she shatters, her muscles pulsing around my cock, making it hard for me to continue moving inside her. I grit my teeth until she finishes, her knees shaking, threatening to give out on her.

Gently, I ease out of her and tug her tight into me, then lift her and carry her over to the bed. "I hope you don't think that's the end of it. I haven't even filled you with my cum yet."

I lay her on the edge of the mattress and shove the makeshift gag deeper into her mouth, then I spread her thighs and slam into her still slick and clenching pussy.

Her hips bow off the bed, and I swear she sucks me deeper. I set a brutal pace, sliding in and out of her, listening to the sounds our bodies make as we come together. I'm not ready for this to end yet so once again I grit my teeth and fuck her harder, faster. Her green eyes flash with lust and hazy pleasure and her tiny nails sink into my thigh muscles.

When she shivers, shaking, so close to coming again I reach down and slap her clit hard. The second time she shatters around my cock, she muffles a scream into the gag, and I close my eyes so close to coming I see lights flashing behind my eyelids.

Not. Fucking. Yet.

I ease her down and pull out, my cock dripping with her juices and pre-cum, the streaks trail down the side of my cock. She reaches for me, and I grab her hips and roll her over onto her belly. Instantly, she lifts her hips, waiting, ready for me. I take a moment to pet her ass, running my hands over her curves, relearning the way she feels under me.

She wiggles back against me, and I slap her ass gently, not hard enough so it makes a noise, but enough that she whimpers again. *So fucking cute.*

When I can't hold back any longer, I situate myself behind her, and I feed my cock back inside her. When she relaxes slightly, I slam inside her again, earning a grunt this time.

I'm not going to hold out much longer. I ease out of her

tight heat and back inside, loving the way her body cups around mine. Like she is fucking made for me.

She mumbles something, and I reach up to tug the underwear out of her mouth. "What's that, Flower?"

"Please. You're killing me," she whispers.

I smile and lean forward to pull her against me, her back to my front. "Then let me put you out of your misery."

I clasp my hand over her lips and set a brutal pace as I fuck up inside her, using her body and gravity to chase my release.

A groan slips out of me, and I press my mouth to the curve of her shoulder and bite down to stifle my next groan, as I come hard, rutting deep inside her. She joins me with no prompting whatsoever, her trembling channel sucking the life out of my balls. Milking me until my knees shake and I freeze, panting, waiting to come down from the edge.

I ease my hand away from her mouth, wet from her lips and the condensation of her breath.

She moans and her head falls forward. "Please tell me you're done. I don't think I can take any more."

I chuckle and gently lay her on the bed. She crawls up to the covers, her thighs slick and shiny with my cum.

"Not so fast..." I growl, this possessiveness taking root inside of my chest. She pauses and turns back to me. "Come here, place your ass on the edge of the bed, legs spread. I want to see the mess I made."

I swear her cheeks have grown redder, but I'm not sure why she cares when she just let me fuck her against every object in her room. Following my instructions, she slowly eases her thighs apart, and I look down at her pretty cunt marked with my release.

I can't help myself. Her clit is swollen, her pussy pink and raw from the brutal fucking I gave it. I look from her pussy and up to Bel's face, noticing that she's watching me with both awe and curiosity.

"I've made a mess of your pussy, but worse than that, my cum is leaking out of you and onto the floor. That's not where it's supposed to go, Flower. It needs to be inside you."

I gather some of the cum up off the inside of her thigh and shove it back inside her. Her teeth sink into her bottom lip as she stifles a moan from the friction. All I can do is smile while I fuck the cum back into her pussy with two fingers, loving the slippery, slurping sounds her body makes as I force my essence back inside her.

"Keep it inside you. That's where it belongs, because someday when I'm ready to share you I'll stuff you to the brim with my cum, making certain you can't escape pregnancy."

"That sounds very psychotic," she groans.

"Baby, I'm absolutely fucking crazy for you," I whisper against her lips, and press those two fingers against her G-spot, while rubbing circles against her clit with my thumb. It takes literal seconds for her eyes to roll to the back of her head and her body to explode.

Once I've made her come a fourth time I press a soft kiss to her mound and crawl up onto the bed dragging her with me, my bruised ribs protesting the entire way.

Her brow furrows as she watches me. "You're staying?"

"For a little bit, yes. Until you're asleep."

She snuggles against me and when my own eyes start to grow heavy and I hear her soft snoring I ease out of the bed, head to the bathroom for a wet cloth, and return to her. She barely rouses when I clean her gently. I marvel at the fingerprint bruises on her hips, and the teeth marks I've left on her throat. *Mine.*

I clean myself, and then redress. Everything in me says to stay with her, but I know I can't. Things aren't settled with Sebastian and my knuckles can't handle another fight tonight.

My lip burns and I brush my finger over the split skin. Then grab another cloth to clean my face up before I have to head out. No doubt I'm going to scare the ride app folks with the bruises already dotting my face.

I crouch next to the bed and brush the golden strands out of her face. "Sleep well, Flower."

Then I slip out through the window and head back to The Mill, leaving what I fear is my heart behind in that bed.

24

BEL

It's been a week since I saw him in person even though he's been texting me every day. A week since he unmade me with his body and left me to sleep it off. I'd woken the next morning feeling sore and sated in a way I hadn't been in a long time.

Even now, so many days later, I get hot all over again just thinking about him and what he does to me. As if he can tell I'm thinking about him, my phone buzzes on my nightstand. I snatch it up and check the text.

Psycho: I'm bored. Wish I was with you.

Me: Sorry, but I doubt it. I'm in dress-picking hell.

He shoots a text back just as fast.

Psycho: Send me a picture, and I'll help you choose. Though I'd prefer if the dress was on the floor instead.

I stare down at my bed and then take a seat on the edge while I type out my response.

Me: Of course you would. I'll send a picture when I figure out which one I want to wear.

His reply is almost instant.

Psycho: You better, or else. ;)

In my mind, I can see the crease in his brow and the sexy mix of arrogance and mirth in his grin. I'm tempted to send another text, but instead, I slide the phone back onto my nightstand. I assume he'll be at the meeting tonight, so I'm excited to see him.

I'd love to sit here and flirt with him all day, but he still hasn't responded to my all-or-nothing request. I let him have me in every way he wanted, but I'm still not sure I can let him all the way in yet. The fear of having my heart broken all over again is paralyzing.

I shift to look at the line of dresses across the end of my bed. All sent by Sebastian for the party tonight. Well, one of them will be, if he has his way. I stare at the ruffles and trains of materials I'm not so sure of. Not a single one of them is my style, and they all scream...frilly in my opinion. Which makes no sense because he's usually meticulous with his style, and what he picked out for me after I moved in was all perfect too.

These dresses scream...*innocence.* Like he's trying to label me as something I'm not. And as I stare at the shimmering fabrics I'm not entirely sure I appreciate it. Him trying to label me, or dress me like some Mafia Barbie.

I tug my robe tighter around my waist and furtively ignore my phone still not announcing a text from Drew. *Dammit.* I can spend five minutes not thinking about him.

I sigh and stand, skirting the end of the bed to stare at the dresses from another angle. Is this normal for these kinds of meetings?

One of the dresses is pink with tiered frills. One is

lavender, one is strapless, and ends in a sweeping train. The other looks like a bridesmaid's worst nightmare. *That's for sure going to Goodwill.* Out of nowhere, the door to my bedroom opens, and I freeze as a woman walks in carrying a stack of towels. She stops dead in her tracks, spotting me.

"Oh my God, I'm so sorry. I thought you were still out."

The horror on her face makes me feel uneasy. Does she think she's in trouble? I push the thought away and give her a smile. She's wearing the usual uniform staff wear, a black button-down shirt and a pair of khaki pants. Her dark hair is tied back in a tight braid and the overhead lighting catches a smattering of freckles across the bridge of her nose and cheeks. I can't pinpoint it but I feel like I've met her before.

I tilt my head to the side as if looking at her from a different angle will help me recognize her.

"Have we met before?"

She shuffles the towels between her hands, and I rush over to help her. When she waves me off and carries the stack into the bathroom, I wait by the bed.

Returning, she smooths her hand down her pants. "Sorry about that. Yeah, we actually might have met. I attend Oakmount."

I snap my fingers and grin. "That's right. I knew I'd seen you at the library a time or two."

She blushes, ducking her chin as if she's embarrassed. "Yeah. I'm just working here to earn money for school."

I chuckle and wave around the room. "It doesn't look like it now, but a few months ago, I understood that all too well."

She nods, no doubt having heard about how my life

has changed, along with everyone else on campus. "I'm sorry to hear about your mom."

I give her a smile and nod. "Thank you. I miss her so much."

She clutches her chest. "I can't imagine. Family is everything to me, and I don't know what I'd do if I lost my mother. She's actually the one who helped me get this job."

I sigh and smile even though I don't feel it, my eyes shifting back to the dresses on the bed. "Since you're here, and I could definitely use the advice of another woman, can you give me your opinion? What do you think of these?"

She steps beside me and peers down at the dresses, a frown twisting her lips. "Well, they are...pretty."

I nod. "Yeah, pretty is right, but would you wear any of them?"

She shakes her head. "Honestly, no. I mean...they are pretty, but like for a sixteen-year-old maybe?"

Yes. That's it. Pretty but far too young for me. They look like the type of dresses that belong at a high school home-coming dance, not for a sophisticated adult event like the one we are about to attend.

There's a noise at the door, and the girl glances up almost anxiously. "I should get back to work. Good luck picking a dress. If it isn't too late, maybe you can order something else?"

I check the clock beside the bed. Not too late, but it'll be pricey. I nod at her and give her a wave as she heads out the door. She gently closes it behind her. When the door closes, a thought occurs to me, and I rush over to yank it open.

"Hey. Did you want to maybe hang out sometime?"

She stops by her cart and glances back. "Oh yeah, I mean, sure, if you think it wouldn't be a problem."

It takes me a minute to realize what she means. If it will affect her job here.

"Oh no, it'll be fine. I'll talk to you later. Elyse, right? You know my name by now, for sure."

"Yes, and I'm looking forward to it." She smiles, and I disappear back into my room, closing the door behind me. First things first, I need to find another dress to wear, because these are just not going to cut it. I grab my laptop off the dresser, settle it on my lap, and open it.

I head to Google and search for local dress stores near me. *Ellen's Boutique* pops up as one of the results, and I navigate to the page. It takes me a total of ten minutes to find a different dress, and I hit the order button, paying extra for delivery. Then I place the laptop on my pillow and leave it open just in case they email back. I'm so full of joy and happiness it doesn't feel like anything can ruin today for me.

While I wait for the dress, I go into the bathroom and prepare for the party. My usual messy bun and mascara aren't going to cut it for this event. I need to be presentable, mature. I take my time putting in my contacts, curling my hair, and smoking out my eyeliner.

A knock on my door startles me, and then I remember my dress. One of the kitchen staff lays it out in the bag across my bed.

"Thanks," I call, as I finish my makeup, slicking on a swipe of bright red lipstick. I smile happily once I'm finished and head back into the bedroom, unzipping the bag to get a look at the dress.

Perfect.

I tug out the black dress and gather it up so I can step into it. The cap sleeves fit over my shoulders perfectly, and I zip the back easily, then the side. The skirt is full with a slit that goes up over my knee. The back is fully open, exposing my skin. The front is the only part of the dress that is fully covered, and the sleeves cutting triangles across my shoulder blades across the back are the only connections between the front and back.

It's sexy and sophisticated, and I wonder if I'll see Drew tonight in this dress and what he'll do when he sees me. I finally give in to the urge and grab my phone off the bedside table again. I missed a text while I was getting ready.

Psycho: I miss you. Where is my picture, Flower? You have five minutes or I'm taking your ass again, and this time I won't be sweet.

Those three words make my heart squeeze in my chest. I angle my foot out of my dress so the slit slides open around my thigh, then snap a picture and send it to him. I don't have time to sit and wait for him to respond. Sebastian will be waiting for me to make my grand appearance so we can get ready to leave. I quickly add a simple bracelet and grab a clutch from the closet to stash my cell phone in.

The strands of my long blond hair brush my bare waist, tickling me as I walk down the stairs to meet Seb. He's standing by the front door dressed perfectly in his tuxedo.

The smile on his lips slips when he catches sight of me. "Uh, Bel, I did not pick out that dress."

I grin back at him. "I know. I did. The dresses you picked out were pretty, but they were for a sister, a *little* sister. And while I'm your little sister, I'm also a grown-ass woman. None of them felt like me."

His forehead furrows, and he stalks around me in a circle. Pausing, he curses. "You can't wear that."

"And why is that?"

Casually, he slips his hands into his pockets and stares down at the floor for a second as if trying to gather his thoughts. "You look like..."

"Like..."

"Prey."

I blink slowly, so slowly I'm pretty sure my eyes close.

"I understand your hesitation, Sebastian, but this dress is me. I'm not hiding, not anymore. I'm going to walk into this meeting with my head held high. I don't care if anyone sees me as prey. They will learn real fast that I'm not to be messed with."

He smirks, and I pin him with a glare. "What?"

"Not a damn thing. You just find a way to shock me over and over again."

"Good. I can't have people anticipating my next move." I grin.

"Nope, let's go."

He extends his arm out to me, and I take it, slipping my own into his letting him lead me to the car waiting for us. I'm grateful for it because I might look like I have it together, but I'm pretty close to falling in these dangerously high heels.

Sebastian holds the car door open for me, and I slide inside. As soon as I'm secure, he closes the door and jogs around to enter the other side, taking the seat beside me. I fidget with my hands, staring straight ahead.

We ride in silence most of the way, but as we get closer, he shifts to look at me.

"It's very important that you stay near me and as close to me as possible. I'm wary about this entire event, and I can't protect you if I don't know where you are."

I nod. "No worries, captain. I'll be right at your side the whole night. Plus, I don't know anyone who will be at this party or meeting. It's not like I'd leave the one person I do know to mingle with people I don't. That's the first rule of being an introvert. Everyone knows that."

"You're such a nerd." Sebastian smirks and shakes his head.

The car slows, and the anxious knot in my belly tightens. We turn right, and I peer out the window, noticing that we've pulled up to a gate. *Not surprising.* Rich people and their fences. Sebastian rolls his window down and hands his invitation to the guard posted outside the gate.

Once the guard waves us inside, the car eases up a long driveway, and I swear my eyes bulge out of my head when the massive fucking mansion comes into view. There's a line of cars waiting for valet, and we wait with them, because why not.

When it's our turn, a valet opens my door and helps me out.

"Welcome to the Marshall estate."

I nod and smile, then my smile slips, and I glance

anxiously at Seb. "Did he just say Marshall? I knew his dad was hosting it, but I didn't think it would be at his house!"

Sebastian isn't paying attention to me, though. He is texting furiously on his phone. I feel bad for whoever is on the receiving end of that message. He's still pounding on the keys when his phone rings.

With a sigh of frustration, he gives me a remorseful look. "Give me a moment." He hits the button and steps away speaking quickly in French.

My high school French is rusty, but I catch a few curse words in the mix. Even so, I can't focus on it because the name Marshall rings in my head like a bell. Had Sebastian told me this party was at Drew's family home? *I don't think so*. Why hadn't Drew told me about it either when I just saw him a few days ago?

Shit. Everything comes raining down on me at once. Am I even ready to see Drew's dad again? I monitor Seb, silently urging him to hurry the hell up on his call. But he only talks faster and moves farther away. So much for making me stay near his side all night.

I look between Sebastian and the front of the house. This strange feeling of being full, content encompasses me. *I can do this.* Turning my attention back to the house, I lift my head, and start up the stairs alone.

I'm no one's fucking punching bag.

Not Drew's, not his dad's. *No one's.*

I square my shoulders and make it to the wide-open double doors. With an exhale, I make the choice that it's time to start this new life properly, by facing down the end of my old one.

25

DREW

Five minutes in and I already want to rip this bow tie off and get out of this penguin suit. While I'd love to skip this party, my father made it clear I better show my face. Since I wanted to check on Mom, I decided to show up and not poke the bear. At least not tonight when he'll be his most volatile.

But the second I arrived at the house, I got dragged into the preparations. My father, as usual, is nowhere to be found until the drinks start circling, or there's someone's money to steal.

I do what I can with zero knowledge, and when my phone pings another text from Bel, I tug my phone from my pocket and duck into the kitchen for a moment of privacy.

It takes a second for my phone to pick up the Wi-Fi and then the picture to load. I smile at the long, sexy line of her leg in a dress. She never wears a dress. It frames her thigh down to the black heels on her feet. What the hell is she doing in heels?

One of the kitchen staff finds me hiding to get the decision on some wine. It all tastes like shit to me, so I just point at one of the bottles and say use the most expensive one. If only to fuck with that asshole and cost him more money.

My mind stays stuck on Bel's leg. *Oh fuck*. No. Seb and I talked about this, or rather argued about it. There's no way in hell Bel should be coming to this fucking meeting.

I rush out of the kitchen toward the foyer. Maybe I can intercept them before they arrive and talk Seb out of it. It'll piss Bel off, but I don't want my wallflower anywhere near these assholes. Not after what happened last time.

People are already arriving by the time I make it out to the foyer. I slow my pace, nodding back to those who acknowledge me. Lots of bodyguards mill around. Most of them are tall with wide shoulders and bulky suit jackets practically advertising their weapons. I have to squeeze through the door around several arrivals.

I make it to the driveway just in time to watch Bel step out of Seb's car. *Fuck.*

The valet helps her to her feet, and I shove forward, intent on getting there. I don't even want this asshole touching her. But she's already free, her gaze over her shoulder and focused on Sebastian, who's talking on his phone near the trunk of the car.

I cut across the lit-up entry and glare at the valet boy, telling him with my eyes to get the fuck out of my way. He skitters around the door while Seb's driver pulls the car away. She hasn't noticed me yet, thankfully, so I take that moment to look at her.

I suck a tight breath into my lungs. *Fucking hell.* She is stunning.

Her stunning blond hair hangs around her waist in long curls, shiny and perfect.

Her bright green eyes pop even more when outlined with makeup and her lips. Damn, I want that red lipstick smeared on my cock.

She turns, giving everyone a smile that slowly dims when she notices me standing there. I take a step forward, slipping my hands into my pockets.

"I'd ask what you're doing here, but I think I already know."

She blinks slowly, and I realize how shitty that sounds only after I've said it. "In case it wasn't obvious, I'm here representing my family."

I narrow my eyes, my own anger flaring. I'm not mad at her. I'm mad at Sebastian for dragging her into the fucking lion's den.

"What's going on?" Sebastian's deep voice fills my ears as he ends the call and walks toward us.

"Really? I thought we talked about this. I told you I didn't want her at this thing. She doesn't belong here. She doesn't belong in this world."

Sebastian's features turn indifferent as he slips on the mask of business. His eyes are cold and dark. It's the same look he's given me for weeks now and doesn't do shit to sway me. I'm not scared of him.

"Thank you for sharing your opinion on what you believe is right for my family," he says, his tone as cold as his gaze. "But I don't give a fuck what you want, Marshall. The only person who matters to me at the moment is Bel."

All I can do is shake my head, turning my attention back to Bel. She hasn't learned how to master hiding her emotions and it's clear she's pissed from the blazing flames of rage in her eyes.

"Excuse me, but you don't get to make these decisions for me. This is my life now and I have just as much right to be here as you do."

It has nothing to do with right and everything to do with belonging, but she doesn't understand that.

"No, you don't. You aren't part of this world, Bel. You're too..."

She arches a brow. "Too what? Too naive, too female, too...what?"

"Good. You're too good for this."

I swallow hard as I admit it because it's almost like admitting she's too good for me too. Which I know is the truth, not that I've been willing to give her up despite knowing that.

"Whatever. I won't stand here and argue with you about whether I should be here when I already am. I'm a big girl, Drew. I don't always need you to worry about me." She shoves past me, and Sebastian follows her, completely ignoring me as he passes to enter the house.

Fucking Christ. The desire to destroy something pulses through my veins like a second heartbeat. I'm so angry with myself and Sebastian. I didn't mean for her to take it the way she did, and now I can't do a damn thing but stand by and watch her enter the lion's den. More guests filter in, and there is no doubt my father will be looking for me soon.

Fuck. I don't need this. Now I have to babysit that asshole's fucking mood as well as keep my eyes on Bel to ensure she's safe. I trust Seb to stand by her side, but there will be parts of this shit show where he'll have to talk to people she doesn't have any need to speak to. I just fucking hope Seb knows the difference by now.

Turning around, I find her without thought and stare at the bare expanse of her back, all that creamy smooth skin on display. Why the fuck did he let her wear that dress?

Someone approaches me from the side, and I can't remember his name, so I just give him a sharp nod and snag a class of something brown off a passing tray.

"Andrew, you're looking well."

Dammit. I don't remember this fucker's name. I think he does something with guns. The majority of these fuckers do. I shake his hand and nod again.

"Call me Drew, please."

He smiles, and his gaze bounces around the room. "Good turnout. I'm a little surprised, considering some of the rumors going around."

Consider me interested. "Rumors?"

He nods toward Seb and the other heads of family gathered in the room thus far. "Yes, the rumors about your father."

I try not to look as interested as I feel. "What sort of rumors?"

Is this what I need? Can it be this easy?

He shrugs. "As his son, you can't tell me you haven't

heard them yourself. I'm sure it's nothing more than gossip."

"Possibly, but I can't confirm or deny what I don't know."

"Right, yes. Well, some members of the family are worried about your father's mental state and if he should be in the seat he's in, given your mother's deteriorating health."

I grit my teeth. "Understandable. I can see the concern, but please tell whoever is spreading such rumors that they should speak with me if they have any issues."

"Of course." Smiling, he walks away, leaving me cursing softly under my breath.

I don't give a fuck what people say about my father, but I refuse to allow them to drag my mother into this and soil her name.

I thought maybe the guy would share something juicy and useful with me that I could use against my father, but of course it would never be that easy for me. None of them are just going to hand me what I need to take down my father. But now that I've thought about it, it's something I might be able to get out of Sebastian. We haven't exactly been friends for a while, but he might know more after this meeting.

I scan the crowd searching for Bel. She's smiling at a woman wearing a red dress and seems okay, but I'm itching to cross the room and talk to her. To check for myself. I know better than anyone that words can hurt her just as much as fists can.

They exchange a few words and then Bel heads toward the bathroom off the foyer. I move to follow just as another man cuts out of the crowd, prowling right behind her.

Fuck no. Not today, or any day that ends in y asshole.

She reaches the bathroom, and he's right there. All I see is his slimy hand on her back, on her bare skin, and I see fucking red. I shove through the mass of people and stalk toward them. The balls this asshole has.

I remind myself that making a scene will do me no good, but then also remind myself that a scene will teach other fuckers not to touch what isn't theirs. The asshole peers at me over his shoulder, then focuses his attention back on Bel again.

His grip curls around her bicep. Bel twists around, trying to escape his touch, and I swear I can smell the panic rolling off her.

"Release her," I hiss through my teeth, trying to keep my damn cool.

Probably too softly with the music playing from the ballroom, but he seems to hear me because his eyes shift to mine, and his mouth turns into a smirk. He's older, probably early thirties, and one of the uncles from the gun-running crew. Paccio, I think, is his name. Not that his name really matters. I don't give a shit who he is or what he does.

"Run back to your daddy and stay out of this." He smirks.

I smile, wide, white teeth, my good ole American all-star smile, then I do exactly what I said I wouldn't do and lose my cool.

Tightening my hand into a fist, I pull my arm back and punch him in the face. My knuckles slam into his nose, and the sound of bone breaking echoes through my ears. It's a glorious sound. Blood sprays from his wound and down my hand. *Dammit.* I hope Dad didn't rent this tux because if so, he's going to be pissed.

The adrenaline pulses in my veins, and all I can see is the asshole in front of me.

I'm vaguely aware of someone behind me shouting, but I ignore the threat until it's upon me. Paccio, or whatever the hell his name is, releases Bel and grabs his nose, while taking a wobbly step back.

That's right, fucker.

"I think it's you who needs to run back to your daddy," I mock and take a step forward, intending to hit him again, but this time a hand closes around my bicep, hauling me back.

"Drew." Sebastian's warning tone makes me pause.

I barely spare him a look, my gaze instead darting to Bel. She is blinking slowly, a mixture of shock and fear pitching her delicate features. I notice her hand on her bicep, touching the space where he grabbed her. I want to remove the memory of his touch for her. I should've broken his arm, hand, shoulder. He deserves worse than a busted nose.

"You okay?" I ask.

She nods, and then as if realizing all the attention is on her, she squares her shoulders. "I'm fine. It was nothing."

The bleeding man shouts at me, "You fucking asshole. I'm going to kill you."

Sebastian steps between us, and right into the guy's face. "Do you know who I am?"

The man's gaze widens, recognition taking place. He

nods and then drops his hands, spitting a gob of blood onto the shiny tile. It wouldn't be a true meeting without a little bloodshed, right?

Sebastian gestures to Bel. "Do you know who she is?"

The man shakes his head. "I thought she was your date or something. A hot piece of ass for the after-party."

Seb's face shifts from perfectly neutral to downright deadly in an instant. I'm ready to step in and stop him from beating this guy's ass, but Seb maintains composure and stops me in my tracks with a hand to my chest.

"This is my sister, Mr. Paccio. My. Sister." There's so much menace in his tone that even I'm a little worried right now.

Fear slowly trickles into the asshole's eyes. "Fuck."

"Yeah, you got that right. Spread the word. Touch my sister, and I will remove your balls and feed them to you while she watches. Fuck with my family again, and it will be the last thing you do. Do you understand?"

The man nods, and Sebastian takes a wavering step backward. Since his grandfather's death, he's been more menacing, colder, and, dare I say, crueler. It's like all the trauma is finally weighing down on him. I can't imagine what it's like to carry that weight, even if he does so well.

Bel looks between Seb and myself, almost as if she's uncertain which one of us is the bad guy. Before she can make her decision, Seb gently cups Bel's shoulder and leads her back into the party.

She glances back at the bathroom door longingly, and I shake my head. Paccio sneers at me, and I'm certain I'm going to have to wipe the floor with his face, but he chooses better of it and turns, heading toward the kitchen as one of the staff scurries to clean his blood off the floor.

"I see you're making friends already, Son." My father's cold voice greets me from behind.

I turn, keeping my face neutral. "Of course, you know how much I love to converse. I'm pretty sure I'll be at master level here soon."

His eyes narrow with annoyance, and he closes the distance between us, shoving right into my face. "You fuck any of this up for me, and you're done. I'll take you out back and put a bullet in your head myself. I'm fucking tired of dealing with you. You're more of a liability to this family than you are good."

I grind my teeth but keep my mouth shut for once. There are so many things I want to say to him, so many things I want to do, but I know my day will come soon enough. Karma is a real bitch, and far meaner than I ever will be.

He turns on his feet, dismissing me, and walks over to greet Sebastian, clapping him on the shoulder. Out of the corner of my eye, I watch Bel, who slowly retreats backward. It's painfully obvious that she doesn't want to be near my father, which is understandable. She looks as if she's undecided on what to do but then walks away, heading toward the bar. *Good girl.* It pleases me so much that she follows her gut instinct. I don't want my father anywhere near her, not after what happened. I can't let that nightmare repeat itself.

I watch casually as my father speaks to Sebastian in a low tone with bowed heads. The conversation lasts but seconds. Sebastian shakes his grip off and laughs menacingly, dismissing my father and whatever he said in favor of going to find Bel. I can't help but smile.

Looks like I'm not the only one screwing things up tonight. It's almost satisfying to see the angry disappointment on my father's face. He turns away, ignoring my existence altogether, and I cut into the crowd to keep an eye on Bel from a distance.

No one touches her.

No one looks at her.

The Wallflower is mine.

I hate to admit it, but I expected more guns and fighting than this. Not that this is bad, but I didn't anticipate a bunch of old men sitting around talking while their wives or mistresses drink themselves into a stupor. Maybe that's the key to getting through these events. Drink until you fall asleep.

I guess, boring or not, I'm here to support Sebastian.

I cradle the glass of wine to my chest and smile at the older woman sitting in front of me. She waves animatedly, telling me a story about a ski trip she just took with her cousin, who I strongly believe is definitely her boyfriend and not her cousin.

At least, by the way she talks about him. I listen just enough to nod and answer any questions she might toss my way, but I'm not involved in the depth of it.

I'm distracted from the conversation when the soft ringing of a bell fills the space. I glance around the room to see where it's coming from. The lady in front of me claps her hands excitedly, drawing my attention back to her.

"Oh, finally, dinner. The best part. At least after dinner, we're closer to being done. I abhor these social gatherings, really."

I give her a nod, not really sure what to say since this is my first one, and maybe my last. Everyone meanders into the dining room, their chatter following them.

My eyes fall onto the massive table set for more people than I care to count. *Deep breath.* It's just dinner. What could possibly go wrong? I take one step forward and find Sebastian by my side. His presence calms me and reminds me that I'm not in this alone. He gives me a slight smile, the best I'm going to get, I suppose, for the night and guides me to our seats. I look at the head of the table and spot Drew sitting right next to his father.

I shudder, glancing away so I don't catch his father's eye. The memory of that night is always there, lingering beneath the surface, threatening to make an appearance.

"Everything okay?" Seb asks, leaning close.

I nod and sigh, pasting on a smile. This is what I have to do. To be pretty, to be a distraction. There is no time for me to have a mental breakdown.

"Yeah, I'm fine. Just feeling a little overwhelmed. Do you know all of these people?"

He takes a sip of water and then leans back in his seat, surveying the room. "Know them? No. Know of them, mostly. Everyone knows the big players in the game."

"And we are...a big player?"

His dark gaze casts back on me, and when he smiles, I feel less like prey that's about to be eaten. "Short answer:

yes. Grandfather would accept nothing less. I've been trained and prepared for this job since I was a little boy."

"Is this what you want to do? Like if you had a choice, would you run the family business, or would you choose to do something else?" I'm not sure why I ask that question right then, but I feel compelled to know if this is what he really wants to do with his life or if it's a sacrificial duty.

He shrugs. "I don't think there was ever going to be a choice. When you're born into this world, the choice is made for you. If I didn't choose this path, I'm not sure I'd know what else to do. Nothing else seems to hold my attention."

I nod and find my eyes gravitating to Drew. Sebastian's response reminds me again that Drew doesn't always get a choice in the matter. There's always someone bigger pulling the strings, ensuring he follows directions or suffers the consequences.

It's hard to be angry with him when I know these things. Yeah, what he said about me not belonging here hurt, but it wasn't a lie. I don't belong here in a room full of criminals. This place isn't me. But that didn't mean he had to point it out so rudely.

I look away but find myself looking back toward him every couple of minutes. Even in a room full of people, I can't seem to stop being distracted by his presence. Thankfully, the staff start to arrive with food. Salad first, then soup, then the main entrée.

I poke at my salad, take a couple of bites, and offer Sebastian my soup. He shakes his head, declining it. The staff make quick work of the dishes, and I feel a pang of guilt watching them carry so many plates and silverware.

By the time the main entrée arrives, I'm ready to climb out the window. The pristine china is placed directly in front of me, and I stare down at the contents. It's some kind of roasted chicken with a mushroom sauce drizzled over top.

"Why are you looking at it like it's still alive?" Seb asks before shoving a cut piece of chicken into his mouth.

"I'm not," I lie.

"You are." He chuckles. "Just try it. It's actually delicious. I mean, it's not your burgers and french fries good, but it's still good."

I smile back at him, and with more hesitation than necessary, I cut into the chicken, spearing a piece on my fork. Like a toddler refusing to eat their vegetables, I cringe, then shove the fork past my lips and into my mouth.

I'm pleasantly surprised by the explosion of flavor that fills my mouth.

"Good, huh?" Seb notices the way my face lights up, and I nod, taking another bite. I'm nearly done with the entire dish before I realize it. When one of the waitstaff circles back to grab plates, I order another glass of wine.

While I wait, I reflect on what happened near the bathroom. It shocked me when Seb stepped in like he did. If he had given me the chance, I would have handled that asshole myself. Now, there's more tension than necessary, and I'm on people's radars in a bad way. I don't want to be the liability here, and I don't want to be seen as a weakness for Seb. I feel like by him stepping in, he's set me up as a weakness to exploit, and I can't help but wonder if others in this room see me the same way.

I know it wasn't meant to be a kick at my ego, but this is my first chance to show I'm a strong leader beside Sebastian.

"Oh, darling, the dessert is divine," Stella gushes.

I glance down and realize my dinner plate has been replaced with a dainty slice of turtle cheesecake, and the glass of wine I asked for sits beside it. *Well, shit.* Was I that disassociated? I didn't witness them bringing dessert.

I shrug and dig into the cheesecake, eating every last morsel. When the dessert is cleared, the conversations grow louder. Many appear to grow restless and choose to stand or walk around the room.

A man with piercing eyes approaches, and Seb steps closer to me. Like the rest of the men here, he's in a tuxedo with his dark hair slicked back. He smiles at Sebastian first and extends his hand. "Mr. Arturo? I'm Henry Salem. I knew your grandfather, but I don't think we've ever met."

Sebastian shakes his hand, his gaze suspicious and heavy. "Mr. Salem."

The man's eyes shift to me, and he leans over to grasp my hand and kiss my knuckles. "And who is this beautiful young woman?"

Sebastian, still suspicious, says, "My sister, Maybel Jacobs."

We hadn't discussed yet if I would use his last name, but it didn't feel right to give up this tiny part of Mom I have left to me.

The man nods once, smiles, and smooths his jacket. "It's a pleasure to meet you both. Perhaps I'll be seeing more of you."

The fact that he spoke to Sebastian the entire time isn't

lost on me, so I cut in. "You will. I plan to help my brother in every aspect of the business. I do have a family name to uphold."

He nods again and tips an imaginary hat, then walks away.

"Are you okay to sit for a bit by yourself? I have some business to attend to," Sebastian whispers into my ear, his eyes still on the stranger's back as he retreats.

I nod. "Yeah. I was just going to walk around a little bit. I'm feeling restless."

"Okay, don't go too far," he warns and then buttons his jacket, stalking off toward the bar.

I walk in the opposite direction, surveying the room. It's beautiful. Silk curtains frame small balconies, and double doors lead to a garden that rests at the bottom of the stairs, going all the way to the driveway out front. It's a shame such a horrible man gets to look at something so beautiful every day.

I look away from the garden, my eyes catching on the sparkling chandeliers and the glittering gowns. My anxiety ramps up, reminding me of that night my entire world changed. Turning on my heels, I choose to make a beeline for the bar, but I don't even take one step before I feel his presence beside mine.

"Avoiding me, Wallflower, or just trying to live up to your name?"

I turn, scanning his devilish face, thankful that he seems calmer now. I look down at his knuckles. They're busted and bruised *again*. I'm both sad and angry at the reality.

I didn't need him to stand up for me, even if it was nice.

Now he's hurt himself again, and for what? I don't want to draw attention to him, and I don't want to look weak for Sebastian. There's a fine line we must walk here.

"Why is it when I'm trying to avoid you so that we don't draw attention, you choose to do the opposite?"

He gives me a lopsided grin. "Guess I'm just a rule breaker."

I roll my eyes but can't help but smile. "What do you want?"

"Oh, Flower. You have no idea how much of a loaded question that is. Did you really expect me to sit across the room and watch that dickhead smile and flirt with you?"

"He wasn't flirting with me. We were conversing. There's a difference."

"As long as he doesn't touch you or get any ideas about fucking with you, then we're fine."

"First, there is no we. Second, I'm a big girl, Drew. I don't need you to be my protector."

He grabs me by the waist and tugs me into his chest. The air wheezes from my lungs, and I feel his hot breath against my lips. "There has and always will be a *we*. If you don't believe me, I will lift you by the ass, set you on that giant-ass oak table, and make certain everyone watches as I devour you from the inside out."

I shiver at the territorial tone of his voice and the image of what he described.

"You wouldn't dare!" I hiss, not even believing my own words.

His green eyes twinkle with mischief. "Oh I would, Flower, and you know it, so don't tempt me."

"Fine, but that's not the real reason you came over

here, right? It wasn't to act like a caveman and show ownership, right? Because you should've just pissed in a circle around me."

"I'll be sure to do that next time." He leans forward, and his lips brush the corner of my mouth. We shouldn't be this close, and he definitely shouldn't be kissing me. Not because it's wrong, but because it's drawing attention.

I can already feel other's eyes on us, and I hate it. It's like being under a microscope.

"I'll be sure to do that next time, but right now, I need you to come with me for a few minutes."

I take a step back and he lets me, releasing his hold on my waist. "Where to?"

"Trust me?"

"Are you joking? Your track record has been less than stellar, Mr. Marshall."

He smirks. "Good thing you don't have an option, then."

Grabbing my hand, he interlaces our fingers, then tugs me behind him as he leads me through the foyer. Everyone is immersed in conversation or drinks, and the few gawkers from earlier have moved on to someone else.

A nervous ball of energy forms in the pit of my stomach, and Drew's gaze swings around the room almost as if he's checking for witnesses. We stop at what appears to be a broom closet door that's hidden under the stairs.

"Where are we going?" I whisper the question as he opens the door, tugging me inside behind him, his hand heavy in mine. The smell of dust tickles my nose, but it's a welcoming scent.

"It's a surprise," he replies gruffly.

I'm momentarily blinded by the darkness as we cut through a long hallway. Seconds later, he releases my hand and grips the brass handles of a set of double doors. Bright light from the other side blinds me for a moment, and I blink a thousand times to get my eyes to adjust.

On the other side, I'm greeted with quietness. Minus the soft snoring emitted from a nurse who I spot resting in the corner and the soft beeping of hospital monitors.

The blood in my veins becomes ice, and my muscles clamp up.

Memories assault. My mother. Dying. Her cold hands. The tears that stained my cheeks. I force a ragged breath into my lungs and swallow the pain down.

It's okay. It's over now.

I often remind myself that grief is the price you pay for love.

With a gentle hand to the small of my back, his fingers splayed across my bare skin, Drew ushers me forward. "I know it's not the standard way of meeting parents but it's all I could offer you and it's important to me, so here we are. I want you to meet my mother."

The softness that enters his voice when he says *mother* makes me lock my gaze with his. "Your mother?"

He nods, and leads me to a medical bed across the room. A woman is laid out on the bed, her body placed perfectly in the center. She's unmoving except for the slight rise and fall of her chest. I look at her face, and find her eyes closed, and it appears that she's asleep. I can't help but wonder if she might be closer to death.

"Is she okay?"

Gently, Drew smooths the hair away from her face, the

dark brown threaded with gray. I'm momentarily shocked at the gentleness and kindness that he shows his mother. It's like flipping a light switch on and off.

"She's alive, so I guess for now, yes, but she went into a coma some time ago, and we are just waiting for her to wake up. I don't know all the details. My piece of shit father refuses to let me see her or have any knowledge of her care."

I melt, witnessing this moment and the look of love that shines in his eyes as he stares down at her.

"Your mom is beautiful. What's her name?"

"Victoria."

I nod and reach for her, patting her hand softly. "It's so nice to meet you, Victoria. I'm Maybel. But you can call me Bel."

His hand eases around my waist, and he tugs me to his side. "I wish we could stay longer, but once my father notices I've disappeared, he'll send his goons to find me, and all hell will break loose if he discovers I'm visiting her when I'm not supposed to."

"You really are breaking the rules tonight." I grin.

"I am. I had to check on her, and I've been wanting you to meet her. It just so happened that tonight was the perfect occasion for all of that."

Calmness washes over me, and I lean into the feeling. For so long, I wondered if there was anything good in Drew, if he cared about anyone else but himself, and while I've wavered in understanding his psychotic tendencies, it's clear to me now, after seeing him with his mother, that he's willing to do anything to protect those he loves. I don't know that I can continue to hold all his bad against him when his intentions are pure.

Drew talks to his mother for another few minutes, telling her about what he's been doing and gushing about me. He smiles at her but even a smile can't misplace the anguish and fear he feels for her. He's a puppet on a string, and his mother's life is hanging in the balance. I wish I could take the pain he's feeling away, that I could hurt his father the way he's hurt him but I can't.

"We've got to go, Flower," Drew whispers into my ear, pulling me back to the present.

"I look forward to meeting you again," I tell her while giving a tiny wave goodbye. Drew is quiet as he leads me back to the party the same way we came. Before we enter the foyer, I give his hand a tight squeeze.

"Thank you for that. For taking me to meet your mother."

He swallows thickly. "I can't wait till the day she's better, and you can both sit down and talk together. She's going to love you. I just know it."

Reality smacks me in the face then. Drew talks as if we're together now, as if everything is better, but it's not yet. *Can it be? Can this all be fixed?* Yes, but it's not an overnight thing. It's going to take time and patience. Still, I doubt I'd be able to walk away again. We remain together, me at his side, as we cut to the bar. The bartender asks for our orders, and Drew gets me a soda while ordering a whiskey for himself.

"I've been drinking wine almost all night," I gripe when the bartender hands me the Pepsi.

"You aren't of age," he taunts and sips his whiskey with a smirk.

His playfulness is surprising, given his father's appearance and the ordeal we had at the last event. At the end of the bar is a commotion, and I hear his dad's vicious voice cutting through the air, a small crowd forming around him.

"She's trash. She came from trash, and she'll go back to it eventually, right? But can you marry trash if it comes with millions? Of course you can."

Drew's hand tightens on my waist, and I swallow hard, realizing he's talking about me. An onslaught of emotions filters through me. Anger. Sadness. Anger again. I want to make him pay for all the pain he's caused others.

Sebastian's voice cuts through the men like a whip. "Well, trash may come with millions, but what does it say about you when the trash decides it doesn't want anything to do with you?"

I catch a glimpse of his face from the corner of my eye. There's a storm brewing in his eyes, but he appears calm, bored even. I look back at Drew whose features mimic Sebastian's. Many of the women and some of the men around the room wear that same face, that same expression. *Do they learn this from the womb?* The ability to lock down their emotions so completely, and if so, how do they do it?

I sip the soda and motion to the bartender, asking for a whiskey for myself. After a while, Drew leads me to speak with a few of the wives, introducing me to them, but I don't hear names or see their faces.

All I can hear is Drew's dad echoing his words from that night.

Trash. Trash. Trash.

Is that all I'll ever be to them? Trash. Trash that might be worth millions now, but nevertheless still trash. As if he can sense my turbulent emotions, Drew cups the back of my neck and leans down.

"You give them too much, Flower. Clear your face. You have to adopt the mask, or they will use that soft heart you carry against you."

Trash. Trash. Trash.

I shake my head and try to get the words to disappear from my brain, but they won't.

"I don't know if I can."

"You can. You only think you can't because you aren't used to it. If you want to support Sebastian and survive in this world, you will learn to master your emotions."

Ugh. Fine. I try to do exactly as he says. I go deep into my brain, focusing on squishing everything that's annoying me, or threatening me at the moment, but the more I focus on those things, the more they threaten to swallow me.

"Would it help if when I fucked you later, I forced you to maintain that mask the whole time?"

His question makes me laugh. "Could you maintain that look through sex?"

He shrugs. "Maybe with another woman. Never with you."

My heart fucking melts a little bit more for this man. *Dammit.*

"What is that look? It's not the mask I just told you to adopt."

I shake my head and stare out at the people, keeping my eye on Sebastian as he talks, shakes hands, makes deals or whatever it is he is doing. He's in his element here, people want to talk to him, want to be near him. And why not? He's young, handsome, and he just took over one of the biggest families.

Drew leans down, his lips brushing against my neck. "You look incredible, by the way. I want to rip this dress off with my teeth and fuck you in those heels."

I smile and then hide the smile in my glass of whiskey. "You're not making it easy for me to maintain a neutral face."

"When have I ever made anything easy?"

Ain't that the truth?

Seb turns, exchanging conversation with another man. He smiles, and it appears things are going well until Drew's father intervenes, clapping him on the back to face away.

I jerk my chin to the pair. "What do you think that's about?"

"Who fucking knows. My father is still trying to court himself into Sebastian's good graces."

I snort. "Seb hates your father, and I think it started long before I entered the picture, or he took over the family."

"Something my father hasn't figured out yet. It's fine. He'll have to figure it out the hard way. If there's one thing you need to know about Sebastian, it's that he's as cunning as he is handsome. He will cut you with the same hand he uses to wipe away your tears. I've known him since we were in grade school, and while I'm not afraid of him, I fully believe he would kill and burn the world to the ground to protect those he cares about."

The opportunity to respond is ripped away from me when Sebastian's icy voice falls over the room. "Fuck you, Marshall. You have a lot of fucking balls to ask me that after everything you've done." Everyone turns to look at what's going on. Seb throws up his chin and glares down his nose at Drew's dad. "You're nothing to me, Marshall. You or your family."

Drew stiffens beside me, and I can't help but fold under the attention that is turned on us with the release of that statement.

Shit. This isn't good.

Drew's dad draws himself off, his shoulders roll back, and there's a predatory scowl etched into his face. My heart cinches in my chest, as he leans into Sebastian and whispers something. I have no clue what he says. All I know is that Sebastian's expression gives nothing away.

I'm frozen. What the hell do I do? There is no choice to be made, not when Sebastian makes it for me. He sets his glass down on a passing tray and turns to face me in the crowd.

Our gazes collide, and I know without words being spoken that he wants me to come with him. I give Drew an apologetic look, and he releases me from his grasp, his touch ghosting against my bare skin. I hate leaving his side, but I can't stay here without Sebastian.

The crowd parts for me, and when I reach my brother, he wraps a protective arm around me.

"If she's trash, then I'm trash as well," Sebastian

announces, loud enough that everyone within earshot can hear. An embarrassment of heat climbs up my neck and into my cheeks. He leads us out the door, and I hold my breath waiting for something, anything to happen, but it doesn't.

No one says a word, nor do they try to stop us. We are in the car before I realize I'm still holding the whiskey glass in my shaking hand and I know from that moment on nothing will ever be the same.

27

DREW

If she's trash, then I'm trash as well.

I can barely contain the smile that graces my lips due to Sebastian's closing remarks. He really knows how to bust my father's balls, and while I know I'll be paying the price for this stunt at some point, I enjoy the satisfaction of watching the man who thinks he's king of all crumble.

Sebastian's departure inspires a few others to leave, and they each cast disparaging glances toward my father as they walk out. No doubt dear ol' dad is keeping a tally of each person who follows him. That's fine though, while he's busy glaring at all his guests, it gives me the opportunity I need to leave as well and I'm beyond ready to get out of here. The only way I managed to stay this long was because of Bel.

Now that she's gone, and I've already checked on Mom, I can leave.

I weigh my options. I could head back to The Mill for

the night, but I didn't get to have the conversation I wanted to have with Bel. I had hoped to tell her everything, to spill my guts to her, sharing my past and darkest secrets, giving her a way to understand why I'm the way that I am. This fucked-up, psychotic asshole.

My end goal is her. For us to be together, and for there to be no more secrets between us. I want what we had before. I want her to look at me like she used to, like she can't bear to be away from me, and she can't wait to see me again.

The night air is cold, and I stuff my hands into my pockets while I wait for the ride app to show up. I need to have this conversation with her and make it clear that I'm ready to move forward.

I already know that Sebastian is going to try to kick me out on my ass, but hopefully Bel will stop him before that happens.

The car finally arrives, and it's a quick twenty-minute ride over to Sebastian's place. I have the car stop outside the gate and approach the guard. It wasn't as hard as I thought it would be when I snuck in the other night, but if I want to make this right and not give Sebastian another reason to kick my ass, I'll go through the front door.

When the guard waves me in, I start my trek up the driveway. As predicted, Sebastian is waiting at the door, his tie undone, his jacket discarded, and his hair shoved back like he's been running his fingers through it nonstop. There's wrinkles of frustration marring his forehead.

"What do you want? It better be fucking good because, believe it or not, I've had my fill of Marshalls for the day.

I'm tempted to shoot you right where you stand." I try not to take his disgust personally.

I nod. "Understandable. My dad is enough for us both."

He studies me for a long moment, his gaze tense. "What do you want?"

"To speak to Bel."

"No."

I sigh and hold my hands out. It takes everything I have left to say this word. "Please?"

For a moment, I swear I see the ghost of a smile curve his lips, but when I blink, it's gone. *Fucker.* I swear he's been waiting for this day, to use my fucking one and only weakness against me. Sucks that it has to be his sister.

He takes one step down the entry and looks me dead in the eyes. "No."

I ball my hands into fists, ready to storm past him if I need to in order to get to her. Nothing and no one is going to keep me from her. No one. She is mine. All fucking mine. Blood rushes in my ears as I think through my next steps, but then I catch a whiff of her floral scent. My gaze darts to the door, and some of my anger recedes.

"Sebastian," Bel snaps from the entrance. She's barefoot and still in that sexy-as-hell dress, but she's got a cardigan on now, her arms wrapped tight around her middle. "Don't be a dick, and stop threatening to shoot people. He came to talk. There's no harm in that."

"No harm?" Sebastian snorts, and his gaze ping-pongs between us.

Waves of tension roll off him. He's not as levelheaded as he usually is. The party wasn't easy for him, and it's obvious he's battling a demon, but he's not advertising a need for help. In typical Seb fashion, he plans to deal with shit all on his own. "There is never no harm when it comes to inviting a Marshall into your home. Have you forgotten that I've known Drew longer than you, and, therefore, I know what he's capable of?"

"I didn't come here with malicious intent, Seb. I just want to talk to Bel." I shake my head, my own frustration mounting.

"What-the fuck-ever." He sighs and waves me forward, finally giving in.

The weight of the world is resting on his shoulders, but I know more than anyone he's not ready to share the burden with me. That's just how he is. He knows I'd help him in a heartbeat, but I can't do a damn thing if he doesn't tell me shit.

"I'm not here to fight," I confirm again, but my word does nothing to ease the tension.

"Just get the fuck inside, and say what you need to say," he sneers at me, and when I start to walk away, he speaks again. "This is my only warning to you, Drew. If you hurt one fucking hair on her head, I will spill your blood on the marble, and no one will be able to stop me, not even Bel."

"Sebastian!" Bel scolds. "Stop it."

"And I'd happily let you do it if I fucked up again, but I won't."

Sebastian rolls his eyes, and once again, he waves his hand forward, a mock of impatience following his movement. I stand tall and climb the steps walking right past him, and into the house. Bel lets out a sigh of relief, and I give her a smile in return. The last thing I want to do is fight with Sebastian, but I'll cross any bridge and break any rule to keep Bel in my life.

"Let's go upstairs and talk," Bel says.

I nod, following her when she swivels around and heads for the stairs. I try not to watch her perfect ass as she walks up the steps, but depriving myself of her is killing me slowly. My cock is as stiff as a board, and I have to remind myself that I came here to talk to her, not fuck her.

At the top of the stairs is a long hall, and we walk until we reach her room. She has no idea that I know exactly where I'm going, and that I spent one too many nights in this house, hiding from my father's rage. Once inside, she plops down on the bed and shifts her feet up to sit cross-legged.

"He shouldn't have threatened you like that. I don't know what's going on. He's worried about stuff, things he's not telling me, and then you saw what happened at the party." Bel frowns.

I nod. "Yeah, that's his MO. When things get tough, he prefers to lock down and turn in on himself. Not that we've been talking a lot or even close as of lately, so I wouldn't have a clue what is going on in his head, but I can guarantee it has nothing to do with you if that's what you were thinking?"

She shakes her head. "No, I just worry about him. Taking over the family business isn't easy I assume, and he doesn't share anything with me about it. Only what I need to know. I think he's trying to protect me, to limit my association with the bad. I don't know."

Her concern and love for Seb makes me rage with jealousy, but it also makes my heart swell. I hate the idea of having to share her with her brother, but it can't be helped. If she loves him, then she does, and I'll do anything to keep her happy.

Even share her with my best friend, who currently hates me.

"If it helps, you're the first person in his life who he seems to give a shit about. The one person he seems to care for other than himself, and that's saying a lot because Sebastian can be one selfish prick when the occasion calls for it."

"I know someone else who can be rather selfish too." Bel looks up at me, her green eyes twinkling. *Fuck, I swear I come in my pants a little bit.* "Anyway, what did you want to talk about?" Her voice is soft. "Must be serious if you came through the front door instead of sneaking through the window."

I unbutton the top button on my shirt and lean forward to brace my elbows on my knees. Talking about this is necessary, but that doesn't mean it's going to be easy.

"As you know, my father is a grade A asshole."

She huffs. "Tell me something I don't know."

I let out a long exhale and stare at my shoes, the serious turn of this conversation makes me unable to look at her. "No, I really mean it. He's really an asshole. I don't even know when the beatings started. When I think back on things, I can't remember a time when he didn't hit me. One day, he shucked me off to the nanny, and the next, he had all these expectations I suddenly didn't live up to."

Her hand glides down my back. "It's okay, Drew...you don't have to do this. We don't have to talk about this."

I shake my head and run my fingers through my hair.

"That's the problem here, Flower. We do. I have to do this, release the demons and the pain. I have to try to heal the fucking wounds if we are ever going to get past everything. If you are ever going to truly forgive me."

Fuck. I thought I could do this, but I don't know if I can. I don't want her to see this side of me, to know the terrible details, but here's no way around this. In order to let go of the past, I have to reveal it, and I'm ready to let go. I shudder out another breath and shrug off her touch. Out of the corner of my eye, I see her flinch and I can feel the shard of glass entering my skin again from that single look.

Reaching for her, I cup her cheek gently in my hand and scan her face, hoping she can understand. "It's not you. I-you can't touch me while I talk about this stuff. The mere thought of what he did to me, and put me through…" I grit my teeth, and my soft grip turns harsh on her cheek. I drop my hand and turn away before continuing. "The memories are strong enough to make me lash out, and I don't want to hurt you."

I don't bother looking at her as I speak. I'm not sure I could stomach it. The pity, and despair, or maybe even disgust that she'll soon wear on her face.

"I think I was five when he first started hitting me. It was for little things at first, like if I failed to listen to what he said or didn't do something perfectly. As I got older, the beatings evolved into something else. They became more frequent and more violent. He went from hitting me with his hands to kicking me. There were even times I blacked out, and when I woke up, I was in the same spot with my blood all over the floor. I learned really fucking quickly that if I wanted to survive I needed to do every single thing he told me to. I went where he told me. I was the best at anything he named. He used me in any way he possibly could to get ahead in business, with friends, colleagues. I was his punching bag and his one-way ticket to all the money in the world," I grit through my teeth, my anger bubbling so close to the surface. I want to give into the burn of it, to let it wash over me, but I can't. I can't let it rule me anymore. I can't let him rule me.

"At the party, when you saw me with that girl. It wasn't because I wanted to be with her. It wasn't because I chose her. It was on his order. It was follow the order or get beat. When you walked into that kitchen and witnessed what he was doing, when you saw what he was doing to me. I..." My heart clenches inside my chest, and I swear I feel what it's like for the first time then to care for something more than you care for yourself. "I was afraid of what he would do to you. I was afraid that he would realize how much I cared about you and use you against me. All I could think about was protecting you, getting you out of that room as fast as I could so he didn't get his slimy hands on you." I growl the last few words, the reminder of that day imprinted on my mind. "It didn't matter though because one second is all it took for him to realize you meant some-thing to me. That's when his motive changed. He wanted to use you to hurt me and I knew I'd rather die than let him get his hands on you, so I did the only thing I could think of. I choose to hurt you myself. I choose to be the villain. I knew that each word I spoke would hurt you, but it would still be better than if my father got ahold of you."

The sound of sniffling reaches my subconscious, and I look up, glancing at Bel over my shoulder. The anguish pinching her delicate features slams into me like a Mack truck. Tears slide down her cheeks, her makeup is ruined, and her cheeks are flushed. I'm tempted to reach for her, to soothe her, and erase the hurt and pity she must be feeling, but I can't. I'm not done yet.

"My father did everything he could to ensure he maintained control over me. As I got older, he realized his beatings no longer held the same power as they had before. I'd become accustomed to the abuse, and in many ways when he hit me it no longer hurt.

"Yes, there would be bruises, and evidence, but I didn't really feel any of it. I'd go into this dark place in my mind where he couldn't touch me, where his abuse didn't hurt me. In that place, no one could reach me. When he realized that, his motives changed, and he started using other, more creative ways to control me. He threatened to toss me out on my ass and cut me off, not understanding that I didn't really give a fuck anyway.

"As my mother's condition worsened, he started holding her over my head. He told me he'd stop offering her pain meds and make certain she suffered if I didn't do exactly what he told me to." I grit my teeth, the shame and guilt resonating through me. I'd always felt strong, above my peers, but I was nothing but a lost little boy when it came to my father. Forever trapped by him.

"That's where he got me. The thought of her suffering because of me. I couldn't handle it. She didn't deserve that. And then you came along, and well, I didn't want to hurt you, ever. I couldn't imagine letting him use you to control me either."

In a flash, she's climbing onto my lap, wrapping her

legs around me, while snaking her arms around my neck at the same time. She clutches onto me tightly, burying her face against my chest.

Her touch burns me to ash. I want to let her heal me, and mend all the ugly, dirty pieces of my disgraced soul back together again, but this isn't my flower's weight to carry.

Lifting her head, she peers up at me, her green eyes shimmering with tears. "I'm sorry, Drew. I knew he was a terrible human and that he hurt you. I saw the marks on your skin and wanted to ask you about them. I tried, but I was afraid you would push me away, and you did. That night you came to my dorm in the tux. He hurt you that night, didn't he?"

All I can do is nod, emotion clogging my throat and making it difficult to speak. Tears prick at my eyes, but I blink them back. The thought of crying over this shit makes me sick to my stomach. Especially in front of her.

"I'm so damn sorry, Drew. I'm sorry no one was there to help. No one stopped those things from happening to you, and I'm sorry that he's using your mother against you. Using her deteriorating health against you. Why? Why would he do that?"

I shake my head because I don't have an answer. "I don't know. I've spent a long fucking time wondering what it was about me that made him hate me so much. I did everything I could to please him. *Everything*," I growl bitterly. "His hate shaped me into the person I am today. I took that pain and anger and hurt others because I could. I was a fucking bully, and no better than my father. When you told me that day that the apple doesn't fall far from the tree, it wasn't a lie. I'm not better than him. I'm the same and I fucking hate it."

She moves her hands and cups me by the cheeks, forcing me to look into her eyes.

"Stop. Don't say that. You're better than him, Drew. You're a thousand times better than him because where your father cares for no one but himself, you care about others. You care about your mother, your friends, and me."

She has no fucking clue how much she means to me. I'd lie, cheat, and steal for her. I'd kill anyone who tries to hurt her. My beginning and end are all her. As she stares at me, I consider telling her the truth about my father, my mother, all of it, and I will, but without all the answers and understanding how it all came to be, I can't. Not yet.

"Maybe you don't think so, but I do. I know I don't deserve you, not even a little bit. But that's the thing. I don't care. I don't give a fuck if I deserve you because I'm far too selfish to let you go. That day in the library, when you stood up to me, you didn't cower in fear or melt beneath me. You were unlike anyone I'd ever met, and when I looked at you, it felt like you were looking at me, seeing the real me, and no one had ever done that before. It both terrified and intrigued me. I was scared you would be able to see parts of me I hadn't shown anyone before. I wanted to control you, to bend you to my will. The darkest parts of me clung to the lightest parts of you, and for the first time in forever I felt in control of at least one thing in my life."

She releases my cheeks and shifts her arms under mine, squeezing me as tightly as she can, pressing her cheek over my heavy beating heart. "I don't know what to say."

The pressure on my chest is lighter, and when I suck a breath into my lungs the weight of my past no longer presses too tightly. "You don't have to say anything, Bel. I just wanted you to know, and my only hope is that by telling you, maybe you'll understand why I did what I did and might be able to forgive me for it."

Strands of blond hair stick to her cheek as she pulls away, her eyes rimmed red as they peer up at me. Her pink lips press into a thin line. "I want to forgive you, Drew, and I'm trying. Every day that passes, it becomes easier to wrap my head around. It kills me to be away from you, and my heart begs me to give in and forgive you because I miss you. I can't even go to the library without thinking about you. It's no longer the same."

"I'm sorry." I stroke her back gently. "I'm sorry for everything."

"I know you're sorry. I feel it in my bones, and in so many ways you're already forgiven. I'm just afraid. I'm afraid that you'll hurt me again, even if accidentally in an attempt to subdue your father, and I don't think I could survive losing you a second time. Your dad still has power and control over you, and there's no saying he won't try to use me again, that he won't make you do something to hurt me simply because he can. I need something concrete that proves your father no longer has a hold on you. That he won't be able to sway you into doing his dirty work. I forgive you, Drew, but I need to make sure your father can't hurt either of us again. Only then can we really let this go completely."

Fuck. She's right.

With my father still in the picture and a part of my life,

Bel isn't safe, and she won't ever be till I get rid of him. There isn't a damn thing I can do to fix this right now, and it fucking sucks.

"I understand," I murmur instead of doing what I really want to do, which is lay her back on the bed, strip her out of this dress, and fuck her into submission until she screams my name and admits how much she wants me. But fucking her won't change anything. It won't make her forgive me any faster. "I want to stay, and fuck you until you promise to forgive me but I should go before your brother comes snooping around. I don't think he would appreciate catching us naked again."

She chuckles. "Yeah, I don't think he would like that very much."

"Me either." I press a kiss to her forehead, and gently lift her off my lap, placing her back on the bed. What she needs is time, and even if it's not what I want to give her, I don't have an option. I won't wait forever. She'll be mine regardless. It'll just make all of this easier if I have her forgiveness.

Shoving off the bed, I smooth my hands down the front of my pants and give her one last look, my heart squeezing in my chest. I turn on my heels and walk out of the room, my insides twisting painfully, my heart urging me to stay with her. The person I'd rip my still-beating heart out of my chest for. I don't. I continue walking, heading back to The Mill, hoping to be greeted by a quiet house. The only way to get Bel back is to get rid of my father, and I'll do anything to make that happen.

∾

A HAND DRAGS me out of bed, ripping me from sleep, and my eyes pop open, my fists clenched and swinging. Adrenaline rushes through my veins, and I peer up at the light shining in my eyes. It takes me a second to realize where I am.

One of my father's goons stands above me, and my gaze swings to the door where I find another standing. "Get up and get dressed. Your father wants to see you."

I shove off the floor and scramble onto my feet. "Fuck you, asshole. He can call me like a normal fucking human if he wants to talk." I say the words as I move on autopilot, walking straight to my dresser to get clothes. I know first-hand what will happen if I don't obey, and it'll be ten times worse if I don't show up.

It takes me a minute to find clothes, but when I do, I shove my legs into a pair of sweats and grab a sweatshirt. My father's two goons watch me with impatience as I slip my feet into my tennis shoes. One walks in front of me, while another follows me as they lead me to the waiting car. I climb into the back seat, and they slam the door closed, locking me inside. My gaze moves to the illuminated screen up front, and I notice the time.

Three fucking a.m. Are you kidding me? I don't know why I'm not surprised. I guess I'd be more shocked if he didn't make a surprise visit or at least send his goons after me. My stomach is a ball of anxiety that grows worse and worse with each mile the car drives.

Ten minutes later, we arrive at the house, and I'm tempted to stay in the car hiding, but there's no way my father wouldn't have one of his asshole guards pull me out of the vehicle by my hair. So I begrudgingly leave the protection of the car and walk up the steps and into the house. The house is quiet, too quiet. Fuck me, this isn't going to be good.

I drag my feet the entire way to his office, one guard in front of me and another behind me, making sure I shuffle along like a good little boy. When we reach the double doors that lead into his office, I exhale. The guard shoves the doors open and then moves to the side, each taking their spots on opposite sides of the doorway. I suck a shuddering breath into my lungs and enter his office slowly. I barely have time to glance toward the desk when something heavy comes flying my way. Pain rips through my temple, and it hurts enough to bring me to my knees.

Fucking prick.

Blood. It trails down my temple and over my cheek. My stomach churns, and I lift a hand to the spot to make certain it's blood and not just my imagination. When I pull my fingers away, they're slick and stained red.

I clench my teeth and scramble to get off the floor. "What the hell?"

Unfortunately, my father is already there, charging across the room, leering in my face. "You ruined it," he spits.

I clutch my head as a wave of dizziness rolls through me, dropping me back onto my ass. God, this is getting old. "What are you talking about? I haven't done anything wrong. I showed up at your party and played nice."

His eyes flash with icy rage, and out of nowhere, he pulls a gun, the glint of it shining in the dim light. He waves it around with his finger near the trigger.

"You're the fucking problem. You ruined it all. You and

that cunt. She convinced that arrogant fuck to withdraw his donations. As of two hours ago, Sebastian Arturo has removed all of his assets from the Marshall Group. I doubt your small brain can comprehend how much fucking money that is."

I want to laugh in his face and tell him I told you so, but practice is the only thing that keeps my face empty of emotion. "What am I supposed to do about it?"

My response isn't what he wants to hear, and in a flash, he lashes out, slamming the gun into the side of my head. The world spins, and my ears ring. Pain lances across my cheek and the bridge of my nose, but I grit my teeth against it, refusing to give him the satisfaction of seeing my reaction.

"What do you think I want you to do? Use your fucking head. Get my fucking money back, Andrew. Go to that fucking house. Find that stupid bitch and tell her you're head over heels in love with her. Do whatever you need to do to make her believe it and have her make her brother return his portfolio. Fix it! That's what I want you to do."

Blood pools inside my mouth, and I spit it onto the hardwood before speaking. A look of utter disgust is cast my way. "How is Bel going to convince Sebastian?"

He spins away from me and reaches for the bottle of bourbon sitting on the edge of his desk. Bringing the neck of it to his lips, he takes a chug and places the bottle back down. I use the time to stand and swipe at the blood on my head.

When he returns his attention to me, he invades my space, gripping my sweatshirt, pulling me into his face. He snarls his lips, and his whiskey breath fans against my cheek. It takes everything inside me not to react or fight back. This man is a ticking bomb and it's only going to be a matter of time before he implodes on himself. Taking us all down with him.

I need Bel and my mom as far away from him when that time comes.

There's no saying the lengths he'll go to get her to agree to something. No one tells my father no, and if they do, they regret it.

"I don't care what you have to do. I don't care who you have to fuck, even if you have to fuck Sebastian himself. Convince them that everything is okay. Make them believe that we respect them, and that we want them to be a part of the Marshall family. Do whatever. It. Takes. The money is everything. The money is the ONLY thing."

He brings the barrel of the gun to my head, the cold steel pointed firmly into my flesh. I don't even blink at his behavior. He's in a fucking mood, and I don't trust his need for me to be greater than the satisfaction of pulling that trigger right now.

"You've never had to live on the street, Son. You've been privileged all your life. You have no idea there are children out there who can't feed themselves or have to sell their bodies to be able to do so. You have never understood how fucking lucky you are to be born with everything you could ever need. So when I say, money is everything, then I mean, the money is the only thing keeping you six feet above the ground."

I swallow hard at what he's saying. He's never...I blink, knowing how he will take it if I ask questions, show him any kind of pity, so I don't.

"Part of the Marshall family?" I ask, softly. "What does that mean?"

He nods, his mouth twisting into a cruel smile as he moves the barrel, tracing down the side of my face with the gun before stopping to press it under my chin. My heart beats out of my chest, and I'm so fucking tired of him making me feel this way. Tired of the anxiety and fear. Of never knowing what he might do next.

"It means you will convince that girl you're in love with her. That you want to marry her. That what happened at the party that night was a misunderstanding. Then once we have her tied to the family with no way of escaping, I'll have my revenge and show that little Arturo bastard what happens when people play with my money. When we've had our full use of the girl, you can toss her in the trash and move on to someone new."

He's lost his fucking mind.

"This is not the 1900s. You can't make someone marry you simply because you say so. What's your plan if she says no? Are you going to kidnap her and force her to sign her name on the dotted line?" I play into his delusional plot. "We can't go into this without a solid plan. Otherwise, it might backfire on us. Sebastian is a loose cannon, and I have no doubt that he will use every bullet he has to try to take us out."

He nods and taps my cheek with the gun, then steps away, returning to his bottle of bourbon. After taking another chug, he places the bottle back down and wipes his mouth with the back of his hand.

"Yes, I agree. I'll have to think of something else. Maybe I'll get rid of your mother and marry the girl myself. She's a sweet little piece of ass, and I'd love to know what it is about her cunt that has my son tied up in knots."

If I wasn't so sure he'd pull the trigger, I'd swing on his ass, but that's what he wants. To see me react, to get under my skin and piss me off. When I do none of those things and simply continue staring blankly at him, he continues.

"It doesn't really matter. I'll find a way to get control of her. Who knows? When I'm backed into a corner, I can be very creative. So tell me, Son, do you want me to take matters into my own hands, or are you going to do what I tell you to? You can still have a piece of the pie. There is still a spot for you here beside me."

I'm backed into a corner. There's nothing I can do but agree. If I don't, there's no saying what he'll do. At least with my agreement, I can buy myself some time.

"Consider it done," I announce, my voice low.

He smiles, and it makes my stomach churn. "Good, and don't fuck this up, Drew! You've caused enough issues. You're lucky your mother is still alive after all the shit you've done. Now, let's fix this. I'll set up a little date for you two. Show me how creative you can be, and maybe you'll get through this in one piece. Although I can't guarantee the same thing for your friends."

28

BEL

A couple of days pass, and I find myself still thinking about the things Drew shared with me. My heart aches for him, bleeds for him even, but there's nothing I can do to help him. It's a potent kind of helplessness.

Forgiving him takes time, and I refuse to rush into a full-blown relationship, especially with his father still actively meddling in his life. If Drew wants a relationship with me, he'll have to find a way to stand up to his father. I refuse to let our love be a secret. There's no way in hell I'll ever allow that. And I don't think Drew would either if the tables were turned.

He wants me and wants us. I can see it and feel it. Every kiss. Every time he slips inside me. He's worshipping my body, saying things he can't put into words. It pulls me a little closer every time. His confession about his father, about all of it, means I need to forgive him.

Hell, deep down, I know I already have, but I haven't

brought myself to tell him yet. Not when I fear he'll revert to his old ways at any second. He's still very fragile, and any little thing could set him off, sending him back to the way he used to be.

Drew never was a snuggly bunny to begin with. There was always a darkness in him. A darkness which drew me in and whispered depraved things in my ear. Maybe accepting that, and forgiving him, means I will finally have to accept this part of me too. The part of me that likes what he does when he takes control, when he uses and commands me.

That part of me is the part I'm afraid to confess to, even if there is no confession needed between Drew and myself. It's the simple fact that I need to acknowledge it and accept it without bashfulness or embarrassment.

I starfish out on my bed and let out a long sigh, just to release some of the pent-up energy that's rolling through me. My stomach rumbles, reminding me that I skipped lunch in favor of studying. *When will I ever learn?* Rolling over and off the bed, I leave the confines of my room and head downstairs, making a beeline for the kitchen.

Maybe I'll make a cup of coffee too. It's almost dinner-time, and if Sebastian sees me drinking coffee this late, he'll give major side-eye, but I'm willing to risk it. The guy is a nut when it comes to his concern over other people, but God forbid you tell him what to do. I walk through the side entrance of the kitchen and pause, my entire body clamming up when I spot Sebastian and Drew together across the room.

They're hunched over the counter, and it looks like they're discussing something. I dart back around the corner because I know both of them will shut down the moment they spot me. And for once, I want to know what the hell they're up to. I swear if this is another macho 'she belongs to me' bullshit talk, I'm going to murder one or both of them.

Mmm, yes, both probably.

As I hide on the other side of the door, Drew's quiet whisper fills my ears, "It's a solid plan, but I don't know if it'll work?"

I crane my neck to hear, trying to block out the low hum of the refrigerator only a few steps away.

"Are you doubting me, Marshall? I think it'll work just fine. My only concerns are Maybel and the effect that it will have on her, but in the end, it's your decision. If you want to go through with it, I'm happy to help."

Worried about me? Happy to help?

They might as well be speaking a foreign language right now. I thought they hated each other? Why are they acting all buddy-buddy? The tiny hairs on the back of my neck rise. Something is going on, and I'm going to get to the bottom of it.

Drew releases a long exhale and scratches his fingers up over his head. It takes me a second to process what he's wearing once I get a decent look at him. Slacks, a button-down with the sleeves rolled up showing off his impeccable forearms.

He dressed up far more than usual. I like seeing him both ways but really prefer his blue jeans, letterman's jacket, and black combat boots. That's the real Drew, the one I've come to know. A hot rush of heat flames my skin all the way up to my ears as I think about those damn boots and the way he made me ride them that day.

"I've thought the decision through, Seb. There's no other way. Maybel and my mom will never be safe with him alive. There's no other option. He needs to die." His words shock me, and a tiny gasp escapes my lips. *Shit.*

As if they heard the sound, their gazes snap from the counter, and they twist around. They both look like predators seconds away from attacking. Well, guess there's no time like the present to walk in. Ignoring the words I just heard Drew speak, I cut around the corner with a big fake-as-shit yawn to give them some privacy, even if I plan to question Drew the second I get him alone.

"Fancy seeing you here," I greet.

Sebastian gives me a wavering glance, but Drew stares at me for a long moment, his eyes roaming the length of my body, lingering over the T-shirt I'm wearing that's now rode up on one side showing off a piece of bare flesh, down to the joggers that hang low on my hips. It's nothing more than comfortable clothing. There's nothing sexual about it but he's looking at me like a man looks after a woman he's hungered for his entire life.

"Bel," he says, but it sounds more like a warning.

I'm momentarily consumed by the thought of him being a killer. Could he really do something like that? Kill his own father? There has to be another way to do this.

"You okay?" Sebastian interjects, his voice dipped in concern. I realize then that I've completely fallen off the deep end and should probably speak now.

I smile and walk closer to the island where they are

sitting. "Of course. What's going on? Why aren't you two murdering each other?"

Seb snorts like whatever I've said is hilarious, then he's out of his chair, shoving the stool back under the counter. I'm not shocked.

"Oh, we were just about to get the knives out and start throwing them to see who has better aim."

"Seriously?" I pretend to be shocked, when in reality I wouldn't even be a little bit surprised if I walked in on them doing something like that. They have a long, turbulent history of fighting, at least according to Drew. Throwing knives would probably be a tame reaction from both of them.

"Don't worry, Bel. You saved his life. Next time, though..." He winks. "Anyway, I'm leaving before I have to dismember him. Don't forget I can kill you and make it look like an accident."

"Oh, I'm so scared." Drew laughs, seeming unfazed by the threat. Are they really joking around with each other? I swear the other day they were at each other's throats but now it seems everything is okay? Maybe this has something to do with the conversation I walked in on?

I look between the two of them, shaking my head. *What the hell is going on?*

"As you should be, and will be especially if you bring her home late or if something happens to her." He gives Drew a pointed glare and then walks out without any further explanation.

Weird.

"First, are you two okay? Second, what are you doing

here? And why is he talking about you bringing me home late?"

He walks around the island and straight to me. I swear I can hear buzzing in my ears. The intensity of his gaze on me short circuits my brain. I can't think when he's this close to me. He smiles and my stomach tightens with excitement. Once close enough he snakes an arm around my waist, dragging me inside his body. The warmth of his body is both soothing, and exciting and I lean into his touch almost desperately.

"Well, the answer to your first question is a loaded one. We're okay right now but give it five minutes and we'll be at each other's throats again." I look up at him and frown, and he cups me by the cheek, his thumb gently caressing my lower lip. I shiver from his touch and breathe his intoxicating scent into my lungs. He smells even better tonight, like teakwood and cinnamon.

"Aren't you excited to see me? I was hoping to surprise you, but you must've sensed me close by and decided to come investigate."

"I had no idea you were here. I was actually coming down to make something to eat because I missed lunch, and my stomach was yelling at me."

"Of course it was. I bet you were knee deep in a book, unable to bring yourself out of the hyper fixation."

I blink slowly at him waiting for him to poke more fun at me, but all he does is smile. "If you think I'm making fun of you, you're wrong. There is nothing sexier than when you immerse yourself in your studies and forget the rest of the world exists."

I narrow my eyes and pin him with a stare. "Stop buttering up to me. What do you want?"

"Nothing, Flower. I came here to surprise you with a date. Then Sebastian and I got to talking, and time got away from me."

"He knows about it already?"

Drew nods. "Yup. It wasn't easy, but he's allowing you to leave your tower for the evening. I have to have you back by midnight, though, or you turn into a pumpkin."

"Funny!" I shake my head but smile.

His emerald eyes trail down the length of my body once more and the diamond hard tips of my nipples press painfully against the thin fabric of my shirt. I wonder if he can see them? See how turned on I become in his presence?

"And while I do like what you're wearing and how easy it would be for me to strip you bare and fuck you raw, I think you should probably change first."

There's a hunger in his voice, and I want to tell him to forget the date, that we can go upstairs and fuck for the rest of the night, but a date with him, an official one. It's something we've never done before, and if we're going to be normal, or as normal as possible, I think it's a good idea.

"You're for real? You came here to surprise me for a date?"

"Yes, Bel. I came here to take you out on a date. The real kind where you get her flowers, and take her out to dinner, and give her a peck on the cheek at the end of the night."

"Where are the flowers then?" I narrow my eyes suspiciously and take a step back from his hold, crossing my arms over my chest, trying to look intimidating but failing.

"Your brother already took them and put them by the window." He hooks a thumb over his shoulder and I spot them sitting on the tiny little breakfast nook table.

The bouquet is a mixture of pink, purple, and yellow wildflowers. It's beautiful, simple, and my heart feels fuller than before seeing those flowers, and knowing that he went out of his way to get them for me.

"Wildflowers..." I whisper to myself.

"There is no other flower that will do for you, Bel." He grabs me by the hips, tugging me into his body, and then I feel his lips ghost against my forehead. Fuck. My resolve is slowly crumbling. Pulling away, he looks down at me, his eyes are bright and hazy with lust. "Go get dressed. I'm not ruining this date by fucking you in the kitchen. I want to do things right."

It's nothing short of an order but I'm too happy about it to complain. With my excitement chasing me, I rush from the kitchen and upstairs to get dressed. When I reach my closet I go through the racks of dresses, using his outfit to determine my own clothing choice.

Wherever we're going is elegant. Not posh, but definitely upscale based upon his own attire. With that in mind, I snag a black sheath dress off the hanger, strip out of my clothes, and step into it quickly. It clings to my body like a second skin, hugging my hips and breasts perfectly. When I first saw it, I didn't think I'd have any occasion for it, but now I can't wait to see Drew's tongue fall out of his mouth when he sees me in it.

After I have the dress on, and in place, I do my makeup

and thank the heavens that I decided to wear my hair down today, making it much easier to deal with. I put a clip in, keeping the hair half up and half down. I'm not sure how much time passes but I do my best to get ready quickly. When I make it back downstairs, he's in the same spot I left him, leaning against the counter while casually browsing on his phone which he nearly drops at the sight of me.

His Adam's apple bobs as he drinks me in. "Fuck me. Bel, you look beautiful."

I shrug, heat climbing up my very on-display cleavage to my neck. "Thank you. You said we were going on a date, and you're..."

He's on me in a blink, and my words are cut off by his lips, which descend on mine with burning passion. I'm melting into his arms, and thankfully, he's there to catch me. His hands come around my waist and slip down over my ass.

It's the touch of a man possessed with need, and my hope is he never stops touching me like this. He gives both ass cheeks a tight squeeze that ignites that low-building fire in my core.

I squeak and break away, breathless.

"Let's go," he growls, "before I lose control and fuck you on the countertop, leaving your release and my cum as proof that we were here."

"Sebastian would not approve." I laugh, already picturing his face if he discovered us.

"I don't care what your brother approves of or not. Not when it comes to you, Flower. There are no rules, and if there were they were meant to be broken anyway. I'll do whatever the hell I want with you and *to* you." The unhinged tone of his voice, mixed with his words, wraps around me like smoke, and I shiver both turned on and excited.

"Lead the way, Caveman," I taunt.

He takes my hand in his and tugs me out of the kitchen. Hand in hand, we walk the rest of the way through the house, stopping only once we're outside. There's a sleek all-black sports car parked a little bit down the drive. I assume it's Drew's since I don't think Sebastian would ever drive something like that.

I've never seen Drew drive nor did I know he had a car, but I suppose there's a first for everything. We walk down the driveway, and he opens the door for me with a smile. There's still that lingering lust in his eyes, but it seems like he's got a better grasp on himself now. After he helps me in, ensuring I buckle up, he climbs in on the driver's side. When he starts the car, I feel the rumbling of the engine in my bones. It gives me a rush of adrenaline, and when he throws the thing in drive and speeds down the driveway, the acceleration pinning me back in the seat, I turn and look at him.

I decide to continue the conversation, hoping maybe that will help. "Is this yours?"

He shifts gears like a professional race car driver expertly weaving through traffic. "Yes, but I don't drive it much. It's temperamental."

I smooth my hand over the soft leather. "Like someone else I know."

He shoots me a cheeky grin, but I can still sense something is wrong. I just can't pinpoint what. "There isn't really a reason to drive. Not when I can use the rideshare app or walk. I prefer the latter because walking gives me time to think and helps to clear my head."

I nod and look down at my hands, which I've placed in my lap. Something feels off, and I don't like it. This uneasiness seems to blanket the air. Back at the house, everything was fine, but now it's not. I want him to tell me if something is wrong, to feel comfortable coming to me.

I want us to be a team.

"Is everything okay?" I look up from my hands and over at him. He glances away from the road, his gaze meeting mine for half a second.

"Of course everything is okay. Why wouldn't it be?"

"Well, for starters, you're strangling the steering wheel like it owes you money."

He lets out a huff and loosens his grip, choosing to drive with one hand instead. With his other, he reaches for me, interlacing our fingers. Whatever worries I had moments ago evaporate into thin air when he touches me.

"I'm just anxious, and I don't want to fuck this up. That's all."

I don't think that's what it is, but I let him believe I do. The car swerves into the parking lot of some swanky restaurant. It looks like one of those steakhouses, but if I had to describe it, I'd say it's a Texas Roadhouse meets a country club.

Drew pulls up, stopping at the entrance. The valet attendant greets us and opens my door, offering me a hand. I'm just about to place my hand in his when Drew comes out of nowhere, glaring daggers at the guy.

"Don't touch her," he practically growls and tosses the keys at him.

The kid, who looks to be about sixteen or so, clams up.

"Sorry." I frown and let Drew help me out of the car. Once I'm standing, I tug him toward the entrance to make sure he doesn't start anything.

Inside, we're greeted by a hostess. The lights are low, and the sound of piano music filters in through the speakers.

It's beautiful and fancy as fuck.

For once, I feel appropriately dressed, if not a little self-conscious as I feel people's eyes raking across my bare skin. My arms, shoulders, and legs are all exposed, and the dress hugs every inch of my skin tightly. Drew doesn't appear to notice their gawking stares and skims his hand down my spine as he speaks with the hostess.

"Right this way, Mr. and Mrs. Marshall."

The woman smiles, and I open my mouth to tell her we're not married but then think better of it. I'm sure it was an accident. The woman guides us to the left of the restaurant into an area that looks like it's been roped off for private parties or high-end guests. Drew's hand on my lower back grounds me, and once we're in the room, the hostess disappears.

The strange feeling is still there, but I ignore it and give him a smile, allowing him to pull the chair out for me. I scoot into the table, my gaze sweeping the room. It's beautiful with the lights dimmed, candles lit, and a bouquet of roses on the table.

I look away from the decor and right at Drew. Where I

expect to see a smile, I find a face that is closer to that of a man who wants to throw up.

What is wrong with him?

He takes the chair opposite of me, and I keep my smile in place even as I slump at the fact he didn't take the seat right next to me. It's not a huge table, but it feels big enough that he seems far away. I try to ignore the bad feeling festering in my gut and put my attention elsewhere.

"This entire place is beautiful and amazing. I'm happy that you brought me here, but what made you choose this place?"

He sucks in a sharp breath and snaps his napkin out to place it across his lap.

"Fuck, Maybel, am I going to have to explain every decision I make to you from now on?"

I blink slowly and swallow around the lump of emotion in my throat.

"Wha-What?"

He shakes his head, and I watch the muscles along his jaw jump as he grits his teeth.

"Just... let's have a good night," he says, his voice a little softer.

I'm bewildered by the change in his attitude but don't get the chance to comment on it because the server comes in right then. She brings a pitcher of water with her and fills our cups, then follows with red wine.

I breathe through my nose and remind myself that while I'm not taking any more of Drew's shit, I also want us to be a team. We can't do that if my first thought is to always fire back and be on the offensive.

"Have a good night?" I question. "This was your idea,

and now you're sitting across from me acting as if you're pissed that you brought me here in the first place."

What the hell is happening here?

Even when he's been mean, cruel, he's never...like this. Not to me at least. It's a red flag. Something is off, wrong.

"Are you okay?" I ask.

As he watches me from across the table, I can feel his eyes sweeping a fiery path over my skin. I see something that resembles panic shining in his eyes. *What's going on? What is he not telling me?* The desire to flee to that safe place in my mind is difficult to fight against but I do it.

I push out of my chair and stand beside the table. "Drew. I need you to talk to me. I know something is wrong."

The door behind us opens, and I twist in my seat. My entire body becomes one frozen block when I realize who walked in. It's not the server that comes through the door but Drew's father.

He saunters into the room in his twenty thousand dollar suit, his hair slicked back, his eyes hard and unwavering. "Well, isn't this cozy? You two are finally taking the time to get to know each other the proper way?"

The proper way? He's kidding, right?

It all makes sense now. The puzzle pieces glide into place, and while I'm angry at his father's sudden appearance, I'm not really surprised. Putting my trust in Drew, I choose to believe that this isn't a setup, and he didn't go through this willingly.

After our heart-to-heart the other night, I have no doubts that this is all his father's doing. I'm tempted to retreat into myself and scurry around the table and hide behind Drew. Especially when his father's beady eyes sweep the length of my body, stopping at my cleavage and the short hem of my dress, but I don't. I won't give this fucker the satisfaction of scaring me into submission.

"My, oh, my, doesn't your little wallflower clean up well? She almost looks...decent. It's crazy how a little makeup, money, and dress can change a girl's entire appearance."

Hot liquid rage makes me clench my hands into tight fists.

"You're a pig." I can't stand to be in the same room with this monster, not with all the knowledge I know about it. "Let me know when the trash takes itself out. I'll be at the bar until then." I move to push past him, but he cuts me off.

His hand clamps tight around my bicep, circling it completely. "Please, you don't have to leave, at least not on my account. I only wanted to make sure my son's date is well taken care of." I cringe, my skin crawling from his touch. He's looking at me like I'm a side of beef at the butcher, and he might want a cut.

There's a noise, and I realize Drew's practically vibrating as he surges to his feet, his knees having knocked into the table in his haste to get to me. The heavy, erratic beat of my heart slows once Drew reaches my side. "Let. Her. Go"

His father releases me and lifts his hands into the air as if to say he means no harm. "Don't get your panties in a twist. I was just ensuring your date doesn't abandon you before the first course, Son."

The server returns with bread and sets it in the middle

of the table. Drew's dad snatches the woman around the waist, one arm anchoring her to him the other circling her throat, his touch possessive.

"Oh, two lovely women in one room. If only my son could handle the bounty."

I grimace and then snap at him. "Leave her alone. She's just doing her damn job."

His eyes flash to mine and then narrow. I can tell he wants to say something, but he doesn't. Instead, he shoves the girl away, discarding her like trash. She skitters out of the room, her chin ducked low, but I don't miss the shades of red painting her cheeks.

We are all standing, eyeing each other. Drew's body is strung tight with tension. His father eyes us both, and it's hard to tell what his next move will be. It's like waiting for a bomb to go off. After a minute, Drew's dad lets out a bois-terous laugh. It echoes through my head, and when he lifts his hands, taking a step back, I flinch.

Drew notices and grits his teeth, anger pulsing through him. He wraps his arm around my waist, pulling me tight to his side.

"I think it's time for you to leave," Drew orders.

After a moment, he senses that neither of us are going to give in to his fucked-up game.

"Okay, well, I'll leave you two kids to enjoy the rest of your evening. I just wanted to make sure things were going well."

It's on the tip of my tongue to ask him why he cares, but inviting conversation with him is like walking a tightrope. A tightrope with piranhas circling a lake below, and I'm not about to step out on that line.

Almost like he wasn't here to begin with, he disappears from the room. The second the door shuts behind him, I release all the air from my lungs. I break out of Drew's hold and walk back to the table. I slump against it, bracing both my hands on it to steady myself.

I TURN TO FACE DREW. "I'm trying really hard not to react, but I really, really want to react. So please, tell me. Was this a setup? Did you willingly agree to play your father's game or...?" When he opens his mouth to speak, all I can do is shake my head. "Drew, I'm trying, okay? I'm meeting you halfway, but I'm struggling because as long as your father has control over you, there will be no us. There can never be an us. How can there ever be? He'll always be there pulling the strings."

Drew reaches for me, his arm wrapping around my waist like a band of steel, refusing to let me escape.

"As long as there's breath in my body and yours, there will always be an us."

"No, there won't. Your father will use me against you for the rest of our lives. I won't be a willing or unwilling pawn to him."

"You don't have to be. Just...I can't lose you."

I tense and force myself to breathe. "Then talk. Tell me what happened."

He slumps forward, his body loosening behind mine as if in defeat, and I hate it so much. I almost turn around to face him but talk myself out of it. He doesn't need or want my empathy.

"It's not something we can talk about here. Can I take

you on a real date? Please? Somewhere that is us and where there's none of this bullshit. If you want to go home afterward, then I'll take you without any argument."

I roll my eyes. As if Drew wouldn't argue. I don't believe that for a second, but I'm inclined to give him the benefit of the doubt after his conversation with me the other day.

I let out a sigh. "Fine, but I want you to give that server an absolutely obscene tip before we go. She deserves it after dealing with your father."

He chuckles, his breath against my neck. "I'm fine with that. Let's get out of here, Flower."

29

DREW

She's right. I know she is, and that's why I have to ensure he dies. It feels wrong to think about my father's death, much less talk about and come up with a plan to kill the fucker and not feel a lick of remorse, but I can't bring myself to feel anything but hatred for the man. I've considered all the options.

From blackmail, to leaving the family behind, to simply disappearing. None of them will ever allow me to be free of him. None of them will protect my mother. There are no other options. I don't try to think about what kind of person that makes me. I'm fucked up in so many ways. I know this. Nothing I do will change that.

Guilt is an emotion I'm still learning to wrap my head around. Many days, when I think of Bel and all that I've put her through, the guilt becomes overwhelming. I don't deserve her, not at all, but now that she's inside me, wrapped around my brain, pumping in my veins there's no letting her go. I'm a piece of shit for bringing her here and playing into my father's game once more. I have to remind myself that it won't be long until he's no longer here to ruin our lives.

It's one small step in the direction we need to go, a necessary evil. It's also something I need to explain to Bel. I was hoping to shield her from the gory details, but there's no way around it now. I can't possibly gain her trust while keeping her locked in the dark.

I can't risk losing her, which means I'll need to tell her everything, from my plan to kill my father down to the fact that my parents aren't even my real ones. If I can make her understand and hold on to her a little longer, then I can fix this.

I just need to make her understand and see it.

I keep my hand on her lower back as I escort us outside, waiting for the minute she shoves my hand away.

Her body is tense, her shoulders set back, chin up, as if she's daring anyone to tell her she shouldn't be here or be with me. Her strength and fury is sexy as fuck, but even I struggle to find a reason to have such a class-act woman at my side. I scan the exit as we wait for the valet in case my father decides to come back and ruin things further.

"Are you still hungry?"

She skims her hand across her belly and shrugs. "Yeah, nothing in there looked very tasty anyway. It looked like the kind of place that serves twelve courses of foam or something."

A chuckle slips out of me, and I tug her against my side. "Yeah, it was that kind of place, but the wine is pretty great."

"You can get wine at the drive-through near campus, and I hear it comes in a convenient box with a spout. Like an adult Capri Sun but with vodka in it."

I smile at her and shake my head. "Are you...teasing me, Ms. Jacobs? That seems unwise."

Her eyes flash with lust and trail upward to meet mine. I swallow hard and consider pinning her to the nearest wall to have my way with her. I'm consumed by her, and there isn't a goddamn thing, or person, that will stand in the way of us having our happily ever after.

"Maybe, or maybe I just enjoy your form of punishment."

Her declaration loosens something in my chest, allowing me to breathe again. I was certain my father had ruined the entire evening for us, but that little sentence makes me think otherwise. The valet brings the car around, and I open her door before the man can get there, glaring as I snatch the keys out of his hand before he gets any ideas.

Mine. He's lucky I didn't remove his eyeballs from his body for looking at her.

Once I'm in the driver's seat, I pull away with a growl of the engine. At the exit of the parking lot, I scan the street ahead and spot the place I'm hunting, a smile tugging at my lips. It's a couple of blocks away, but we speed down the road like a bullet. I watch Bel out of the corner of my eye, her cheeks pink, her eyes bright and shimmering in the shadows of darkness. I swing into the fast-food burger joint ahead and notice that a little bit of the light in her eyes dims.

She tips her head back and blinks furiously like she's

trying to stop herself from crying. Fuck, what did I do now?

"What's wrong?" I ask as I steer into the drive-through line.

"Nothing. Nothing is wrong. It's just this was my mom's favorite place. We'd come here anytime we could afford it, so it just holds a lot of memories for me. That's all." She dabs at the edge of her eyes before looking at me with a half smile. I'm undecided about whether we should get food here or not. I don't want to ruin the date further. As if she can see me wavering in my decision, her smile widens. "Stop overthinking it, Drew. This place is perfect. Really. Much better than overpriced wine and meat-flavored foam."

"If you're okay with it, then yes, but I don't want to ruin the night further."

"You didn't ruin the night to begin with. Your father is the one who tried to, but I refuse to let him get that satisfaction."

That's my girl. I order for both of us, getting a few burgers, a couple of orders of fries, with some mayo for her since I know she likes to mix it with her ketchup for dipping. She leans over the center console and whispers, "*Milkshake,*" in my ear when we pull up to the window to pay.

With a shake of my head, I turn to the window and lay on the charm to get a couple of milkshakes added to the order as well. Bel is beaming with joy and takes the bags of food and milkshakes happily when we get to the second window.

With the goods in hand, I drive to a nearby park overlooking a small river. It's perfect. I put the car in park and kill the engine, wishing I had brought her on my bike instead. Sighing, I turn in my seat and find her digging in the bags. She pulls out the mayo and ketchup packets and a thing of fries.

"I'm going to get this all over my nice dress." She frowns but then shrugs, shoving a fry between her pretty pink lips. "It'll be worth it."

I scan the sexy curve of her waist and down over her hip, and when she offers me a paper-wrapped burger, I shake my head.

"No, you eat. I want to explain everything first."

She nods and takes a huge bite of her burger. A moan of pleasure escapes her, and I swear the sound goes straight to my cock.

"I'm going to need you to stop moaning like that if you want me to get any explaining done because all I can think about right now is replacing that burger with my cock."

She lets out a snort and continues chewing while rolling her eyes. This feels so much more like us. She's relaxed and happy. That's all I could ever ask for, as long as I'm by her side for it.

"My father is pissed off because Sebastian removed his funding from the firm the other night."

"Hwee thid?" she asks through a full mouth, and I can't help but grin at her.

"He did, yes. Since then, my father has got it in his head that he wants us to get married so he can get back into Sebastian's good graces and hopefully gain access to the extensive Arturo fortune if something were to happen to one or both of us. It's a fucked-up plan, but I'd expect nothing else from him."

I watch her face as what I'm saying sinks in. She swallows hard and wipes her mouth with a napkin. "You mean, he's trying to pimp you out again, but this time to me instead?"

I shrug. "Yeah."

Her brow tugs together, and she looks like she's trying to solve a puzzle. "I wasn't supposed to find out, I'm sure, since you didn't mention it to me, but is this why you want to kill him? Why you asked Sebastian for help?"

Fuck. I had hoped she didn't hear that conversation before she entered the kitchen, but I guess she did. It doesn't matter because I knew after what happened tonight I'd have to tell her the entire plan. There was no getting out of it. Yes, I wanted to protect her but I need her to know that I was serious.

With a long exhale, I slump against the seat. "I wasn't trying to keep it from you, but I also didn't want to drag you into it. It's the kind of situation that if the wrong people find out I could end up in prison. I don't want you to be an accomplice to a murder. And on the off chance my father didn't die, he'd do anything to destroy us."

"I don't like it. I know you want him to die, and I'll be the first to tell you he deserves whatever is coming to him, but the idea of you killing your own father. There's no coming back from that. I'm worried you might fall off the deep end."

I reach for her and swipe some of the ketchup that sits

in the corner of her lip with my thumb. "I'm more concerned about the effect my father's living will have on you. He won't stop until he gets what he wants, which means I'll either be forced to follow his orders or risk retaliation. I won't put you or my mother at risk anymore. I'm tired of fighting him, tired of being his punching bag. He deserves to die. He's a ticking time bomb, and I don't know when he's going to go off. All I know is that I have the power and resources to end this, and I will. There is no other option."

She scans my face, the food forgotten for now. "There has to be another way, blackmail, or..."

I cut her off, trying to rein my anger in. "There isn't. Nothing will stop him. He's on a power trip, and no one is safe from him. Not me or my mother. He's threatened to kill me so many times. What happens when it's no longer a threat? He wants to drag you into the mess too, and I can't let him do that. I refuse. I've lost so much because of him. I won't risk losing you again."

I watch her eyes and the way she swallows thickly. I know she wants to fight me on this, but she doesn't understand. There's nothing he won't use against me. "Okay, and Sebastian? How does he fit into all of this?"

"He's got access to resources I need, and while he won't be the one pulling the trigger, he's helping me come up with a plan that solidifies everything. He wants him dead as much as I do, and I know he'll do anything to ensure your safety."

She shoves her food into the bag and drops it at her feet, then leans down to unstrap the sky-high heels she's wearing. Once she's done, she shimmies her dress to sit crisscrossed in the seat, her knees pressed between the console and the door. It looks uncomfortable as fuck, but she seems to need to shift in order to think.

"I don't want to know anything, I think. It's one thing to know you are planning or might do it, but another to hear all the details. My biggest concern in all of this is the impact it will have on you and Sebastian. If something happens to either of you..." Emotion clogs her throat, but she continues, "I don't think I could handle losing both of you."

"Shhh, you aren't losing either of us," I soothe, reaching for her.

She shakes her head and clenches her tiny fists, slamming them down on her thighs. "You don't know that. There's always the risk of the unknown. What if someone finds out? What if you don't succeed in killing him? I'm so angry right now. Angry for you, for us. It feels like we'll never be free of him."

"Which is why I have to do this, Flower. It's why I have to take the risk. Because if I don't, then the outcome is the same. You were right when you said there is no us as long as my father is a part of my life."

"I didn't think you'd take that as an opening to have him murdered," she squeaks, and I can see tears shining in her eyes when she turns to face me.

"If it makes you feel better he's not even my real father."

"What?" Her mouth pops open, "What do you mean he's not even your real father?"

"It's a long story, but I found out when I had them run some blood tests on me after my mom was admitted to the hospital. I was hoping that if she needed a transplant that I would be a match, but what I found out instead was that neither of them were my parents."

I didn't think Bel's face could fall any further, but it does, and I hate the way she's looking at me with pity and sadness. Is it sad? Of course, but it's life, and I'm grateful to discover he's not my father. It explains his hate for me all these years. There's no way in hell he doesn't know.

"Wait, so your mom and dad aren't your parents?"

I shake my head. "Nope. They aren't my parents and before you ask I don't know who my parents are. My plan was to ask my mother at some point and time, but she's been in a coma since she came home, and the piece of shit refuses to let me see her."

"Have you talked to him about it?" She whispers the question, almost as if she knows the impact it will have on me.

"I haven't. I'm afraid he'll use it against me. That he'll find a way to hurt me or Mom worse if he finds out that I know. The only way for me to find out would be for me to have blood tests run, and if he thinks I know more than I should about her condition or what he's doing to her, then it could ruin everything. He'll never spend time in jail for what he's done, but before he takes his last breath, I'll make certain he knows that I knew everything."

"I'm sorry..." Bel says crawling over the center console and into my lap. I don't even attempt to stop her. I could use the distraction because there's a lot of darkness in my head right now. "I'm sorry for all you've lost and all you've gone through. I know it doesn't change anything, that my apologizing doesn't fix it, but I want you to know that I see you and hear you. You aren't alone."

Bel has a way of calming the storm before it becomes uncontrollable. She doesn't run from my storm clouds but instead dances in the rain. She takes the bad and turns it into something magical, and I envy the person she is.

"I don't deserve you, Bel, but I'm never letting you go. Never," I whisper against her lips while cradling her head between my hands. So fragile, so fucking perfect.

She licks her lips, and her eyes flash to mine, a little wide, a little hot.

"I want you."

"You have me. Always." I run my thumb along her bottom lip.

"No, I want you..." She licks the tip of my thumb, making my nostrils flare and my cock grow harder. I look up and find her cheeks a crimson color. Is she embarrassed? I hope not. I'll give her whatever she wants, but only if she begs prettily for me.

"Do you?" I lick my own lips. "How bad?"

"Really bad," she answers, her voice husky.

"Hmm... and do you trust me, Bel? Trust me to fuck you however I want. To do whatever I want to your body because it belongs to me, as does your pleasure?"

She's looking at me now with wide, soft eyes, and I can't help but stare back, waiting for her answer. It almost burns that it takes her so long to answer, but I guess I deserve that.

Finally, she nods the best she can while in my grasp. "I trust you."

Her words slice through me, leaving behind little cuts of satisfaction, each one a tiny release. "Good because only I can make you feel this way." I quickly hit the button to slide the driver's seat back as far as it will go.

I release my hold on her face and trail my hands down her body until I reach the hem of her dress, which I shimmy up higher so I can feel the heat of her pussy on my slacks. I'll be inside her very soon, but that doesn't mean I want to go without feeling her against me.

I glide my hands up her hips, over her trim waist, and higher until I reach her slender throat. Like a cobra, I strike, wrapping one hand around the delicate column, noticing the way her pulse spikes and her breathing increases. She loves it when I play the predator, when I unleash all her wicked fantasies.

"Do you think you could fight me off? Do you think you could escape me?" I whisper against her ear, nipping at it.

She tenses, her entire body trembling with pleasure. I pull back and look into her eyes. Her pupils are dilated, and she wants this so bad I can feel her leaking on my slacks.

I apply the barest hint of pressure, and her eyes pop open, her pupils blown wide. "Drew..." she whispers.

"You'll never be free of me, Flower. Never be free of the darkness. I'll always find a way to possess you, and if I can't, I'll hunt you down and fuck you until you beg me to take mercy on you. You're mine. All. Fucking. Mine," I growl the words against her throat, and then suck on the tender flesh hard enough to leave marks.

I want to mark her flesh. Brand her so everyone knows she's mine, and I want her to brand me in return so everyone knows I'm hers.

"Yours," she moans, grinding against me, seeking out relief to the pleasure building in her core.

"Do you trust me?" I repeat again.

With a gulp I feel against my palm, she nods.

"Good. If you need me to stop, tap my thigh with your hand, do you understand?"

She nods as much as she's able, then I squeeze tighter, until her shoulders drop and she leans even forward, her entire body pressing against me. I arch my hips up into hers because I just can't help it. "A little more, Flower."

I tighten my grip on her delicate neck, all at once realizing I could snap it so easily. But she is giving this to me —to me— after everything I've done. She trusts me enough to make this good for her, to put her life in my hands.

She's forcing breaths heavily in and out of her nose now, at almost a pant. I can't hold out much longer. Sliding my free hand down, I nearly moan at the heat of her pussy before flicking the scrap of lace against her cunt aside. She's dripping, and I sink two fingers deep into her cunt without warning.

"Fuck, Bel. Your pussy was made for me. You clench so tight around my fingers, and do you hear that?" I fuck her with the digits, letting the wet indecent sounds fill the vehicle. "You like this, don't you? Being at my mercy, letting me choke you while I fuck your pussy."

A moan slips free from her lips, those full, lush lips I dream about, and with my hand wrapped around her throat, I kiss her. Gently at first, small sips of a kiss until she opens her mouth to me, and I slide my tongue along hers, tasting ketchup, salt, and the sweetness that is just my wallflower, my Bel.

I tighten my hand the tiniest bit, and she wiggles in my lap, sliding forward like she might glide along my cock if she had access. And I fucking want her to have everything she wants.

I tug the two fingers out of her slick heat and bring them to my mouth. I suck the glistening arousal off my fingers and then grapple with my belt, jerking my slacks open. I tug the belt off and release her throat.

She lets out a whimper of displeasure, and all I can do is smile. With my other hand, I take both her wrists and hold them together. This angle causes her to thrust her tits into my face, and I inhale the scent of her, my chin in her cleavage, as I take the belt and wrap it around her wrists, securing her hands behind her back. Then I reach up to cup them gently before sliding my right hand higher and my left hand lower to release my zipper and pull myself free.

She licks her lips and stares at me with hooded eyes. *So fucking beautiful.*

"You want my cock, Flower?"

She nods once, and I squeeze her neck a little and skim the head of myself along her wet slit, teasing us both. "If you want it, you have to tell me you want it. Beg me, Bel. Be a good girl and fucking beg me to choke you, beg me to fuck you, beg me to make you come."

She's panting now, all but writhing against me, and I loosen my grasp enough so that she can get the words out. "Please, Drew. Please. Fuck me."

"And?" I prompt, not even hiding the deep edge to my tone, the need coursing through me.

"Fuck me. Choke me. Do whatever you want to me. You can have it all."

I lean in and nip at her jaw. Her eyes are squeezed shut, and I tip her face down and press my forehead into hers. "Open your eyes and say it again."

Her beautiful green eyes flutter open, and when she speaks, I nearly come then. "Fuck me, Drew. Please. Please, fuck me."

I smile and skate my mouth across hers. "Such a good fucking girl, that's only bad for me." I've teased us both enough. I take my cock into my hand, bringing it to her entrance, and I thrust deep. At the same time, I press my lips to hers, kissing her hard, taking her mouth with the same brutality as I take her pussy.

She moans into my mouth, and I swallow it all while her body tightens around mine like a vise. *Fuck, she feels so good.* I'm not going to last long, and I need to make this so good for her.

"Look at how beautifully you bloom for me, my Little Wallflower," I murmur and arch my hips enough to drive deep. I keep a tight grip on her neck and slowly constrict her air supply, watching as panic bleeds into her eyes. I grit my teeth and pound into her from below until that panic fades. She starts panting, and her nails dig into my knees from behind her back.

She's so close I can already feel her pussy tightening. I

clamp my other hand across her mouth and nose. "Trust me here, Bel. When I tell you to breathe, I want you to take big full breaths, got it?"

She nods softly, and I shift my hips higher, harder, and deeper until I feel her right on the edge. Her eyes roll back, and I feel the spasm of her orgasm starting. I give one last tight squeeze to her airway, then release her completely. "Now."

She sucks a ragged breath into her lungs, like she's been dying for it, and her pussy milks me as she comes. Small screams slip out between her gasping breaths. It's the greatest thing I've ever heard.

"Use me, Flower. Fuck me. Take from me. I'm at your mercy, forever and always." I brush the blond strands from her face so I can see her eyes. Then I drop my hands down to my sides, and she rides me like a bull, her body writhing against mine.

When the last flutters of her orgasm come to an end, I grip her by the hips with bruising force and slam deep, fucking her hard, embedding myself inside her, just like she's embedded herself under my skin.

"Drew! Oh shit," she mewls, and I don't take mercy on her. If anything, I fuck her harder, holding her to my chest, bending her, forcing her to take more of my cock.

"I'm going to come. I'm going to fill your pussy with my cum."

"Yes! Yes!" Bel cries against my throat, and then, out of nowhere, she bites me. Her teeth sink deep into my shoulder, and I lose my fucking mind. I slam into her over and over again, following the searing pain in my shoulder and the rising pleasure in my gut.

In seconds, I'm exploding, coming so hard I see stars behind my eyes as I empty myself deep inside her. I float back down to reality slowly, and when I open my eyes, I see her. She's watching me, and there's a softness, a serenity in her gaze as she scans my face.

I cup her by the cheeks, kiss her lips gently, and whisper the words I've been unable to because I wasn't ready or aware of what it really meant to love someone.

"I love you, Flower."

Her eyes go wide, and her mouth pops open. "You...?"

"You don't have to say it back. I don't need you to, not until you're ready. I just want you to know that I love you. I'm sorry I didn't tell you sooner. I didn't know what it felt like to love someone until I lost you, and I had to endure the concept that you might never give me a second chance."

"I..." She struggles to find the words, and I can see her beautiful mind trying to wrap itself around my confession, but I don't need her to say the words to me. I don't need to know that she loves me, because her actions prove it to me.

"Shh. You don't have to say anything," I repeat and undo the belt that's wrapped around her wrists, then I gently massage them until the blood returns to her limbs. I don't dare look at her face because I'm afraid that what I'll see there will hurt far more than the thought of never getting a chance to fix things with her. After holding her for a bit, I ease her back into the seat and grab some wipes from behind the seat. I clean her up gently, as best I can.

I check the time on the dash, realizing I need to get her home soon.

"Buckle up. I need to get you home before you turn into a pumpkin."

She laughs softly and settles back into the seat.

The drive back to the mansion is quiet, too quiet, and I wonder if I made a mistake telling her. When I pull up to the house, her fingers hover on the door handle and I swear my heart is about to beat out of my chest. She turns to look at me, a tiny little smile tugging at her lips.

"I don't need to wait to tell you that I love you, Drew. I loved you even when I knew I shouldn't. I loved you when you weren't deserving of my love, and I love you now."

She slips from the car and closes the door behind her, leaving me with that parting admission. I squeeze the steering wheel with both hands, stopping myself from following her inside the house. *Fuck, she loves me. She loves me.* She loves me even when I don't deserve her love, and that's why my father must pay. That's why I have to do this.

To protect her and my mom.

It'll kill me to bring her deeper into this, but she's strong, stronger than Sebastian or anyone gives her credit for, and if she trusts me like I know she does, she'll see right through the bullshit. *Don't worry, Flower. I'll protect you. I'll end this for good and give you the happily ever after we both deserve.* I tug my phone out of my pocket and scroll to my father's contact.

My fingers tremble as I type out the words. The element of surprise is what's going to make this go as smoothly as we need it to.

· · ·

ME: Tomorrow at sunset. I'll bring her to the house. Have everything ready.

I DON'T EXPECT to receive a text back right away, but three little dots appear on the screen, and then I find myself squeezing the device hard enough to hurt my fingers as I read his response.

DAD: Good. Come by the house. I want to discuss everything for tomorrow.

ME: K. On my way.

AS BADLY AS I don't want to go, I don't have any other option. I need to make this look good, like I'm on his side. If I make him think I'm in agreement, then his guard will be down, and he'll never see the attack coming.

MY SKIN IS clammy when I arrive at the house, and I wipe my hands on my dress pants. I hate what I'm about to do, but I remind myself that this is the last time I'll ever have to play his warped games. This is the last time I ever bow to him. The house is quiet, almost eerily and when I reach my father's office, I see his guards missing from their usual posts.

He's sitting behind his desk, a glass of whiskey in his hand instead of the entire bottle like the time before. I shudder at the memory. I hate being here in his presence.

"I'm glad you've finally decided to see things my way."

"Well, I realized tonight at dinner that no matter what I do, I'll never get her to agree to marry me. Knowing that, I knew there was no reason to wait."

The smile that twists his lips is depraved. "I can't wait to see the look on Sebastian's face when he realizes his whore of a sister married you. Once we get rid of both of them and inherit the family assets, you'll be free to find any woman you want."

I force myself not to react to his horrible words. The way he talks about disposing of them as if they aren't real living, fucking people.

"What's the plan?" I grit out.

His eyes narrow, and it looks like he's trying to look through me, to find any holes in my exterior so he can rip me open. Easing out of his chair, he walks around his desk, stopping a few feet in front of me.

"I thought you would've come up with a plan. It is your wedding day after all."

"If I had it my way, I'd drug her, bring her to the house, and have everything finished before she wakes up so I don't have to deal with her struggling or fighting."

"Maybe you are more like me than I thought." He smiles and tugs something out of his pocket, extending his hand out to me.

Internally cringing, I open my hand and take the small syringe with a needle attached to it. Then I look up at him. "What's in it?"

"Midazolam. It's a preoperative sedative and should make her lucid enough to agree but not enough to be combative."

"Is it safe?" I cock a brow in question.

He shrugs. "Depends on how much you give her. Too much and she'll stop breathing on her own. Not enough and we'll have to use other methods to keep her quiet."

My stomach churns at the thought of him touching her or being near her. There's no other way, though. Hopefully, she'll be knocked out long enough for me to get the job done. "Okay, I'll make sure I give her enough."

"Good, just don't kill her. Not yet. I need to get her signature on the marriage certificate first, and then we can figure out how we'll get rid of her and her brother."

"No worries." I swallow around the anxiety clawing up my throat, pushing it down as far as I can. Even the briefest hint of weakness and he'll jump on it.

"I'm glad you decided to see things my way. It's a shame it took this long..."

"I thought Sebastian was my friend, and I thought I loved Bel. Turns out, it wasn't love. It wasn't anything. It needs to be taken care of."

"Love is a fickle thing. It's much easier to fuck and leave them instead."

"I'll make her regret ever crossing paths with me." I grit my teeth, ensuring he can see the venom behind my words.

"By the time we're done with them, regret will be the only thing they can focus on. I promise you that. Now get out. I'll have it all in order for you tomorrow. You can thank me later." He motions at the door, the whiskey in his glass sloshing up the side.

I don't wait for him to tell me again. I'm out of his office in a flash. It will take every last ounce of courage to get this done, but once finished, it will be worth it. Bel will be safe. My mother will be safe. Everything will be as it was always supposed to be.

30

BEL

The following morning, I roll over in bed, wondering if the events from the night before really happened or if they were a dream. It was the most fun I'd had in a long time, and our date showed me that I had already forgiven Drew for what happened. I was simply afraid and using that fear as a crutch.

Now, my biggest concern isn't that fear alone; it is a fear of a different type. A fear for Drew and Sebastian and what might happen to one or both of them if they decide to go through with this plan. I know I said I didn't want to know anything, and I still really don't want to know, but standing by and letting them go through with it without trying to give them other ideas or stop them seems stupid.

Yesterday, Drew seemed more determined than ever that he was going to go through with it, and while I hesitate to try to have another conversation with him, I won't shy away from it. This is our future together, and his actions will directly impact both of us. I love him and I don't want to see him or my brother go to prison, even if his piece of shit father deserves nothing short of death. I hold my cell phone in my hands, contemplating who I'll go and question first, Sebastian or Drew.

Fate steps in at that moment, and my cell chimes with an incoming text from Drew.

Psycho: Come to The Mill at 5.

IT'S NOT A QUESTION, but a demand. I'm tempted to reply with a smart-ass remark but choose against it. The time on my phone says three, and while I know his message says five, I've already spent the entire day letting my thoughts on the conversation run rampant.

If I show up earlier than expected, who cares?

There's a frenzy of fear in my gut. I hate the thought of losing either of them over some stupid-ass shit. Not now, not when things have been better. Drew's dad would find a way to fuck everything up. The longer I've thought through it, the more I'm pulled in two directions.

Part of me wants to tell Drew that I'll do anything I can to help him get rid of his father, but the other part of me, the part with the moral compass, feels disgusted at the thought.

Death is something the horrible man deserves more than anyone I know, but...

Do I really have it in me to be an accomplice to murder?

It's hard to think about because the thought reminds me of my mother and how fresh that loss still is. I miss her every single day, and I'd do anything to get her back, and here is Drew preparing to kill his father just so he can be free.

It hurts my heart the longer I think about it, so instead of doing that, I make the executive decision to go see him early. I ease away from my desk and the stacks of books, and stand to stretch. Sebastian is probably in his office right now, so if I sneak out the front door, I'll have like a fifteen-minute head start until the text barrage of "where are you" commences.

Instead of bothering the driver who will most likely tattle to Sebastian—not that I have to answer to him really —I order a ride through the app. It's only a short drive to The Mill, and I huddle into my black peacoat as the car inches up the driveway.

When the car pulls away, I'm left standing there facing the front door of the mansion. I'm not sure what to do with myself. *Do I knock?* I almost laugh.

Usually the door is half open, people or a party spilling out. I guess I'll just go inside. With a shrug, I push it open and step inside, letting the warmth of the house lead me. The juxtaposition is almost painful between the deadly chill outside and the blasting heat indoors.

It would be a wonderful day to be cuddled on the couch with hot cocoa and a book. I vaguely wonder if I could get Drew to read one of the romance books I'm reading. I save the thought for another time and walk a little farther inside.

The house is mostly silent, and I don't like it. It's odd and makes me think there's something bad about to happen. I tell myself it's nothing but nerves. I tiptoe toward the staircase, but freeze, my heart thudding into my throat when I spot Lee standing in the kitchen, his dark gaze on me.

The normal boyish grin and charm he exudes are replaced with something far more menacing now, and the energy that rolls off him makes me shiver. My gaze roams his shirtless chest, not because I'm checking him out, but because of what I see there. Even in the dim lighting, you can't miss the numerous scars that dot his chest, sides, and arms.

Are they from fights? Is someone hurting him? Is he hurting himself?

The questions stack up, and all I can do is frown at him, afraid that if I open my mouth, I'll end up regretting it.

"Wipe that look off your face. I don't want or need your pity."

I steel my spine. "I was just going to ask if you've seen Drew."

"Sure you were." He rolls his eyes. "He's upstairs, or maybe he's not. I don't know."

I take that as my cue to leave and turn on my heels, giving Lee one last look as he holds the bottle of rum to his ripped abs. It's half gone already, and I know someone needs to help him. I can see the pain in his eyes, but everyone else is so absorbed in their own issues that no one seems to notice their friend drowning in his sorrows.

I jog up the stairs, heading straight to Drew's bedroom. The door is cracked, so I take it upon myself to walk inside. The first thing I notice is the smell of burning wood, and I spot the small fire that's going in the grate.

I look from the fireplace and to his bed, noticing that

the covers are twisted and mussed, and his dirty clothes are tossed across one well-worn armchair.

There's no sign of Drew, though.

I pad across the bedroom and peek in the bathroom, but it's empty too. *Well shit.* I tug out my phone, clamber up onto his huge-ass bed, and settle into the pillows that smell like him. Then I shoot him a text. I wait and nearly startle, tumbling out of bed when his phone dings loudly on the bedside table.

Jesus. I have to relax a little. Getting my heartbeat back under control, I figure it's unlikely he went far without his phone, so it shouldn't be long till he gets back. I slip off my shoes and snuggle under the covers, reveling in his warmth and scent of teakwood and mint. If life was perfect, this is what it would be. Him, me, us spending time together, and not worrying about all the other bullshit.

I know I shouldn't have to be concerned that my boyfriend is about to kill his father. That shit isn't normal. None of this is normal. *So how do I fix it?* If I told him not to do it, would he even listen? *Doubtful.* Drew is the single most hardheaded person I know. Telling him not to do something is the ammunition needed for him to do it just to spite you.

What if things go wrong? What if he fails, or worse, what if he doesn't? Who will he be if he succeeds? Will killing his father push him closer to damnation, or is it the saving grace he needs to climb out of the dark?

These thoughts swimming in my head are the reason I barely slept last night. I inhale long and hard, using his scent to chase away some of my doubts and fears.

It's not easy with our history, but after yesterday, after he's been so transparent about everything, how can I not give him the benefit of the doubt? He's changed. I know it. I see it when he speaks to me and touches me with reverence and respect. He touches me with love. Something I don't think he could have fathomed when all of this started months ago.

And I know he's noticed the changes in me too. The way I don't roll over and take every blow, every slight. I'm no longer a wallflower. I'm a fucking wildflower. I'm his wildflower.

I roll over on the mussed covers and climb out of the lush bed to wander the room. I'm restless and need to move around to get some of the energy out. Yes, I trust him, but just because I trust him doesn't mean that I'm not worried about him.

His father is a monster, and Drew is, admittedly, also a monster. I guess it takes one to kill one, but how much of a monster will this turn him into?

I pace by the edge of his bed, back and forth, back and forth. I continue pacing, and as I do, I scan the shelves around the fireplace, dark thick wood lined with battered paperbacks, textbooks, and a few old classics. Somehow, the old classics look fresher than the paperbacks. It makes me smile, and I skim the lines of books with my fingers reading the titles, tilting my head as I walk to scan each one of them.

Drew knows how much I love books and reading in general, but we've never talked about any of these books. He's never indicated an interest in reading.

I continue, my smile growing wider and wider until I

reach the end of the shelf. At the very edge of the shelf my entire body clamps up. My heart hammers in my chest, and my thoughts take a nosedive into the dark.

Lying there on top of one of the hardbound books is a syringe, with its clear blue cap over the needle tip. The contents are clear from what I can see. I twist around and peer over my shoulder, half expecting him to jump out of the shadows, but he's still not here, and that only intensifies my worry.

I've seen him drink several times, but I've never considered that he might use drugs. I blink, and without thinking, I pick up the syringe to inspect it closer. What would he be taking that's in a syringe form? God. I need to stop thinking about this. It's probably nothing. Maybe a steroid for football or maybe it's a shot for some type of illness.

I hear his footsteps a heartbeat before he enters the room, and as I whirl around, I see the ghost of a smile on his lips. It slips off his face the moment he sees the syringe in my hand.

"What are you doing?"

I gulp around the ball of anxiety that's now formed in my throat and gently place the syringe back on the shelf. He stalks toward me, and I take an involuntary step back right as he reaches me. I don't know why I do it. He doesn't appear angry. If anything, he looks sorry, which makes no sense to me.

Snatching the syringe off the book, he repeats the question he asked a moment ago. "What are you doing?"

"Nothing. I was... I was waiting for you. You seem to enjoy going through my things, so I thought I'd return the favor." I force myself to smile, but he doesn't return it. My gaze shifts back to the syringe, and I can't stop myself from asking. I trust him. I love him, so why am I so afraid to know what this is all about?

"What's in the syringe?"

His mouth folds into a thin line. "It's something that I didn't want to have to use, but that I no longer have an option not to use."

It's neither an answer, nor a question.

I chuckle and shake my head. "Is it some kind of steroid, a football thing?" I try to make my tone teasing, but instead, it comes out shaky with what...fear?

"Bel." He sucks a deep breath into his lungs, then exhales with a slight rumble through his chest. When his arm snakes around my waist and he drags me against his chest, I'm unable to resist. "I hate that I have to do this to you, and I promise I'll be able to explain everything when it's over, but right now...I can't. I know I don't deserve it, but I need your complete trust."

I pull away enough so I can see his face. "I told you I trust you, and I do. I'm just confused and worried. You're speaking in riddles."

"You're looking at me a lot like you did that first night in the woods, so I don't really feel like you trust me."

I blink and swallow. "I don't know. I trust you, obviously. I just...why would you have a syringe? And what's in it? Why are you talking like you're going to use it on me?" I force myself to look away from the syringe that he's just uncapped. Like if I don't look at it, then it means he won't do what I'm suspecting he will.

"Bel...Wallflower, look at me."

I do, only from habit, the sharp bite of command in his tone. "You either trust me or you don't. Say you trust me."

"I do." The words slip from my lips with ease. The sharp jab of a needle hits the side of my neck, and I hiss out a breath. "What the hell?"

"Trust me, Bel. That's all you need to do right now, okay?" A slow tingly warmth moves through my veins, and my knees wobble.

What did he inject into my body?

There's an undercurrent of sheer panic, but beneath that is the reminder of trust. Peering into my eyes, he tightens his hold on me and moves me to hold my complete weight. There isn't anything malicious in his eyes. In fact, he's looking at me with more yearning than I've ever seen before.

"Drew," I murmur as a heavy fog clouds my mind. "I might trust you, but that doesn't mean I'm not super mad at you right now."

He chuckles softly, gently brushing strands of hair from my face, and I feel the heat of his breath against the side of my neck. "Fair enough, Flower. We'll settle up when you're back on your feet. Just remember, I love you, and I'm doing this for us."

With those last words and his beautiful green eyes swimming in my mind, my eyes flutter closed, and I slip deep into darkness, losing myself completely.

31

DREW

Choosing to bring her into the lion's den wasn't an easy choice but the only option. I hate that I'll be putting her in the same room as my father all over again, but I remind myself that this will be the last time. It has to be.

My stomach roils, and bile rises up my throat. I'm sick with grief and anger. I really don't want to fucking do this, but now that I've administered the drug, I need to go through with it. I have no idea how long it will stay in her system. I have to take her to my father's house while she's still knocked out to sell the plan.

I need him to be arrogant and secure in the fact that he's won before I rip his head off his body and burn it in the woods behind The Mill house.

Okay, that's not the actual plan, but it's one of the many endings I've envisioned for him over the years. Now that it's finally time, I'm nervous. Not for myself since I haven't been able to protect myself properly in years. No, for Bel.

If she somehow gets hurt in the crossfire, I'm not sure I can live with myself. She's an intricate part of the plan, a way to put my father at ease. A way to ensure everyone but my father walks out of that room alive.

I swallow down my emotions and remind myself one last time that I'm doing this for us. Then I hike her unconscious body up a little higher and carry her down the stairs. I'm near the door when I spot Lee in the kitchen, a bottle of his alcohol of choice halfway to his lips. His gaze darts between me and Bel's face, and I can't miss the concern that appears in his eyes.

"Should I even ask?"

"No, you shouldn't. The less you know, the better."

His eyes narrow as he takes in the scene. "Since you assholes have been exceedingly anti-social and don't tell Aries or me anything, how can we help?"

"I don't want your help," I bite out, only realizing a few seconds too late how it sounds. But I don't have time to soothe his temper.

"Whatever, be that way, but know that if something happens to her, that's on you. This might be our own shit hole of lives, but we don't have to drag those we care about into the pits of darkness with us."

"Look, I'm sorry. I'll explain as soon as I can. I'll be back later... If—if I'm not, then you need to step up for The Mill."

"You know Sebastian is next in line."

I say nothing because the less he knows, the better.

"What are you planning to do, Drew?"

I shake my head and walk out the door to the car my father sent over for us. I cradle Bel's sleeping body in my lap, breathing her scent in, wishing I could take this moment and encapsulate it forever. It's short-lived, of course, since we get to the house faster than I'm ready for. Bel shifts in her sleep and every twitch makes me fear she'll wake too early. At the house, the driver opens the door, and I step out, quickly clasping Bel to my chest so he doesn't get any ideas about taking her.

She's far too light as I carry her inside, reminding me of how fragile she is in this whole thing. Even though I don't want to, I take her straight into my father's study as he instructed me. When I enter, he looks up from his desk, the double doors of the office slamming against the walls behind me.

His desk sits across the room, his back to a bank of windows, shelves line the opposite end of the room crammed with books I'm pretty sure he's never touched. An antique rug stretches the length of the room with a large leather couch, end table, and lamp near it. There's a bar built into a shelf near his desk, and he's cleared something out just beyond the doors. I stop dead and stare at the open space. "What's this?"

He waves at the empty space. "I moved some things around so we'll have room for your wedding guests."

He's fucking delusional, so I don't even bother asking about the guests comment. His beady eyes scan me from head to toe, and I try to keep any lick of emotion off my face. Any show is something he can use against me, and he's taken enough as it is.

"Well, shit, Son. I didn't think you had the balls."

Of course he didn't.

"I told you I was going to do it."

"I understand that. I'm just impressed. Not only did you stick to the plan but you got her here in one piece. Maybe there is potential in you after all."

I watch him cautiously as he walks around the desk straight toward me. There's a crystal glass of whiskey in his hand, the brown liquid near the brim. Great, he's drinking. I try to do my best to hide my response to the way his eyes move over her limp form, almost hungrily. "She is rather pretty when she tries. Not that it matters. You won't have to be married to her for very long." He waves at a clothes rack to the side of the room that I hadn't noticed when I walked in. "There are clothes for both of you. Put her on the couch, and I'll take care of dressing her while you put on your tux."

I clutch her tighter to my chest and nearly growl in response. "No. This is your party, sure, but I'll be dressing her myself. She's mine at least until I choose to dispose of her."

The usual ember of rage flickers to life in his eyes, and I expect a punch to the face for my defiance, but after a moment, the corner of his mouth lifts, and he nods.

"Fine. The white lace will look good on her, I think. She's a little too skinny for the velvet."

I carry her to the rack and pull the first white lace thing off I see. None of it matters since it's all for show. The next time I see her in a wedding dress it'll be on the day of our real wedding and my father won't be in sight. With the dress in hand, I carry her to the far corner of the room near the bookcases. It's still out in the open, and yes, he can see her, but I will do my best to shield her body as much as possible.

I quickly learn it's really fucking hard to undress and dress an unconscious person. Every time I move her, I fear she's going to wake up and freak out. I'm not sure what the hell I'll do if she wakes too early. Not that I'd blame her for freaking out. I'm just not sure I'll be able to calm her down enough to keep her in line.

The last thing I want is to see the fear in her eyes and worry that this time, this time, is when she decides she can no longer trust me.

I dress her in a white lace dress with a full gauzy skirt that bells out around her thin waist. I hurry to make sure she's covered, not worried about straightening anything out. It takes half the time to get into my tux as it took to dress her, but I still keep my body firmly between his gaze and her body. I turn to tuck the gun I brought into the small of my back once I slip on my belt and the jacket.

Then I face Bel again, if only to hide the shaking of my hands as I quickly button my shirt and tuck it into the pants. This is fucking ridiculous. Why dress us up like dolls if the marriage and wedding mean nothing more than a piece of paper and contract?

There has to be more going on, and that thought alone leaves me suspicious. I finish dressing and lift her gently to lay her on the nearby leather couch. At least she'll be more comfortable when she wakes up freaking out.

My heart is in my throat, choking me at the thought of her waking, seeing the fear on her face and the mistrust in her eyes. She'll be terrified and hate me all over again, and I don't know if I can handle that.

She trusts you.

I square my shoulders and sit beside her, then I gently

lift her head and place it on my thigh. I look away from Bel's sleeping form to see my father wheeling a hospital bed into the room. My mother's hospital bed. *Fuck.* I didn't anticipate this.

What the fuck is he doing?

I'm tempted to go over to her and make sure she's okay, but Bel is still in my lap, and I don't want to risk moving her again, not yet. "What's going on?"

He doesn't even look at me as he maneuvers my mother's bed near the bar on the far wall by his desk. I'm shocked that he even takes the time to engage the brakes on the bottom once he has her where he wants her. "I know your mother isn't one-hundred percent with us, but I would assume you don't want her to miss your big day?"

I bite the inside of my cheek until I taste blood. I'm beyond angry, and even more concerned with her here. If something goes wrong, I'll have two people to protect, instead of one. Deep breath. I count back from ten in my head. *Ten. Nine. Eight. Seven. Six. Five. Four. Three. Two. One.* I let the anger clouding my thoughts go and remind myself what the endgame in all of this is. "Fine. Whatever."

Out of nowhere, a man I vaguely recognize walks through the door. I'm tense and jumpy. If I don't calm down, I won't be able to pull the trigger when I need to. The man's tall, taller than either my father or me, with a heavy five o'clock shadow, and he's wearing a long dress coat over a nice black suit. My father cuts across the room to shake his hand. "Richard, thank you for making it on such short notice."

I've seen this man before at my father's events. One of his allies, but not really a friend.

My father turns to me with a sneer. "Richard here is going to be our officiant. He's a lawyer, naturally, and brought the contract, but he'll be doing the vows too."

I flick my gaze to Richard and back, not quite sure of him yet. "Is that legal?"

Richard smiles, and it makes him look younger than I thought. "I assure you, Mr. Marshall, the contract is perfectly legal, and I'm a state-certified officiant."

I gulp, hoping neither of them see it. None of it matters. We won't actually get that far anyway.

Bel stirs on my lap, and her whole body stiffens, telling me she's awake but pretending she's not. "So what's the plan?" I ask, knowing she's listening intently.

My father stalks over, hands in his slacks pockets, scowling down at me. "The plan is for you to marry this brat, gain access to all that Arturo money, and that's really it."

I don't bother keeping the doubt off my face. "That's it?"

He chuckles and shrugs. "I mean yes. That's all I'm going to say with a lawyer present, that is."

The lawyer in question heard every word. I glance his way. "Richard is it...what's your last name?"

He smirks. "Bellago."

Well, that explains it. One of the "community" so he wouldn't care if my father pulled out his gun and shot me in the head right now. I skim my hand down Bel's forearm. Her skin is colder than usual, and I place my arm over hers to try to warm her up. She shivers, and my dad's eyes drop to Bel's sleeping form.

"Ah, perfect timing. Our bride is ready to join us. Wonderful. We should get started."

Everything in me revolts at this plan. Yes, I agreed to it. All of it seemed like the easiest way to put my father at ease and let him drop his guard, but fuck, if Bel and I marry one day, when we marry one day, she will be fully awake, alert, and present. Not to mention, I'll spend every cent I have to give her the wedding she's always dreamed of.

Not this rushed bullshit affair in my father's fucking study.

I rub her arm again and then cup her chin gently. "Wake up for me, Flower. We'll get this over with, and you can get some rest." My voice is low and gentle, and I don't miss the sneer on my father's face or the muttered, "Fucking soft," as he heads over to his friend to whisper and confer.

It's not a moment alone like I wish I had, but it's all I know he'll give me right now.

Her eyes fly wide, and immediately, her gaze chases across my features. Tears welling. "Drew?" I don't miss the waver in her voice or the way her fingers clench on my tuxedo jacket.

"It's okay. You're safe."

Her voice cracks as she whispers, "Safe?"

"Bel, look at me." I hold her chin tight in my hand and resist the urge to spread her hair across my lap and soothe her. "Do you remember what you said to me in the car the other day? You told me that you trust me. You trust me, right?"

I keep my voice low, and the fear and pain in her eyes

are like an ice pick to my heart. "I.... I do. I just... I don't know. What's going on?"

I gently ease her into a sitting position and wait while she clutches her head in her hands, no doubt dizzy from the drugs. Dropping her hands from her face, she slides her eyes down over her body before meeting my own.

She's looking at me with a mixture of confusion and fear, and there isn't a damn thing I can do to ease her worries. "Drew. Please. Tell me what's happening. What are you doing? Why am I in this dress?"

Here goes nothing. Giving her knee a squeeze, I raise my voice and smirk at her, hoping she sees through it, like she always does. "It's your lucky day, Maybel. Today, you become a Marshall. You get to marry me."

My head feels like a fishbowl, and I'm greatly confused but there is no way that I just heard him say what I think he did. *Marry me?* I give the room we're in a glance over. I've never been in his room before, but the style reminds me of Drew's family home, and if Drew's father standing there scowling is anything to go by, at least I know where I am.

I run my hands down to my neck, further stopping when my fingers meet the edge of lace. *Lace?*

"Did you undress me?"

He gives me another smirk that I want to smack off his face. "Nothing I haven't seen before. If it makes you feel better, I changed too. We want to look good for a couple of pictures, right?"

There's something in his tone that I don't understand. Something telling me to play along. Except even if I were playing along, then I wouldn't just sit here and stand by while his psychotic father marries us.

I put steel in my tone when I speak again. "What the hell is going on, Drew, and give me a straight answer this time."

Drew's father or what-the fuck-ever his name is, Lucian, Lucious, something sinister sounding for sure, speaks instead. "Why, my dear, we are welcoming you to our family, as my son says."

My gaze catches on the hospital bed across the room. Drew's mom is still unconscious. At least one of us is. I wouldn't put it past this asshole to force me into this thing even if I were knocked out.

I let out a long breath before I push off the couch to stand, and then I glower down at Drew who's somehow in the seconds I've been sitting there had slouched into the couch, looking every bit the villain. "Take me home, now, and we'll forget this ever happened. I won't even tell Sebastian, so you won't have to worry about him coming in guns blazing."

Not that I've seen Sebastian with a gun on him. I spotted a couple in his desk drawer once, but I'd never seen him actually hold one. Even when he had murder in his eyes. My statement is more of a means to scare them, which isn't really working.

Drew stands, buttons his black tuxedo jacket, and smooths his hair back away from his face. "Relax. Let me grab the contract. You can read it and know you'll be well taken care of."

He's joking, right? "You call this charade well taken care of?" I shake my head. "After everything, you're really going to stand here and force me to marry you?"

His eyes go a little wide as he studies me, and I have no

idea if he knows that I'm only trying to sell this. Whatever the fuck this is.

In the car the other night, he asked me to trust him, and I realized I already did. I already do. So this situation must be some kind of plan. I just wish he'd trusted me enough to reveal it in the first place instead of drugging me.

At the reminder of the drugs, my stomach roils. I force out a long breath and place a hand against my stomach. Yep. Going to need a minute. Maybe if I puke on Drew's dad, then he'll let me walk out of here.

Something tells me it's not me he wants but Sebastian's money.

When Drew crosses the room to the other man lurking near the door, he opens a small envelope and passes over a thick folded stack of paper. I barely spare the paper a glance because at that moment I spot the outline of something at Drew's back. The glint of metal is barely noticeable, but I see it. *A gun. He's got a gun?*

My breath stalls, my lungs starving for oxygen. What the hell does he want me to do here? Fight, play along with the ceremony? I assume he won't let things get far enough that we are actually hitched for life. There's no way he would want that. Right?

As I'm thinking about it, Drew returns to my side and holds out the papers. "Take a look at it, read it, front to back, and we'll sign it before the actual ceremony."

I'm not sure what he sees in my face, but his mouth turns down, the slick grin slides away, and he studies me. "Bel? Take it."

I snatch it out of his hand, glaring now. I might trust

him, but that doesn't mean I'm not pissed as hell. The memory of the jab in the neck returns slowly, and I remember calling him out the same way. *Asshole.* As soon as we're done here, I'm kicking his ass.

I snap the papers folded in thirds open and skim the first page. It seems to be a standard marriage contract except all the stipulations about what is mine is Drew's and what is Drew's is his family's. Ridiculous. I'm not signing this bullshit.

He kneels in front of me, his tuxedo pants stretching across his muscular thighs obscenely. I can't help but stare, and his smirk this time is real. "Bel?"

I lean in, and he tugs me forward, pressing a kiss to my mouth. It's so quick it's over before I can comprehend it's happening and those wicked lips of his skim from my own across my jaw, stopping at the shell of my ear.

"Stall for time," he whispers.

When he pulls away, I glare and then turn the contract page as if I'm reading very, very slowly.

"Oh, for fuck's sake, it's a marriage contract. There's no need to review every page. Now get your ass up so we can do this," Drew's dad grouses from across the room.

I'm about to give this man a run for his money.

I slap the contract at Drew's chest hard enough to send him back on his ass on the fancy carpet. There's a flash of a grin, then his eyes harden. "Is this you telling me you want to play? Because I can fuck you right here on the carpert for the world to see. Or you can be a good girl, get up, sign the contract, and marry me."

When he's distracted trying to stand in his fancy clothes, I scoop up the full skirt of my dress, relieved he at least put my Converse back on my feet, and I race toward the door. The man standing near it watches with a smirk but does nothing to try to stop me as I reach the open double doors. The rubber soles of my shoes slap on the marble floor in the foyer. I don't get far before an arm circles my waist, dragging me backward. My back crashes into a hard body, and I know without even looking back that it's Drew.

"Bel," he whispers. His hands come around me, and it's all I can do not to lean into him, fall into him, and let him carry me out of this.

He might not have trusted me enough to be a part of his little plan, but he needs me to do something now, right? I can't let him walk back in there alone. Knowing what will happen if he lets me run. His father will hurt him, and I don't know how that will go, seeing as he's armed. Yes, I imagine he's going to kill his asshole father very soon, but I don't want things to go wrong for him. I don't want to make it worse.

I allow myself one blissful second of soaking up his strength and his force of will. Then I turn around, pull my hand back, and slap him hard across the face. There's a stinging in my hand, but it's a welcome sensation. It reminds me I'm alive.

"I hate you," I growl.

His lip quirks, and I spot the other two men watching from the study doorway. "That's okay. You don't have to like me to fuck me or even marry me. Plus, we both know how much your hate turns me on."

There's so much conviction in his tone I have to really meet his eyes to see underneath. Damn. He missed his calling on the stage or with his stupidly good looks in movies. Maybe this plan needs whatever level of devotion he's now bringing to pull it off. I move to slap him again, but he grabs my hand and tugs it down to his chest, then spins me and lifts me, all in seconds, carrying me back into the study, my body bouncing on his shoulder. "As much as I love a good chase, I want to get this done and over with," he says, passing his father and the other man.

He sets me back on my feet near the open space off to the side of the room. "Don't do this," I plead with Drew. Then to his father and the other man. "Don't do this."

His father sees my request as a weakness, I can tell, as his lip curls. "Stop begging, girl, or I won't let you enjoy your wedding night. There has to be some consolation prize, right?"

Him speaking about his son that way, like something to be used and discarded, makes my already queasy stomach clench harder. Yup. Definitely might puke on one or both of them.

The absolute disgust refuses to leave my face, and Drew's father must notice this as he steps toward me, the same predatory slow walk that Drew has sometimes. "You will learn your place, Bel, or I'll make sure that place is six feet under the dirt."

"Don't fucking threaten her," Drew snaps from a foot away now. "I did exactly as you asked, and while this is me following your directions, don't think for a second that I'm letting you touch her. She will be my wife, and she will be respected as a member of this family. Let me know if you have a problem with her, and I will take care of it. That's my duty as her husband."

I hate how Drew speaks about me as if I'm a disposable object, but I also know this is part of the plan. He's got to play the part and walk the line.

Drew's father has no respect or regard for women besides what they can offer him. It's obvious from the way his wife lays in that hospital bed, barely alive while he sleeps around with women half his own age. It's disgusting, and creepy. I might think Drew is a villain, but his father is evil. Pure evil through and through. He deserves to die. And that brings me some measure of solace as I stand toe-to-toe with him.

I hold the trust I have in Drew tight in my hands. I have to believe he will interfere if things get out of hand, so I take this chance to say what I've been dying to say since I first saw the bruises on Drew's skin. "You're nothing but a bully. And eventually, the bully gets bullied by someone who is bigger and stronger."

He grins now. "Oh, I like it. She has teeth now. How cute. I'm glad you've steeled up that spine of yours. The last time we talked, you were a weeping, pathetic mess. At least you aren't crying this time."

I clench my hands into tight fists. What would happen if I punched him in the face?

"And I'm far worse than a bully. I'm a monster, sweetheart, and I will destroy you without even blinking if you try to fuck any of this up. I'd much rather be the person who does the stepping than be the one who gets stepped on. So far, things have been working out just fine for me." He waves at the room and the opulent furnishings.

"Yeah, I'm sure life for you has been fucking peachy," I growl, barely recognizing the venom in my own voice. "It says so many wonderful things about you when you take your anger and frustration out on your son. Hoping that one day he will turn into a version of you. News flash, he did. A better version. A man I'd be proud to take as a husband, but only when we decide to do it on our own, and not when we're forced at the hand of some psychopath."

Drew's father holds his hands wide and smiles a slimy smile. "Well, in a perfect world, sure, but you can thank your bastard brother for forcing our hands. If he didn't make such stupid choices, we wouldn't be in this situation."

He reaches out to touch my face, and I jerk back, stumbling. Drew's there, his chest against my back, keeping me upright. I can feel the anger rolling off him, the energy in the room laced with malice and intent.

The mention of Sebastian has me on pins and needles. I know he's part of the plan, but I can't determine in what way.

"Stop bickering with each other. Can we get this done and over with so I can get out of this fucking suit?" Drew says over my shoulder. "Shall we?"

Drew's dad smiles, and this time, I have nothing to say to stall things further. Fear of the unknown slithers up my spine. I glance back at Drew, hoping to see something, anything that might give me a hint on how far this is going to go, but there's nothing to be seen. His mask is firmly in place.

He won't actually follow through with marrying me, will he?

33

DREW

I can feel Bel's eyes on me, but I don't budge. The slightest change in my demeanor could cost me the entire plan. While I want to soothe her worries, I can't risk messing up. Instead, I look anywhere but at her.

I lock eyes on Richard, the officiant, who looks bored. He's mastered the indifferent smirk most of us learn from childhood, but there's something about the way he clenches and unclenches his hand in his coat.

I'm more aware of my surroundings than most people think. To others, his demeanor might seem normal, but he hasn't even bothered to remove his hands from his pockets. It's almost like he's waiting for something to happen. Like he's going to make a run for it the second his duty is done.

We move into position, and I wonder if he's here voluntarily or if my father coerced him in some way. I also wonder if he'll be an ally the second I put a bullet in my father's head or a hindrance. I'm grappling with the idea of killing one person. The idea of killing two feels exhausting.

Then there's Bel. I fear her seeing me so cold-blooded will just give her another reason to walk away, and it kills me. A person can say they understand all they want, but there's a huge difference between saying and doing something, between watching a bullet enter someone's brain, and watching life leave their eyes, and simply saying you're going to kill them.

My father steps behind me, and I remain as still as a statue, hoping he isn't close enough to feel the imprint of the gun at my back. I nearly sigh with relief when his hand clamps down on my shoulder, his fingers digging hard into my flesh.

I barely restrain snarling at him as the pain from his grip ripples across my shoulder. He needs to take his fucking hands off me in the next three seconds or this is all over.

When he steps away to my right and waves at Richard, I breathe out a long exhale. "No point in dragging out the inevitable, so let's go. I have plans this evening that I don't want to miss."

Which is code for I have a woman I'm waiting to fuck. *Fucking asshole.*

Richard lets out a sigh, then tugs an index card from his pocket, his gaze dancing between Bel and myself. "I guess we should make it official, then. I took the liberty of truncating the ceremony so we don't have to waste anyone's time."

I assume on my father's order, but I keep my mouth shut. We're getting closer to the finish line. All I need is a clear shot. The second he cuts in front of me, I'll end him. Right here. Right now. My only regret in all of this will be dragging Bel into this mess, but there wasn't any other option. I just hope she can forgive me afterward. This isn't going to be easy to witness.

The weight of my choices weighs on me. *Hurry.* I want this to end. I need it to end. My nerves are fried, and I'm barely keeping myself standing upright. The sound of shuffling feet over marble meets my ears, and then the closed office doors fly open, slamming against the wall.

Both Bel and myself startle at the intrusion. The goons my father usually has circling him like vultures stalk forward, two of them dragging a very pissed-off Sebastian. He thrashes his body back and forth, one of them nearly losing their grip on him. *Fuck.* The tension in my chest makes it hard for me to breathe, and I risk glancing at Bel, who looks fearfully between Sebastian and myself.

As if that's not enough, a third guard comes stalking in behind them, his hand clamped tight around a man I recognize immediately. My mother's old doctor. The one I went to the hospital to get answers from.

What the hell is he doing here?

He wasn't a part of the plan. At least not my plan.

The guards release Sebastian with a shove, and he falls to the ground a few feet away from us. He's pushing up off the floor and onto his feet in seconds. There's no fear in his eyes when he makes a rush at the guard nearest him. The hulking giant gets him in a headlock, his thick muscled arm wrapped tight around his neck. "Give me a reason, pretty boy. I hate rich little assholes like you. It would be my pleasure to relieve the world of one more entitled rich kid."

Sebastian's deadly gaze finds mine as he claws at the man's forearm. I give my head a little shake, trying to ward him off. We might still be able to salvage this, but only if he keeps it together.

My thoughts take a nosedive into darkness when my father takes a step toward Richard, then turns to face us. All the air in the room is sucked out when I see the glint of metal as he pulls out a gun. Of course. I should've expected him to have a weapon. I'm so fucking stupid. The plan is crumbling in my hands.

With a murderous glare, he trains the muzzle on Bel, and I instantly grasp the hilt of my own handgun, pulling it free of my waistband. I point the muzzle directly at his face with my finger on the trigger.

"If you want to play whose cock is bigger, I'm pretty sure I'm going to win."

My father narrows his eyes at me. "I don't know why I had any belief in you. I should've known something was up when you agreed so easily to my demand."

All I can do is shrug. "What do you want me to say, *Dad*?" I hope he doesn't miss the emphasis I put on the name. "You opened that door and pushed me inside. I don't think you have any idea how long I've been waiting for this day to happen."

His eyebrow arches. "And what day is that, Son? The day I finally put you in the ground?"

My father and I are lost in a stare off, our guns pointed at one another. It's only a matter of time before one of us pulls the trigger. One of us is going to die, maybe even both of us. All I know is that when this is over, even if I die, the fucker is going to die too. Shouting off to the left of the room gathers both of our attention.

I turn my head the briefest just enough to get a peek at what's going on, refusing to take an eye off my father and find Sebastian behind one of the guards, who is kneeling, a gun in his hand, the barrel pressed to the back of his head.

The other is standing as Sebastian holds a wicked-looking serrated blade against his throat. In the all-black sweater, jeans, and combat boots he's rocking, with his hair falling forward over his eyes, he's giving some serious badass assassin vibes right now. I can't help but smile despite the fucked-up situation.

The air in the room becomes hotter, the tension rising, making it even more difficult to breathe. Focus. Don't let him get to you. Movement catches my eye, and I swing my weapon toward Richard, who tucks his cards into his pockets before raising his hands palm up.

The guard holding the doctor has his gun pointed at Sebastian.

"Well, one of us will have to make a move soon or we'll be standing here all night," I say.

Bel makes a small sound beside me, and I shift away from her. The movement leaves her unprotected, but I'm not stupid. She's not really the one my father wants to kill, at least not until he gets every penny Sebastian took from him.

No way in hell will that happen, not when I have a Desert Eagle pointed at his head. It will make such a satisfying hole too.

"Let's discuss this like adults. What do you want, Drew?"

"You. Dead."

"Hmm, and what do you think the outcome of doing that will be? I have guards, more on the way likely. Do you really plan to murder me in cold blood right here in my own office, much less in front of an officer of the court?"

"I'm not scared. I'm prepared for this to end in the worst way. All that matters is making certain you take your last breaths in this office."

Out of the corner of my eye, I spot Richard, whose face definitely says leave me the fuck out of it. He keeps quiet, letting us carry on without his input.

"My death will not fix whatever it is that you're trying to fix. Killing me solves nothing."

"It solves everything!" I growl. "The only thing you deserve is death, and I'm going to make certain you get nothing short of that."

Even when facing death head-on, he still doesn't have the balls to admit his wrongdoings. Red-hot rage blisters through me. I hate him for destroying me and ruining my life. For hurting my mother. For taking every good thing in my life and killing it.

I know I'm letting him get the best of me, and I need to keep a clear headspace, but I can't stop the reaction from bubbling up and out of me.

A bitter laugh rips from his throat. "Do you really think you can end me and walk out of this office without your own death taking place?"

I shrug. "You fire, I fire back, and if you somehow manage to kill me or hurt me enough that I can't shoot you, then Sebastian will kill you for me. Either way, you will die here. Today. By my machinations. Your luck has run the fuck out, and I'm done being under your control."

My father smiles, and it takes me a minute to realize he's always smiled like that. Slightly unhinged and ready for anything. It's why I've never really been able to fight back. I've never known which side of him I was going to get. One day, he might take me to the movies and treat me to anything I want. Then the very next day, he might beat me to within an inch of my life for looking at him wrong.

Has he always been this unstable and have I just been blind to it?

"I know you don't want to kill me. All this is, is built up anger and resentment. Think rational, Son." His voice drops low, becoming almost soothing.

I shake my head, my sweaty finger moves against the trigger. "That's where you're wrong. I do want to kill you. I want to kill you like you killed me. I want to put a bullet deep inside you for every time you ripped a piece of my soul out of my body, for every beating I had to endure, for every hateful word slung at me. I didn't deserve to be treated like I did as a little boy, but you didn't care. You still don't. The only thing you care about is yourself." I'm like a dam breaking. All the pain and sadness rips through me like water escaping through the cracks. "Even now, while facing death, you only care about yourself. It's pathetic, sickening, and I'm ready to end your pitiful life so I don't have to deal with you anymore, and I can be free."

"Killing me won't change anything. You'll still be the pathetic piece of shit you've always been, regardless of how much I tried to fix you. It's a shame your mother and I couldn't have children of our own. I always wondered if I had a son with Marshall blood pumping in his veins if things would be different." There's a new thread of malice braiding his tone.

His words sting. They sting so bad. Like he's beat me with them.

A smile tugs at his lips. "Did you think I didn't know?"

"I don't give a fuck what you know," I grit through my teeth, reminding myself that all he's trying to do is sway me, to anger me into submission.

"Do it. Ask me the questions I know have been weighing on your shoulders, Son." My hand trembles. The gun feels heavier in my grasp now.

"Do it!" he demands, his voice booming. "Ask me, Andrew. Ask and you shall receive."

Even though I shouldn't, because I know it'll lead me nowhere, I give in to the impulse to ask him the questions weighing on me. As badly as I want to end his life, I also desperately want to know what it is that I've done to deserve so much hate.

"Why? Why did you pretend I was your son for all these years? Is that why you hated me so much? Because I didn't have Marshall blood running in my veins." I keep my face blank. He might've pushed me into asking him, but I'm not that trapped little boy controlled by him anymore.

"I thought you figured it out years ago and were just too chickenshit to confront me about it. That or you didn't give a shit. You being a bastard child might've been the obvious reason for my hate toward you, but it wasn't the only reason. You were born with everything that I had to claw, cheat, and steal to get. I came from nothing, less than nothing, less than your little wallflower. You've been oblivious to that fact, always a spoiled, entitled brat all your life. One I raised, admittedly, so part of that is on me. I thought maybe a little discipline would help, and it only made you more arrogant. The harder I tried to get a rein on you, the worse you became. Soon, I realized that it wasn't that I just didn't like you. I didn't love you either. Not like a father should love his son. Those feelings never changed."

I can't hide the flinch that time, and I hate him even more for it. "I was only a child. How could you hate a child?"

He shrugs. "I didn't want you. I didn't want kids at all. Your mother was the one who made the decision to adopt you."

My mother. My sweet... hanging on by a damn thread mother.

I don't miss the way he glances in the direction of her sleeping body with a sneer. "Your mother, the useless fucking lump who does nothing. I never grasped how she could love you like you were her own. She wanted children so badly and refused to lay it to rest. It destroyed our marriage. I tried to give her what she wanted, but I failed. Nothing was ever good enough for her."

Part of me is worried he is oversharing to stall, and another part of me wonders if he's lying just to fuck with me. Could be both.

I wave my gun at his face. "If you hated me so much, then why didn't you just leave? Why beat me? Why stick around for years?"

"It's simple really. After a while, I came to the conclusion that there was no getting rid of you. I decided then that it was my responsibility to toughen you up. I couldn't change that your mother wanted you, but I could make certain you turned out to be the man I needed to take over the family business when the time came. Unfortunately, you proved over and over again how useless and pathetic you were. I held out hope until that trashy little slut came into your life." His gaze shifts to Bel, along with the muzzle of his gun. "Hopefully, your shot is as good as you think it is because if you don't kill me with one bullet, I'll make certain you get to experience firsthand the ways I plan to make her suffer."

Bel's entire body shudders beside me, and she wraps her arms around her middle like it'll hold her together. I want to say something to comfort her, but doing so would only draw his attention to her further.

I shake my head. "No, you don't want her. You want to kill me. Haven't you been dreaming about that day as long as I have? It's not just because I'm not your biological son."

His gaze swings among Bel, Sebastian, and me. "Whose death would be the most impactful here?" He shifts his stance, one foot behind the other like an old-west gunslinger.

God, if he goes for Bel, this is over. I'll have ruined both mine and Seb's life, whether we walk out of here or not. I shift to match his position, inching closer to her so if he decides at the last second to shoot her I can try to jump between. I notice Seb doing the same, his knife somehow gone, two guns drawn now. One on either guard. When did he get so good at this?

I force air into my lungs and focus my attention on my

father. This is my only chance. One shot to take him out and end this all for good. Inside, questions linger. I want more answers. To ask who my real parents are and find out why they put me up for adoption. And unfortunately, the only person with answers at the moment is the fucker standing in front of me.

"Well, are you going to pull the trigger?" my father snaps.

Seconds tick by. All I can hear is my own heartbeat in my ears. Why am I hesitating? I tighten my grip on the gun, the sweat clinging to my palm.

He lets out a long sigh when I don't immediately take the shot. "Just like I expected. So fucking pathetic and weak. I think this is the real reason I always hated you, because you have no concept of what it takes to survive in this world." He raises his gun and points it at my face. "Let me demonstrate."

I don't breathe.

I don't blink.

In an instant, I'm assaulted by emotions that are soon drowned out by the deafening bang of the gun as the shot echoes through the room.

34

BEL

The bang of the gun is deafening, and my ears ring to the point that I lift my hands, placing them over my ears to eliminate the sound. Fear holds me frozen in place, and time ticks by slowly. *What happened?* A heaping dose of adrenaline fills my veins, and awareness trickles back into my body.

Drew's been shot. He's going to die.

I'm going to lose another person who I love and for no fucking reason whatsoever other than selfishness. My heart clenches in my chest when I lift my gaze to Drew and find him standing there, perfectly still like a statue.

Oh god. I move to take a step toward him, but my feet, legs, they refuse to move. The thunking sound of metal on wood drags catches my attention, and I watch as the gun in Drew's father's hand clatters onto the hardwood a few feet away, stopping at the edge of the rug.

I look from the gun and back to Drew's father, who is

slumped against a sideboard, his hand clutched tight to his side. Bright red blood blooms against his white button-up, and nausea rolls through me. There's no missing the wide-eyed look on his face, a mixture of shock and anger.

It happens in slow motion, as everyone in the room turns to look in the direction he's looking. I blink, wondering if what I'm witnessing is really real. It can't be, can it? There's no way. Yet the image before me doesn't change.

I can't seem to unsee Drew's mom sitting there, her feet dangling off the edge of the bed, a gun clutched tight in her hand that she slowly drops as all the attention in the room turns to her.

This... I can't wrap my head around it, and I don't know who's more shocked. Lyle or Drew himself. At this point, I think everyone is shocked, and I can't swallow past the hard lump that's formed in my throat.

What the hell do we do now?

No one makes a sound. It's so quiet you could hear a pin drop. Victoria lists to the side, fisting the sheets with her free hand to keep herself upright. Her skin is ghostly white, and her long dark hair fans out around her biceps, only accenting her pale complexion. She's wearing the same blue hospital gown I saw her in before.

I'd only seen her one time, but even then her beauty shined bright. Now, holding a gun in her hand, with fury flickering in her eyes, I feel a different level of respect for her.

Victoria waves her hand in a come-hither motion, and the doctor, still on the far side of the room, rushes across the room, stopping once he reaches her side. He quickly checks a bunch of the cords and then quickly plugs some things into the machines.

The puzzle pieces slide into place so easily now. She had herself unplugged from the machines so she wouldn't give herself away, but how did she do so without going unnoticed? I can't even begin to understand what's going on.

I can still feel my pulse on my tongue, leaving my mouth dry and my hands shaking. I'm helpless. This isn't my fight, my revenge, none of it. Yes, I hate that man, but I sure as hell wouldn't be able to kill him. Mostly. Probably.

Drew's dad makes a feeble attempt to sit up, and coughs, blood sputtering out of his mouth as he does. When he speaks, his voice is labored. "Looks like you didn't have the balls after all, Son."

Even dying, he has to disparage him.

Okay. I could probably kill him.

My legs are heavy, and my knees quake, threatening to give out on me. If I don't sit down soon, I'm going to pass out. Ungraceful as hell, I slump to the floor, spreading my legs out in front of me. Relief courses through my veins.

Drew's concerned gaze falls on me before pinging back to his mother.

"I don't understand what's going on? What's happening, Mom? How did you get a gun? I thought you were in a coma?"

The questions boil out of him, but he's not getting answers, not yet at least.

She flicks her eyes to Drew for a heartbeat, then

focuses her attention back on her husband. "A mother's love knows no bounds, Drew. Even on the verge of death, I knew I'd do whatever I had to do to protect you."

Drew jolts and looks shocked. "What...? I don't understand."

Again, his mother doesn't explain further and sneers at Lyle. "I'm glad the first shot didn't kill you, so I can tell you what a damn asshole you are. I can't fucking believe you."

Like an angel avenging those she loves, her gaze darts around the room, over each person. Drew. The guards. Sebastian. Me. When she reaches the officiant, whatever the hell his name is, who is standing to the side with a strange look on his face, something changes in her features.

"Richard, is it? Do you think it's self-defense if you kill a man who has been slowly killing you for years?"

Richard blinks and focuses on the wall opposite like he doesn't want to draw attention to himself. "I mean...I could probably sell it in court if you had some kind of proof, and the person in question had a track record of being a bad person. There's a lot of things to take into account, though, especially when in court."

Drew takes a staggering step toward his mom. "No, we won't be inviting the law into this. Sebastian agreed to take care of things. We already have a plan in place."

Her pensive gaze swings back to Drew, and a smile touches her lips, making her face appear brighter. "Sweetheart, I hate to break it to you like this, but Sebastian and I also had a plan."

What? I'm as shocked as Drew is, and his face is a

portrait of sheer surprise when he turns toward Sebastian. "What the fuck, man? My mom, really?"

There's a shuffling of boots on the floor, and I skitter back as Sebastian stalks over, kicking the gun Drew's father was trying to snatch off the floor with the toe of his boot. It flies toward the wall and bounces near the door, out of reach of everyone.

The guards shift on the hardwood like they want to do something, but Sebastian is there in a flash, his guns pointed back at them.

His voice is low and dark as he stares them down. "I don't think you want to do that. I'm itching to make one of you bastards hurt for all the beatings you've inflicted on my friend."

Drew's hand brushes my shoulder, and I focus on him again. "What do you need from me?"

He shakes his head, keeping his eyes on his mom, though. "I don't think there's anything you can do right now, Flower."

Fuck. I feel useless. I don't know how to fire a gun, or fight, or do any of these things that seem integral to this world. Am I useless to him too?

Victoria slides off the side of the bed until her bare feet settle on the hardwood. Dr. Brooks rushes around flustered, helping her to stay standing.

"Victoria, you should stay in bed. I understand you need to do this, but you shouldn't be moving if you don't have to be."

She glares at him for a second, and it's the look of a lover, frustration and hope? "I do have to be up because that asshole isn't dead yet."

He sighs long and deep, and simply helps her forward. She limps and wavers every step of the way. When she reaches Drew's dad's feet, she stops and waves the gun at Seb. "Lock the door. I don't want any more surprises. This ends now."

Another gunshot rings through the room. I flinch and draw my knees up to put some distance between me and them, but the second I move, Drew stops me, keeping me close. Drew's dad jerks, and blood pools around him more. He coughs and sits up, wincing as he does. There's something crazy in his eyes, like he still might try to fight back even though he has two holes punched through him.

I should be more horrified, more scared, but right now, I feel Drew is finally getting the justice he deserves, and apparently, so is Drew's mom.

"I've been sick for ten years. Ten years you've been slowly killing me. Ten years you've been murdering me."

There's so much venom in her voice even I'm a little scared right now.

"And you know what?" She speaks louder. "I'm not the only one he slowly killed. Although I think it took a lot longer for your mom, Bel."

I flinch at the sound of my name and then process what she's saying. "Wh-what?"

Her gaze skims Sebastian who is standing jaw set tight. He knew. He knew, and he didn't say anything to me. "What do you mean?"

"The first woman he poisoned was your mom. She knew she was in trouble and ran. And that poisoning stayed with her, making her sicker and sicker over the years."

I gulp, hot tears building and falling down my cheeks. But I'm focused on Seb now. "You knew?"

"It's not his fault. I asked him not to say anything until we could figure out a plan. Sebastian's private investigator is the one who uncovered the information, mostly from your mom's doctor. Please don't blame him. It's my fault. I asked him to keep it a secret until we knew everything."

I gulp and swallow my rage down. I sure as hell can be mad at him, but I'll wait until we get home to discuss it with him. Like Drew, he didn't trust me with his plan. Neither of them did. Because they think I would have ruined it? Or because they thought they were protecting me? I don't know.

Drew's dad coughs up more blood. "Just finish it if that's what you're going to do. If you..." He coughs again. "Just want to talk me to death, this entire event is going to take fucking forever."

Drew walks over and kicks him hard in the ribs, spraying blood in an arc out of his father's mouth. His eyes flutter closed, and Drew kneels. "You don't get to die yet. Not until we say you do. We aren't done getting our answers."

Victoria places her hand gently on the back of Drew's neck, and for a heartbeat, I see the broken boy in his face. The one who only wanted one parent to love—actually love and care for him.

I wrap my arms around my legs and hunker further into myself. How did I get here? This feels like a nightmare none of us will ever wake up from. I'm in a fucking wedding dress, for fuck's sake.

Victoria resettles her feet to keep her balance, and Dr.

Brooks is right there at her side, clutching her close, keeping her upright. And when her arm droops with the weight of the gun, he lines his own up with hers and helps her carry that weight too.

I bet he got to know the plan. Then almost instantly I scold myself for being a child. This is life and death, actually life and death. It's not that he didn't trust me. He needed things to go off perfectly, and with me knowing, it was one more variable to manage.

Another wave of nausea rolls through me. I might still be mad about the drugs, though.

I breathe deep and then regret it with the scent of iron heavy in the air. How is Drew's dad still alive after being shot twice?

Victoria steps closer, and Drew's dad slowly, so fucking slowly, pushes off the floor and stands. Blood smears down the front of his white shirt, and across his mouth and cheeks. It would almost be admirable if the man wasn't possessed by a demon or something right now.

"Any last parting words, Bel or Sebastian?"

I shake my head instantly. Funny how hours ago, I considered convincing Drew not to go through with his plan to murder his father. Now I couldn't care less what happens to this man. He's the reason my mother suffered up until the day of her death.

He deserves everything he's about to get and more.

Sebastian clears his throat. "Why would I have anything to say to him?"

"Don't play coy. You know the truth. No matter how deep you dig the hole to bury your secrets, they'll eventually be unearthed. The answers you seek are right here. I thought I'd give you the courtesy he never did with your mom, and let you say whatever last parting words you might want to before I kill your father."

ather? I'm not sure my brain is comprehending my mother's words. Everyone appears to be wearing the same shocked expression. *Holy shit.* We miscalculated all of this. In a few ways, I myself feel duped, but I'm grateful to have my mom at my side and to finally end this once and for all.

I glance at Bel and notice the burning rage in her eyes. She's glaring at Sebastian like she wants to rip him apart, piece by piece.

"What the fuck, Sebastian! I knew you were hiding stuff, trying to protect me, but this is a pretty big thing."

He exhales through his nose, a flash of guilt in his eyes. "We can have this conversation after we take the trash out. I'm not talking about it right now."

"Sebastian," I whisper. "Give her something here."

He flicks his cold eyes to mine. "Like you always do?"

She lets out a sigh of defeat. "When this is over, we will be talking about this."

Sebastian growls low in his throat, the tone sheer frustration. "Our mother and Drew's whatever he is now were set up in an arranged marriage. I was the result of said marriage. Once I was born, she started planning her escape. During that time, she met someone new, got pregnant with you and made a deal with my grandfather—our grandfather—to trade me to him in exchange for her being able to run without being hunted, for her to disappear with you."

Bel's expression grows bleaker, and tears shimmer in her green eyes. I can only imagine how this all looks, like we've all been hiding the truth from her. "How long have you known all this? How..."

Sebastian sighs this time. "Not long. It was uncovered by the PI. He found some of my grandfather's paperwork, and it was laid out in it."

"Mom wouldn't do that. Mom wouldn't trade one of her kids to save another. That wasn't her." There's a note of panic in her tone.

I step closer to try to comfort her, but she swats my hand away. "No, don't try to soothe me right now." She shuffles to the side, away from both of us. "I wish she would have told me all of this before it was too late. I could have..."

"What?" Sebastian supplies. "You could have what? There was no threat then."

Turning, she waves at my dad, or should I say Sebastian's dad. "He was always a threat. To you, to me, and obviously to Mom."

"Okay, and you would've done what about it? Walked in here and killed him yourself?" Seb asks. I'm nodding along with him because over my dead fucking body would she have come here to face that asshole alone.

My mom turns to look at me, and I'm shocked all over again. She's spoken more words today than she has in years. As much as all those that I care about have lost, is it selfish of me to be grateful that I still have my mother?

Am I finally going to get my mom back?

When she steps closer, the doctor always guiding her, she shakes her head. "I'm so sorry, Drew. I should have protected you, tried harder. I should have realized sooner what that asshole was doing."

The dominos keep falling, revealing a new image, right behind the next one.

"This wasn't the way I planned on telling you we adopted you. Not in a million years. As a matter of fact, around the time I started mentioning to him that we should tell you is when I suddenly started getting sick."

"Why?" I'm so fucking lost right now.

She smirks and shoots my father a glare. He has the audacity to raise his chin even though he's the one dying right in front of us. "Because of the money of course. Why does he do all the things he does? My money is what powers our life, it's the only thing he has. The only reason he was able to get engaged to an Arturo was because he lied and charmed his way into their lives. It worked on my family too, and once the deal was done, it was too late to correct. He'd already sunk his talons in."

Sounds exactly like him. Driven by greed and the desire to be in control of everything. He could charm anyone into believing him. Nevertheless, I'm going to need some time to decompress with all these new revelations.

"I'm sorry... this is just a lot to wrap my head around right now. "

Mom nods. "I understand, but I need you to know why he treated you the way he did. It had nothing to do with you, Drew. Nothing. You were and still are a wonderful son. That man..." She growls toward the man responsible for most of the people's pain standing in this room. "It was always about the money. It took me some time to see that. He knew that if I died, every penny and dime would go to you. He needed complete control over you to ensure the money would continue to flow. That's why he abused you, and forced you to fit into the mold he wanted."

Her voice shakes now. "I'm sorry for the pain I've caused you, and if you decide you don't want to be a part of my life anymore, I get that, but please know that you're my son. You've always been mine, and I don't need something as trivial as blood to confirm it."

My heart stutters in my chest, and I reach for her, my hand grazing her cheek. She looks so fragile and breakable. I'll do anything to protect her in the future.

"I don't want you to apologize, Mom. You've been there for me, and yes, there are things you couldn't protect me from, but you've always been and always will be my mother."

There's a short coughing laugh that comes from the other side of the room. "Isn't this touching, you two catch up so sweetly over my corpse."

"Shut up!" I snarl at him, both wanting to kill him right this second and watch him die slowly as he bleeds out on the floor.

He struggles to suck air into his lungs, and I notice the

pool of blood around his body growing bigger. It shouldn't be long. Then again, with as big of a pain in the ass as he is, I doubt he'll go out quietly.

"Killing me won't change what happened... but..."

I watch my heart leave my body, as he uses the last bit of strength he has and lunges forward, his hands outstretched for—Bel.

I'm moving without thought. The doctor tugs Mom out of the way, and Sebastian rushes toward her too. A gunshot goes off and the echo of it rings in my ears, creating a staccato tap along with my heartbeat.

No! For half a second, I fear the worst. Bel's been shot. I don't know what the hell I'll do if she doesn't make it. That sheer panic is short lived when I notice my father's body slumped to the ground, his open eyes vacant and lifeless.

In the center of his forehead is a perfectly round bullet hole. I know I should feel something akin to sorrow or sadness, but I don't. Does that make me a monster? I don't know.

Sebastian sneers at him, and I wonder if he's going to shoot him again. Maybe. I would. Just for safe measure.

Reaching Bel, I wrap my arms tightly around her slender body, vowing never to let her go. "Are you okay?"

She nods, as tears slip freely down her cheeks. "I'm fine. He didn't get close enough to touch me. I... It just scared me."

I tighten my grip on her, terrified that if I blink, she'll disappear, and I'll look down to see her body in place of my father's. *It's okay. She's okay. It's over now.* I repeat the mantra over and over again inside my head, holding her as tightly as I can to my chest. I relish in her sweet floral scent, and allow the steady thud of her own heartbeat to bring me back to a normal state. I need this moment with her, to know that she's okay, that I'm okay. That this nightmare is fucking finally over.

"Fuck, Bel. I'm sorry. I'm sorry you had to witness all this. It was supposed to be simple, straightforward, and quick. I was trying to outsmart him, to make him think I was going to go through with it," I whisper into her hair. "I'm so sorry for putting you in danger."

My gaze catches on Sebastian, who stands over Lyle's body. The gun is still in his hand, his finger still on the trigger. It's hard to read him right now. I can't tell if he's numb, or if what I'm seeing is a mixture of guilt and anger.

He's lost so much. What happens when the dam breaks?

"You okay?" I ask, even while knowing he's not.

"As okay as I'm ever going to be. My only regret is not getting answers to questions I might have wanted answers to. I didn't think about that until after I'd pulled the trigger. Not that I think it matters anyway. He wouldn't have told me anything I wanted to know, not without bloodshed. Everyone else's lives were games to him. If he could fuck things up or leave you reeling with emotion, then he would."

"I know. I hate that you won't ever get the answers you want, but I'm glad he's dead. It's what he deserved."

He doesn't say anything, but then again, he doesn't have to. He lost his mother without any closure, and now he's lost his father—even the piece of shit that he is. And I thought my life was fucked up.

To be in his shoes right now. I wouldn't wish that on anyone.

"Let's go lie back down. I think you've had enough fun with the gun for today," Dr. Brooks says. I turn just in time to watch as my mother slumps forward, Brooks catching her gently under the elbows.

I give Bel a squeeze, then release her and march over to my mother. I pick her up gently, like she's made of glass, and carry her over to the bed again.

"I agree. I think you need to rest. I don't want to lose you because you put all your energy into getting rid of him, especially when he's already gone."

A sigh slips past her lips, which I swear are pulling up into a smile as she lies back in the bed. The doctor bustles around to plug in her monitors, and the IV I only just noticed, that's still hanging out of the joint in her arm.

"No matter what happens in the future, this moment was worth it. Worth every hardship, secret, and ounce of strength. He deserved to pay in blood after hurting so many and destroying their lives. I just hate that he died so quickly."

I lean forward and press a kiss to her forehead. "It's done now. He's gone, and he'll never hurt us again. Now we can focus on moving forward."

"Oh I know, sweet boy." She smiles up at me, her eyes twinkling.

"I've missed you so much. I thought I was going to lose you."

She sighs softly, the tiredness returning to her face. "You weren't going to lose me. I was in good hands all along. Alan, here, realized what was happening, told me, and we came up with a plan to break me free from his control. Got me out of the endless loop of crooked medical staff he hired and made sure I could finally get the help I needed."

The thought hits me like a punch to the gut. "You...are you going to die? Or is this curable?"

The doctor leans over and checks some vitals, his fingers grazing my mother's wrist dare I say intimately. I don't have the mental bandwidth to open that can of worms at the moment, so I choose to keep the thought to myself, and I'll ask about it at a later date.

"No, she won't die. I think whatever he did to your girl-friend's mother was where he started. It was worse at that time since he didn't know how to control the doses properly. I've implemented a plan to get your mother back to health, but it's going to take some time."

I nod once and turn back to face Bel, who is now sitting on the couch, her eyes carefully avoiding the dead body on the floor.

I kick one of the guards in the side with my boot before spouting off a demand. "You help, or you die, it's as simple as that. Get his body out of here. I don't care what you do with it."

The two goons push up off the floor and rush toward his body without question. I feel nothing but relief as they lift him by the arms, and drag his deceased carcass out the door, leaving a trail of blood behind.

It's over. It's really fucking over.

I suck a ragged breath into my lungs, and it's like I'm breathing for the first time. The weight on my shoulders, on my fucking heart, has lifted. I'm no longer held down by this imaginary brick. Tears prick my eyes. It's the most fucked-up thing ever, and I can only describe it as a blanket of calm overcoming me.

I snap out of it, and blink back the tears before they can fall. I notice Richard standing near the door. He looks like he's about to bolt.

"Are you going to be a problem we need to get rid of?"

He shrugs, and then pulls a pack of cigarettes out of his pocket, along with a lighter. He lights one up right there, sucking on the end of the cancer stick like a straw. I can't really blame him. At this point, I need something stronger than whiskey to drink.

"Nope. I won't be a problem to you or your family. As far as I can tell, your father deserved it. When it's time to do the paperwork and transfer everything over, feel free to reach out. I'll even do it without charging you."

Bel cuts in beside me. "How can you say you won't be a problem when you just witnessed what you did? When you tried to force us to marry each other? A person willing to do bad things doesn't just change."

Barely glancing at Bel, he replies, "You're right, but a person who is smart and doesn't want to die does what they must to adapt. I don't know about you but when someone holds a gun to your head and says do this or else, you choose the option that's going to keep you alive the longest. I have a daughter who needs me more than I need a bullet in my head. I won't be a problem."

I'm reminded in an instant that we all make choices. We all do what we must, choosing between the lesser of two evils in our lives simply to get ahead and protect those we love. It's never personal. Sometimes it's kill or be killed.

Bel's body sways against me, like she's lost the last of her fight. I feel a similar exhaustion threatening to take me out at the knees, but I need to be strong, at least until everything is cleaned up and any potential risks are dissolved.

I circle an arm around her waist. "I got you, Flower," I whisper, lifting her, and cradling her in my arms. She lets out a grumble but doesn't try to stop me.

"I'm okay, just a little tired. Someone injected me with a tranquilizer." Sarcasm clings to her words.

I cringe. "Yeah, I'm sorry about that. I'll make it up to you. I promise."

Bel turns, resting her cheek against my chest, and in her eyes, I see the trust and forgiveness I've been fighting for since the very beginning.

"Oh, I'm counting on it." She smiles.

I hold on to her a little tighter, just to confirm this is all real and not a dream. That we made it out of this unhurt and content. With a sigh, I can only smile with tears in my eyes. It's finally over. I'm finally free. And Bel is mine.

BEL

I'm adrenaline and fear braided to a fine point, and I know once it wears off, I'll be nothing but an exhausted mess. My hands tremble, and my brain reels with all the information revealed. Drew's father, Lyle, is really Sebastian's father, and my own mother was arranged to marry him? My father is a man who my mother fell in love with after he saved her life, but that's disappeared off the face of the earth? I can't wrap my head around it all. It feels like someone took my brain and put it in a blender. Even thinking about it now gives me a headache. Still, I wish I had my mother to ask these questions.

All the lies, hate, and pain. There's so much darkness in this room.

I'll never say Lyle didn't deserve every bullet, but that doesn't mean I don't mourn the scar his death will leave on Drew's and Sebastian's souls. More than anything, I feel bad for Sebastian, for the loss he's suffered, and now I worry about the impact it will have on him. He already carries the weight of the world on his shoulders.

Drew holds me in his arms, and we sit on the couch and wait for the car. The doctor already wheeled Victoria back to her room so she could rest. I know at some point Drew will need to discuss with his mom who his real parents are, but after everything that came out tonight, I don't know that we could handle another reveal.

At least he'll get the answers he's been seeking, even if it won't happen tonight.

"Our ride will be here soon. I figure we're both a little shaken up, a ride is the safest bet," Drew says.

All I do is nod.

I'm a ball of nerves right now, and I'm trying not to be bothered by Sebastian's icy demeanor. He has a lot of shit going on. I couldn't even fathom being in his head at the moment, but that didn't mean I was willing to let him slip into the dark abyss.

I feel helpless, watching as he paces the room, his phone stuck to his ear. I don't know who he's talking to, but I can make assumptions based on recent events. A moment later, Sebastian ends the call and turns toward us.

I hate how tired he looks.

"Cleanup crew will be here soon."

"Okay. I ordered a ride while you were on the phone. I'll take her back to your place, and then I can come back here and help with anything."

Sebastian shakes his head. "No. Go back to the house with her, and I'll be there shortly. I don't want her to be left alone."

Even facing all that he has, his concern for my well-being shines through the darkness the brightest. I'd planned to talk about the drugging and what happened once Drew and I had a moment alone together, but I didn't know if I wanted to leave Sebastian here by himself. I can only imagine how far off the rails this is all going to take him.

At some point we will need to discuss the new information revealed, but I think that can wait till another night. I might be upset with being left in the dark but I think Sebastian has had enough shit tossed on him today.

"Whatever you want. I just didn't want to leave you to clean up this whole thing on your own."

It makes me feel good to have them both on the same page, at least for now. I know it won't stay that way forever but I was terrified for a little bit, that their friendship might end because of me.

"Are you okay?" I ask even while knowing he won't give me an honest answer.

Sebastian's been a pillar of strength for me from the beginning, supporting and encouraging me after losing my mom, *our* mom. It's my turn to return the favor. To be the strength he needs.

"I don't think you could handle my answer at the moment, so I'll say yes, and we can discuss it later." The steel of his voice vibrates through me.

"I'm just worried. I can't lose you too." I hate how vulnerable that admittance makes me but I need him to know that I can't lose him. That I won't survive if I do.

He gives me a smile, the one that he saves just for us, and some of the weight on my chest lifts by seeing that little bit of light shine in his eyes. "I'm not going anywhere, and nothing will happen to me. I promise. In a couple of days, we can discuss the findings from the PI. I'll make sure I have some fast-food on standby."

"Don't try to butter me up." I playfully grin at him.

"I have to have at least one form of protection against you."

"And french fries is your weapon of choice?"

He shrugs. "Yes. I'll just toss them at you like grenades, and eventually, you'll be so full you'll forget about getting revenge."

Laughter bubbles out of me. "Oh, I'll get revenge, but you'll never see it coming."

Sebastian rolls his eyes in a playful way, and then his phone chimes with an incoming text. He stares at the screen for a full minute, his demeanor changing in an instant. He's wearing the same expression he wore that day when his stepmom/aunt showed up.

"Our ride's here." Drew's voice drags me away from my thoughts, and before I realize it, we're moving. He cradles me in his arms as he pushes off the couch.

"You know I can walk, right?" I grumble while secretly enjoying his caveman demeanor. It's crazy to me that I'm happy instead of sad right now. Someone just died, yet I'm smiling. I try not to think about that, or the person it might make me for not feeling remorse, or guilt at the loss of his life.

"If I want to carry you around for the rest of my life, then I will. You're my woman, Bel, and I'll do whatever I please with you." He smirks, carrying me outside to the waiting car. He gently sets me on my feet, then opens the door. We climb inside together, the driver giving us a strange look as he takes in our attire.

Shit, I forgot we were still wearing wedding clothes. Thankfully, he doesn't say anything on the way over to the house.

"I can't believe it's over..." I whisper to Drew.

"Me either. It's going to take some time before I can wrap my head around him being gone."

It feels wrong to be discussing death like it's the weather, but I need to talk about what happened. Otherwise, it might eat me alive. A calmness blankets us, and I lean into Drew's side, pressing my head against his bicep. Our fingers are laced together, and all I can do is stare down at them.

He'll never hurt anyone ever again. It's over. I'm bitter that his death was so quick when my own mother had to suffer for years through hers, but at least he's gone.

I don't even realize we've pulled up to my house until the car rolls to a stop, and Drew gives me a nudge on the arm. I sit up straight and give him a smile. He thanks the driver and opens the door, but he doesn't let my feet touch the ground.

He grabs me by the waist and tosses me over his shoulder, carrying me into the house, and I don't even object. There's no point. He walks inside like he owns the place, and the guards don't even blink in his direction. We make it to my bedroom at breakneck speed, and I let out a short laugh when he plops me down on the bed. He turns and slams the door closed behind him, flicking the lock into place.

"Now," he says and turns back to face me before stalking back over.

Gently, he sets our phones on the bedside table. If I didn't know him I'd be skittering away by the feral glint in his eyes. "I know there are a million things to be said, and that a lot happened tonight. I also know you're mentally and physically exhausted, and that you're most likely pissed off at me. I owe you answers, and an apology but I'm begging you. I'll give you all those things, but please, right now, I need to touch you, feel you, to make sure you're really here with me and that this isn't a dream." There's a note of pleading in his tone, and I know this is something we both need.

I gulp hard, and give him a nod. "Oh, I'm more than angry, and we will have a conversation about how you can make it up to me, but for right now, you can start by touching me."

He does exactly as I ask and roughly shoves my thighs apart, the gauze of the dress stretching across the space. I let out a gasp but am prepared when he throws back the material so he can step between my bare thighs.

My phone vibrates on the bedside table, and with an irritated huff, he snatches it up. I'm about to tell him my passcode when he enters it with a wink.

Of course he knows my passcode.

"It's a text from Sebastian. He says the doctor is taking my mom back to the hospital."

Immediately, I'm filled with concern. "Do you want to go? We can get a ride back."

Drew shakes his head. "I can check on her in a little bit. There's nowhere else she would be safer than in the hospital, and I'm not a doctor. Plus, all I need right this second is sitting in front of me."

He quickly texts back and then tosses my phone on the far side of the bed. "Now that we've got that out of the way, let me look at you."

I shove the worry and concern for his mother to the back of my mind and shift so he can access the zipper on the back of the dress.

He peels the bodice off from around my shoulders and down to my waist. Then shoves the bra straps down my biceps and tugs it off at my elbows.

Goose bumps erupt across my skin, and he rubs his hands up my arms to warm me. It's not necessary, not with his fingers pressing into my flesh and his eyes locked on my bare chest.

"Look at you. Still so fucking beautiful even after all the destruction and chaos," he whispers. "Do you have any idea how strong and amazing you are?"

As if he can't get me out of the dress fast enough, he tugs it down, ripping the material in his haste. It doesn't bother me. I'd be fine if he burned the damn thing. I never want to see it again.

"You too," I whisper, grasping his tuxedo jacket at the collar to shove it off his broad shoulders. I tug at the loose bow tie until I can strip it away and start on the buttons in a long line down his chiseled chest.

He tugs his shirt out of his pants and I rip it off his arms leaving him in his slacks. His shoes and pants go next until he's standing in front of me in nothing but black boxer briefs. Damn he looks good. He always has but now,

now that I know how so completely he is mine, he looks even better.

I swallow hard and meet his eyes. "Touch me."

He licks his lips. "I'll touch you but we are going to do it my way. You trust me with your life, now trust me to give you what you need."

I lean forward, hoping for a kiss, but he just flashes me a quick smirk and sinks to his knees in front of me. "I'm going to spend the rest of my life worshiping you, and proving how much you mean to me, and I can't think of a better spot to start than right here." He grabs me by the ankles and tugs me forward, roughly placing my legs over his shoulders. "Now be a good girl and let me please my pussy."

Psh...I laugh. "Did you just say please your pussy?"

He smirks and it hits differently as I meet his eyes over the curves of my body. Damn he's beautiful, and free. So free, like a bird escaping a cage. I spear my fingers through his dark hair, as he places a kiss to the inside of my thigh.

"Yes!" he whispers, almost to himself. "Mine. My pussy."

There's an urgency to his words, to the way he touches me, like he's afraid I might disappear beneath his fingertips if he doesn't hurry.

His fingers sweep through my folds, moving lower, and then all at once he enters me with two thick digits. I'm not quite wet enough for the rough treatment but the slight sting and the way he does it with absolute confidence means I take it anyway.

"Fuck..." I hiss out, throwing my head back, squeezing my eyes closed.

He makes up for the roughness by sucking my clit between his lips, his teeth grazing the sensitive skin.

I lift my hips, begging for more, needing more. "Drew!"

He flicks his gaze up to meet mine and speaks against my pussy. "What did I tell you, Flower? It's my pussy. Every inch of you belongs to me."

When he ducks back down, he takes no mercy on me. His teeth graze my clit with every swipe of his tongue and when my body grows wetter, the muscles relaxing and adjusting he adds another finger. He fucks me with those three fingers, making me climb higher and higher.

I'm full, so deliciously full, but I love it.

All I can do is whimper when he gently eases in a fourth finger. *Oh fuck.*

"Can my pretty pussy take the whole thing? Can you take my fist in your cunt, Bel? Will you cream all over my fingers, and scream my name while you explode?"

There's no other option but to take the pleasure and pain that he gives me. The sounds my body makes as he slips in and out of me, they're embarrassing yet so hot they intensify my pleasure.

"Can you feel it, feel your pussy tightening around my fingers? God, I love seeing you stretched like this. At my mercy... hanging on the edge, waiting for my command."

My toes curl, and I'm walking a tightrope of pleasure. There's a burn in my core, and I know what he wants. There's still one more finger to go. He's going to stretch me as far as I can go, and make me take it even if I whine, whimper, and beg for him to stop.

He knows my body better than even I do.

His green eyes lock on mine. "Don't take your eyes off

me, Bel. Don't you fucking dare. Your pleasure is mine, and you'll come when I say you can come."

I grit my teeth and blink up at him, knowing exactly what he expects of me. He smiles and oh-so slowly adds his thumb to the other four fingers already inside me. The tinge of pain from being stretched so thoroughly tugs at my nerve endings.

Oh god. My arousal drips down my thighs and his hand. I can feel the pleasure building, threatening to consume me. I fist the sheets below my hands and try to escape the pleasure, but I can't.

"Drew! Please! I need to come... please..." I whimper, nearly on the edge of tears. With a chuckle, he disappears again, and his lips latch onto my clit again, sucking, drawing the orgasm out of me like a peel carved around an apple. I convulse, my hips lifting on their own, as the juices spill out of me like a damn waterfall.

It's a damn miracle that I keep my eyes on his, even as mine well up and tears slip down the sides of my cheeks. The pleasure ripples over my body, until it becomes almost painful, and I have to push at his shoulders to get him to stop eating my pussy or risk dying from post-orgasm pleasure.

He takes mercy on me finally and lifts his head from between my thighs. I watch mesmerized and in a haze as he licks the arousal glistening his lips.

"You're such a good girl, creaming all over my fist."

All I can do is huff out a breath, my heart still hammering against my rib cage. With a tenderness, he eases his fingers out of me, and I'm left with an emptiness that only he can fill. I reach for him, wanting to return the favor, but he merely shakes his head.

"I'll fuck you and fill you with my cum real soon, but first we need to have a little talk."

"I'm still mad at you for drugging me."

"As expected."

"It hurt my feelings that you didn't trust me enough to tell me."

"It wasn't that I didn't trust you. I wanted to tell you. I needed the element of surprise, and if you followed along with everything I did, I wouldn't have been able to sell it to him. I needed him to believe that I was finally following along, that I was going to listen."

I understood that and knew I'd have to accept that the men in my life would occasionally do things to protect me and not tell me because they wanted to ensure I was safe. That didn't mean I had to like it, though.

"Don't do it again."

"Which part? The drugging or the hiding information until the very end?"

I pin him with a glare. "Both. I didn't like not knowing what was happening, and I was scared when I woke up and we were in your father's office."

Drew cradles my cheeks in his hands, his lips hovering above my own. "I'll do my very best in the future to tell you every single detail of every single thing. Unless it's unsafe for you to know."

"Fine." I smile and press my lips against his. There's no use arguing, he won't change his mind on this. I can tell by the rigid set of his jaw and the spark in his eyes. There will be things I can fight him on and things I can't fight him on.

I know this, and I need to learn to compromise with him, but it's difficult when he's such a caveman.

The kiss becomes possessive, searing. Like he's trying to destroy me and piece me back together at the same time. I fall deeper into the kiss, letting it consume me. I'm completely breathless, and tugging on his shoulders, begging for more, when he breaks away from me. I whimper with disapproval, and he shakes his head at me, his restraint barely intact.

"Shower, dinner, and then I'll fuck you. In that order. It's my job to make sure you're taken care of, and I take my job really fucking seriously, Flower."

His dark tone is delicious and makes me want to disobey him just to see what kind of punishment he'll give me. "What do you want to eat?" he asks.

A smile pulls at the corner of my lips. "Cock," I whisper.

His gaze darkens tenfold, and he shoves a hand into my hair, tugging the strands hard. I see the lustful haze that appears there and the zing of pleasure I get from speaking to him that way, but more than any of that is the trust and warmth I feel when he touches me. I feel safe with him, and while I've always been safe with him in one way or another, it's never been something I could be one-hundred percent certain of. Now there's nothing in our way. No hurdles to jump. No secrets or lies to be discovered.

It's just us.

"I love you, Maybel Jacobs, but if you keep taunting me, I will show you what it's like to be hate fucked. Now stop teasing me."

He releases me, and all I can do is smile.

"Fine. Let's shower, and then we can go downstairs and find something to eat."

Drew carries me into the bathroom, placing me on the edge of the counter. He opens the glass shower doors and turns the water on, twisting the dial to hot. It doesn't take long for steam to fill the space, and when he returns, he picks me up and carries me into the shower with him.

"I feel like I've waited my entire life for this moment," Drew whispers against my lips.

"To shower?" I giggle.

He glares. "No. To hold you in my arms without the fear of something dark and sinister hanging above us."

"Only the most hard-fought love is worth it," I soothe, wrapping my arms around his neck.

"Fuck, I can't get over hearing you say that you love me."

"Well, you better get used to it because I'm never going to stop saying it." I smile and fall deeper into his penetrating gaze. After a while, we take care in cleaning each other and washing away the weight of what happened today.

I'm not sure how long we stay under the stream of water, but we remain wrapped up in one another until the water turns cold. When we get out, Drew wraps me in a fluffy white towel and dries me off before drying himself off.

My belly rumbles loudly, and I grin at him, knowing he heard it too. I grab a T-shirt, pair of panties, and sleep shorts from the dresser, and turn back to Drew. *Shit.* He doesn't have anything to wear.

"Why don't I stay up here, and you go and get the food.

I'll be waiting here with a reward when you get back." He playfully wiggles his eyebrows at me.

Drew's awakened a sexual beast inside me.

"Fine. I'll go get something from the kitchen. You stay here."

"Hurry..." he teases, and I disappear from the room with a smile.

I'm almost in the kitchen when the sound of shouting filters into my ears. It's getting late. No one else should be here except the couple of people who stay on for the night if we need anything.

Just inside the threshold of the kitchen, I pause. I take in the entire scene in an instant. Sebastian stands near the black granite countertops, and the maid, Elyse, is near the stainless steel fridge, her small body hunched over, her bleeding hand clutched tight to her chest.

There's blood on Sebastian's hand, which I assume is Elyse's. Did he hurt her? I can't fathom him doing that, but then again, we all do things differently when the stress on us is different.

"I told you not to touch it, and you did anyway. The only person you have to blame for that cut is yourself!" Seb's voice is a shout that fills my ears.

The maid turns, tears slipping down her cheeks, dragging mascara with them. "I'm sorry. It's my job. You can't just leave broken glass on the floor. It's unsafe."

He drags a crystal glass filled with something off the counter beside him and takes a long swallow. "I'm not safe either, but that doesn't seem to scare you."

It's a whip crack of a response, and I gasp.

"Sebastian."

His eyes find mine, and for a flash, I see guilt there. "Just go, clean yourself up," he tells her. "If you need stitches, I'll make sure you get to the hospital."

The maid gives me a quick glance, then rushes out of the room toward the employee wing.

I'm considering going after her when the back kitchen door swings open and a wave of chilly air slams into me. I'm both stunned and concerned when a tall brunette comes walking, her body teetering on sky-high heels and the tightest red dress I've ever seen. *Who the hell is this person?* A man with a shaved head follows her, wheeling several stacked suitcases in.

"I'm home," she greets in a liquid honey voice, her eyes all for Sebastian.

"What the hell is going on?" I ask, marching over, instantly seeing the way Sebastian's shoulders go rigid.

Seb looks worse than he did when we left him. His usually lovely curls disheveled and shoved out of his face. He's changed, his dress shirt partially unbuttoned, and the black sweatpants he's wearing are totally out of character.

"Sebastian? What's going on?" I whisper, barely sparing the new woman a glance.

"Nothing. Everything is fine," he grits out.

The woman steps forward and extends her hand like she wants me to kiss it, but I shake it instead. "Don't be rude, Sebastian. Who is your little friend?"

Sebastian looks like he's going to blow a blood vessel at any second, so I save him from defeat and answer myself.

"Maybel Jacobs," I tell her.

"Mmm, nice to meet you. I'm Tanya Arturo."

For once, I consider using the Arturo name because

she looks like she doesn't give a shit about anyone without money or power. Her makeup is perfect to accent her brown eyes, her hair perfectly straight down to her butt, not a gray in sight even though she has to be in her late thirties. Something in my gut tells me this woman is bad news, but I have no confirmation or reason to believe it other than Sebastian's silence and desire to look anywhere but at the woman or even me.

It hits me then. Was this the aunt Sebastian mentioned one time before? What is she doing here? Not that I have much say in if she comes or goes, as this isn't my home, but if this was a planned visit, indeed Seb would've told me ahead of time, right?

"Tanya, I told you not to come here. There are a number of hotels to stay at. You could've chosen any one of them."

"And miss seeing you?" She pouts. "I think not. Plus, this is my home. I deserve to be here as much as you do."

"Whatever," he sneers. "Make yourself at home."

"Great," she beams and turns, giving me a smile. I'm temporarily frozen, unsure what to do. I feel this unruly desire to protect Sebastian, but I have no idea what I'm protecting him against. Certainly not this Tanya woman. "It was nice to meet you, Maybel. Maybe I'll be seeing you around?"

"Definitely," I reply and make a note of the flash of anger that flickers in her eyes.

"Excellent. Let's go, Marcus."

The woman snaps at the bald man with her luggage and starts walking, her high heels clacking as she disappears from the kitchen.

What the fuck was that?

"What's going on? Are you okay?" I step toward him, but he shakes his head, waving at the shine of glass still littering the floor like he needs the distraction.

"Nothing. I got careless. As I told the maid, I'll clean it up."

"Her name is Elyse, and I'm not just referring to the glass. That woman, who is she, and what happened?" I take a deep breath, realizing I've just hit him with a lot all at once. "No one would fault you for losing it after everything that happened today."

"I don't give a shit what her name is," he snaps and then sighs almost as if he's defeated. "I'm fine, Bel. Don't worry about me, and don't worry about Tanya. She's no one, and she'll be out of our lives as fast as she entered it if I have anything to say about it."

I feel like there's this vast distance between us, and I hate it. I know he's only being an asshole to push me away, and he can be however he wants to be, but I want to make certain he knows I'm not going anywhere. Against his wishes, I take a step forward and wrap my willowy arms around his middle, hugging him as tightly as I can.

"Sebastian. I'm here. When you're ready, I'm here. And I love you. I'm not going anywhere."

At first, it's like hugging a two-by-four, his entire body tense and unmoving, but then he presses his face to the top of my head, the tension easing from his body. I wish the moment would last longer, but it ends as quickly as it happens.

Taking a step back, he severs the connection.

"Try not to worry about me. I'll be okay. You have your

hands full enough with the psychopath." He gestures toward the way I entered, no doubt indicating Drew.

I hate it, but I can't make him talk to me. I can't make him take my support or help. I have to wait until he's ready, and it sucks so much.

"If you need anything, you know where I am."

He nods, but I'm not convinced he'll come to me if he needs something. I leave the kitchen without anything to eat. My appetite is mostly ruined now anyway. Entering the bedroom, I find Drew sprawled out on the bed, one eyebrow raised in question.

"Was the pantry empty?"

I shake my head and cross the space, needing to be closer to him. "No. I didn't even look."

"That's fine. Let's order a pizza or something," he whispers into my ear, dragging me onto the bed beside him. I let him, mainly because I'm not sure what I can do to help Seb's situation right now. I twist out of Drew's hold and turn to face him.

He stares at me, concern etched into his features. "What's wrong?"

"I'm really worried about Sebastian. I'm worried about the behavior I just witnessed downstairs, and how he acted toward Elyse. Then Tanya showed up." I let the frustration pour out of me. "She gives me a bad feeling, and I don't even really know her."

Drew nods. "Well, she's the stepmom/aunt. I'm actually surprised she didn't show up sooner, given the death of Sebastian's grandfather."

I shrug. "I don't care. I don't like her. And I don't like how Sebastian treated Elyse, the maid. She was bleeding."

Drew doesn't seem surprised. In fact, he's as calm as a cucumber. "It's going to be okay. Bad situations bring out the worst in all of us, and with the added stress, I'm sure whatever happened was an accident. I've known Sebastian almost my entire life. He's as hardheaded as you and even crazier, but he's strong and smart. He'll be okay, and if he isn't, then we will be there to help him."

"I know, but what if he's not okay... what if it's so much worse than we think it is? What if he doesn't ask for help?"

"Shhh," Drew soothes, feathering his lips along my throat. "Remember, you can't save everyone. Let him figure out his problems the same way he let you figure yours out. When he's ready, and if he needs it, then we'll be there to help him. He's never alone, Flower. Not with us, Lee, and Aries at his side."

The combination of words and his touch melts away the fear and worry inside me. All I can do is be there for him, be the pillar of strength he needs, and when he's ready he'll share with me whatever he wants to.

"I love you," Drew growls, nipping at my ear and dragging me from my thoughts. I look up into his sparkling green eyes, and I know there isn't a single thing he won't do for me. He's gone through so much to keep me at his side, and I've never been prouder to call him mine.

"I love you too," I whisper and let him drag me into his darkness.

THE END

Read on for a bonus epilogue, as well as the regular epilogue and don't forget to pre order Sebastian's book The

Prey in ebook, and paperback on my website which
releases in July 2024
If you enjoyed this book please consider leaving a review
for it. Reviews not only help consumers but I enjoy reading
them as well.
While you wait for book 3 to release, consider checking out
some of my other works that are similar in genre. Worse
Than Enemies, Blackthorn Elite, and North Woods
University.

EPILOGUE

Drew

SIX MONTHS LATER

The forest is loud as the crunch of old sticks, leaves, and bark breaks under the procession's feet. The four of us—Lee, Sebastian, Aries, and I —guide the line behind, robed in black, blending into the night, even with the full moon overhead bleeding through the gaps in the canopy.

Bel trips next to me, and I clutch her hand tighter, keeping her upright. Her friend Elyse trails just behind her, and I can feel her weary gaze scanning over each of us as she follows.

There's a grumbled complaint somewhere behind us. "Shut the fuck up and keep walking," I snap.

The person goes quiet, nothing but the sound of the forest greeting us again.

Ahead is the small clearing ringed with four-wheelers, and I stop, guiding Bel off to the side, gently pressing her against the tree trunk before kissing her softly. "Stay here while I get them ready."

She grins, eyes wide behind her glasses.

There's a rush of excitement in the air, of darkness, and I clutch it tightly in my hands, letting it ripple across my skin. I can feel her eyes on me as I march back to this year's freshman recruits. They stand in a semicircle with black bags over their head, ropes loosely looped around their wrists to connect them, leading up to Lee, who strips off the rope and drops it to the ground.

Aries, Lee, Sebastian, and I grasp two of the recruits each by the arms, lead them to the four-wheelers nearby, and shove them roughly to the sloped cart on the back of each. It lays at an angle like a surfer's pickup sled after a wipeout. They realize what's happening and resettle, propping their feet up on the edge so they don't hang down.

Once the eight new mill members for the year are all secured, we each hop on a wheeler. I gesture to Bel, who comes running over, climbing on, and taking the spot beside me. Elyse slides gingerly beside Aries, who studies her closely in the soft moonlight. He looks curious and surprised while she keeps her gaze straight ahead. Her body is as stiff as a board. I remind myself that she's not my problem. It's not my job to babysit her. Bel wanted to bring her, and I'm fine with that, but she's responsible for herself. I spare a quick glance at Seb and Lee to ensure they are ready.

Both give me a nod, and we head through the trees. It's several miles out to the cliffs. We used to make the new members walk out blindfolded, but things changed after a leg break from a fall.

It's fine. They will get their dose of ceremony when we get there. Bel holds on tight to the top handle. "Faster."

I smile and shake my head but oblige, laughing as the recruits on the cart curse for every jolt and jostle over sticks and the uneven forest floor.

It doesn't take too long to reach the clearing by the cliffs. A line of citronella lanterns stands in a circle, lighting the space, obscuring the edge just ahead. Let's see if we get anyone to pussy out tonight.

Bel hops off the moment we stop, and she doesn't bother hiding the smile of wonder on her face as she takes in the lanterns and the rock on the far side of the clearing opposite the cliff edge. The rough granite is carved and pockmarked with names from every generation of Mill members.

I raise my voice and line the new members up in a row facing the rock. "The time has come to take your place among your brethren. Step up to the rock and carve your name. There's no backing out now."

I rip the hoods off their heads and nudge the first skinny kid forward. "Step forward, carve your name, and take your place."

The skinny bastard scrambles forward, and he falls against the rock in his eagerness to grab the pick on the ground nearby.

I shove two more, and Seb does the same on the other end of the line.

They step up, each carve their name, and once they finish, they turn back eager-eyed and grinning.

I hand the hoods back to each of them. "You can put this on if you're going to be a pussy, but...there's one final rite that you must complete in order to be considered a member."

"Adios, fuckers." Lee grins and runs toward the open space between the lanterns, disappearing in a soft mist.

The new recruits mutter among themselves, and I shove a couple of them forward. "Go on."

Bel leans into Elyse, her bright hair a contrast to Elyse's dark braid that's hanging over her shoulder. "You don't have to do it if you don't want to."

Seb wanders over, his hands shoved into his robe pockets. "She's here, isn't she? She can either do it, or she'll be stuck out here by herself."

Elyse takes a tentative step back, and I march over and cut between them. Seb hasn't stopped pushing her since that night in the kitchen six months ago. Lee, Aries, and I have an ongoing bet that she's going to punch him square in the face and quit before the summer ends.

I snag Bel's hand in mine and lead her to the edge. "Together?"

With big, bright eyes, she peeks over the side of the ledge, then tugs her glasses off her face and hands them to me. "Keep these safe."

I smile, and she jumps, dragging me along by the hand.

There's a moment of panic, of pure free fall, until my boots hit the water, and we sink below. She releases me, and I swim up to the surface. It's not a long drop, but with the mist from the small falls nearby, no one can see the water below.

Lee swims on his back a few feet away, his robe, shirt, and shorts on the rocks nearby. "Think we'll have some rejects this year?"

I glance up, and with the light above and the slivers of moonlight, I spot Elyse on the edge of the cliff, scanning the water below.

Bel waves up at her, but Elyse doesn't see her.

"He won't really make her jump, right?" Bel asks, a hint of worry in her voice.

"Make her? I don't know about that. If you ask me, Sebastian has it out for her for some reason. I wouldn't be surprised if he..."

A shrill screech cuts through the night, followed by a splash.

"He pushed her!" Bel shakes her head. "What an asshole."

I can't help but chuckle. He's in for a fight with that one. She hates him so much.

"I called that a mile away," I mutter under my breath.

Elyse pops up out of the water, and I don't need to look at her face to see how pissed off she is. I can feel it vibrating through her and into the water.

A second later, there's another splash, and I watch Seb's body disappear beneath the water. The only people up top now are Aries and the eight recruits. His gruff voice echoes into the valley, but I can't make out the words.

"You okay?" Bel calls to Elyse.

"Fantastic. Never been better," Elyse practically growls.

"Oh, don't act like I'm the bad guy here. If I didn't push

you, you never would've jumped. I think, if anything, you owe me since I did you a favor technically." He splashes water at her.

"I know where you sleep," she mutters under her breath.

"Are you threatening me?" Seb taunts.

Jesus, these two are like fire and gasoline.

Bel swims around me in a circle and lets out a relaxed sigh. "The water is so warm. Nothing else could make this night better unless maybe those two stopped their bickering."

"It's called foreplay, and that's why we do this in the summer. I don't want to freeze my balls off by doing it during recruiting season in the fall and winter. I'm an asshole, but even I have things I won't do."

She leans in and licks a drop of water off my cheek. "We should come out here again, but next time alone."

Lee splashes us both. "I'm warning you now that if you two start fucking, I'm going to sit here and watch. I have zero shame."

"I wouldn't expect anything less, but if you look at Bel, I'll have to remove your eyes from their sockets. The only one who gets to see her naked is me."

"Whatever..." He grins.

There's a shout, followed by a splash signifying that at least one of the new guys has enough balls to jump. Once the first one goes, it doesn't take long for the remainder to follow. I count each splash in my head while I tread water.

Finally, all eight make it down, and Aries follows with a singsong bellow and launches far out off the cliff. We all shift out of the way so he doesn't land on us. *Fucker.*

Bel clutches onto my shoulders, using me to hold herself up and out of the water. "Have you ever checked behind the waterfall?"

I shake my head. "Check for what?"

She shrugs, the water sloshing. My gaze strays down to her T-shirt that has molded against her shoulders and chest. "I don't know. Treasure, fairies, witches. Who knows what could be back there."

The look of excitement and mischief in her gaze is intoxicating. I love seeing her like this, the happiness radiating out of her.

I snort. "If anything is back there, it's probably rocks."

She swims away from me, going in the absolute wrong direction. I wait a second, then snag her ankle and drag her back, letting my hand slide up her bare leg to the hem of her shorts. She yelps, and I clutch her core in my hand.

"Oh sorry, I slipped."

"Sure you did." She giggles.

I release her and snag her glasses out of my robe pocket, then slide them onto her face gently. Water droplets spot the lenses but she swipes them off.

Then, with another grin, she swims off in the direction of the waterfall, leaving me to follow. Catching a glimpse of her creamy inner thigh, I can't help it. I give chase, swimming after her. There's a rocky ledge ahead, and I warn her.

"Be careful. It's not as deep right there, and the rocks make it super slippery."

"Okay, Dad." She snorts. "Why're you so worried?"

Like a disobedient brat, she barely listens to my warning and climbs up onto the small outcrop of rocks, her feet slipping while she tries to gain footing. My heart thunders in my chest. Fuck, she's going to give me high blood pressure with her damn antics. She puts her hand through the rush of the falls. Water cascades over her arm in a fan as she places it through the wall of water.

With a grin, she ducks under the spray and disappears.

"Bel! I swear to god. You need to wait for me," I growl. There might be a fucking bear or something in there. I don't know.

I scramble up the rocks and chase her. The small chamber beyond the falls is cool, and the hush of the steaming water echoes all around us. It's empty, but there is enough space to lay flat on your back. Puddles pool around the floor, and I crawl over to her and take the spot beside her.

"Do that again, and I'm going to spank your ass."

She doesn't appear fazed by my response, and that's fine. Once we get home, I'll teach her a lesson about patience and safety.

"Joke's on you. I like your spankings." She sticks her tongue out at me, and I'm tempted to bite it.

"No treasure, huh?"

She shakes her head, grinning. "No fairies or witches either. But that's okay. This is cool enough."

I pull her in to rest her head against the crook of my shoulder. "Come here, let me keep you warm."

She settles against my chest with a heavy sigh. "This is magic."

Light flickers beyond the curtain of the falls where Aries is no doubt setting up more lanterns now that everyone has jumped. We brought beer, food, and music as well. Not a soul will hear us this far out. It's a celebration after all. The recruits are officially members. I lean over and kiss Bel gently, tasting the river water on her lips. I'll never get over the fact that she is mine. That we're free, that I'm free.

"No, you're magic, and I love you, my beautiful Wildflower."

Made in United States
Troutdale, OR
05/12/2024

19825461R00279